ALSO BY ALEX SHAKAR

City in Love

The
Savage
Girl

a novel

Alex
Shakar

HarperCollins*Publishers*

This is a work of fiction, and any similarity between imaginary characters and living people is coincidental. Where well-known real people are mentioned, their activities are often imaginary, and where real companies are mentioned, the activities, products, advertising campaigns, and characters connected with them are also often imaginary and should not be construed as real.

HarperCollins books may be purchased for educational, business, or sales promotional use. For information, please write: Special Markets Department, HarperCollins Publishers Inc., 10 East 53rd Street, New York, NY 10022.

FIRST EDITION

Designed by Jessica Shatan

Library of Congress Cataloging-in-Publication Data is available upon request.
ISBN 0-06-620987-0

01 02 03 04 05 RRD 10 9 8 7 6 5 4 3 2 1

For Saint Olivia of the Catfish

. . . After looking curiously over his panes of glass one by one, I exclaimed: "What! You have no colored glass, no pink, no red, no blue! No magic panes, no panes of paradise? Scoundrel, what do you mean by coming into poor neighborhoods without a single glass to make life beautiful!" And I pushed him toward the stairs.

Going out on my balcony I picked up a little flower pot, and when the glazier appeared at the entrance below, I let my engine of war fall down perpendicularly on the edge of his pack. The shock knocked him over and, falling on his back, he succeeded in breaking the rest of his poor ambulatory stock with a shattering noise as of lightning striking a crystal palace.

And drunk with my madness, I shouted down at him furiously: "Make life beautiful! Make life beautiful!"

—CHARLES BAUDELAIRE, from "The Bad Glazier"

Smirkers

Stitching

The savage girl kneels on the paving stones of Banister Park, stitching together strips of brown and gray pelt with elliptical motions of her bare arm.

The sleeves and sides of her olive-drab T-shirt are cut out, exposing her flanks and opposed semicircles of sunburned back, like the cauterized stumps of wings. A true redskin, more so than any Indian ever was, her skin more red than brown. It must have been pale once. And her Mohican is whitish blond, her eyes blue or possibly green.

Her pants are from some defunct Eastern European army, laden with pockets, cut off at the knees. Her shins are wrapped in bands of pelt, a short brown fur. Her feet are shod in moccasins.

There is a metal barb about the size of a crochet needle stuck through her earlobe, and a length of slender chain hangs from her scalp, affixed in four places to isolated lockets of hair.

Each time the girl bends forward to make a stitch, her tattered shirt drapes and reveals her breasts, full and pendulous, whereas the rest of her is lean and unyielding. Down the bench, the man with the greased hair and mustache and forty-ounce beer, and his friend, the man with the Afro and mustache and forty-ounce beer, watch the ebb and flow of her flesh with sleepy smiles, lulled by the savage girl's mysterious, eye-of-the-hurricane calm, while around her the rest of the park gyres and caterwauls with trick bikers, hat dancers, oil-can drummers, chinchillas, rats, drunks, kendo fighters, shadowboxers, soccer players, a couple of cardsharpers, and, of course, one trendspotter, Ursula Van Urden, who has been circling the savage girl all morning, moving from bench to bench to get a better view, trying to work up the nerve to speak to her but unable to rid herself of the ridiculous idea that the girl simply won't understand, that she communicates only by means of whistles, clicks of the tongue, or tattoos stamped out on the cobblestones, and that even this rudimentary language she reserves solely for communing with the spirits that toss in the rising steam of hot-dog and pretzel carts.

Superheroes

The kiddie playground of P.S. 179. Children toss and tumble, a maddened sea of screams and limbs, in the middle of which, high and dry, sits Ursula's boss, Chas Lacouture. Atop the back of a cement dolphin. A good choice, the dolphin, she thinks. Better than the lion, the turtle, the orangutan. It goes with his sharkskin suit, pressed to a cold perfection beneath his trenchcoat. He looks more natural here than in his natural habitat, the rarefied crags of upslope office buildings, the blue-lit hallways and slate-gray conference rooms of the Black Tower. There he's too perfect, a weathered masterpiece of brilliantined gray hair, pulsing jawline, and leathery skin. He doesn't look like other men; he looks like their impossible expectations for themselves. But here he's just another fantastic fixture. You'd almost expect the children to hurl rubber balls off him, the pigeons to settle on his massive shoulders.

As Ursula approaches, her fellow agent Javier Delreal sails down the main schoolyard ramp on rollerblades, waving to her as he circles through the kiddie playground's entrance. He is just a little too tall and too thin for verisimilitude. He cuts ahead of her and slaloms around the playing children, his trenchcoat flapping behind him. Then he pirouettes neatly and hops up to a seated position on the dolphin's back next to Chas, who, without looking at him, begins to speak.

"I saw a guy with a neck beard masturbating in a cybercafé," he says curtly.

Ursula pulls herself aboard on Chas's free side, the curvature of the dolphin's back sliding her closer than she wants. Her fingers find the smooth spout hole between her legs. Its position strikes her as lewd, and a little neurotically she covers it up with her palm.

"I saw a sorority girl reading a book called *Subcultures*," Javier responds. Even his head is tall and thin, bracketed by a high, bony forehead and a long, tapering jaw, as though his face were a rack designed to torture his elongated and slightly broken-looking nose. His skin is olive-colored, his hair is dark and frizzy, his eyes are hazel. She can't begin to guess his ethnicity.

"I saw two fat men in black suits get into a pink Cadillac," Chas says.

Javier flips through the pages of a notebook.

"In the last seven days I've seen twenty-nine people wearing shirts with images of anthropomorphic suns, and only two with anthropomorphic moons," he announces.

"*Astrological* iconography," Chas mutters, shaking his massive, square head. "The *simpletons*."

He falls silent, retreating into the runes and cursives of his squint and furrowed brow. Meanwhile, Javier watches the children raptly, a hieroglyph of big nose and big, unblinking eye. Ursula feels that if she can ever manage to decipher the mind of either of these men, she just may begin to understand all the other things that currently baffle her: what her schizophrenic sister means when she says that fashions are messages from the future; why a pretty teenage girl lives in the park and wears primitive clothing and never speaks to anyone; how to dress for success; how to win friends and influence people; how to bring the system to its knees. . . .

Chas tocks his tongue five times, takes a breath.

"Kyle Dice from Nestlé called this morning. He let me have it about the carob-egg breakfast cake."

Javier looks up worriedly. "It's not selling," he ventures.

"That was *your* thing, Javier, cake for breakfast. They followed you on that."

Javier's fingers grope around in his unruly hair. "Damn. It's their own fault. They did it all wrong, Chas. It's too dark. People want bright foods in the morning: fruits, juice, eggs, cottage cheese, yogurt." He pauses, concentrating. His tongue bulges his lower lip from left to right and back. He holds out his hands, palms parallel, and stares into the space between them. "Drab morning foods need brightening," he formulates.

Chas closes his eyes, presses two fingertips to his forehead. "Cereal gets milk," he says. "Bagels get cream cheese. Toast gets jam."

"Donuts get glaze or powder."

"Did we tell them that? Was it in the report?"

Javier doesn't answer for a moment. "It seems so self-evident," he hedges.

Chas shakes his head. "Those people live in a lead-lined box. Their windows are darkened with sheets of Mylar. They breathe recirculated air. They can't tell a falcon from a flying toaster."

A tiny incubus wearing a Superman shirt totters up and clings to Chas's dangling legs, clutching the creases of his slacks with small, grimy fists. Chas narrows his eyes and aims a forefinger-and-thumb pistol between the kid's eyes.

"Pow," he says thoughtfully.

The boy narrows his eyes as well, returning the stare defiantly until two little girls in 'N Sync and Ricky Martin shirts catch him and pull him away. He squirms between them as they kiss him all over his flushed, pudgy cheeks.

"Not much of a kid person," Javier says, "are you, Chas?"

"So what?"

Javier whips an aquamarine silk handkerchief out of his trenchcoat and noisily blows his nose, then blinks dizzily from the exertion. "I'm totally a kid person," he declares.

"The hell you are," Chas says.

"I *am*. Kids are great. Kids can do anything."

"Like what?"

"They can tie the skyscrapers into Krazy Straws. They can shake the sea and the sky into Seven-Up." His long, nervous fingers agitate the air in front of Chas. "Kids are about *possibilities*," he goes on excitedly. "Limitless possibilities. Know what I'm saying?"

Chas nods. "They're dumbasses all right."

A little overwhelmed by their routine, Ursula stares at the swarm of children, unfocusing her eyes. Her brain begins playing tricks on her the way it does when she stares at TV static, resolving the kids' senseless caroming into neat helixes, rings, figure eights. The human brain comes hardwired with a mania for order, and Javier and Chas, she's decided, have cultivated this unthinking compulsion into a weltanschauung, a metaphysics, an endlessly snarled and compendious street index of the human condition. They have theories for everything from children's games to breakfast foods to the patterns of sneaker soles. She herself has been on the job less than a week and has only one theory so far, which is that when they were experimenting one day in their secret lab, Chas replaced his skin with a coat of Fleckstone, and Javier lopped off his arms and legs and attached a dozen industrial-strength rubber bands in their place, and ever since then they have been only nominally human: Granite Man and his sidekick, Rubber Man—superheroes, supervillains, superfreaks—two lurking, smirking, life-size action figures of themselves.

"Listen," Chas says, "I want to make it up to Kyle with a good lead on kid food."

"Kid food," Javier repeats.

"I'm thinking candy in a gun." The barest hint of a smile encloses his bloodless lips in parenthetical stretch lines.

"Candy in a gun," Javier solemnizes.

"They could shoot it into each other's mouth, that sort of thing. Refills would come in clips."

He goes on smiling that subzero smile of his. Ursula has already acquired a healthy fear of the man. His logic is so efficient it could be something instinctive, reptilian. She resists an urge to jump up and warn the children, to gather them up and hide them away in a wildlife preserve.

"I know what you're thinking," Chas says to Javier. "Injuries. Lawsuits. But they'd make the candy really light. Little wafer balls. They could even get some of that cream filling in there, I bet."

"Keep it light." Javier nods.

Chas nods back. "Like I always say."

A thunderclap draws their eyes up Middle City's southern slope to the volcano's peak, where storm clouds mix with the crater ash above the jagged metal and glass of the marketing offices. The rooftop crenellations of the Black Tower rise the highest, from this angle anyway, grazing the dark bruises of the sky. Chas regards the clouds with satisfaction. Perhaps, she thinks, he has summoned them. He turns up the collar of his trenchcoat—an especially tall collar. No doubt within months half the city will be wearing this collar. It will make the wearers appear to themselves more dramatic, more intriguing, for they will have become the kind of people who wear trenchcoats with tall collars. Ursula will not get one herself. But only out of obstinacy. She will want one.

Chas breaks their reverie with a snap and a tight twirl of his index finger. "OK, Ursula, what do you got?"

She takes her sketchbook out of her bag, then hesitates.

"I'm not sure if these are the kinds of things you want."

He replies with an impatient, outstretched hand. She relinquishes the book, wondering if this, her first week as a trendspotter, will also be her last. It would be a giant disappointment but not a big surprise. She lied her way into the job, lied like never before, with all the death-defying virtuosity of a bullfighter, inventing all sorts of experience in advertising and market research, peppering her speech with jargon she'd gleaned from a stack of out-of-date library books. For the first few minutes of her pitch, Chas sat watching her with suspicion; clearly he wasn't expecting to be hit up for a job. He had gone out with her sister Ivy over the months leading up to Ivy's breakdown and had probably agreed to this meeting only out of curiosity, not anticipating that it would turn into a request for employment. But she had him cornered and pressed the advantage; she'd stayed up the whole night before, preparing this routine, and she was determined to see it through to the bitter end. A little cynically, she had assumed from the beginning that any job having to do with marketing would require, more than anything else, an ability to bullshit without shame or respite, and she wanted to show her stamina in this regard. *My market-research experience,* she said, *is fairly extensive, as you'll see from my résumé, taking into account my job at Tolson, which wasn't just telemarketing, though that was a substantial part of it. . . .* When Chas saw that she wasn't about to stop anytime soon, his expression changed. It was the look a cat might wear upon seeing the mouse it was getting ready to eat suddenly break into a tap-dance routine. He leaned back in his chair and didn't interrupt, silently daring her to keep talking. The more she talked, the more naive and ridiculous she sounded, but she kept at it, straight-facedly enthusing about fashions she'd never seen in countries she'd never been to, bragging about the keen powers of observation she'd honed in learning how to paint. She boasted about what she called her interpersonal skills—*If you'll notice on my résumé, my experience at Tolson really was great training in terms of giving me the ability to communicate with consumers of diverse ages and educational and financial backgrounds. . . .*

To her lasting shame she even declared herself a "people person," at which point Chas held up his hands to silence her. A full, nerve-wracking minute passed, with him just watching her, his eyes narrowed once more, cold, appraising—who knew what he was thinking? Was this the way he'd treated her sister? No wonder Ivy had gone nuts. He was probably some kind of Fascist in bed, the kind who liked to sit in a chair, loosen his tie, and bark out orders to a twenty-year-old aspiring fashion model: *Take off your clothes, Take off my shoes,* and so forth. He certainly hadn't cared enough about Ivy to visit her in the hospital. Nor did he now bother to make even the slightest gesture of sorrow about her breakdown to Ursula. He just sat there in his big, flare-backed leather chair, studying her as if he were not seated across a desk from her but rather on the other side of a one-way mirror. Finally she gave up all hope of getting a job and glared back at him angrily.

Then his expression changed again; he acknowledged her with a look of bemusement and a slow nod. He buzzed his secretary. A few minutes later she was filling out a W-4 form and he was giving her the only three instructions she'd gotten so far:

Go out there, he said. *Find the future. Bring it back to me.*

And now, sitting between her and Javier on the cement dolphin, he goes through her guesses at the future without a shred of interest. He shakes his head and turns the pages roughly, dismissing sketch after sketch of teenagers in baggy pants, clown shoes, floppy hats, rolled pantcuffs. When he comes to the first sketch of the savage girl, though, he stops. His mouth remains set in a line, but his eyes don't quite conceal his surprise.

"What's this?" he grumbles. "Some kind of punk hippie?"

"An urban savage," Ursula says.

"I tell her to bring me the future, she brings me a cavewoman," he mutters. "Take a look, Javier."

He and Javier pore over the pages, sharing an amusement Ursula decides must be at her expense.

"She really this filthy?" Chas asks.

"She lives in the park."

"What are those things on her feet? Paper bags?"

"Moccasins."

"Aha." Chas shakes his head.

"I'm pretty sure she made them herself," Ursula offers.

"Sure," Javier says, still looking over the sketch. "That's . . . evident."

The two men fall silent. She considers trying to lead them back through the other sketches, but that would seem desperate, she knows, and she doesn't want to give them the satisfaction of seeing her squirm.

"Well, that settles it," Javier says, stretching and cracking his overlong fingers. "Don't you think?"

Chas thinks for a moment, then nods.

"What?" Ursula says. "Are you going to fire me? You told me you were going to train me—'Find the future,' you said. You call that job training?"

"No, I don't," Chas says. "Training starts tomorrow."

Javier leans forward to reenter Ursula's field of vision, fortuitously avoiding a foam rocket that sails over his head from behind. "Your savage girl is *postironic,*" he says. From his tone of voice she guesses this is a good thing.

Chas grunts agreement, examining the sheen of his squared-off fingernails. Then he taps the sketchbook with them.

"You're a good artist, Ursula," he says.

"Thanks," she says.

"No. You're *too* good. There's too much dirt here. You've got to clean it up. We need it colorful, light, airbrushy. Can you use an airbrush?"

It takes her a moment to realize what he means. He doesn't want a good artist; he wants a bad one. She tells herself that this will be a new kind of challenge, requiring a new kind of skill.

"What's this jewelry she's wearing?" Chas asks. "What's it made out of?"

"Little bones," she explains. He seems impressed, and she feels a surge of excitement. "Actually," she goes on, couching the boast in the form of a modest admission, "I just made that jewelry up. She didn't really have it on."

"Then where's the warpaint?" he asks. "Why didn't you give her warpaint, too?"

"I—I didn't think of warpaint."

"You didn't?" he asks, his tone incredulous. He stares at her as though she'd just admitted to being a Flat Earther or an alien abductee.

"Great idea, Chas," Javier whispers.

Finally Chas relinquishes her from his gaze and turns to Javier.

"Not mine," he says. "Avon's got it in the pipeline."

"Really? Even better," Javier says. "We've got synergy on this."

Chas nods.

"Couch won't be happy about this hide-and-fur stuff, though," Javier goes on. "His last report was all about animal-friendly clothing, plant-fiber alternatives to leather, remember?"

James T. Couch is the other member of the team. Ursula has yet to meet him. She was hoping he'd be here today, on the assumption that whoever he is, he can't be as strange as these two.

Chas shrugs, claps the sketchbook shut, and hands it back to her. "Stay on this savage thing."

"Chas," Ursula says. She was planning to be an absolutely ruthless bull-shitter, a salesman among salesmen, but this is happening too fast. "I don't really know about this. I mean, I picked it almost at random."

Chas watches the storm clouds crawl downslope toward his cetacean throne, his face impassive. "This is not random," he says. "You picked this for a reason. And it's the same reason I picked you."

A teacher with frown lines around her mouth and a real butcher job of a haircut walks out the cafeteria door and spots their position on the dolphin. Her head cocks as she goes into Indignant Citizen mode and comes at them through the gate, the knife pleats of her heavy wool skirt flaring like a nun's wimple. Chas and Javier turn and retreat in a single, fluid motion, hopping through a hole in the fence and rounding the corner, their trenchcoats snapping behind them like the booming wakes of jet planes. With a final, embarrassed glance at the approaching teacher, Ursula casts her lot with absurdity, slipping off the dolphin and darting after her coworkers.

Candyland

Ivy is sitting by the unopenable window, in a wooden chair with arms that scythe around her like the pincers of a giant beetle. But she is too slight a prey to come to any harm: the chair seems made for someone twice her size, so the pincer arms can't grasp her, and she rests her bony elbows on them, hunching her shoulders into nonexistence. She's gained a little weight in the three weeks since she was admitted to Lady of Nazareth Hospital, due to the medication, Ursula's been told—her face has rounded out a bit, giving her naturally sulky, petulant expression an even more childlike cast—but she's still too skinny, or maybe just enviably skinny: when it comes to Ivy, Ursula distrusts her own judgments. Her slightness is accentuated by the oversized clothing she wears, castoffs from their father: a plain white button-down shirt, a pair of khakis she keeps from falling down by rolling the waist over a few times. She'll wear only men's clothes now, and of those only the most shapeless and nondescript. Her hair is still long, though since the last time Ursula saw her she has sawed into her bangs to make a jagged window for her improbably wide-set eyes. The job is so crudely botched that she must have done it herself. They can't have given her a pair of scissors. Maybe she used a plastic knife.

She eyes the shopping bag in Ursula's hand in undisguised hope, and

Ursula holds it up in response. Ivy slips out of the chair, and the two of them leave the room and walk through the maze of corridors, Ivy keeping her eyes on the rainbow of painted lines, stepping only on the gold, taking care to avoid the green and the purple to either side. The terrace deck just outside the cafeteria is empty, the late-afternoon sky faintly drizzling and dark enough for the metal caging enclosing the deck to take on the bluish glow of the three-story-high Lady of Nazareth icon affixed to the hospital's outer wall above them. Ivy selects a table by the edge of the deck, hitches up her pants, and folds herself monkeywise into a metal chair. Her body is all bones, but still she has no definite structure. Chin propped on her knees, she reaches for the bag Ursula has laid on the table, removes the contents, and arranges them in front of her: two cartons of Sobranies, a lighter, two plastic spoons, a couple of napkins, and a half-gallon carton of ice cream, Ivy's favorite kind, with separate sections of vanilla, chocolate, and strawberry.

"So, how's it going?" Ursula asks, trying to sound casual.

Ivy seems confused by the question, and to avoid answering she concentrates on working the cigarette packaging open with her clawlike fingers. She takes out a green cigarette and then puts it back, preferring to start with a pink one. She smokes rhythmically, bringing the gold filter to the center of her full lips at the beginning of each inhalation, then exhaling to the right. She can finish off an entire pack now in an hour and a half.

"Are you still feeling scared here?" Ursula asks.

"It keeps them away sometimes," she answers in her wispy and whispery voice. She's had this strange half a voice for as long as Ursula can remember. When she was a child it sounded merely frightened and tentative, but as she grew older it acquired an undertone of paradoxical assurance as well, a breathless theatricality befitting a movie starlet who knows that the whole world, craving any opportunity for intimacy with her, will always lean in just a bit closer to hear what she has to say. The voice has become especially appropriate of late, for Ivy now understands herself to be continually watched, photographed from without and surveilled from within. She is the golden goose at the center of the universe. Her menstrual cycles replenish the World Bank. Her breath commodifies the air. In her more communicative moments she has explained these things to Ursula. More often, maybe on the assumption that everything she thinks is already generally known, she speaks in a kind of shorthand that Ursula has to painstakingly unpack word by word.

"What keeps who away?"

Ivy shakes her head, looking down at the table.

"You can tell me," Ursula says. "I won't say anything."

This is a formula that has worked before. Ivy won't open up to anyone else, not even the psychiatrist.

"The smokescreen," she says, taking in and releasing another quick puff. "It's a subterfuge. Oldest trick in the book."

She scrunches her eyebrows, peering down some branching inner path.

"Oldest dick in the nook," she adds.

Ursula has talked with Ivy enough to know there is an elaborate mental process going on beneath everything she does. The smoking, too, she now sees, is connected to some complex internal ritual.

"The Imagineers can't stand it," Ivy says, waving the smoke around. "They turn away."

"Why do they turn away?"

"It reflects badly. The image is tarnished. The tarnish mucketies the reflection. They turn away."

The doctor has instructed her not to humor her sister. She's supposed to talk Ivy out of her delusions immediately as they come up. But Ivy seems so isolated, so desperately lonely in her world, that sometimes Ursula can't help but provide a sympathetic ear. Besides, she's curious. Ivy's world is an interesting place, a complicated place, and the only way to understand it is to draw her out whenever possible. So far she's managed to piece together that Ivy believes herself to be a cavewoman high priestess kidnapped from her prehistoric time by people called the Imagineers. As far as Ursula can make out, these are not the actual Imagineers—the writers and theme park conceptualizers employed by Disney—but rather some kind of cabal of evil businessmen from the future. After snatching Ivy out of her idyllic time and steeping her in the nefarious ways of their own, the Imagineers then sent her to the hapless present to advertise their products. How exactly they sell products to people in other times is one of those nuts-and-bolts matters that don't seem to interest Ivy. Perhaps, Ursula speculates, future corporations have shell subsidiaries in the present. In any event, the Imagineers are continually feeding her stage directions, telling her to cross or uncross her legs, to toss her hair, to keep her eyes focused on certain colors or shapes or parts of people's anatomies. From what Ursula has put together so far, the products Ivy is made to promulgate don't seem to be limited to physical objects but rather include all manner of less tangible things such as gestures, opinions, desires, locations in space, and times of day. Apparently Ivy can sell just about anything, and she's a terribly influential force in the world. Her every action sends powerful messages and brings about massive shifts in worldwide patterns of production and consumption, and correspondingly in the patterns of people's private thoughts, fantasies, needs.

Simultaneously in a low office building across the street and in a tall, thin one high up the mountain's face, horizontal bands of lighted windows go dark. Ivy shakes her head quickly, as though responding to this somehow, brightening the tip of her cigarette with an intake strong enough to collapse her cheeks. The cuffs of their father's old shirt are unbuttoned and flap around her arms, exposing the bandages on her forearms, where, among other places, she cut herself on the night of her crack-up. Ironically enough, it was only her descent into madness that gave her anything approaching her delusory fame. She chose to do it in a very public way, slashing herself bloody and then running naked through Banister Park. The next day her picture was in the local papers. By the time Ursula got to town, a couple of tabloid TV shows were picking up the story as well.

"They want me to sit up straight and push out my chest," Ivy whispers, hunching over further. "They want me to advertise for the Bodies. But it's really for the Antibodies. My belly button lies along the i-axis. I'm the drain magnet in the glamour continuum."

She looks up at Ursula, hoping for comprehension. Not finding it, those strange eyes of hers wander off again. Ursula's own eyes are a little more wide-set than average, but Ivy's are wider still. When she was a child, her wide eyes, small mouth, and pale, bulbous brow gave her face the underdeveloped look of popular conceptions of aliens. When he had them for a weekend once, their father joked around with Ivy, telling her that when she was born, her eyes had been on stalks; that they'd swiveled around independently of each other and seen everything coming and going; and that their mom had performed the surgery to put those eyes back inside her head, where they belonged—or almost, anyway. Later Ivy asked Ursula if it was true; their mom was, after all, a plastic surgeon, and the two sisters had sneaked looks at informational videotapes of procedures that seemed far more unlikely than that. Out of a combination of malice toward Ivy and loyalty to their dad, Ursula swore it was true, and for weeks afterward Ivy wore a baseball hat low over her face to hide her alien deformity.

She stamps out her cigarette and lights another, a pastel-blue one this time, her wide eyes crossing slightly as she brings the flame to the tip.

"The Imagineers are gunning for Total Control," she whispers, staring with suspicion at the plastic spoons on the tabletop. "They've interfiltrated the compound. They monitor all the desire lines. Except the gold."

"That sounds serious."

"I'm keeping the gold open for the trendspotters," she says. "They're my *onlyhope*." She pauses, processing. "My *lonelymope*. Ace-in-the-sleeve. Let-me-leave."

Ivy's predominant facial expression since she was admitted has been the shell-shocked look she wore when she was four, in the months after their parents got divorced, when she'd sit in the backyard day after day gazing at the insects amid their giant blades of grass, her neck twisted, her lower lip pushed out, her eyes adamantly bulged. But now, as she speaks, that other, far rarer look appears. It happens like it always does, all at once and for only a few moments. Her pale, delicate face clears. Her forehead smoothes. Her pout recedes. Her lips curl into a slight, secret smile. This is the look she gets when she talks about the trendspotters. The first time it happened was two weeks ago. She said the trendspotters were with her, hidden but always present. She said they would never abandon her. And they would help her complete her mission and save the human race.

By that time Ursula knew about Chas—not from Ivy, but from her friend and slightly more successful fellow model Sonja Niellsen, who other than telling her his occupation only described him as an "old guy." Ursula had already called him to set up a meeting, with no other plan at the time than to try to get some perspective from him on what Ivy had been going through during the period leading up to her breakdown. But after Ivy started talking about trendspotters, looking as hopeful and com- forted as a child being paid a visit by imaginary friends, Ursula's own hope-starved imagination began to take comfort in the thought of them, too. She pictured the trendspotters as creatures wrapped in mantles of newness, always in the know, always one step ahead of their culture, living perpetually at the gleaming edge of the present, where it sparks and glows fresh from the future's forge. They began to symbolize for her all the ways in which Ivy's life had become different from hers, all the new thoughts and dreams and expetations Ivy's more glamorous existence as a model in Middle City must have entailed, everything that separated them and could conceivably, if only Ursula were initiated, bring them back together.

Ursula had spent the last four years on the outskirts of a small college town, trying without much success to be an artist, having sporadic friendships and relationships with transient grad students, often depressed and all but broke. In many respects her life had been organized around the principle of distrusting glamour. But her sister's illness jarred something loose in her. Wandering the endless skein of Middle City streets after visiting hours, she felt completely disconnected from her past, as though she'd just woken up from a long slumber, a dream of a life that she was relieved to find was not her own—or at least not *necessarily* her own, she thought. It didn't have to be. She could change it all, starting here and now. She could move to the city. She could have a career that was fashionable and relevant and exciting and financially rewarding. She could be successful, stable, secure—the kind of sister in a position to do Ivy some good, the kind who could be a positive presence in her life, who could take care of her, nurse her back to health.

She leans closer to Ivy, basking in the sudden brightness of her eyes.

"*Why* are the trendspotters your only hope?" she pleads, unable to contain her excitement. "How can they help you?"

Ivy points with the cigarette around the room. "The trendspotters *see*. They've got coder-sponders." She points a pinkie at her right temple. Then she winces and clutches her head, moaning uncontrollably. Ursula jumps up and rushes around the table, bends over and hugs her sister, asks her what's the matter, if she's in pain, if she needs a doctor, but already the moaning has subsided into a very quiet, high-pitched noise, like a shriek heard from a great distance. Ursula rocks Ivy against her, feeling guilty for letting the conversation go this far again. She half wishes she could tell Ivy about her new job, let her know that she has the trendspotters close at hand, that whatever help they can possibly bring her, Ursula herself will obtain. But of course this would just nail Ivy's delusions all the more firmly in place.

Gradually Ivy calms down, and Ursula pulls a chair around next to hers and sits down. After looking at the ice cream carton for a minute, Ivy reaches out and tears off the perforated strip, lifts the top, and gazes at the fat, pristine stripes of white, brown, and pink. Years ago Ivy declared that the three colors arranged in the box this way looked like the flag of Candyland.

"This is future ice cream," she whispers. "Isn't it?"

"I don't know. What's the difference?"

"Squibb-Bryer's is the difference. They use the ideal ingredients."

"What are those?"

"Breast milk and semen. Mummy cummy yummy."

She picks up a spoon and grasps it by the base of its handle for leverage. The ice cream is still hard and comes off in small flakes. She works on it intently, excavating the band of chocolate, taking care not to disturb the other two flavors. Watching the tiny crease of concentration appear in the vast, milky expanse between Ivy's eyes, Ursula is reminded of a game they used to play in which they'd act like robots, trying to get each other to smile while keeping their own faces serious and saying absurd things in expressionless voices. Being eight and a half years older, Ursula always had the upper hand, but even so, Ivy was exceptionally good; sometimes she'd hold out all day, even after Ursula had lost, even when Ursula no longer wanted to play. Ursula keeps expecting her to come out of the act now, to let her soul once again reassert itself behind those lost eyes. But all that emerges is little pieces of the former Ivy—here a knitted brow, there a tongue tip poking from flattened lips, occasionally even the trembling top half of a toothy smile—momentary shapes half recognized in choppy water, continually raising and dashing Ursula's hopes. The doctor has told her that Ivy will probably have periods of remission, perhaps even very long ones, but that even in these times she will never be the same person she was; henceforth her mind will be more like a weather system than a transit system, and living with her will be a matter less of regular time-tables than of perpetually shifting forecasts. It will be up to Ursula to find a way to give this convocation of clouds that once upon a time was a sister some semblance of a worthwhile life.

Picking up the other spoon, Ursula joins her sister in the excavation, making a couple of minor forays into the strawberry. Ivy redoubles her efforts, swallowing a heaping mouthful, puffing her cigarette, and then digging into the chocolate once more. She leans over the carton as she digs, and her hair gets between the spoon and the ice cream. By the end of the visit her fine honey-blond hair will be a cloying mass of chocolate and smoke. Ursula has never seen Ivy eat with such determination, and this actually pleases her a little. At least in this one limited sense, Ivy can enjoy herself more than she has ever been able to before. It was always a struggle getting Ivy to eat. When she was in kindergarten, a round-cheeked child full of smirking secrets, she'd hide in the coat closet to avoid snack time. It drove the teacher crazy. Ivy never explained this behavior to anyone's satis-faction. It had something to do with the sharp odor of the apple juice, the sound of the Graham crackers cracking apart between fingers and teeth.

"We won't touch the vanilla today," Ivy whispers, her voice as arid as the smoke rising and dissipating from her lips.

"Why not?" Ursula asks.

"Looks cleaner than it is," she says.

Her eyes go hollow. She puts down the spoon and rests her chin on her knees, rocking her head left and right. A frozen, fleshy chunk of strawberry that Ursula can't swallow bleeds coldness into the center of her tongue as Ivy looks away into that other dimension, that cold, conglomerous future from which all the trouble comes.

Training

Sure, trendspotters are supposed to blend in, Javier explains as they cling to the pole of the jostling subway car and Ursula's rollerbladed feet scramble out from under her, like chameleons in the urban flora, wearing gray suits in the banking district, green toothpaint down on Bissel Boulevard, fleshtone leather pants in the galleries, and so on, sure, one wants to observe without influencing, but he for one has no time for that anymore, *no time,* things are changing too fast, new species of trends evolving, slithering through the underbrush, taking wing, spinning iridescent shapes, bellowing at the moon, some even going extinct before they're ever recorded, puzzled over, learned from, appreciated, and, yeah, sure, *loved,* loved by someone who understands them for what they truly are, those draped necklines and hemp pumps and zydeco rap tunes and poppy perfumes and gingko colas—namely, the pure dialects of human desire, the untrammeled expressions of the cultural unconscious, signs and symbols from the ideal world in which we hope someday to live.

He likes to go fast sometimes, he explains as they hand-over-hand the handrail, rollerblades splaying up the subway steps. He likes to shake things up so he can see them anew. For a while he switched to a go-ped, like everyone else, but the skates allow him more access, and he's confident that everyone else will soon switch back as well. He likes to take the subway to the peak of Middle City and skate all the way down the mountain. Some days he skates down the streets of the West Slope, through the theater district and the upscale residences along Richard W. Held Park; other days he circles around to the South Slope and skates down the broad shopping thoroughfares—down Hull Avenue, say, or Kline Boulevard. And some days he sails all the way down past the old mines and the mouth of the Shackley River and on down to the flatlands, breezing through the Disney townships, Heartland USA, Bogart City, Hipsterville.

Today it's the East Slope. Haloed in sunlight, he holds out his hands and pulls her up the last few steps, his long fingers enveloping her forearms, his spindly frame somehow supporting her with ease, making her feel strangely weightless. For the first time since they sat on her stoop while she put on her skates and he downed a baggie of vitamins and other more mysterious prescription-type pills with his grandissimo frozen coffee drink, Javier is not talking, and the consequent emptiness of Ursula's brain is a little terrifying. His voice has been a constant, there has been no escaping it, she can't even plug her ears, occupied as they already are by earphones that broadcast his giddy whisperings stereophonically in either ear. There's no microphone on her headset, only on his. The tactics of brainwashing.

He pulls her out of the pedestrian traffic, and they stand facing each other on the cement plaza of the Angleton Banking Center, then he lets go of her hands, letting her wobble in place while he skates perfect circles around her, rotating forward and backward as he revolves. Her confidence in these things is already badly shaken from the subway platforms, where she got knocked around and had to wrap her arms and legs around urine-corroded metal beams to keep from pitching into the tracks. If only she'd brought along a pair of normal shoes—but of course out of all the ten thousand things Javier considered worth mentioning, the fact that they'd be getting on a subway and traveling all the way upslope wasn't one of them.

He begins to float away from her backward, beckoning her forward. A bald man in a pastel-yellow suit scatters from his path. Gritting her teeth, she kicks out after Javier across the plaza. He slaloms around the columns of the Angleton building, sails across Colby Street, and spins through a revolving door and into the rainbowed glass atrium of the Hilton. Whereas it takes Ursula's complete attention to keep up with him and not fall down, Javier, for his part, seems to look everywhere but where he's going, all the while mouthing his ongoing quasidialectic of style into the microphone, postulating that rustic-brown tie, worrying however that slate-gray tie with ebony clip, realizing that perhaps—yes, irrefutably—amaranth tie, umber tie, jade-and-sapphire-stippled tie . . .

They skate through Maheu Square and past the Museum of Postmodern Art, with its sculptures of water oaks, weeping hemlocks, and sweetbay magnolias along the curb. He is saying bolero jacket, tunic dress, bee-striped skirt, kid with the bubblepipe, the look in the chauffeur's eyes, sparkly, wistful hint of tear, yes, just cut it and print it and there's your ad for obscurantists—plastics, mutual funds, health care, and sky-blue pipe must match mother's shirt, none of that sepia, must be vibrant, the trend is colorful, not just any colors, shimmery yet guileless, oh, the kind of colors they wear in Heaven.

"The Light Age," he whispers ecstatically as they float over the Snepp Viaduct. He presses his palms together, like a pope on wheels, blessing the flea-market crowd below. "It's all falling into place."

"The Light Age?" she shouts. Startled, he snaps his head toward her and consequently loses his balance, has to wheel his arms wildly to keep from spilling out. Apparently he forgot she could hear him talking. Maybe he forgot she was there at all. He stops himself over the back of a mailbox, then gestures her over. She joins him, grateful for something to hold on to.

"It's the megatrend me and Chas are tracking," he says. At this range his amplified voice feeds back, searing her eardrums. Cursing, she pulls off the headset.

"Oh. Sorry," he gasps, taking his off as well. "Chas is better at explaining it." He whispers now, as if to make up for the previous volume, thereby forcing her to lean still closer to his unusual face. "Chas is a real philosopher, used to teach at MCU and everything. But if you'll bear with me, I'll give it my best shot, OK?"

Chas? A philosophy professor? She tries to picture Chas in a tweed jacket, talking about transcendentalism. She simply can't. The man barely talks at all; *he grunts.* A fact that makes Javier's reverence of him seem a little absurd—and a little touching, too, in a way.

"I'm all ears," she says.

"OK." He pauses to blow his nose. The blue-green silk rag disappears into his trenchcoat as quickly as it emerged. He clears his throat and begins:

"See, niche marketing is getting really sophisticated now. That's part of it. We can subscribe to ever-more-personalized newspapers, magazines, satellite channels, clothing catalogs. We can pop in a CD-ROM and learn how to practice Sufism or Swedenborgianism or Santería. We can choose from dozens of different antidepressant and antianxiety pills, so we can even tailor our moods and perceptions to taste nowadays. With the Internet, we can choose the very communities we want to be a part of as well. You with me so far?"

From the twinned exertions of skating and explaining, his skin is flushed, and his eyes are bright. She thinks she can even feel the heat pulsing off his face. He has a tendency to sniffle, and dark circles under his eyes. She wonders if he's got something contagious. But his face is sort of fascinating from this close up. She doesn't back away.

"The way me and Chas see it," he goes on, "we're on the cusp of something really wonderful. A renaissance of self-creation. In the Light Age we'll be able to totally customize our life experience—our beliefs, our rituals, our tribes, our whole personal mythology—and we'll choose everything that makes us who we are from a vast array of choices. The last barrier is our persistent irony, which fills us with doubt about the validity of our relative truths."

"Our 'irony'?" she asks.

He nods, his grown man's face as open and earnest as a child's. Apparently he himself has transcended this last barrier of which he speaks. She can't help smirking at the thought, and in turn his expression changes to one of confusion and possibly even hurt.

"What?" he asks.

She begins to apologize, but suddenly his attention is elsewhere. She tracks his gaze and discovers a dark-haired woman halfway down the block, sitting on her haunches and peering down through a subway grate. The woman wears an off-white cotton top and black jeans, which separate to reveal two vertebrae of her pale lower back as she bends closer to the sidewalk. Meanwhile, a bike messenger with a three-day beard and a heavy pack is pedaling vigorously up the street toward her. He slows, and the woman cranes her head and gives him a plaintive look, but he passes her without stopping. The woman watches him go by, then stands and wanders off, gazing up disconsolately at the canyon of glass and steel.

When the woman is out of sight, Javier skates over to the grate and drops to his knees. Ursula follows him over, holding his shoulder for balance as she bends down to gaze with him at what the woman lost: a pearl earring, sitting on a bed of dust and cigarette butts on a ledge five or six feet below. Without a word, Javier gets to his feet, skates to a nearby stoop, sits down, and takes a sketchbook and a box of colored pencils from his satchel.

"That cream top was all wrong," he mutters when Ursula sits down next to him. "With those jeans it made her look so stark and abject."

He seems genuinely upset and intently begins designing a new outfit for the woman, explaining how it would stand up to the dramatic shafts of urban daylight and the sidewalk's glare. He gives the woman a purple Indian-print silk tunic with gold embroidery around the collar and sleeves. He gives her a pair of red capri pants. He accessorizes her with a Chinese drawstring hip pouch, red flats, and a playful silver charm bracelet with miniature hearts, horns, and horseshoes to twinkle as she waved for help. His drawing hand trembles a little, but he uses this to his advantage, transmitting a shivering energy to the lines. He's a decent artist, and he details the outfit for her calmly and pleasantly as he draws, and not for the first time today it occurs to Ursula that the man, despite his idiosyncrasies, is not wholly unlikable. To complete the look, he straightens her hair and ties it simply back in a red ribbon that would have shown off her nape as she turned to the bike messenger for help.

"If she'd been wearing this," he says, tapping the sketch with the red pencil, "he would've stopped. Anyone would've stopped. A whole crowd would've gathered."

She pictures the crowd peering downward tentatively, an odd moment of suddenly not quite trusting the ground.

"And then an old woman would've taken a spool of thread from her purse," he enthuses. "And a teenage boy would've taken a piece of gum out of his mouth. And working together they all would've gotten that pearl back for her."

Ursula sees the event happen as he describes it. It takes about half a minute, the length of any commercial. She is half inclined to go out and buy a purple Indian-print silk tunic or a pack of chewing gum. The other half of her is annoyed at the first for being so easily sold.

"That's the kind of world people deserve," he reflects.

"People deserve a world where it wouldn't have mattered what the woman was wearing," she says. "Where people would have stopped to help her anyway."

"But beauty can inspire people to be better. Beauty . . ." He pauses to shade in the ground around the figure of the woman, tilting his head as he draws, thinking, nodding to himself. "Beauty is the PR campaign of the human soul."

He continues smiling as he sketches a few rising squiggles that transform the buildings behind the leggy, crouching woman into a whimsical print pattern. For a moment Ursula is drawn into the calming geometry of his sketch, and then she's back in her own body, conscious of her own appearance, her flushed face, the smell of her sweat. How easy it is for men to talk about beauty, and how subtly intimidating when they do.

"That's where *we* come in," he goes on, shading in the air. "That's our job, Ursula. To give people the beauty they deserve. And from the beauty they deserve will come the love they deserve. And from love will follow truth."

"You don't really believe that, do you?" she asks, squinting at his face against the afternoon sun.

"Sure. Probably. Maybe, anyway." His overlarge, scruffy head blots out the sun when he turns to her, making visible his sad, crooked-toothed smile. "Meanwhile, beauty alone will just have to do, right?"

The question hovers between them. She wants to say no. But his tender eyes and lopsided cross section of teeth make her think just maybe. She laughs, and Javier shrugs and looks at his drawing again, amused as well.

Postirony

. . . Find the future, Chas Lacouture said, leaning back in his chair and allowing Ursula the view, the cloud-capped spires and fog-stockinged spindles of Middle City in breathtaking disarray all the way down the mountain's face, bending and arching and standing on tippytoes, a troupe of colossal robot ballerinas prepping for showtime. And in that moment she felt as though she might do just that, she might venture into the streets of her brand-new home and find the future there waiting for her like an outfit in a window display, and it would be as easy as that: new outfit, new career, new life. She hadn't known she'd give up on trying to be an artist after she moved here—a *real* artist, she had thought, whether idealistically or snobbishly, she's no longer sure, not just a commercial artist—but she must have secretly been hoping she would, hoping she *could* give up, otherwise why would she now feel so little regret and so much relief? Her foray into the world of art had been a serious miscalculation, a boondoggle, her own personal Somalia, an effort to save a seething mass of humanity with a compass and a bowie knife. It's only now she's out that she realizes the profound and pitiless extent of her desire never to return.

In retrospect there was something more than a little monomaniacal about her last four years, spent painting and repainting the same theme in dozens of variations. They were all triptychs, some actually consisting of three separate panels, some divided in more subtle ways, but all presenting three distinct views of the subject at hand: in every painting there was an idealized world and an infernalized world and the everyday world in between—three takes on the same objects, or people, or landscapes, or even abstract geometries. It was odd stuff, it now seems to her, but she sent it out into the world full of hope of understanding and ambition for recognition. She allowed herself to imagine that her paintings would be accessible to and even resonate deeply with people, but for one reason or another her work never caught the attention of more than a handful of minor galleries, and only a couple of the pieces ever sold. And meanwhile, her kid sister moved to Middle City and began peddling her own little triptych: of wide-set eyes, perky tits, and long, skinny legs. This was the visual art, it seemed, that the world had use for. In the few brief phone conversations they had in the year before her breakdown, Ivy told her about all the work she was getting—she was slated to be on every runway, in every magazine, she bragged and bragged. The boastfulness was some-thing new, uncharacteristic, but Ursula was too full of resentment and self-loathing to question it, and when Ivy stopped calling, it only fed Ursula's bitterness even more, and she herself made no effort to renew their contact. Had she known that Ivy, in all her time in Mid City, had gotten just one major print ad and other than that only an intermittent stream of less glamorous jobs, mostly for foreign clothing catalogs, and that furthermore she was losing her protracted struggle to hold on to her sanity, Ursula would have acted differently, of course. But this doesn't make her feel any better now. She knew there was no one else in the world to look after Ivy, certainly not their parents, and that alone should have been reason enough for her to keep tabs on her sister.

Looking after Ivy has pretty much always been Ursula's job. Even before the divorce their father was never really a part of the family, and as for their mother, motherhood just never ranked among her various engross-ing interests. So Ivy ended up mostly in Ursula's charge, and despite their substantial age difference, they did what they could together. They walked to school and home from school. They entertained each other with story-tellings and games of make-believe for which Ursula was a little too old and Ivy a little too young. They sat under a tree in the backyard and made marathon courses for bugs. In time it would fall to Ursula to answer all the body questions—when and what to shave, what to do about men-struation. Ursula took her job as surrogate parent seriously, as she took

everything seriously. She was diligent in schoolwork and sports and hob-
bies, responsible to a fault, carving out self-imposed rules and parameters
to which she would arduously adhere in an attempt to counteract the
chaos of her largely parentless childhood. Her expectations of Ivy were
likewise exactingly high, as was her disappointment when Ivy failed to live
up to them. At a time when Ursula had enrolled herself in drawing classes
and was spending two hours a day afterward working on her sketches, Ivy
would sit on her own in an unused corner of the room, making drawings
as well. To Ursula's consternation, Ivy's drawings were all the same drawing, the same exact cartoon mouse, over and over again. She filled book
after book with this mouse, or rather mostly just fragmentary beginnings
of it, sometimes just a line or two, the curved side of a face, a couple of
eyelashes, a solitary whisker, at which point she'd abandon the drawing
because something about it just wasn't right, and she'd need to start again
on a fresh page. Finally one day she put down her sketchbook, never to
pick it up again. This would become a pattern. Ivy would obsess over something every waking minute for weeks or even months and then abruptly
walk away and forget all about it.

From an early age Ivy was branded the spacey one. Other kids made fun
of her for her indifference toward their games and their company, and
Ursula, incensed, would stand up for her time and again, but Ivy herself
never took offense. She never got upset, never defended herself, never
seemed to care about anything deeply. She didn't do sports, didn't make
friends, didn't do well in class. Ivy's behavior galled Ursula at the time, but
over the years she would come to realize that it stemmed from the fact that
deep down Ivy thought that nothing she did could possibly matter. Her
self-esteem was so low that she was less a child than a pale, flitting ghost,
both to herself and to everyone around her.

After Ursula graduated from high school, she decided to attend a local
college and keep living at home so she could be there for Ivy, but over the
next four years Ivy herself was there less and less. She made a couple of
friends, a pair of precociously sophisticated and alienated girls from the
neighborhood, and spent all her waking hours in one or the other of their
homes. Over that time her body grew from scrawny to lithe; her wide-set
eyes went from weird to exotic; and suddenly she was the prettiest girl in
school. Wherever she went, boys tracked her motions with longing, and
girls with jealousy. She visited Ursula's campus once, and even the college-
age guys couldn't help themselves from staring, their desire pathetically
plain on their flushed, confused faces, while Ivy, to Ursula's rage and

amazement, demurely encouraged them, flirting with shocking expertise. Her looks had given her something that, if it was not exactly confidence, at least resembled confidence from afar. She could playact any way she wanted now, and people would more or less follow along. She became almost inhumanly self-sufficient, her own best friend, doing and saying whatever she felt like and never thinking of the consequences. Back in the neighborhood, a mystique began to grow up around her. Kids would tell stories about her, mostly involving drugs, and after a while Ursula stopped refuting them. She doubted they were true, but she was no longer completely certain. Ivy slipped further and further from Ursula's control, and fairly or not, Ursula felt unappreciated and even, in a way, betrayed, and finally she washed her hands of her sister altogether and left for grad school in another state.

From then on she would see Ivy only through the time lapse of summers and holidays, and the rest of the picture would be filled in through tales she'd hear from friends, about Ivy's monthlong school absences, her failed classes, her nomination for homecoming queen and subsequent nonattendance of the ceremony. When Ivy told her that everyone said she should be a model and so that was what she was planning to do, Ursula made one last attempt to guide her, telling her she didn't have to do that, necessarily, she was capable of other things in life. But by then Ursula was bitter about her own life, about her own lack of success of any kind, and her bitterness turned to jealousy when she saw Ivy's Hugo Banzer ad in *Glamour* magazine—a cool, gorgeous, disaffected Ivy slouching on a Mid City subway car in a stretch silk slip dress with her knees haphazardly parted, next to a chiseled guy in a T-shirt and snakeskin pants. In that moment she decided that Ivy epitomized all the things about the culture that conspired to make people unhappy, all the glitz and shallowness and materialism and facile beauty worship. Underneath this lay a more personal sense of outrage at the idea that Ivy had coasted through life without making the slightest effort and was now a success, whereas she herself had always worked like a dog, and still there was no reward in sight for her. It took Ivy's crack-up for Ursula's bitterness to melt into all the old feelings—the duty, the sorrow, the guilt, the rending, hopeless love.

So Ursula has taken up the old mission to save her sister one more time. She doesn't know whether her learning about trendspotters will end up giving her any further access to Ivy's inner world, but it may at least give her some access to an outer world, a world beyond her ever-shrinking sense of the possible in life. Chas and Javier will teach her to read the future in the colors of ties and the flavors of snack foods and the lyrics to pop songs, and maybe this future really will be different from anything she has previously thought possible, maybe it really will turn out to be more than just a fairy tale, more than an idle longing, a fatuous idealization, a story she tells herself when her life gets too oppressive, when she's walking along a busy avenue trying not to inhale the more or less constant car exhaust and a homeless man is walking alongside her talking about how his limousine broke down and he needs change for the train, or when she's on the train just before it goes around a curve so loud it makes her want to scream to equalize the pressure in her head, or in the sad silence when she turns off the TV after wasting an hour of her life watching celebrities promote their latest hairdos and personalities, or when she's in bed at night, like now, desperately needing to clear her mind of thoughts about money and fame and respect and other things she doesn't have and will never have and will never stop hating herself for wanting. She takes a breath, and another, lying on her back, the soft weight of the pillow over her eyes, and tries to imagine the future, the postironic future, the future of the savage girl's dreams. What will it be like, this future? There will be no Middle City, for one. There will be no Lady of Nazareth Hospital, no airless, windowless psycho wards smelling of steamed eggs and antiseptics, no corner-mounted TV sets bristling with snide, self-satisfied car salesmen and fashion models, no fashion models period—self-satisfied, self-loathing, schizophrenic, or otherwise.

She takes a breath, and another, slow and deep, exhaling the present, exhaling her anxiety, her loneliness, exhaling the stale air of her still coldly unfamiliar apartment, breathing the future in. It starts with a warm energy like sunlight in her lungs, gently massaging her muscles. The warmth flows into her nerves, her veins, until she can feel her heart beginning to glow. She closes her eyes. It's a warm, breezy, sunlit day in the Light Age, and the trees are ten feet thick and a hundred feet tall, and she's lying in a canoe, looking up into the glimmering, flickering scalework of leaves on the underbelly of the sky, and the whiff of wild roses cleanses her from the inside out. On the riverbanks, flowers are now blooming luxuriantly and sending delicious waves of summer scent over the eddying water. The trees are broad-based and sturdy, and the forest goes on forever, with trees of all kinds—pines, hickories, chestnuts, oaks, willows—interspersed with meadows and ponds. Sustainable living has made of the forest a lush garden of fruits, spices, and medicinal herbs, teeming with deer and elk and foxes and ruffed grouse. There is no hunger, no want: it turns out that poverty was something created by money, and there is no money here, no mass production, no advertising, no entertainment industry. Work is an opportunity to feel the power of the muscles and the health of the mind, and play is meaningful, a ritual for reconnecting one's spirit to the spirit of nature. Both the work and the play are something to look forward to, but at the moment there is nothing to do but enjoy the gentle motion of the boat, the intimate trickle of water against its sides, the warmth of the future sun on her eyelids, the coolness of the future breeze in her nostrils, as Ursula's boat rocks and drifts her peacefully, lovingly, almost unironically, even, to sleep.

Warpaint

Ursula came here as a teenager, one of the thousands comprising the nightly spectacle that was and still is Harvey Street, a heady blend of tourists and suburbanites who make the pilgrimage by the busload for the pleasure of dressing up in system-buckingly cheap thrift-store outfits, or the harrowingly expensive designer knockoffs thereof, and promenading up and down this quasi-world-famous strip in order to gawk and scoff at the other dressed-up or dressed-down tourists and suburbanites who, in turn, are gawking and scoffing at them.

All of this is just as she remembers it, but there have been some changes, too. The customary "Mid City Sucks" T-shirt has evolved into several hardier, more virulent strains, such as the "I Paid a Malaysian Textile Worker's Monthly Wage for a Middle City T-shirt" T-shirt, and the still more eye-straining "I Got Insulted, Robbed, Raped, Jailed, Hooked on Crack, and *Gang* Raped in the Mid" T-shirt. The Narcotics Anonymous meeting hall and the Scientology recruiting office have been supplanted by two theme restaurants: Medea, where you can have a meal vaguely resembling your murdered offspring, and GrossOut!, where you can dine surrounded by blown-up photographs of rare skin diseases, Siamese twins, radiation victims, flamethrower victims, cannibals gnawing on roasted hands, women eating feces from men's anuses or menstrual blood from other women's vaginas, jars of pickled mutant fetuses, cross-sectioned heads, and maggots feasting on cats' carcasses. And the old wino mime with the sign saying he was trying to raise $1,000,000.25 for wine research has been forced out by an invasion of slicker operators: the mime who screams at passersby, the mime who mimics different people using exactly the same mannerisms, the mime who feels for a way out of an actual glass box.

It was never exactly a cultural mecca, but still, Ursula can't help feeling there's something insidious about the changes here. In high school the one thing she learned in her blow-off Earth Science class was that Earth and Venus started off almost exactly the same, the only difference between them being a temperature variation of about four degrees, which tiny difference caused a tiny bit more water to evaporate from the oceans, trapping a little more carbon dioxide in the atmosphere, which trapped a little more heat and caused the temperature to rise a couple more degrees, which caused more water to evaporate, and so on, until the planet was a seven-hundred-degree hellhole of corrosive gas. The lesson concerned a brand-new theory known as chaos, and she never forgot it: in chaotic systems, slight differences in initial conditions can over time produce massively divergent outcomes.

Ursula has the eerie feeling that she's now witnessing the early stages of a similar kind of experiment. There's something off balance here, and that certain something—she's almost prepared to admit it—may very well be irony. Excessive amounts of it have been released into the atmosphere. The city is already too cool for its own good, and the temperature is dropping. Soon it will be supercool, too cool for living tissue. The only survivors will be a race of disaffected, lounge-posing, ad copy–writing, indie film–watching androids.

The epicenter of the impending catastrophe may in fact be this very stoop, overlooking a cappuccino and tattoo parlor on one side and a combination religious-icon and sex-toy shop on the other, to perch on which her tireless trainer, Javier Delreal, has unerringly brought them for the purpose of people watching. Apparently this is a ritual of his, and it involves not only sitting on this stoop but also drinking beer. They have the stoop but not the beer, which is making him anxious.

"You know," he says, "it isn't just a matter of beer. It's a matter of tallboys. In paper bags, the little paper bags designed specifically for tallboys."

She pretends not to listen, having by now determined she can do this without risking her job. He doesn't seem to take offense. She leans over the book on her lap, sketching the various new hairstyles bobbing past and giving them fanciful names: The Whirl. The Deep-fry. The Porcupine. The Pan-o'-Jell-O. It's been a long day. Her legs are aching and her feet are sore from two days of rollerblading, and Javier gave her only an hour off to shower and change and eat before making her meet him again for this nocturnal outing. In her sketchbook, her pencil marks come out deep and jagged, the emergent faces vulgar and discomposed, the trunks like shards of flint, no arms or legs. The figures are so mean- and disturbed-looking that she almost laughs at herself. Eventually she'll have to turn them into airbrushed marketing fodder, and it's not so much an aesthetic revolt as a perverse moral impulse that makes her want to render that job as difficult as possible for herself.

"The can of beer has to be in the paper bag. Right up to the rim," he goes on. "So when you take a swig your bottom lip touches the paper, not the can. And that little bit of paper gets soaked with the beer. And you taste the brown paper bag as well as the beer."

It's not because she doesn't want a beer that she's resisting. She likes beer, and the way he describes it actually makes her gulp with anticipation. But for some reason she suspects that Javier *doesn't* like beer, that he would never even think of wanting one if he didn't happen to be sitting on a Harvey Street stoop on a Saturday night, the same way he'd probably opt for a piña colada on a tropical vacation or a Pernod in the bar at Charles de Gaulle Airport.

"It's not a good precedent, to forgo the tallboys," he explains. "Things like that have consequences. People who sit on stoops without tallboys come to bad ends."

"Like what?" she says.

"They end up donating kidneys. Filling out place-mat puzzles. Rooting in cockfights."

"So go get a beer. I'm not stopping you."

"No. You've got to have one too. It wouldn't be right with just me drinking. We've got to sit here and be like two synchronized pistons. Slow-motion-like. Me drinking, you pausing. You drinking, me pausing. That's just the way these things are done."

She closes her sketchbook. "Hey, Javier, what do you say we go get some beer?"

"Check."

They get up and walk to the corner store, which Javier refers to, with due reverence, as a *bodega*. Apparently this bodega is part of Javier's ritual as well. He talks about what a good bodega it is, how it's one of the last of its kind, well lit but not overlit, how the narrow aisles are stocked almost all the way to the low ceiling, allowing you to shop with a feeling of privacy and even intimacy.

"They put the little cookie bags up there on the top shelf," he says, pointing. "If you see them, it's only by accident. They're almost out of reach, even. That's great, really great."

"Why?"

"It's so innocent. Everyone knows you put the impulse items right by the counter. They teach you things like that in grade school nowadays. But it works here, don't you think? It makes you feel secure. It's exactly where your parents put the cookies, way up in a jar on the top shelf behind the bag of flour and the box of oatmeal." Javier gazes moonily at the bright packages.

"Is that where your parents put the cookies?" she asks.

"My parents? No. We didn't have cookies."

For a moment his face goes slack, losing its hyperintensity, becoming, she thinks, what it must really look like. It's a strange face, sad and a little beautiful, even, every feature—eyes, nose, cheekbones, lips, chin—a little too big or too long, like an Eastern Orthodox saint's. But then he smirks, and his eyes dart at her puckishly.

"I was raised by Gypsies."

He picks a can of cat food off the shelf. "Filet mignon–flavored. Take a look."

The cat on the label is wearing a miniature robe, tall gray wig, and crown, in the style of Catherine the Great.

"There's actual filet mignon in it," he says.

"That's kind of sick."

"Cats are there to be indulged. That's their function: to receive the love and devotion we never fully gave our parents. Not like dogs. Dogs are there to give us the love and devotion our children will never fully give *us*. You've never seen a dog wearing a tiara on a dog-food can, right?"

"Not that I can remember," she admits.

"Well, now you know why. What about you?"

"What *about* me?"

"Did you have cookies in cupboards?"

"I guess so."

"Loving parents? Happy childhood?"

"That's kind of a sore subject," she says.

He looks at her expectantly. She gives in.

"They divorced when I was thirteen," she begins. "Standard story. My dad left my mom for a slightly younger woman, moved away with her, and started a slightly younger family. Not very inventive, but then, he's not the interesting one. That's my mother Gwennan's job. Pretty much her full-time one since she lost her real job."

"What was her job?"

"She was a plastic surgeon, until she did a few operations on a woman who wanted to look like Betty Boop."

"Betty Boop," Javier repeats. "Sure, she's pretty hot, for a cartoon."

"I guess I'm not making myself entirely clear. The woman didn't just want to kind of resemble her; she wanted to have the exact same proportions as the cartoon character—her face, her body, everything. She was a performance artist, or wanted to be one. The operations were going to be a publicity stunt for the Postfeminist Movement. Her life-character would be known as the Boopleganger, and her mission would be to disrupt media events."

Javier nods somberly, bulging his cheek with his tongue. "And . . . your mother did the operations."

"My mother is a supporter of the arts. That's more or less what she told the jury when the woman sued."

"She didn't do a good job?"

"No, she did a *very* good job. She obsessed over the job. She did eleven operations on the woman over four years. She planned out each one for months. She stopped taking other clients. She'd sit in her study poring over medical books, making notes and sketches, screening Betty Boop cartoons against the window shade using an old movie projector. The result of it all—the Boopleganger, I mean—was, well, something less than human, more than cartoon."

"'Less than human'?"

"It's not easy to describe. Her nose was just a kind of fleshy tab. Her lips were sort of sectioned off, and collagen was pressure-pumped into the centers. Her cheekbones were like the bony faceplates of a rhinoceros. Her breasts, I'm pretty sure, were unrivaled by anything in history except for maybe a couple Indian fertility goddesses."

"Wow," Javier mumbles. "So did she do her performance art? I never heard anything about it."

"No. She stayed indoors, mostly. At first she wanted everything complete before she made her appearance. And then . . . she just didn't want to go out. The final operation was going to be on her eye sockets, which my mom was planning to expand so they could contain plastic replicas of Betty's giant moonpie eyes. These would be removable, for the Boopleganger to use primarily during performances. In court the Boopleganger's lawyer argued that no ethical and responsible plastic surgeon would ever have collaborated in the plans of a woman so clearly deranged—which, according to the Boopleganger herself, she'd been all along."

"And then she . . . um . . . *stopped* being deranged?"

"She testified she got her sanity back suddenly one day and found herself hideously deformed; a couple psychiatrists explained her condition. But none of the testimony was really necessary anyway. The sight of her alone probably would have convinced any jury. The clincher was when Gwennan admitted under cross-examination that she'd encouraged the Boopleganger to go on with the operations even after she started expressing doubts. Gwennan basically confessed she'd become emotionally invested in the project."

"I can see how that wouldn't look too good."

"My mother was a postmodern Dr. Frankenstein, and the Boopleganger was her creation, her true daughter, a monster that returned to destroy her. The newspaper editorials called it a lesson to any and all who would presume to overstep the natural limits of taste."

Javier looks at her—a little fearfully, she thinks.

"What happened to your mother after that?" he asks.

"She became a Buddhist, joined a bridge club, and in her one or two hours of spare time a week devoted herself to raising her children."

He smiles weakly. "Good thing for the bridge and Buddhism, eh?"

She laughs, and a look of something, understanding or solidarity, passes between them. Ursula is happy for this—she hasn't had anyone she's felt she could talk to in a while—but their quiet moment is interrupted by two women in party dresses and teased hair who saunter between them and over to the beer coolers. After a little comparison shopping, they pick out two six-packs of Corona.

Javier leans over and whispers in her ear.

"How about I show you an old trick Chas taught me?" He winks at her, then strides over to the cooler.

"Hey. You guys headed for the party?" he asks, reaching in for a six of Dos Equis. One of the women hesitates, but the other says yes.

"So are we. I'm Javier, and this is Ursula."

They respond with their names. The one in the skunk-print slip is Bettina. The one with the pointillist landscape dress is Tammy.

"So who do you guys know?" Bettina asks Ursula on their way to the counter.

"We're part of John's contingent," Javier explains.

"John?" Bettina says. "Which John?"

"John Hayden."

"Oh. I don't know that John."

"He's in sales."

"We're in sales," Tammy says.

"Really? Are we talking the same company?"

"General Foods?" she asks.

"Right. Well, he's mostly regional nowadays." He tosses a Payday bar down next to his six-pack on the counter. "You probably wouldn't see him much. Hey, Santos."

He shakes hands with the weary Latino man behind the counter and asks him to break a hundred, talking about Middle Eastern counterfeiting rings as Santos holds the bill under an ultraviolet lamp. By the time the group gets out onto the street Javier has already changed the subject a few times over, with a little help from the headlines on the row of newspapers next to the door. Tearing into his candy bar, he brings up a recent murder mystery in Richard W. Held Park, about which the two women profess fear and exhibit excitement. He tries out yesterday's capture of a guerrilla leader in central Africa, but they aren't too keen on politics, so he shifts back to the familiar: the British royal family, the latest fun-loving-hitmen buddy movie.

They turn uphill on Singlaub and are met by the full moon, nestled beside a low cloud of crater ash above the volcano's mouth, its cushiony underside illuminated by the jeweled city lights.

Tammy and Bettina gaze at the tableau.

"Full moon," Tammy says softly. "Anything could happen tonight." Bettina nods, her eyes misted, her face newly serene and hopeful. It's as though the two of them had been sprinkled with pixie dust. Javier gives Ursula a look that says, This Is Significant.

"What's it *mean* to you?" Javier asks the two women. "That bright big moon up there?"

Tammy and Bettina give each other an amused, questioning look, silently conferring, probably, on the issue of whether Javier is weirder than he is cute or cuter than weird. They seem, at least provisionally, to settle on the latter, and begin trying to answer his question. Javier keeps eyeing Ursula as the women talk about travel, adventure, romance. He begins to prompt them. Does it mean newness or oldness? They talk about childhood camp-outs under the stars and about ancient mysteries and decide it means both. Does it mean belonging or separation? Again they decide it means both. Wholeness or emptiness? Wholeness, definitely. He asks them if they're superstitious, and at first they don't think so, but then Tammy admits that her horoscopes are often quite accurate, and then Bettina talks about her frequent déjà vu experiences and the dream she had about flying, which was a lot like the skydiving scene in the TV movie she saw the next night, and then Tammy relates *her* recent dream of going to a shoe store and being fitted with a pair so soft she couldn't even feel the ground. She thinks it might mean something, but she isn't sure.

To Javier, of course, it means something.

"Superstition is on the rise," he whispers to Ursula.

They turn up the driveway of a luxury high-rise and take the elevator to the seventy-seventh floor. She wonders how Javier can be so sure they won't be stepping into something they can't possibly fake their way through— a dinner party, a bridal shower, a living room in which four people are playing Scrabble—but as it turns out, he's judged the women well: the party is large and well under way, the apartment a duplex in which seventy or so people are milling around in the main rooms of the lower floor and a dozen more are out on the back terrace. The crowd is midtwenties to thirties, professional, the men wearing regulation dress-down Friday khakis and audaciously baggy sport coats, the women dressed on the whole more casually than Bettina and Tammy. The front room is decorated with cartoon stills, and the back with vintage liquor and cigarette ads.

A stocky man in a black satin shirt and black jeans strides over to bellow hello to Bettina and Tammy and stick a hand in Javier's direction.

"Ed Cabaj," he announces.

"Javier Delreal. And this is—"

"Ursula," Ursula cuts in.

Cabaj appraises her, his bushy eyebrows furrowing toward the center of his broad, red, balding head. "You look familiar," he says. "Have we met before?"

"We probably met at some other party," she says, looking off through the terrace window. "Octoberfest? Mardi Gras? Day of the Dead?"

"They're friends of John . . ." Bettina pauses. "What did you say his name was?"

"Hammond," Javier says, at the same time Tammy says "Hayden." "Hammond," he corrects her.

"And he invited you here?" Cabaj says.

Javier looks back at him innocently, opening his hands. "Well, he lives here, doesn't he?"

"No," Cabaj says. "*I* live here."

"You're kidding!"

Ursula begins scanning for exits. Javier turns to her and says, "You know what, Ursula? I think we've come to the wrong party! Isn't this Four eighty-four West McCone?"

"No. It's Four eighty-four West *Wisner*," Cabaj says.

"Aha! This is fantastic! They'll crack up at John's place when I tell them about this. I'll tell them all what a great party you're throwing over here. Tell me, Ed, what is it you do?"

After a bit of formalized modesty, Cabaj reveals that he's the head of marketing for General Foods' New Beverage division. As it turns out, this is a very challenging job. It is a very exciting time for new beverages. You have to be very creative nowadays in marketing. Javier keeps feeding him questions, he and Ursula going into Very Interested mode, eyes widened 14 percent, nodding every 3.7 seconds. Cabaj hammers the ball back into Javier's court.

"So now tell *me* what *you* do."

Javier gives the one-word answer, which of course doesn't satisfy. Sensing no end to the conversation in sight, Ursula excuses herself to get a drink. She finds the wet bar in the kitchen and makes herself a vodka tonic in a tall glass, happy at long last to finally have a minute alone—ridiculously happy, downright giddy, in fact. She can't believe Javier scammed their way in here like that, can't believe he got away with it. The drink, she sees, looks just as it should—the tall glass, the rough-cut ice cubes, the slight rainbow brightening the faint tonic fizz. She moves over to the garnish bowls and finds Bettina and Tammy behind her. She holds up her drink for their inspection.

"Have you ever seen a vodka tonic that looked so much like a vodka tonic?" she asks.

Bettina and Tammy exchange an ambiguous look. Ursula goes on.

"It could be in an ad for vodka, or for tonic, or for glassware, or for investment services. This vodka tonic has star potential." She addresses the drink: "Stick with me, kid. We'll *go* places!"

They smile. And cut her, turning to talk to a man who's just walked up, an effete-looking guy with octagonal-lensed glasses and a trimmed hedge of curly hair. Mission accomplished. She returns her attention to her preferred companion, the drink. Lemon wedge or lemon peel? The wedge would taste better, but the peel would look better. The choice might have seemed obvious to her before, but no longer. Appearances *mean* something, after all. They offer a pleasure all their own. Ultimately she hits upon the solution of squeezing the wedge over the drink, disposing of it, and then dropping in the peel. Who says you can't have it all?

But the operation takes too long. Cabaj and Javier have appeared. Cabaj is pressing close to Javier, asking him to explain what he means about something. Javier hesitates, then steps up to the bar.

"OK, this is kind of what I mean," he says. "This is the world." His hands pass over the glittering rows of bottles and then flutter over a silver serving tray, clearing it off. He picks up the tray and balances it on top of the bottles. He then begins to place things on the tray—the bowl of pretzels, the martini shaker, the plate of limes.

Cabaj laughs nervously. "That's several hundred dollars worth of booze you're playing with," he says.

"Exactly," Javier concurs. "And *this*," he says, gesturing quickly at the upper level, "is the world above the world."

Around the pretzel bowl he places four more bottles, then balances the cheese tray on top of *those* bottles. He does all of this quickly, recklessly, but the balance is perfect. Cabaj watches, hypnotized by the movement of his hands.

"You see? The world above the world," Javier says. "Our world exists only to hold up this other world, this ideal world. It's the world of our dreams, our desires. It's elaborate, it's heavy, and we carry it around with us everywhere. But we don't mind. The more that's up here, the better. Because up here is where we keep all that's best in us. The more that's up here, the richer our imagination becomes."

Behind Ursula a small crowd of people has gathered. They all watch expectantly, murmuring and laughing, waiting for catastrophe to strike.

"Now the limes," Javier says, leaning in and pointing, "and the pretzels, and the bowl and the plate, these are *products*. Products are the materials we use to build our world above the world."

Cabaj nods, and Javier runs a hand through his tangled black hair, the two of them gazing teary-eyed at the ramparts and pinnacles of the wet-bar metropolis.

"It's nice to hear someone talk about marketing positively for a change,"

Cabaj says, reaching for a bottle safely off to the side and pouring out a couple of neat tumblers of scotch. "It's refreshing. In this business it's so easy to forget the bigger picture."

Javier accepts a glass from Cabaj. "Market researchers are public advocates," he says. "We bring consumers' desires to the attention of private companies. We're like congressmen: we represent the public."

Cabaj nods, thoughtful, then looks to Ursula. "You think of yourself this way, too?" he asks.

"Not so much like a congressman," she says. "More like . . . a missionary. Or maybe a saint. Like Mother Teresa, kind of, but with an expense account."

Cabaj begins to smile, but she keeps a straight face, and the gears of his own face slip, leaving his mouth half open and his eyebrows half cocked.

Javier holds up his glass.

"So. Here's to marketing," he says cheerily. The glass trembles slightly in his hand, and he quickly brings it to his mouth. She remembers the bag of pills and the handkerchief in his pocket, and she wonders what's wrong with him. The idea that he has some kind of terminal illness takes a sudden, frightening hold of her. As she watches him swallow the drink and wipe his forehead with his sleeve, the idea gains strength in her mind: his frenzied pace, his almost spiritual need to find meaning everywhere, his complete lack of cynicism—these could very well be the qualities of a man who knows he has only a short time to live, a man who's determined to soak up all the love he can in the time remaining to him.

Javier and Cabaj look at her. She realizes she hasn't joined in the toast to marketing. She raises her glass and drinks, inwardly laughing at herself. The fact that she can understand optimism only as a desperate response to terminal illness no doubt says more about her own cynicism than it does about Javier.

"So, Ed," Javier says. "What's this revolutionary new product of yours you mentioned?"

Cabaj hesitates, looking back and forth between them. He scans the kitchen to make sure no one else is listening.

"All right, kids. I guess I can let you in."

He rechecks the room and then leans in closer.

"Diet water," he whispers.

"Diet water," Javier repeats sagely, and the two of them nod.

Ursula studies Cabaj's face feature by feature. She finds evidence of booze in his flushed cheeks and the faint skein of capillaries on the tip of his nose. She finds evidence of poor grooming in the form of a couple of recently clipped nose hairs beached on the reef of his upper lip. She finds no trace of irony. She feels the vodka beginning to burn a hole in her stomach.

Javier keeps nodding sagely for a moment longer, then shakes his head. "I don't understand," he admits.

Cabaj smiles. "No problem. Think about it: water is fattening. Not literally, of course. I mean, it doesn't contain or produce fat. But still, you know, it does keep those dieters from losing as much weight as they could, right? Because the water is *retained*. I mean, how often have you heard women complain about water retention? How much heavier it makes them, how bloated it makes them feel?"

"Diet water," Javier repeats, his forehead showing the struggle beneath to join these two words into a single idea. He turns to Ursula, a small, troubled knot on his brow. "Is it true, Ursula? Does water make you feel bloated?"

"Sure. Every time I drink from a fire hose." As punctuation, she downs her vodka.

Cabaj acknowledges her wit with a laugh and a hot hand on her back.

"We've perfected an artificial form of water," he says, a keen blaze in his eyes. "It passes through the body completely unabsorbed. It's completely inert, completely harmless. It's extremely simple to manufacture, and we've got all the compounds used to make it on the fast track for FDA approval. But of course, with a product this . . . as I said, *revolutionary*, there might be some entirely . . . foreseeable degree of reservation on the part of the consumer. So I've got to figure out just the right pitch. I mean, the thing's gonna take some finesse, you dig?"

Cabaj is now leaning in so close that his aftershave vapors sting Ursula's face.

"But . . . ," Javier says, "but won't people be thirsty?"

Cabaj guffaws, his bulk rippling beneath the satin shirt. "No problem. They'll buy more. They can drink all they want, guilt-free."

Cabaj is in high spirits. Javier's smile is weaker.

"Well. . . ." Javier laughs, scratching his head. ". . . Well, Ursula, diet water. What do you think of that?"

Ursula looks at him, at his strained half smile, his liquid, frightened-looking eyes. It occurs to her that he may be feeling the same hole in his stomach that she is.

"It had to happen eventually, I suppose."

Her response seems to cheer him.

"That's true," he says, smiling a little more genuinely now. "I'm amazed I never thought of it myself."

"If you had, you'd be a pretty rich son of a bitch," Cabaj says. "Or whoever you worked for would be, anyway."

Javier nods. "Our agency can help you with this," he says.

Cabaj smiles slyly. "You think so?"

"We'll tell you exactly the kind of pitch people are in the mood for. As I told you, we've got contacts in every major city in the world, and a research department that can tell you everything there is to know about your target market." He hands Cabaj his card. "Give us a call. We'll make your beverage go down so smooth people won't know how they lived without it."

Javier's crooked-toothed smile loiters on his face like a vagrant who doesn't really want to be there but has nowhere better to go. He glances at Ursula and quickly away, again his eyes retreating to the comforts of the liquor-bottle landscape. Cabaj, she now sees, is staring at her.

"Excuse me—Ursula, did you say your name was?"

She nods.

"You're a model, aren't you?"

"No, sorry, never done that."

"Oh. I was almost sure. But I've been looking at head shots for two weeks straight. I look around and see nothing but head shots. Still, I could've sworn. . . ." He pauses, his jaw slightly unhinged. Without looking away from her, he holds up a finger and calls out to the hedge-haired guy, who's still standing nearby with Tammy and Bettina: "Hey, Lucien."

The man looks up and then floats over, carrying the women in his wake. He has a sinuous way of walking, as though propelled by small snakes fastened to the bottom of his shoes.

"Couldn't we get someone like her?" Cabaj asks him.

Lucien presses his octagonal glasses up his nose, and he and Cabaj set about examining Ursula, tilting their heads this way and that. Bettina and Tammy follow suit, regarding her with renewed interest, and Javier begins dumbly staring as well.

Meanwhile, Ursula smiles like she doesn't have a thought in her head, like she doesn't know exactly what's coming next.

"She looks like Ivy Van Urden," Lucien concludes.

Cabaj furrows his brows, trying to place the name.

"She does, doesn't she?" Bettina says.

"The name sounds familiar," Cabaj says.

"*You* know, Ed," Bettina says. "That wannabe model who went nuts last month?" She smiles at the memory.

Cabaj laughs. "Oh, yeah. She was some kind of streaker or something, right?"

Javier glances worriedly at Ursula.

"She ran stark naked through . . ." Bettina pauses. "Which park was it?"

"Ray E. Davis Park," Tammy says.

"Richard W. Held Park," Lucien says.

"Banister Park," Ursula corrects them.

"Right!" Bettina enthuses.

"Of course!" Cabaj says gratefully. "And she cut herself, too, or something, right?"

"Carved herself like a pumpkin," Ursula says. The others laugh, except for Javier, who runs his hand through his hair nervously.

"And . . . ," Cabaj says, "didn't she have on . . . warpaint?"

Ursula freezes. The memory of Chas's reference to warpaint comes back to her. And the way he stared at her when he said it. She didn't make the connection then. She'd never thought of it as warpaint.

"She painted her body," Tammy confirms.

I hired you for a reason, Chas said. What reason? The fact that she's Ivy's sister? Why would that give him any confidence in her abilities?

Lucien picks up the conversational slack left by Ursula, a serene smile oozing across his face. "She marked the places on her body she was going to cut with red paint, and then she cut them with a straight razor. Except for the marks on her cheeks."

"Her cheeks?" Cabaj smirks. "Which cheeks?"

Tammy laughs. "Her face cheeks."

"Why didn't she cut her face cheeks?"

Tammy widens her eyes. "Nobody knows."

"She probably forgot," Ursula says. "She seemed like kind of an airhead."

They all laugh and fall silent, the attention then gravitating back to Ursula, who stands stiffening, shoulders tense, feet taking root in the floor.

"Do a lot of people tell you you look like her?" Cabaj asks.

She takes a breath and looks at him—calmly, she hopes. "Yes. I've been hearing that lately."

"Too bad she lost her marbles," Cabaj says. "She would have been perfect for this one."

"Why not use Ursula, then?" Javier says.

Asshole. She shoots him a look that obviously scares him.

"Oh," Lucien says. "No, she's a bit too smart-looking. Too, um, wise."

"Too old, you mean," she says.

Lucien titters, caught out.

"But I'm sure people must tell you that you should be a model all the time," Cabaj insists.

Ursula nods. "It's not my style. Not that Ivy Van Urden doesn't make the whole profession seem quite glamorous."

They all laugh.

"Excuse me," she says. "I've got to go find the bathroom."

"The one right upstairs is probably less crowded," Cabaj offers.

She thanks him for the tip and heads for the stairs. There's no line for the bathroom, and two men with smallish eyes are just leaving. She goes in and locks the door and commences her ritual of self-inspection, searching her reflection for the latest punishments, meted out in the form of tiny lines, freckles that increasingly resemble age spots, slight droopings of jowl and sallowing of skin. There remain the rallying points—the dark-blond hair, the broad cheekbones—those features Nature got right the first time, before going back to the drawing board and perfecting the mold, eight and a half years later, in the form of Ivy. Ursula's pale-blue eyes are sharp and focused, a little too shrewd-looking, her brow and jawline a little too bony. Ivy's face, by contrast, is round and delicate, her forehead high and smooth, her eyes more widely spaced, which makes them look larger, glassier, and gives them that sought-after cast of vulnerability. The differences don't stop at the neck. Ursula is broader in the shoulders, thicker in the arms, curvier around the hips, buttocks, and breasts. Seeing herself in pictures next to Ivy has always made Ursula feel physically excessive. Ivy is so straight and slight, with nothing wasted; there's simply less of her, making what substance remains all the more precious.

Standing before the mirror now, she tries to duplicate the smile she gave Cabaj and his entourage downstairs as she said those things about Ivy. The smile looks as false as it is, making her entire face seem arbitrary, haphazard, slapped together. She thinks of Ivy's face, her new, insane face, a palette with all the colors mixed, bleeding into one another. Pieces of smile, of frown, of pout, of glower, emerging briefly in an eyebrow or a bent lip or a delicately thinned nostril before sinking back into the undifferentiated confusion, like a tumor growing bits of tooth and brain and hair and liver and skin all jumbled together. What are those bits of brain thinking? What are those bits of skin feeling? Whenever she visits Ivy in the hospital, she has to resist the urge to put her fingers on Ivy's face and physically resculpt her lips into their usual gentle pout, her cheeks into those adorable balls they used to form when she smiled.

Which cheeks?

She pulls open the cabinet mirror. Cabaj's shelves support a variety of colognes, antacids, antidiarrhea pills, an electric nose-hair trimmer, an electric razor, an electric toothbrush, a box of multicolored condoms. She takes the toothbrush and rubs it under the rim of the toilet. Then she unscrews a bottle of Drakkar Noir, douses the bristles with it, and puts everything back in place.

Still not ready to go back downstairs, she walks down the hall and cracks open a door at random. Cabaj's study. Bookshelves lined with bound reports and neatly labeled videocassettes. A small, chartreuse vinyl loveseat kitty-corner to a mammoth TV and stereo console. A silvery fiberglass desk against the window. She closes the door behind her and walks to the desk. His computer whiles away the time with a screen saver showing a cartoonish Middle City getting trampled by Godzilla and King Kong. She slides the monitor to one side, then clambers onto the desk, stands, and presses her forehead to the windowpane.

For some reason these few extra feet make all the difference. The altitude becomes something palpable. The city ceases to be an innocuous array of baubles and takes on depth: a spiky, glittering chasm. It has to do with how the window now spans from head to toe, how the wall disappears. If the pane dislodged or broke along some invisible fault line, she thinks, she'd be taking a swan dive, eight hundred feet, into a sidewalk puddle.

Of course, there are people who fall farther—fall from airplanes, even—and live.

Then again, there are people who fall five feet, having slipped on a stair, a spent condom, a patch of ice, and split their skulls open like watermelons.

All that glass, all those windows. Behind each one she imagines some loser like her, staring out the window with muted outrage, thinking about all the talents she possesses, all the capacity for loving, for shining, for doing things both uncommonly great and commonly good, thinking about all the ways those personal talents and capacities are squandered in this world, never put to use. Ursula sees it vividly, sees all of them, the millions, the isolate, seething hordes of one, in offices, standing on desks, foreheads pressed to a windowpane, putting their whole frustrated, useless weight against it, waiting for it to dislodge, waiting to plunge into the chasm, and statistically, some will, they will fall, and they will think to themselves, This is my last moment, I should be enjoying it, living it up, feeling the wind in my hair, but they won't feel the wind because even as they fall, the pane will still be in front of them, falling below them, their hands and feet and foreheads still pressed against it, and they will console themselves that the pane will break before they themselves will break, and maybe in that gap, in that moment, they will be freed into some larger context, some larger meaning, though of course the gap will be almost unmeasurably slight, and perhaps the best thing to hope for is the momentary satisfaction of seeing it shatter.

Losers.

She turns, hearing a noise. Javier stands in the doorway.

"Hi, Ursula."

On the computer screen at her feet, Middle City is rebuilt and then leveled under a mushroom cloud.

"I thought you were long gone," he says. "Good thing I'm a snoop, too."

She turns back to the window, hears him walking up to the desk, peripherally sees him sit on its edge, lean back against the window, and gaze up at her face. He reaches up and takes her hand.

"Sorry about that, Ursula. Sorry if I said the wrong thing."

His hand feels surprisingly delicate and soft. The way it grips hers gently communicates something unexpected to her, an essential care that belies his frenetic behavior. She feels suddenly warm toward him, and embarrassed about the appearance of her own hand, with its ragged nails bitten almost down to the cuticles—not a proper businesswoman's hand, she supposes. She remembers the military precision of Chas's squarely manicured fingers, steepled between his eyes like a warship's prow. She imagines them on Ivy's face, pressing it from either side like vise grips, and feels a chill.

"Did you ever see my sister with Chas?" she asks.

"Just twice. Neither time for long."

On the screen, Middle City is rebuilt and again destroyed, this time simultaneously by a volcanic eruption, an earthquake, a tsunami, and a tornado.

"He was crazy about her," Javier adds. "Deeply in love. Still is."

"What?" She scans his eyes for duplicity, deviousness, or mere idiocy, but all she sees is wide-open earnestness. "Did he tell you that?"

"No. It was obvious."

He stares up at her moonily, the way he looked at the cookies in the store. She believes him.

"Why hasn't he visited her?" she asks.

"He tried once. Her first day there. Before you got here. She screamed her head off."

On the computer screen, Middle City is rebuilt and then flattened by the sandaled foot of God. Ursula crosses her arms and presses her forehead into the cool pane, wondering what Chas and Ivy were like together, wondering whether he could have done something to stop her from cutting herself and running through the park. But it doesn't really matter. She knows Ivy's schizophrenia isn't something any boyfriend could be blamed for. It's all in the genes. Ursula is probably prone to it herself. She, too, may wake up one day and believe that the entire world is an elaborate lie meant to mask an even more elaborate conspiracy.

She turns back to the city.

"It looks pretty from a height," she says. "Like it's nothing but light. Like it couldn't hurt you if it tried."

Javier reaches up and places his hand on her arm, firmly, then makes her lean back a few inches from the pane.

"Ursula," he asks, "what do you see?"

"I see the world *below* the world." She laughs, on the verge of crying. "I see a nightmare made of solid steel. I see a hundred square miles of compulsion, delusion, and death. Where does *that* fit into your philosophy of marketing?"

"No," he says, "change your focal length. What do you see?"

She sees herself, in the ersatz space of the pane's reflection.

"Oh." She sighs. "Just some loser, looking out a window."

"I see a beautiful woman who can be anything she wants," he says. "Who never needs to touch the ground. Who can take off and fly. And the city will be as beautiful as you want it to be, as beautiful as you. I promise you."

She looks at him, suspicious as always of compliments about her appearance, but his face is flushed with embarrassment, and his eyes are luminous with awe, and his overall demeanor is so earnest she could kick him, and she feels a silly, weak, reprehensible smile spreading over her face—he thinks she's beautiful, this weird, not entirely unbeautiful man—and he smiles as well. He holds out his hand and she lets him help her down from the desk, while on the screen gravity fails a freshly rebuilt Middle City, which detaches from Earth and floats forlornly into space.

Continuum

A squad car creeps along the paths of Banister Park, its headlights slowly sweeping around, sparking along the fence bars. The police lock the gates now at midnight, a Pyrrhic victory for the neighborhood landowners, who must have hoped the homeless would spontaneously vanish instead of merely shuffling out through the exits and settling on the surrounding sidewalks with their bedrolls, overcoats, garbage bags, and carefully laid newspapers. Ursula treads along lightly, breathing minimally, the way people walk through graveyards.

It's getting harder, visiting Ivy; the frantic haze of Ivythink takes longer to wear off every time. She's been wandering for hours now, and her thoughts are still jumbled, unfamiliar—half frightening, half funny. One of her favorite phrases of Ivy's—*the glamour continuum*—has been bouncing around in her head. It's such a good phrase she half suspects it came to Ivy before and not after its definition, whatever that may be. Possibly that glamour is a zero-sum game, that the creation of a single Hollywood celebrity requires the squalidification of hundreds, maybe even thousands, of inner-city dwellers—a thousand warts on a thousand noses, a thousand ill-fitting knockoff jeans, ten thousand lamentable haircuts, dinners at McDonald's, greasy complexions, pounds of fat. In which case these homeless people's problem boils down not to poverty per se but more essentially to a desperate, terminal lack of glamour. Perhaps Ivy anticipates the establishment of charities for the redistribution of this commodity. Celebrities could donate designer gowns and invitations to awards ceremonies. Society matrons could donate money for the homeless to attend fund-raisers where they in turn could donate it to *other* charitable causes—the opera house, the botanical garden, the Exeter lacrosse team.

Ursula stops, having found the human mound she's looking for: the savage girl, swaddled in a bedroll sewn together from old leather and suede coats. She is curled up like a question mark, with Ursula's own feet forming the dot. Her stiff platinum Mohican sets off her head like a lunar eclipse—dim moon, corona of jagged light. She looks so peaceful asleep that the sparkling sidewalk beneath her could be hewn from a cloud. Ursula herself feels a wave of drowsiness. She could curl up next to her. It might not be that much less comfortable than the lumpy futon mattress in her cramped apartment. But of course it would, she corrects herself—a reflex of guilt or simple self-hatred, she's no longer sure which. Of course she's lucky to have that futon and that apartment and this cushy job, and all the other privileges that more often than not just feel like burdens to her. Splitting the difference between sidewalk and futon, she crosses the street and sits down in a doorway, turning up the not-so-tall collar of her trenchcoat and watching the savage girl through the space between two parked cars.

She opens her book and begins to sketch, trying to remember the look of calm determination on the girl's face the day she observed her stitching pieces of hide. The expression is elusive, and soon Ursula is drawing her sister instead, the way she looks in the afternoons, hunched over, bony-backed, the plane of her oval face angled toward the circular tabletop, reflecting its blankness. In the background, the disembodied, unfinished face of the savage girl continues to float like it does in Ursula's mind, like the abandoned beginning of an idea. In the empty space above Ivy's right shoulder, Ursula begins penciling in her own face, emphasizing and even exaggerating those features of which she was ashamed as a teenager and of which she now makes a point of being proud: the ridge on which her eyebrows are set, her muscular jawline, the elongated slope between her nose and her upper lip. It's important to have these features, she thinks, for the same reason it's important to live in a cramped apartment with a lumpy futon. With a face like this, in a place like that, she's never in danger of feeling glamorous. She can sit on a pile of moldy pillows on the floor of her windowless living room, so dark the ceiling lamp needs to be on in the middle of the day, and she can pull up the hem of her nightshirt, as she did this afternoon, and look down at her thighs and not feel sexy, not feel attractive at all, feel quite *un*attractive, in fact, whereas if she were on a white couch in a spacious room with oversized windows and sunlight warming her thighs, who knows? She might look at those legs and think of those legs' being looked at and think of herself as being sexy and even glamorous, too. Because glamour is a matter of context. And white, empty space, as she learned from her pile of out-of-date library books, is the number-one glamour cue in advertisements. Anything placed on a white, empty background is instantly glamorized, be it a perfume bottle, a watch, a hair-care product, an upscale toothpaste, or a woman's body. This was what Ivy wanted, white space, nothing but white and space. Ursula marveled at all that white space when she went to break the lease on her sister's apartment, too white and spacious for Ursula herself to afford. A white couch, a bed with white sheets, a small white table and white chairs, symmetrically placed amid four white walls: Ivy aspired to the absolute zero of glamour. Her ideal was to have no context at all, only weightlessly to crowd-surf on an endless sea of strangers who would hold, fondle, and pass along every facet of her glamorous existence. A kind of utterly passive immortality.

The bar on the corner shuts down.

Sounds of bottles shivering in bags, chairs jumping onto tables.

Ursula thinks again about getting up and going, but just then, as if her brain were commanding the wrong body, the savage girl pops her head up and starts wriggling out of her bedroll. She's still wearing the usual tattered T-shirt, but the cutoff army pants are gone, replaced by an improvised skirt of uneven, variegated flaps of pelt. She gets ready quietly, slipping into her shapeless, makeshift moccasins, tying the tattered loose ends of them up around her ankles, bundling her bedroll, and strapping it to the bottom of her hide pack. Then she humps the pack and starts walking west.

Ursula follows. The streets are empty, so she has to hang far back and stick close to the buildings to avoid detection. Up ahead, the savage girl moves warily, catlike, responding with her whole lithe body to every change—a traffic light going green, a lamp snuffed in a third-story window. She walks as though the city were alive with spirits, gurgling from sewer grates, rustling in stray leaves of newsprint, alerting her to dangers and guiding her along on her mission through the night. Her world is in love with her, will do anything for her, generating no end of meaning, dressing every last inch of itself up with significance. And Ivy's world, too, Ursula reflects, for all the pain it causes her, does essentially the same thing: the more it persecutes her, the more importance it ascribes to her. After spending all this time with these two self-styled cavewomen, Ursula is beginning to feel like she herself is the abnormal one. More and more she's coming to feel the outlines of an unnatural growth inside her, something pathologically resistant to even the meagerest infusions of religion, nationalism, racialism, humanism. The extent to which people find their lives meaningful is directly proportional to their ability to allow themselves these kinds of delusions, but this intractable thing inside her, this immune system gone awry—this overactive *bullshitological* system—allows her no meaning whatsoever. She can feel it gnawing away day after day at the very organs it was supposed to protect: the organ that lets people live as part of a particular clan or group or effort, the organ that lets people orient their beliefs along some particular axis, the organ that lets people feel some particular sense of purpose. Ursula increasingly lacks these normal, healthy functions, and her life has become correspondingly meaningless, and she generally feels so lonely on Earth she could die.

At the end of the block the savage girl stops. Shoulders hunched, hands tensed and open at her sides, she follows with her eyes the course of a metal gangway zigzagging up the face of a windowless brick building. Possibly a power station. Ursula edges closer, moving hunched over from car to car. The savage girl turns back to scan the street, and Ursula freezes, too afraid even to duck. But she doesn't seem to spot her and continues what she's doing, taking off her pack and crouching over it, her hand emerging with what appears to be the sawed-off top of a coatrack attached to a coil of rope. Holding her arm out to her side, she swings the hub of coat hooks around on the rope, widening the arc until she releases it, sending it up and over the railing and onto the gangway. She pulls the rope gently until the hooks catch on the railing, gives it a couple of tugs, then begins to climb, twining her bare legs around the rope and hoisting herself with her arms. She scoots up over the railing and takes the stairs the rest of the way up.

At the very top of the gangway, she hops back onto the railing, and for a moment Ursula thinks she's planning to jump, but instead she wraps herself around a support pole and inches up it until she can clamber onto the gangway's tin roof, her legs kicking out behind her like a frog's. The tin gives off a muted clangor, like a cracked gong, and the half-dormant pigeons in the stonework at the building's crest cluck and flutter.

She crouches. Then springs. The birds squawk and tear off madly, but she's managed to catch one in either hand, pressing and trapping them in their niches. She pulls them out and brains them against the wall, quickly, again and again, until they stop flapping. The tin roof continues reverberating as she kneels and twists the birds' necks around like bottlecaps.

In a dark, weedy, junk-strewn lot, the rest of the night passes in staggered, disjointed time as Ursula hides between two parked vans and watches, transfixed, at once horrified and exhilarated: the savage girl plucking the birds, their dark heads dangling from the skin of their broken necks; the savage girl roasting their pale-gray bodies on an umbrella-pole spit over a garbage-can fire; the savage girl ripping at the steaming meat with her hands and teeth, her face wild and orange in the glow, the whites of her eyes blazing behind the mean iris hillocks like a jack-o'-lantern's, ash and pigeon grease encircling her mouth; the savage girl squatting in a corner of the lot, her face proudly impassive as she excretes a loose stream of waste.

Surfaces

Chas unrolls the airbrush painting on his desk, pinning the corners in place with his desk phone, his cell phone, his Palm Pilot, and a bottle of Pepto-Bismol. He leans over it, forming an arch of tanned forearms, ironed sleeves, muscular shoulders, greased gray hair. A vertical crease bifurcates the horizontal creases of his forehead into two columns, doubling the look of physical strain, as though at any moment he might kick his feet up onto his chair and start doing marine-style pushups over the painting.

Instead he simply lowers his head, a couple of wet-looking kilostrands coming loose and pointing at her like the horns of a bull.

"Ah, shit," he mutters. "You just don't get it."

To allay her dread she searches for something about him to laugh at: she studies the top of his head, looking first for a combed-over bald spot, then, a little more desperately, for evidence of implantation. But his hair is receding in an altogether dignified manner.

"What's wrong with it?" She was shooting for a tone of affected concern, as though she were masking a secret confidence about the picture. But she sounds simply hurt.

"That face," he says. "Only a mother could love that face." He pauses. "A mother wombat."

"You think she's ugly?" Her voice rises. Now she really is hurt. Not just because it's her work, but because it's the savage girl's face, and she's not sure if she loves that face, but she *is* conscious of feeling a little maternal about it.

"Her expression is," he says. "And how you've got her hunched over like that. It's nasty."

"It's not nasty. It's tough."

"Tough is all right," he concedes. "But where's the softness? She's got to be soft, too. And this dirt. What's with this dirt?"

"She's a *savage*, Chas. That's the whole idea. You want her to smile and look all glassy and drugged like a centerfold?"

"No," he says, and then adds under his breath, "not exactly."

"*'Not exactly,'*" she huffs, hoping for an advantage.

He shakes his head, turns, and looks out the window. In a rare swath of sunlight the buildings bristle, bright and dangerous-looking, all the way down the West Slope. His trendshop, Tomorrow Ltd., occupies a small but prestigious suite of offices. The view from the Black Tower is one of the best there is, partly because of its position at the very peak of the volcano, partly because it's one of the few places in town from which you can't see the Black Tower itself.

"This painting, Ursula," he says, spinning his chair back around to face her. "It's so . . . *real*. Even with the airbrush. It's like she's right here getting fleas all over my desk."

"I take it that isn't a compliment."

"Contradictions," he says. "You need contradictions to make an ideal. There are no contradictions here."

"Contradictions?" Ursula stares unseeing at the picture of the savage girl. She wants to take it and tear it up, childish as that would be.

"You don't get it," he repeats.

"I guess not."

His voice softens. "It's not your fault. We threw you into the deep end. Look, I've been busy courting a big new client, otherwise I'd've helped with your training."

The sudden sympathy, so unexpected, makes Ursula's eyes begin to tear, to her embarrassment. She always used to think of herself as being tougher than all the other artists she knew. But now that she's a businesswoman, she seems to be crying all the time.

"Come on," he says, seeming not to notice her little internal crisis. "Let's take a field trip."

He tosses on his jacket and leads her out past the unused reception area to the hallway. There are other people riding the elevator, and neither of them speaks again until they're out in the street.

"Where are we going?" Ursula asks.

He doesn't answer. He leads her right on Cook Street, left on Ulner. Women and men, young and old, eye Chas as they walk by. She sees them trying to peg him. At first they look at him and think, A powerful business-man; then they keep looking, and then they think, A *perfect example* of a powerful businessman. Most are satisfied at this point, but those who look for a few seconds longer—those who, like Ursula, look long enough to ask themselves how someone gets so perfect—begin to suspect he must be a maniac of some kind. His obsessive nature betrays itself in a hundred dif-ferent ways. Even his robust health seems like a sickness. A build like that on a man in his fifties. He must work out regularly—more than regularly; he must have an utterly inflexible regimen, alternating muscle groups according to the day of the week to provide equal attention to every square inch of his sun-basted, weather-beaten flesh. It's an image that might even have been sexy if it weren't accompanied by those other things—the omnipresent creases in his brow, reticulated like a second muscle-bound abdomen on his head; the constant tensing and pulsing of his jaw; those narrowed, razor-blade eyes.

He leads her to a supermarket built into the ground floor of a high-rise apartment building and gestures for her to go in ahead of him. The doors slide open as she walks across the mat and into the store.

"Go ahead," Chas says. "Lead the way."

"What are we doing here?"

"Shopping. Get a cart, get moving."

She does as she's told, but as soon as she starts pushing the cart, he stops her.

"Eighty percent of shoppers turn right," he says. "Like you just did."

In a low voice he continues to talk as she maneuvers the cart past the produce section toward the sliced meats.

"What do you smell?"

She inhales, closing her eyes. "The flowers," she says, opening her eyes again and looking at the small island of potted plants. "And there's a kind of sweet, citrusy smell. I guess that's coming from the fruit."

"You guess wrong. Stay aware of the smells as we go."

So what? They pipe in smells or something. Ursula already knew they probably played tricks like that. But even so, with Chas next to her, whis-pering conspiratorially in her ear, she finds herself walking more tenta-tively, as though the linoleum floor might be mined.

"Here," he says, "watch this woman. Don't let her see you watching."

They pretend to price the ricotta cheeses while to their right an obese woman with a pink, shell-shocked face and a huge violet jogging suit spends two minutes comparing salamis, finally selecting the longest. Chas turns and faces Ursula squarely.

"What did that woman just put in her cart?"

"Are you going to say it's some kind of phallic symbol?"

"Train your mind, Ursula. Don't categorize and dismiss. Think rigorously. Look. A long stick of salami can give the illusion of security and safety because many slices can be cut from it. It's a phallus, yes, but a phallus like none other that woman has ever known. It's her dream phallus. It offers long-term security, not just fleeting gratification. This phallus sustains her," he says, his tone fierce, urgent. "It lasts and lasts."

A dream phallus. Maybe this guy really did used to be a professor of some kind. She eyes the glistening, packaged meats, mainly to avoid his nailgun eyes. They don't look appetizing, those meats. She recalls the smell of bologna, the slimy, metallic taste of it on her tongue. Not for the first time she decides to become a vegetarian. They start moving again, the cart gliding effortlessly ahead.

"All right," he says, "what do you smell now?"

"Coffee."

The scent draws them into the next aisle. It comes primarily not from the prepackaged coffee but rather from the gourmet stuff in plastic dispensers.

"What's the paradessence of coffee?" Chas asks her.

Paradessence? She came across the word *essence* in a couple of the marketing books she skimmed, usually attached to some glib distillation of the product's selling points. But *paradessence*? What could that mean? Something paradiselike, perhaps.

She takes a shot. "I guess something about how it wakes you up, maybe. Or the way it warms you up on a cold morning."

"Waking and warming," Chas says. "Very close. Now think. Locate the magic. Locate the impossibility."

"'The impossibility'? I don't know. Being warm. That's kind of like being sleepy, I guess."

"The paradessence of coffee is stimulation and relaxation. Every successful ad campaign for coffee will promise both of those mutually exclusive states." Chas snaps his fingers in front of her face. "That's what consumer motivation is about, Ursula. Every product has this paradoxical essence. Two opposing desires that it can promise to satisfy simultaneously. The job of a marketer is to cultivate this schismatic core, this broken soul, at the center of every product."

Chas starts walking again, leaving her frozen in place. After a few steps he stops.

"What's wrong?"

"Ice cream," she says. The two words are no longer familiar to her ears; they sound like a foreign language.

"What? Where?"

"What's the paradessence of ice cream?"

Chas closes his eyes and pinches the bridge of his nose between thumb and forefinger. "You tell me. Hint number one: Licking and sucking. Balls on wafer shafts. Twin mounds on a tray. Served with bananas and cherries."

"Sex?"

"Eroticism, that's half of it. Now the other half. Hint number two: Malt shops. Small towns in summertime. Running to the ice cream truck after a game of stickball. All those other childhood memories you've been told you have. Tonguing your cone too hard and losing the scoop on the parlor floor, and the nice lady gives you another scoop for free."

"Innocence," Ursula says.

"Eroticism and innocence."

"Semen and mother's milk," she says. "The ideal ingredients." The memory of eating it sends a coldness down her throat to the base of her chest. Chas looks at her askance. She keeps pushing the cart and doesn't say anything more. She can hardly blame Ivy for reacting to Chas the way she did, for blowing up his theories into some totalizing system of delusions. Ursula herself is shivering with revelation. She feels like she's getting a glimpse into the secret laws of reality. This must be the way the physicist who discovered quantum mechanics felt when he worked out the last decisive equation and realized that the basis of all the universe's laws might very well be a set of fundamental flaws. Around her the supermarket has transformed into something rich and strange—a metaphysical playground, a fantastic space station at the bottom of a black hole where all the light and color goes. Light and color everywhere, and not a single shadow—the fluorescence is like some eye that sees every inch of you from every angle. She feels giddily powerful, nauseatingly vulnerable: the paradoxical sensation of vertigo.

"All right. Next lesson," Chas says. "Listen. What do you hear?"

"Muzak," she says, trying to concentrate. They are pushing their cart through yet another aisle. She wants to ask him about every product she sees. What's the paradessence of a mayonnaise substitute? What's the paradessence of pinto beans? But his demeanor doesn't invite questions. He walks next to her tensely. He doesn't seem to be comfortable here. When he's not speaking, she can see his jaw working, grinding his molars to dust.

"Muzak." He nods. "What's it for?"

"To make people shop more?"

"Good guess. How?"

"I don't know. I guess it's kind of happy and upbeat. It probably makes people feel more at ease, not in such a rush, makes them look around more, count their pennies a bit less?"

"That's the prevailing theory," Chas says. "The dissenting opinion is that it makes people shop more because it makes them more anxious. Either way, it works—better than silence, better than any other kind of sound that's been experimented with yet. I could show you a hundred studies."

He pauses, his eyes moving uneasily along the shelves. Then he goes on, his voice rapid and terse:

"To really understand why it works, you've got to think about what Muzak is. Pop music is all about the time it's composed in. It becomes a way we measure our decades here on Earth. A way we distinguish one era from another. Muzak, conversely, is all about timelessness. It takes pop tunes out of time. Cans them, pickles them, preserves them for eternity. This is the paradessence of Muzak: *eternal transience*. Different people react to this contradiction in different ways. Some find it comforting, because it reaffirms a fatuous hope that every insignificant event in their piddling little lives is actually important, is actually being recorded in some cosmic database somewhere. Muzak-likers are immortal souls traveling through a material wonderland, and so what the hell, why not buy anything pretty that catches their eye? Muzak-haters, on the other hand, are terrorized by the stuff, because it turns everything unique about every era into the same homogeneous mush, and moreover does so with ease, thus reinforcing their suspicions that there's essentially nothing unique about their era or themselves; that their cherished individuality is nothing but a merchandised illusion begrudgingly maintained for them by marketers; that when you get right down to it, it's all the same crapola."

Chas stops talking, as though he'd lost his train of thought. Eventually it becomes clear he isn't planning to add anything further.

"But how could *that* feeling make people want to shop more?" she asks.

He shrugs. "Nihilists make for fairly avid consumers. Plenty of studies on that one, too."

"But aren't there people out there who Muzak makes so anxious that they end up shopping *less?*"

"Statistically insignificant. Besides, nowadays we've got medications for people like that." He smiles grimly. She's not sure, but she thinks he's just made a joke. The smile vanishes instantly, his face newly impenetrable, jaw bulging, molars gnashing as before.

"Chas, all this stuff about products and marketing—how exactly does it help you spot trends?"

"Same principle. A trend is like a big product. A metaproduct. You wanna understand *War and Peace*, you learn the alphabet first." He waves his hand in a tight arc. "This is your alphabet, Ursula. Consumer-motivation research. Spend a month here in the supermarket and you can pick up a lot, if you can keep from slitting your wrists in the process. Think you could make it?" He looks around, exhaling heavily through his nostrils. "I did. Spent a whole goddamned month of my life in a Key Food just like this one, back when I was a lowly market-research assistant. Every day, open to close. Wore a stockboy jacket. Followed people around. Charted their paths. Watched their eye motions. Mounted hidden cameras in the freezers. Put NOW FAT-FREE stickers on boxes of laundry detergent and watched the fat ladies pick them up and toss them in their carts. The whole bit. I vowed never to set foot in a supermarket again, have my food delivered, etcetera. But no, I came back. Too much at stake not to. Besides, I had to train Javier. Trained him in these very aisles. I remember the day I told him that surfaces were all people had." He shakes his heavy head. "You should have seen the poor kid. He was in tears."

She stares at him, trying to process everything he's saying.

"'Surfaces . . . ,'" she repeats. "What do you mean?"

"Look around you. How many of these people do you think ever get to experience a great passion, a great love, a great cause? A product can stand in for those experiences. A surface can stand in for the depths most people will never know. That's what it all comes down to: *surfaces*."

The word is sibilant on Chas's tongue, accompanied by an asymmetrical hitch of his upper lip. Ursula pictures Javier standing where she is now, pictures Chas telling him this, pictures the tears forming in his eyes. The pair of them must have been a sight: two immaculately groomed stockboys with delusions of grandeur, one young and the other not so young, father-and-son perverts lurking in the feminine-hygiene aisle, watching women choose their douches from behind their Key Food jackets and clipboards, a leering, sneering Mephistopheles and his young, frightened, but determined protégé, bent on mastering the arcane signs and symbols in which everyday reality is written.

"Yeah," he chuckles. "Javier's got some romantic notions. I'm sure you've found that out for yourself by now."

"What's wrong with him, Chas?" she asks.

"'Wrong'?"

"He takes pills. His hands shake. He's always got a runny nose. He's so skinny."

Chas shrugs. "Nothing life-threatening. A mood disorder. He's a little . . . volatile . . . emotionally."

"'Volatile'? What kind of mood disorder? Is he getting help?"

"'Help'?" Chas's eyes widen, his nostrils flare. "You don't fuck with genius, Ursula. The man's a magician when it comes to trendspotting. He looks at a fashion and immediately grasps the underlying desire. His ideas about postirony and the Light Age have put my own investigations years ahead of where they might have been."

"Those were his ideas?"

"He lives and breathes trends. He's a cultural divining rod. Have you seen his apartment?"

She shakes her head.

He smirks. "Never mind. Anyway, I can't really blame him for getting a little weepy that time. I made him serve two straight weeks here; that's enough to unhinge even the not-so-sensitive souls. Don't worry, I'm not gonna make *you* do that."

He drops a hand onto her shoulder and gives her a shake, the first time he's ever touched her, and she feels her legs go slack. She is suddenly confused, unsure what this gesture means. Is he attracted to her? Of course she'd never do it, but she wonders what dating a man like him would feel like, whether it would mean security in his arms or terror under his gaze.

"I don't want you to crack," he goes on, "doing supermarket duty on top of psycho-ward duty—no, that's too much. How's your sister doing, by the way?"

Despite the casual way Chas tosses off the question, he's anything but casual. His smile is forced, she sees now. He looks away, looks back.

"What?" he says. "Can't I ask?"

"Sure you can ask. It just caught me by surprise." The hand on her shoulder was an expression of affection not for her but for Ivy. She feels that selfish reflex of disappointment she's never been able to help whenever men reveal their preference for her sister. But Chas's sudden vulnerability makes her feel a little powerful, too, now. She finally has him at a bit of an advantage. And perhaps he isn't as inhuman as she once thought.

"Well, how is she? In your opinion."

"Could be worse," she answers.

He nods, evidently interpreting this statement as good news. "Make sure she gets better," he says without looking at her, his tone all business, as though he were asking her to bring him a demographics report or a cup of coffee. But she can see the strain. His jaw is a knot of muscle and bone. His fists are clenched at his sides. Her own heart is racing. She can't bring herself to pursue the subject.

They enter the cereal aisle. From the other end, a father and son enter and ferry their craft through the treacherous currents, the boy spotting from ten feet away a brightly colored box positioned on a lower shelf halfway into the aisle.

"The sweet spot," Chas says, indicating the location of the box. "Child height. Middle of the aisle."

Ample time for the boy to petition his father, eight cries of "Daddy." Daddy caves, watching with a weary smile as his son pushes the box up over the side and into the cart.

"Fathers are twenty-eight percent less adept than mothers at turning down their kids' product requests. And the rate is even higher when it comes to cereal. Why?" he asks.

"I can't imagine," she admits.

"*Cereal,*" he says bitterly, sweeping the aisle with his hooded eyes. "An opportunity for fathers to bond with sons. Fathers who regard each day as a struggle. Who meet the day with a fighting attitude. Kids like it because it's sweet. But daddies like it because it's crunchy, hard. Because it offers resistance, however chimerical, to the teeth."

Falling silent, he rubs the back of his neck, a moment that let's show his age, his fatigue, the creakiness of his joints.

"I hate this goddamn place," he says.

Paradessences

Ursula crouches against the wall at the end of one of the long corridors at Middle City Airport, an unused clipboard propped against her knees. Chas has sent her out here to make meticulous records of clothing colors. Companies in every line from textiles to automobiles to foodstuffs are relying on trendspotters to predict next year's colors, he explained, which can be forecast based on the color choices of early adopters. When she asked why food makers cared, he told her about 1985, the blackest year on record, a year so black even the food was black: black tortilla chips, black bean dip, pasta dyed with squid ink. Color is serious business. Representatives from Benjamin Moore and Ralph Lauren have been known to come to blows at the annual Color Association meeting. Dye must be ordered more than a year in advance so it can be planted and grown and shipped, and a faulty forecast can leave retailers with racks of unsellable colors. Investors and growers can lose their shirts. People can starve, as they did in the Peach Bust of 1912, when peach was predicted and fields upon fields of coral-colored poinsettias were grown all over Mexico, and then purple boomed instead. Picking the right color is not only a matter of prestige, Chas growled at her; it's a matter of survival.

But his lecture was mostly in vain: grave though the task at hand may be, she can't keep her eyes on the clothing. The tyranny of the human face is too great: she can't help watching them, the faces, the endless stream of them floating toward her along the peoplemover.

A man with an overlarge forehead and jaw looks out the window at the airstrip. His head tilts, his vast, smooth, whalelike brow catching the light. Trying to gather in some vestige of his childhood love of airports, maybe. That trip to Peoria would have been an unmitigated thrill to him back then. He wears a gray suit, the jacket draped limply over an arm. Red tie. He is part of the thrilling world now. He rubs the back of his neck, bulbous head bent.

The paradessence of air travel: *sanitized adventure; exoticism and familiarity.*

A man with thick, light-trapping glasses and pale, freckled skin looks at the Mid City tourism ads posted in the freestanding light boxes lining the corridor. His gaze fixes on a picture of a couple in evening dress sitting at a table in the Top Room; they lean their structurally perfect profiles toward each other, into the candlelight, foregrounded against a breathtaking western view of city lights. On their plates, beneath the luminously lit tops of the woman's breasts overflowing her dress and set off against the starched white shirt of the hovering waiter, the food glistens: lobster, rack of lamb. The ad-gazing man's head turns, staying with the image as the peoplemover trundles him toward Ursula. He sees her watching him and looks away, embarrassed. He wears a brownish short-sleeved shirt and loose, poorly tailored jeans. He is obese.

The paradessence of fine dining: *Your animal needs are divine.*

A youngish man with sand-colored hair and stubble looks around, slightly stunned. His shoulders slump under the weight of his army-surplus backpack. He wears a black baseball cap bearing the logo *Ark, Inc.*—whether this is an actual company or a band name Ursula remains unsure. He looks at the ads, at the other arriving passengers. He looks down at the device conveying him along the corridor and chews the inside of his mouth. He is thinking, she imagines, of the shacks and shanties of the Third World from which he has just returned. He is both relieved and disappointed to be back. Here in the Mid he has an entirely different order of problems to face, desires to try to satisfy. As he steps off the peoplemover, she notices his boots: scuffed, watertight leather bound by an elaborate network of red laces and yellow straps. He looks over and sees Ursula. He looks at her white suit, at her blond hair. He shakes his head slowly, pawing his rough jaw. Dismissively. It riles her. She spent a good deal of thought deciding on her outfit. She wanted to blend in with the sterile corridors of the airport.

"Excuse me," she calls out. He stops, then shambles over, hoisting his pack. "I'm taking a survey," she says, not quite knowing why. "Do you have a couple minutes?"

"OK."

"I like your boots," she says. "I've never seen any like that before."

"They're Mauritanian jungle boots," the young man says, not without a hint of pride, and then catches himself. "That's what the salesgirl said, anyhow."

So much for her powers of intuition. He's probably come from Peoria as well.

"OK, good," she says, pretending to make a note on her clipboard. "Next question—"

"Was that the first question?"

"Yes. Next question: Is your yearly income less than twenty-five thousand, twenty-five to fifty, fifty to a hundred, a hundred to five hundred, five hundred to—"

"Less than twenty-five," he cuts in.

She feigns disappointment, makes a check in an imaginary box. "OK. Last question. What's your mission in life?"

The young man is silent for a moment, then regards her with a strange intensity.

"To save the planet," he says.

"Wow. That's quite a mission."

"I guess it is," he says, a little defensive now.

"OK, that's it. Thanks for your help."

He stands there, surprised at being dismissed so suddenly.

"What about you?" he says. "What's *your* mission in life?"

He's blurted out the question abruptly, but in the ensuing silence he regains some of his composure, staring down at her and waiting.

"My mission," she replies, "is to make the Mauritanian jungle flourish like it never has before."

For a moment he seems suspicious, but she widens her eyes and doesn't blink, and after a moment he nods.

"Good for you," he says. "Good luck."

"Good luck to you."

She looks down at her clipboard and does some doodles as the young man rejoins the dazed procession bound for the baggage claim.

Good for you, Ursula.

She closes her eyes. The pressure of airport noise builds in her head: the hum of the peoplemover, the murmur of conversations, the steady succession of mispronounced names being paged. Who was she to make fun of him? He's proud of those boots—so what? They make his life a little more bearable. Even though they're only a surface, a stand-in for heroic adventure. Even though there are no jungles in Mauritania.

The Light Age.

The way Javier talks about it, he seems to think it will actually mean something, will actually give people great passions, loves, causes, will change more than the surfaces of things. She wonders about his momentary sadness when Ed Cabaj announced the plans for diet water; she wonders about Chas's story of his crying in the supermarket. Chas was probably exaggerating. Javier's eyes tear up sometimes, but so do her own; whose wouldn't around Chas? Looking through the window at the planes curling off the runway, she draws a mental portrait of Javier against the sky, trying to assemble his odd medley of features, the quality of attention in his overlarge eyes, always accepting, never mocking, never judgmental. The way they look at everything as though everything were brand-spanking new. The way they look at everything with admiration, compassion, even love. The way they look: earnest, comical, passionate, sad, however it is they do when the tears that aren't really crying appear.

Teeth

Their mother is here today, sitting by the bed in the only chair and reading a four-month-old issue of *Self* magazine while Ivy sits curled into a ball against the headboard, a wax sculpture, eyes glassy and wide.

"Well," she says dryly from behind the magazine, "looks like Ivy's really taking to the new medication."

"Hi, Gwennan," Ursula replies. Other kids always thought it was strange that she and Ivy referred to their mother by her name, but that was what Gwennan preferred. It bespoke her hands-off approach to motherhood. She told her daughters that she didn't particularly care for children, and that anyway childhood and adulthood were not factors of age but states of mind. With Ursula Gwennan at least went through most of the maternal motions, but by the time Ivy showed up, she made no further concessions to convention. She treated them like adults, which meant that half the time they simply had to pretend they knew what she was talking about, had to pretend they really had the full-blown personalities she bestowed on them to speed things along. Ursula would get to be the personification of Gwennan's left brain—an eagle, sharp-eyed, world-weary, and proud—while Ivy would get to be the right: some shy, reef-dwelling creature, beautiful, overdelicate, dreamy, awkward.

"Hi, Ivy," Ursula adds. Ivy doesn't respond. She is catatonic. Ursula has never seen her like this, but Dr. Shivamurti has warned her that it's happened with her a couple of times already—a medical rarity, especially in schizophrenics of the paranoid variety.

"I have to leave in a few minutes," Gwennan says. "There's a tournament. This magazine's a piece of trash, incidentally." She tosses it onto a pile of other magazines lying on the floor next to the chair.

Since her forced retirement twelve years ago, she's become nationally ranked in bridge. Bridge and Buddhism continue to be her only interests in life, though even these are not so much interests as modes of impartiality. They provide her with respectively the distraction and the philosophical justification that allow her not to watch the news, not to keep up with old friends, not to pursue any career or cause, and not to feel guilty about any of it; with the aid of bridge and Buddhism she's pretty much succeeded in washing her hands of the world, which may be another reason Ivy's illness hasn't fazed her all that much: withdrawing from an unpleasant world is, after all, a perfectly logical course of action, and in her opinion that's more or less what Ivy is up to, albeit in a more weak-willed way than herself.

"They say that even if this medication works," Gwennan observes, "the effects probably won't last. Their hope is that someone will have churned out another medication by then. And then of course that one won't last, either. There's no money in cures, you know, just in treatments—interminable treatments, keeping you hooked, each new pill more expensive than the last."

"She's not unconscious, Gwennan. She can hear you."

"Can you hear me, Ivy? Blink for yes."

Ivy doesn't blink. Gwennan sighs, a sigh not of impatience but rather of acquiesence to the circumstances. She is in the process of accepting her child's failure as part of that larger, natural order of failure she perceives the universe to be.

"I know she can hear me," Gwennan says. "She did the same little trick when she was a kid. I'd have to tickle her to bring her back. But she's not ticklish anymore."

She runs her hand through Ivy's hair. Her chosen demeanor of fatalism and wry bravado doesn't entirely exclude elements of maternal affection. Ursula notices that Ivy's hair is different again. The sides and back have been cut in a choppy, raggedy shag. This time it actually doesn't look bad.

Abruptly Gwennan stands and puts on her jacket.

"Found a job yet?" she asks Ursula, blinking away the wetness in her eyes.

"I've been working for two weeks now."

"Doing what?"

"Telemarketing. They say there's a big future in it."

Ursula has planned this response in advance. The fact that keeping her job a secret from Ivy also affords her an opportunity to lie to her mother is an added bonus. For her part, Gwennan nods, undisturbed. Obviously she was expecting nothing less wretched than this.

"Yes. I suppose they would. Well, good-bye, Ivy," she says. "I'll be back tomorrow sometime. Good-bye, Urse. Wish me luck with my tournament."

"Good luck, Gwennan."

"Maybe I can come over and see your apartment sometime?"

Ursula lets the question hang in the air for a moment, unsure whether the hesitancy in her mother's voice is coming from a lack of actual desire or from a vulnerability at having expressed an actual desire.

"You probably wouldn't be too comfortable," she replies. "I haven't gotten chairs yet."

Gwennan's face clambers back into the armor of its bleak, knowing smile. "Another artist's garret, eh? I should have guessed. Remember, Ursula, a real artist knows that poverty is just another form of self-indulgence."

She leaves without a backward glance.

Ursula collapses in the chair.

"What a . . ." She completes the sentence with something between a groan and a howl, strangling the air in a way she knows from experience will make Ivy laugh.

But Ivy doesn't laugh. A heavy silence fills the room. Ivy's face remains a mask of itself, and a strangely poor mask at that—flimsy, indistinct, with the overall look of being mass-produced.

Ursula pulls her chair closer to the bed, puts her hand on Ivy's knee, and tries to breathe slowly, tries to remain perfectly still, so as not to tax her sister's nerves. When she first heard about it, Ursula assumed that catatonia was a kind of temporary brain death, but from what she's read since then she understands that the opposite is the case. Ivy's brain is hypercharged, too much sensory data leading to too many thoughts, so many she can't find her way to the surface, no neurons to spare for movement, coordination, speech. She knows Ursula is here; she can see her in the periphery, she can hear her clearing her throat, hear her chair squeaking as she leans forward. But at the same time she's hearing a hundred other things: the hushed, conspiratorial voices of the interns talking across the hall, the bragging and nagging tones of a TV commercial in the next room, the papery skeleton of a pop tune jangling from the earphones worn by a patient shuffling past the door, the bowel-moving hum of the air-conditioning, the teeth-tickling buzz of the fluorescent lights, the squeak of sneakers, the rattle of mop-bucket wheels, the sound of her own breathing. All of it heard in the same moment, with no difference between hearing and listening, the normal filters not functioning and everything becoming just as important as everything else. Catatonics are forced to listen to it all as though it were all meaningful to them, with the result that it all does become meaningful to them, bearing directly on their existence. Their only defense against it is to remain perfectly still, to slow things down just a little, to create fewer ripples in time, fewer unforeseen repercussions, because the slightest motions are causes leading to effects that become causes of other effects which bring on the future all the more quickly, bring on all manner of suffering and strife: monsoons off the coast of Manila, typhoons over Trinidad and Tobago, tsunamis roaring over Tokyo, speculative raids on Third World currencies, massive prison economies, imperialistic wars on the Moon, monopolies stretching to the end of time.

"You can relax, Ivy," Ursula whispers, "she's gone now."

Ivy makes her lungs pump, makes her heart beat, makes the universe expand.

From behind Ursula comes a gentle knock on the open door, and she becomes aware of the slight, white-jacketed form of Dr. Shivamurti.

"I was hoping she'd come out of it on her own this time," she says, walking up to Ivy and feeling the pulse on her wrist. "But I'll give her something to help."

She unbends Ivy's arm and bunches her fingers into a fist. The arm stays obediently outstretched while she prepares a hypodermic needle.

"What are you giving her?" Ursula asks.

"Sodium pentathol."

"The truth serum?"

"It's used for that also. It will help her relax."

The effects are dramatic, almost immediate. Ivy's head bobs, then catches stiffly again. Her eyelids droop and reopen. Dr. Shivamurti helps her along, putting her arm at her side, massaging her neck and rotating her shoulders, stretching out her legs and bringing her into a reclining position on the bed. The simplicity and kindness of this ritual make Ursula's heart rise achingly to her throat.

"You can talk now, Ivy," the doctor assures her. "Say hello to your sister."

Groggily, Ivy looks over at Ursula.

"Hello to your sister," she mumbles.

Ursula and the doctor laugh.

"How are you feeling now?" Shivamurti asks.

"Cold."

Shivamurti pulls the covers over Ivy as she nuzzles herself deeper into the bed.

"She might sleep soon," she tells Ursula. "I'll leave you to talk."

"Thank you, Doctor."

"Have them page me at the desk before you leave," she says on her way out, "and we can have a little talk."

"I will. Thanks."

Ursula reaches under the covers and finds Ivy's hand. "I like your new haircut, Ivy."

Ivy nods and then mumbles something Ursula can't make out.

"Can you speak louder, Ivy? I can't hear you."

"Mr. Teeth cut it for me," she says, her voice childlike and hoarse.

"Mr. Teeth? Who's that?"

"A trendspotter. First one's ever come." Despite her stupor, she manages to convey her excitement by squeezing Ursula's fingers.

"But I thought you saw them all the time," Ursula says.

She shakes her head. "Not saw, only heard. Coder-sponder." She takes her free hand from beneath the pillow to point a limp finger at her right temple.

"And his name was Mr. Teeth?"

Ivy smiles. Her eyes flutter heavily.

"What did you two talk about?"

"They want me to get well."

Ursula has never heard Ivy speak of herself as unwell.

"That's good, Ivy," she says.

"They *need* me. They need me to model again," Ivy explains.

"Who? The trendspotters?"

"They showed me pictures of me," she quietly confides. "The way I was. The way I will be. I will be *so so so beautiful.*"

Ivy reaches over to the nightstand, picks up an oversize Snoopy get-well card sent by her agency, and hugs it to her chest. "I need to get my beauty rest," she says. "That's what Mr. Teeth said. Kiss me good night, Ursula?"

She closes her eyes. Ursula leans over and kisses her on the cheek, and Ivy sighs. Her face softens and sinks deeper into the pillow, and Ursula is left alone again, perched anxiously on the hard plastic chair, every muscle stiff and aching.

"*I* need you," she whispers.

Superstition

The savage girl sits Indian-style, her back to the statue's sun-warmed marble pediment, calmly but diligently scrubbing a large bone—a femur, or a tibia, maybe—with a damp cloth, making it white and smooth. Peace reigns in the park this time of day; the morning sunlight domesticates the feral squirrels, reconciles rival gangs of pigeons and sparrows, and renders the flaring eyes and nostrils of old Guy Banister more comical than fearsome—which was more likely the sculptor's intention anyway—so that for a moment one might even mistake his haughty glower for a smile.

Ursula dunks a currant-speckled scone, sending brown rivulets over the lip of her cup and down the bare chests of the discus throwers on its side. Next to her Javier slides down the bench like a trail of jelly until he can rest the back of his head against it. He gropes in his omnipresent trenchcoat, extracts a pair of wraparound burnt-orange sunglasses, and pushes them up his long nose into place.

"Out partying last night?" Ursula asks.

"Working. Work work work."

"Where at?"

"A rave. Sponsored by Camel. Free cigarettes, T-shirts, sushi, sesame noodles, portable ashtrays—little velvet pouches lined with asbestos or something. Free cocktails."

"How'd they stop half the city from showing up?"

"Same way as the noncorporate raves. You've got to be in the circuit, in the know, you know?"

"So how did Camel get in the circuit?"

"Hiring people like us. Once they're in, it's a great opportunity for market research. They photocopy driver's licenses at the door and pack the place with plants."

"I assume you don't mean ficuses."

"Undercover agents. One of them struck up a conversation with me. She was good. It took us a while to realize we were both market researchers, pumping each other for information."

"Wow," Ursula says.

"Wow what? What wow?"

"That sounds really, really creepy."

"Creepy? Why creepy? Creepy how?"

"'Creepy how?' Luring those kids in there under false pretenses, that's creepy how. It's satanic."

"Satanic?"

"If surfaces are all people have, like Chas says, then isn't it a little bit satanic? Stealing their poor, broken souls? I mean, doesn't that bother you sometimes?"

Javier sits up. He thinks for a moment. She wishes he weren't wearing sunglasses. This is her chance to figure him out, to determine what he really thinks. Beneath his superhuman optimism there's a vulnerability, a secret sadness, and Ursula feels a need—whether out of bitterness or tenderness she isn't really sure—to lure that sadness out into the open.

"Stealing their souls," he says. "That's an ugly way of thinking of it."

The adjective strikes her like a fist to the solar plexus. Her mind knows he's not calling her ugly. But her heart aches nonetheless.

"Sometimes the truth isn't pretty," she says.

He runs a hand through his hopelessly bed-headed hair. "Sometimes ugliness is totally unnecessary; sometimes it's just a bunch of self-flagellation."

"You think that's what having a conscience is? Self-flagellation?"

"Can I have a sip of your coffee?"

"Careful, it's hot," she says, too late. He howls and grips his throat in a chokehold.

"Listen," he rasps, "you've got to take those things Chas says with a grain of salt."

"Well, at least I didn't cry when he told me surfaces were all people had."

Javier reddens and touches his forehead, smiling a little.

"Chas words things darkly sometimes," he says. "But if you think about it, what he's really saying is that products are . . . are *magical* things in our lives, you know? This world forces us to be so damn logical all the time, forces us to think like robots. But when it comes to products, we can let loose just a bit, you know? We can buy a car that makes us feel both impulsive and safe. We can go to an amusement park and feel both terrified and reassured. Products . . ." He ponders, then smiles, finding the image he's looking for. "Products are the fruit of the human imagination! The supersweet, magical fruit! And we need that magic. Don't you think, Ursula? Don't you need a little magic now and then?"

He smiles at her. In the lenses of his shades she sees only her own reflection.

"'Don't you need a little magic now and then,'" she repeats. "So what pop song did you cull that fascinating bit of pop philosophy from?"

Javier turns away, and Ursula wonders for the millionth time why she has to be so negative.

"I'm sorry I'm not deep enough for you," Javier says, folding his arms.

"*I'm* sorry, Javier. You are deep. I'm the shallow one. All I ever see is a world of surfaces."

Javier seems to consider this, then borrows her coffee again, slurping carefully this time from the top.

"We've almost finished this year's trendbook," he says. "Once you read it you'll understand."

"'We?' You mean you and Chas?"

"I mean all of us. Me and Chas and you and James T. Couch. We all contribute with our reports. But I guess mostly it does come down to me and Chas," he confesses with a hint of pride. "This year's book'll be something else, I'm pretty sure. More ambitious than anything we've tried before."

"Wow. So how do you split up the writing?"

"We talk, and then Chas writes it up."

She knows she shouldn't, but she can't help herself. "So when you say 'we,' you really mean Chas."

He clears his throat, forces a troubled smile. "Well, I'm no writer. But the main ideas are really all mine this time."

"The Light Age," she says. "Postirony."

His smile becomes assured, and he regards her intensely over the top of his sunglasses. "Total imaginative freedom," he says. "Total fidelity of outer fashion to inner self."

As she looks into his hazel eyes, the greenery behind him blurs into a forest, a river, the primitive community of her now all-too-frequent day-dreams. She looks away, shaking her head to clear it of this foolishness. Over by the statue the savage girl works placidly on her bone.

"Where do you think she got that?" she asks. "Can you get bones that big in pet stores?"

"Why? You think people would go for them?"

"I don't know. Maybe. It seems to make *her* happy."

They watch her rub the cloth along the cleft knob at the bone's end, inches from her eyes.

"Javier," she begins, tentatively. "A couple weeks ago you told me you thought people were becoming more superstitious."

"Sure. It's everywhere. Don't you see it?"

"Like where?"

"Like everywhere. Like the way my bank manager looked out the window at the sky when he talked about deregulations of capital flow. Like the way at Ed Cabaj's party a woman kissed the Band-Aid she wrapped around the index finger of her boyfriend after he had an accident with a corkscrew in the kitchen. . . ."

"Are you superstitious, Javier?" she asks.

"Totally. You?"

"No. I wish I was, I think," she says softly. "I think I do need a little magic in my life."

He studies her for a minute. "I'll show you how."

"How to be superstitious?"

"Right."

She laughs. "You can't just show someone how, Javier. It isn't like rollerblading."

"Sure it is."

Without warning he takes her hand. She barely has time to grab her handbag before he's pulling her across the park. Reaching the sidewalk, he stops abruptly, and they teeter there as though over a precipice.

"Wait. Be careful. Don't step on a crack."

"Why not?"

"Jeez, don't you know *anything?* You'll break your mother's back."

She thinks about this. "Tempting," she says.

They walk for a time like extreme picnickers in a minefield, eyes glued to the terrors underfoot. After a while he declares them free from danger, and they move on to other challenges. They stop in at a drugstore and buy half a dozen pocket mirrors not to drop and an umbrella not to open indoors, and the minute they emerge, it begins to rain. They head up Roselli into the hotel district, on the lookout for ladders not to pass under, sneezers to bless, evil eyes to avoid, heads-up pennies in the gutter.

At dusk they wander into a reader-adviser's parlor and offer their palms to an old woman after crossing her own with green. She has a sleepy eye and cracked plum lipstick and claims to be a Gypsy but looks more like a Slav. She tells Ursula that there is a good man in her life and a bad woman in her life. She asks her if this is true, and Ursula nods, uncertain. She then tells Javier there is a good woman in his life and a bad man. She asks him if this is true, and he doesn't contradict her. They hurry out of the parlor and break into a run. Once they have put enough distance between themselves and the old Slav, they duck into a Turkish fast-food place popular with the cabbies, where they eat kabobs and read each other's fate in the syrupy dregs of their Turkish coffee, Ursula seeing in Javier's a villa in Majorca with a plump wife and seven sons, him seeing in hers a return to painting later in life and a small farm with seven orange tabbies, represented by the seven orange specks of the sticky Punjabi cake they bought next door in order to have something to dunk.

They cross over to the traffic circle around the giant statue of Manuel Noriega. His broad, pockmarked face, angled down at the orbiting taxi-cabs, retains a look of stony impregnability, but emerging from the side of one eye the sculptor has chosen to affix a large, utterly incongruous silver teardrop, which gleams in the streetlight against the bronze. On the gray slate of the plaza surrounding the plaque, fellow revelers in the munici-pally sponsored irony have spray-painted accompanying slogans:

FREE NORIEGA!

MANUEL IS OUR MAN!

NORIEGA FOR STATE COMPTROLLER!

She sits down, happy and exhausted, on the plaza floor, against the statue's pediment. Javier collapses next to her, and silently they watch the cabs spin by, bejeweled with cigarette ads on light-board displays, the drivers and passengers mere shadows underneath. A strong wind begins blowing from the south, and Ursula turns in the wind's direction to catch the coolness on her face. Down the mountain slope, between the mis-shapen, toroidal dunce caps of the Volcanoville tenements, the Lady of Nazareth icon glows blue atop the hospital, her face an empty circle, her sleeves draping from arms held slightly out from her sides in an open-palmed gesture of welcoming, which, upon continued viewing, always seems to transform into a kind of apologetic shrug.

Sorry, she appears to say. *No insurance, no service.*

Nothing we can do.

Our hands are tied.

Talk to your congressman.

Ursula laughs to herself and in the sting of the wind feels a wetness on her cheek. With her hand she confirms a couple of windblown tears. She runs her finger under the bottom of her eye and feels more wetness pooling. She blinks a few times. The false tears blur her vision a bit, spreading the yellow lights from a nearby liquor-store sign over the bottom of the sky, spreading the green and red traffic lights over the blacktop, doing magic tricks with the wind, making of it confetti, whirling ashes, a star garden, a flamingo waltz. And for one perfect moment, she sees the city as the savage girl must see it, as Ivy must see it, as Javier must see it: every nub of masonry and huddled shadow and dopplering rhythm ready to burst open like a jack-in-the-box with some new message, every alley and lot and building ready to serve as a mystical testing ground for the human spirit, every square inch of concrete and tar replete with a meaning after all, and it's not ugly, no, not really, it's actually quite beautiful, this ugly, ugly place, and then her throat becomes thick, and she is sobbing.

Javier looks at her searchingly.

"I'm sorry," she says, her voice catching painfully in her throat.

Javier says nothing as she struggles to pull herself together, his eyes luminous, sympathetic.

She takes a few breaths, wipes her face on her sleeve.

"I've always wanted . . . ," she begins, "I've always longed to see the world the way I think you see it, Javier. Like it's something more than it is. But I just can't. I can't do it. Not for more than a minute. And then it's gone again."

He nods. "I know how that feels," he says.

She smiles miserably. "Chas says you have some kind of mood disorder, but as far as I can tell, *I'm* the one with the disorder."

Her words seem to fluster him. After a moment he seems ready to speak but she cuts him off.

"All I mean to say is I don't want to bring you down. It's nice of you to be so nice to me but I'll just bring you down, Javier. I bring everybody down. So really, thanks for everything you've done but—"

He reaches over and takes her hand lightly in his, and her thoughts scatter. After a moment the warmth of his hand seeps into hers, and she watches, mesmerized, as their hands become the whole world. His slender fingers slide around the backs and fronts of her own, wrapping them slowly, carefully, in an invisible cocoon, suspending her hand limply in space. Then, with the tips of his thumb and forefinger, he explores the entire length of each of her fingers, starting at her thin, pointed knuckles and tracing his way up the back and down the front of her palm. He holds his hand out for her to explore in turn, and she traces the lines of his palm with her fingertips as the palm reader did a while ago, and then moves to the back of his hand, tracing the strong lines of his veins.

Their hands are the world.

The wind is chaos.

The cabs are order, orbiting moons.

He presses his palm into hers, and she returns the pressure. She parts her fingers, allowing his into the more intimate regions between. A warm shiver shoots from her opened fingers up through her arm and down her legs. Their fingers slide into each other's, lock, clasp, and retreat, touching tip to tip. And then his hand passes around behind hers and cradles it from behind, and she can't remember a time she ever felt so comforted by a man, so safe, so tended to, and she feels so much meaning in this little gesture that she's afraid, and she has to pull her hand away, though the moment she does, the rest of her slides into his arms.

Suit

U is the axis of the woman in the man's bed that is nothing but a bed.

i is the axis of the woman in the hospital bed that is also a bed of sand, that is also a bed of air, that is also the bed of a truck making its way through a sandstorm in a trackless desert.

Chart a vector in the U-axis and grid yourself into a city, a neighborhood, a house, a room, a side of a bed, the arms of a man. Slip into the i-axis and slip off the grid. The arms of a hospital chair are also the arms of a carnival ride, are also the arms of a meter measuring your proximity to the truth, are also the arms of a broad-bellied djinni gyrating in a sandstorm against an obscured horizon.

Ursula opens her eyes.

A new day, another sun, rising to the top of a tall window, tall curtains billowed by a breeze.

Life is tall that way, attenuated, longer than it is wide.

Maybe.

No, that makes no sense.

Not enough sense, anyway.

A tall window belongs to a tall man.

That much is true, but it doesn't mean anything really, it's just a coincidence.

A tall man.

Her musings gather into a solid wave of dread.

A tall, spinning, skating, gesticulating man. . . .

She closes her eyes again, not daring to look. They slapped together a romance overnight like some Hollywood Western set. Now, in the light of day, she knows she'll be confronting all the telltale signs of fakery: hastily painted morning smiles, places marked with gaffer's tape for a stiff parting hug. Stupid stupid stupid—

"You were dreaming something," he says. "What?"

She turns over.

He is on his side, gazing at her, an arm folded beneath his pillow.

And she knows the taste of his skin now. The smell of his neck. The feel of his chest against hers. And the things he now knows about her . . . But his eyes are sleepy and calm, and his voice is casually solicitous. As though nothing too catastrophic has happened.

She relaxes into the bed, which is softer, actually, than anything she's slept on in years.

She still can't quite look at him.

"It's hard to explain," she answers. "Ivy was telling me things, kind of."

He waits for her to go on. He is still. The room is silent.

"She wasn't talking, really. She was thinking for me. She was lending me her thought patterns."

"What was that like?"

"It was different. There was some math terminology."

"She thinks in math?"

"I don't know. We used to think so. For a while in high school she had all these math notebooks she kept. But when the doctor asked to see them, we discovered they were just page after page of weird symbols and equations that didn't make sense. To anyone but her, I guess."

The silence seeps back into the room.

"What was she telling you in the dream?"

It's an antique of some kind, the bed, with posts of carved, stained wood. A galaxy of motes drifts in a clearly delineated swath of sunlight. The bourgeois propriety of the room makes last night seem even more improbable.

"That what we did might have been a big mistake," she admits.

"I was dreaming about that, too, sort of."

"You were?"

He turns onto his back, covers his eyes with his pillow. "It's kind of silly."

"Tell me."

"I dreamed we didn't make love at all, but only kissed a little and then told each other things till the sun came up."

"What did we tell each other?"

"Well, you told me about your childhood."

"I did? What did I say?"

"You told me your gym teacher dressed like a lawyer, gray suits and tasseled loafers. And that he never ran and never touched a ball, and you never understood why. Let's see, what else. . . . You said your favorite thing on earth was Edward's nose."

"Who's Edward?"

"Your pet puppy. You liked the texture of it. How it felt like a tongue but colder."

"We never had pets. Our mom was a total neat freak."

"Not even an ant farm?"

She laughs. "You dreamed I had an ant farm?"

"So you didn't?"

"In our house? Not a chance."

"That's too bad," he says. "I bet you were the kind of kid who would've liked an ant farm."

"What kind of kid is that?"

Javier is silent for a moment. "A quiet, serious kid," he finally says. "The kind who stares at colors on soap bubbles until her eyes glaze over."

He peeks out from under the pillow, and she looks at him, speechless for a moment, because for what it's worth, this is true. It wasn't just Ivy; she was like this, too, once, something her own mother never even recognized. And she misses never having had a dog named Edward now. And maybe he does understand something about her, maybe this isn't entirely fake after all.

"And what did you tell me?"

He smiles with embarrassment. "Can't remember."

"Come on," she laughs, "I told you all that stuff about my childhood and now you're gonna hold out on me?"

He takes a breath. "OK. I told you that I . . . I liked you from the minute I saw you."

"You did?"

"I told you how you didn't see me," he says, "but I watched you leaving

Chas's office the day of your interview. You walked out of there so proud, steady, perfectly put together."

"I did?"

"And I was so happy just watching you, but I was also miserable because I was sure you'd never want to have anything to do with a goofball like me."

She laughs. "No, certainly not."

"But then I learned about how you'd come to the city to take care of your sister. And over the weekend before you started your job—before we even met—I skated down to the hospital a couple of times, just to watch you coming out at night. And I saw how hurt and sad you looked. And I realized that you weren't just strong and cool; you were caring and good, too. And you would never abandon your sister or anyone else you loved. And I said to myself that if you ever let me be your friend, I'd never abandon you, either."

Javier is still smiling. He has said all this very calmly, holding her gaze. She, for her part, is too stunned to say anything, too stunned to move; all she can do is look into his eyes and marvel that he's real.

"Breakfast," he declares. A second later he's up, a flash of dusky buttocks, semierect member, and muscular limbs as he tosses on a robe.

She explores the apartment while he makes breakfast. The living room is large and high-ceilinged, with the same tall windows and ornate moldings as the bedroom. It's the kind of room that's difficult to make look anything but tasteful, but Javier has risen to the challenge, using it for a kind of medicine show of outmoded furnishing technologies: A divan and a méridienne vie for floor space with a fan-backed wicker throne. A leather chair shaped like a human hand and a couple of candy-colored beanbag chairs nuzzle like a mother wolf and her young by the fireplace. The job of timekeeping is squabbled over by a grandfather clock, a cuckoo clock, and a cat clock with eyeballs and tail swinging in opposite directions. The shelves, bureaus, and end tables run the gamut from Egyptian Revival to fifties space-age and are filled with a Byzantine population of curios she can't even begin to classify. The room is by no means chic, but it isn't quite horrible, either. The overall effect is simply fanciful, naive, a cross between a museum and a playground.

She flips through his music collection, a couple of long shelves of dusty albums and several more of CDs, finding everything from Brazilian jazz to Ugandan court music to Mexican reggae. More than a few of the hundreds of CDs have never even been opened. She picks out one of these at random. On the cover, a monk wearing a cassock and a large pair of earphones smirks at her from behind a mixing board. She opens the plastic with a ragged fingernail and pops the CD into the player, unwittingly unleashing a postmodern Inquisition, a choir of chanting monks getting scratched on turntables, beaten by synthesized drums and bounced between speakers.

The bass line makes her bowels ache. She finds her bag and retreats to the bathroom. After shitting and washing and making herself halfway presentable, she opens his medicine cabinet and checks the prescriptions: a bottle of Hismanal; a tube of something called Nizoral; a bottle of pills called Augmentin, the expiration date on which has passed; a bottle of something called Eskalith, with instructions to be taken daily. She's looking primarily for information about his alleged mood disorder and secondarily, as she always does with men she's slept with, somewhat uselessly and after the fact, for any possibility of venereal disease. She commits the names to memory.

On her way to the kitchen she stops at the doorway to a large room, in the center of which sits a worktable littered with paper scraps and art supplies. Aside from the table, the room is empty of furniture, but the walls themselves are covered with a staggeringly intricate collage of scribbled notes, swatches of fabric, pages torn from magazines, sketches of people, buildings, and garments, and long, curving arrows connecting one item to another. Walking into the room and taking a closer look, she discovers to her burgeoning amazement that the thing is rigorously ordered. It appears to be some sort of trend time line that runs around all four walls, beginning at different points in the antiquities of Greece, Egypt, China, and other cultures she doesn't immediately recognize, then progressing through millennia and centuries, slowing down to decades, years, the present year, and finally projecting beyond to the future. Covered on the chart is the emergence of fashions, social mores, scientific and philosophical ideas, in a series of ever-diverging and -regrouping colored lines and boxes marked by red, orange, and green sticker dots and hastily scribbled notes on ledger paper. The words *Tribalism, Virtualism, Elective Affinities, Mysticism, Spiritism, Self-Creation,* and *Invented Origins* are given color-coded boxes just below the ceiling. At the very end of the fourth wall—above the space where the little swaths of color, movie stills, typeface samples, advertisements, and fashion plates peter out and the hair-thin colored lines end in boxes left mostly blank—the words *The Light Age* float below the elaborate molding markered in gold cursive script.

Before she has a chance to examine the walls more closely, Javier calls out to her. She follows the scent of coffee and browned batter into the dining room, where he stands in a sky-blue apron worn over his bathrobe, setting a long table surrounded by a half dozen mismatched high-backed, gilded chairs.

"This place is too much" is all she can say at first.

He finishes filling the coffee cups, then looks up. "Not what you expected?"

"More or less. Actually I expected an astrolabe somewhere. And a big sepia globe. You really dropped the ball on the whole nautical-theme thing."

Javier nods thoughtfully. He disappears into the kitchen, returns with bowls of blueberries and sliced strawberries, and sets them down on the table.

"And I expected a mincing servant in a white jacket and red astrakhan," she goes on. "And a parrot."

"A parrot?"

"I thought you'd have a parrot in a big golden cage who'd bid me good morning in five languages."

"You're mocking me," he at last decides.

He says this so earnestly that she laughs. He goes off to the kitchen again and comes back with a plate of crepes and a bowl of whipped cream.

"My God!" she exclaims. "You can cook, too?"

"'*Too*'?" he asks, pulling out her chair. "What else can I do?"

She smiles, preferring to let the other skill go unmentioned. Instead she sits down and asks, "So what else did the Gypsies teach you? Can you hypnotize bears? Escape from locked boxes?"

"The Gypsies?"

"Where do you really come from, anyway? Tell me about your childhood, Javier."

He sits down and helps himself to a crepe. "It wasn't all that interesting, really. Probably not that much different from anyone else's." He pauses, his eyes losing their luster, his expression flattening. But immediately he brightens again, reaching for the berries and powdered sugar and sprinkling them onto his crepe. "Except for the aviary, maybe."

"The aviary?"

He nods. "The aviary in the west wing of the castle. My mother, the grand archduchess of Borogrovia, was mad about birds. She was mad about many things. She was quite mad, in fact."

"All right, I give up," she says. "You obviously had some kind of horrible traumatic childhood you don't want to think about."

He looks up, a little startled.

"An abusive baby-sitter, I'll bet," she goes on. "Or maybe a rat ate your baby brother."

He smiles. "Both. You found me out."

"Just shut up and eat."

For a minute they cram themselves with crepes and berries and cream and coffee, and then they start talking again. She prompts him about the decor, and he explains, a little apologetically, that over the last few years he's made his apartment into a kind of ongoing exhibition of trends, both living and dead. He points out the shimmering red and gold curtains lining the kitchen door, a manifestation of the seraglio theme currently in vogue. This is a trend he predicted, he tells her, based on the growing popularity of Arab music and cuisine. He points to an Arab headdress draped over a sinuous-necked liqueur bottle in the display cabinet.

"Kaffiyeh," he says. "Two years from now they'll be wearing these in the inner city. One year after that, middle-class Jewish kids will be pissing off their parents by wearing them to raves. You'll see. The drama of this flowing headgear is going to bring down anti-Arab sentiment to a thousand-year low."

"You really believe fashions can change things that actually matter?" she asks.

"They can and do. All the time. You see those moonboots?" He gestures toward the pair of large, puffy, silver boots occupying a silver cake stand on the serving table in the corner.

"How could I miss them?"

"Kids started wearing those things to school four years ago. Chas spotted them and advised our clients. The next season silver jackets showed up in the nightclubs. Sci-fi movies boomed that year. Last year Congress approved an increase in NASA's space-exploration budget. And this year in the nightclubs it's sparkling neon polyester and transparent plastic. In their minds these people are already colonizing other planets. It's part of the dawning of a global consciousness. Those outfits will lead to trade agreements with North Korea, international peace accords!"

Ursula laughs. "How do you figure that, exactly?"

"Think about it," he says, leaning back in his chair. "What can national boundaries possibly matter to people who wear sparkling pink jumpsuits?"

He leans over and kisses her on the cheek, then blushes at his own boldness. She laughs again. He smiles.

"You ready to go do some shopping and fine dining?" he says.

"What do you mean? It's a weekday. Don't we have work to do?"

"Sure. Work. What do you *think* I'm talking about? If you're too tired, though, I'll understand."

"Too tired for shopping and fine dining? Are you kidding?"

"The main thing is I just want to make sure you don't get tired of *me*."

"I'm sure you'll get tired of me first."

"No," he says with a quiet laugh. "I don't think so."

An awkward, tender silence follows, in which they can't quite look at each other.

Once they've secured a cab, Javier lays out the agenda: a brief stop by the office, a visit to an upscale clothing store or two, and then some people watching over lunch.

At the office they find the Roman bust in an Italian suit that is Chas Lacouture in particularly good form: the grain of his gray-marbled hair stands out under an extra coat of polish, and a grim rictus, newly chiseled into his bloodless lips, accentuates the malevolence of his smile. He and Javier begin their meeting in their usual fashion, eyes gleaming, static electricity crackling in the air around them as they parlay their respective energies into a juggernaut of agitation, trading the bits of information they've culled from the street that for some unfathomable reason seem noteworthy to them. Javier has seen audience members stand up to a stand-up comedian who was making fun of someone in their midst. Chas has seen a woman point out her daughter's bad posture on a security monitor. Javier has seen a group of drunken college kids stop in front of the plate-glass window of a hospital waiting room and fall silent at the sight of the sad people inside.

"Ursula," Chas says. "You reeled in a new client. Good work."

"I did?" she says. "Who?"

"Ed Cabaj at General Foods. You impressed him."

Javier shakes Ursula by the shoulders. "Way to go," he says.

She feels her face flushing. "Me? But Javier's the one—"

"He admired your 'poise,' as he called it, once he found out who your sister is."

"But . . . ," she begins, feeling, for some reason she can't name, betrayed. "But how did he find *that* out?"

Chas stares at her, perhaps a little mockingly. "Just came up." He drums his fingers on the desk. "Anyway, it's a big account. And they want a presentation pronto for the diet-water brand image. Ursula, I want you to present the savage girl. Put together a little speech, something personal and touchy-feely. Next thing. Javier, I've just about finished our trend-book."

Javier leans forward. "Really?"

Chas taps the side of his head with a square-nailed finger. "Burst of inspiration this week. It's all coming together."

"Great," Javier says, and then, with a nervous glance at Ursula, adds, "Um . . . maybe I should take a look at it—you know, see if I have any suggestions."

"I've already taken all your suggestions into consideration," Chas says, reclining in his chair. "You helped me see things this year, Javier. You helped me put all my theories together. This year our clients are getting more than a trendbook; they're getting a fucking *treatise*." He leans forward. "I'm not dumbing it down this time, Javier. I'm through spoon-feeding pap. This time I'm taking my fellow marketers to *school*. You remember my university lectures?"

"Of course," Javier says.

"Well, I'm gonna give it to our clients just as straight. Gonna enlighten the shit out of them. This trendbook is my best fucking work ever."

"You were his student?" Ursula asks Javier.

Javier smiles. "He taught me everything I know."

"All right," Chas mutters. "Enough dawdling. Go do your job."

He picks up a sheaf of papers and spins in his chair, eclipsing himself from view. Silently, Ursula and Javier get up and leave. Out on the street they catch a cab to Hugo Banzer to check out the fall line. Javier points out the prevalence of ethereal colors, soft fabrics, and draping cuts. One dress suit catches her eye, lapis lazuli with rough onyx buttons—a long, fitted jacket and pants.

"Yes," Javier says. "There's something in that one. Try it on."

"Why?"

"Please," he urges. "I need to see you in it."

His black hair is still wetted down from his morning shower, making his eyes even more luminous than usual.

"Well. If you need to see me in it."

A saleswoman shows her to the dressing room. She puts it on and stares at herself in the mirror, taking in the drama of the cut against the curves of her body. The transformation is astonishing, and her first reaction is confusion. She looks like her mother, smug and untouchable. She looks like her sister, the way they made her look on glossy catalog pages. She realizes that the suit scares her. She thinks of her sister in the hospital, curled up in a ball, terrified of being forced into a dress lest she inadvertently bring about some kind of fashion Armageddon. Maybe she and Ivy aren't so very different. This suit is a kind of power, a pair of wings that could carry her too high too fast. But the woman in the suit, the woman staring back at her from the mirror, seems to feel otherwise. This woman isn't afraid of her power. Ursula wants to get to know this woman.

She takes a breath and steps out of the dressing room. Javier's eyes widen comically. He sinks to his knees and guides her with his fingers, turning her slowly around and around. Reflecting the ceiling lights, his eyes take on a teary slickness.

"It's not bad, is it?" she says, amused at his reaction.

"Not bad!" he whispers. "You have to wear it to lunch."

"Javier, I can't afford this."

"This one's on me," he declares, getting to his feet.

She laughs nervously. "What are you talking about? This thing is twenty-five hundred dollars."

The figure stops him in his tracks, but only for a moment. He calls the saleswoman over.

"I'm buying this suit," he mumbles, extracting a deck of credit cards from his wallet and fumbling through them. "Which is higher? Platinum or titanium?"

"Titanium," the saleswoman says.

Javier thinks for a moment. "What about tungsten? You think that would outdo titanium?"

She tilts her head. "I don't know. Is that like radioactive or something?"

"Hey, even better: the plutonium card. Has a real ring to it."

"I'm not going to wear this," Ursula insists.

"Then it'll hang in my closet until the moths devour it."

The saleswoman enjoys a private smile at the scene before vanishing with his card.

"Look, you'll need this suit for the presentation," he says. "You can pay me back when you've made your first million. It won't be long now."

Despite her misgivings, she's thankful to be wearing the new suit at Pablo's, the poshest restaurant she's ever set foot in. The place is on the roof of the Kermit Roosevelt Jr. Building, at the peak of the city, just across the volcano's mouth from the Black Tower. Designed to resemble the grounds of a sprawling Colombian mountain villa, the deck has been heavily landscaped with trees, vines, and waterfalls, the sound of which serves to drown out that of the humming bank of giant fans blowing the bitter crater ash away from the diners. Stocky Latino men in suits and sunglasses are planted evenly around the perimeter of the dining area, providing both security and decoration. The day is sunny and temperate, and the polished palmwood tables around them are crammed with power lunchers.

Javier sits next to her so he can discreetly point out the things he observes. In his quiet, serious way he indicates the ruffled yoke of one woman's blouse, the pagoda sleeves of another's. The cuts are more fanciful and flowing, he asserts. The men's suits are still boxy and dark, but this doesn't bother him because men's fashion is always the last to change. He observes the new accessories in evidence: a cloche, a cartwheel hat, a pair of ocher-yellow ballerina slippers.

As he talks, he takes her hands in his, and she shakes her head sadly at the contrast between her elegant, onyx-buttoned cuffs and her grubby, nail-bitten hands.

"I'm wasting all our time with this savage thing, aren't I?" she asks.

"What are you talking about?"

"I don't know. Can you see any of these people dressing like Tarzan?"

"I can, yes. So can you. Just squint." He demonstrates. "Try it."

The two of them, squinting and swiveling their heads around, must look to the other diners like Chinese impersonators, or baby birds.

"No Tarzan outfits so far," she says.

"Look at the colors. What do you see?"

"Red, yellow, green, blue," she reports, ". . . violet. . . ."

"Bright colors."

"Uh-huh."

"Brighter than you'd expect."

"I guess."

"But natural. Not synthetic colors."

"Yeah."

"Jungle colors. You see that now, don't you?"

"You really think so?"

"Open your eyes. Look at the food on their tables. The dishes are getting simpler. Fewer sauces and garnishes. More nuts and berries. Tropical fruits, too. Fish served whole rather than filleted. Meat on the bone."

The waiter arrives, and Javier politely asks him to bring them everything that's popular this week. Ursula thinks the waiter will just laugh at this, but instead he responds with an efficient nod and vanishes.

They listen to the conversations going on around them. He instructs her about what to listen for. Adjectives are often a reliable indicator. Javier is surprised to hear a nearby tableful of portfolio managers using the words *good* and *bad* to describe everything from investments to golf courses to political candidates. A year ago the adjectives were more guarded—*sensible, inadvisable*, and the like. People are growing less afraid of value judgments, he tells her; they are feeling nostalgic for a simple, moral universe. At another table a middle-aged woman with long, frizzy hair in a lilac suit is telling a story about a business trip she took to India, the day when a squatting beggar in the street smeared his feces on her shoes. She's gained enough distance from the event to laugh about it, though it's obvious the memory still disturbs her. What catches Javier's attention is the highly descriptive way she tells the story, pantomiming the beggar's posture and motions, fanning herself to convey the infernal heat and the stench of waste, savoring the warbling timbre of native words in her mouth. It's quite clear, he whispers, that the woman actually envies the beggar somehow, envies his intimacy with his own shit. The three younger women at the table listen eagerly. For these few minutes the frizzy-haired woman has become their village elder, Javier suggests: a communal story-teller, keeping the oral tradition alive.

Ursula watches Javier's performance with wonder and unease as the corporate lunchers around them transform into toucans, orchids, and flying dragons wherever he points his magic wand. She feels like Wendy in Never Never Land, a place continually and effortlessly conforming to the shape of people's dreams. Well, perhaps this is the way things work, she thinks. Perhaps we really do live in a world where imagination and reality merge. Where a pair of silver boots is all the pixie dust required to set in motion the colonization of Mars. Where a humanity clad in sparkling pink jump-suits may one day strike the national boundaries from the maps, pave the Moon with mirrors and Earth with colored lights, and proceed to boogie the nights away till the end of time. Why not? Culture, much like nature, is subject to chaos. And poor Ivy, afraid even to stir the air by brushing her hair, is onto something, isn't she? After all, the brushing of a model's hair in Middle City might cause a hurricane in Polynesia, where in turn the storm-appeasing dance of a savage could cause a heat wave in Middle City.

And *the savage girl?* Ursula thinks. What changes could *she* bring about?

As Javier talks on, she squints her eyes again, putting the impressionistic blotches of color together in new ways, bringing off a world of savage girls, their moccasined feet communicating with the earth, their far-seeing eyes peering into the ether, a world of people committed to authenticity, people with no interest in buying or buying into anything that commercial culture has to offer. The thought is crazy, but she can't get it out of her mind. Could she really sell Cabaj on the savage girl? Could she use his ads for a useless product to spread the savage girl's message of autonomy from consumerism? Could it turn out to be her message, and not his medium, for which people would ultimately find use?

It wouldn't be any kind of death blow to consumerism, of course—most likely it would barely register at all—but it just might be the beginning of something, she thinks, something a little bit meaningful, a little bit exciting, even a little dangerous. A kind of guerrilla campaign, waged behind enemy lines.

A team of waiters converges on the table with silver platters and sets about spreading a kaleidoscopic palette of food on the table, every dish brightened with some exotic garnish or sauce—plantains with red guava paste, dark meats with white yucca, blackberries with glistening caramel, figs with coconut shavings. Ursula tries not to show it, but the sight of all this festive food being laid before her makes her feel unstoppable, as though it were not just food but raw power waiting to be put to use. She's going to do it, she decides: she's going to unleash the savage girl upon the world and let her wreak whatever havoc she can. And she's going to keep wearing this blue suit, and other suits like it. And she's going to make a point of ordering everything that's popular. And she's going to accept all the love this strange man is prepared to give her—this man who rhapsodizes about bubble pipes and weaves divinity into fishtail hems, who is just mad enough to think she's strong and steady and cool and caring and beautiful, who seems ready to say or do just about anything to make her happy.

Wampum

The savage girl on the screen is both voluptuous and strong. Her thighs are soft, while her haunches are muscular. Her legs are long but not overly thin. Her Mohican stands up straight without looking stiff; on the contrary, it is silky and golden, adorned with downy blue feathers. Her hip juts boldly, though her eyes are down-turned, almost demure. Ursula has worked as hard on this airbrushed thing as she used to work on her art paintings, but this is nothing like her art paintings. This is magic. You can look and look and never see it, never as a whole; your eyes shift restlessly from paradox to paradox. High-heeled moccasins. A fur loincloth over waxed legs. A midriff-baring animal-hide top that looks as light and comfortable as rough-woven silk. A necklace of menacing incisors arranged in a floriated pattern. Warpaints of pastel pink and amber along her cheekbones. You can look and look and look and look, an endless whirligig of unsatiated desire.

Cabaj sits at the far end of the table. His in-house staff and his hired guns from the Mitchell and Chennault ad agency have arranged themselves around the table not by company but rather by job description—marketers to the left in skirt suits, hypererect postures, power ties, hair gel; creatives to the right in cotton and poly shirts, bangles and clips, canvas boat shoes. Chas, seated unobtrusively in the corner, settles back in his chair and nods at Ursula to begin. She gestures toward the screen.

"Call her the savage girl," she says. "That's what *I* call her, anyway. No one knows what she calls herself, because she doesn't speak. Language is full of lies, and the savage girl wants nothing to do with lies. She's sick of modernity, sick of all the cynicism in our culture that passes for sophistication. She tries to live authentically, honestly. She tries to live simply, in tune with the earth."

The woman with the spiky hair in the charcoal dress suit knits her brows. The man in the black shirt with the gold stud in his ear nods agreement.

"You and I may find her glamorous, but she cares nothing for glamour. In this way she may be deeper than the rest of us. She may be superior. She doesn't spend money. Rather, she makes things herself, using materials at hand. The experience of making things herself is valuable to her. It gives her power."

The thin, gray-haired woman in pinstripes leans forward. Lucien, his curly hair pomaded flat against his temples, looks at his glittering watch. Ursula fights a moment of panic. She knows she's reached the point of no return. She takes a breath, trying to flatten the tremor in her voice.

"So what do you have to offer her? The truth is, I'm not sure. Maybe nothing. She doesn't trust you. Maybe she will never accept you, no matter what you offer. Maybe she will sense you're the enemy, smell it on you, know you're out to steal her secrets, to mine her resources. She knows your kind: you're just one more emissary of the Imperium, trading wampum for sacred land, chintzy porcelain Buddhas for the treasures of ancient temples."

The young Asian executive with the crooked tie and the nasty underbite blinks rapidly, almost psychotically. The spiky-haired woman leans back and frowns, tapping her nails against the tabletop. Chas pinches a centimeter of flesh at the bridge of his nose.

"The thing people are beginning to want more than anything else," she continues, "is to be free of you. *They want to not want you; they want to not want anything you have to offer.*"

An uneasy murmur. She looks for Javier's reaction, but he's standing next to the projector and its light obscures his face. Chas, however, she *can* see, and he is glaring at her—she didn't know those perpetually hooded eyes of his could open so wide. He has no idea what she's doing. He's actually nervous, a discovery that fills her with unexpected joy. For the first time since she met him, she feels completely in control.

"Of course, on the other hand," she says, in a more casual tone, "those Indians and temple priests were quite happy with the deal. Those Indians loved wampum. It gave them a lot of prestige in their tribe, at least until the market was flooded. And as far as those temple priests were concerned, the shiny porcelain Buddhas lit up their temples like beams of divine sunlight."

She pauses. All eyes watch her expectantly.

"Value, as we all know, is relative," she says. "Right now people are nostalgic for simpler times, times when people felt pure and complete in their bodies, when their bodies were all the power they required to satisfy their needs. People today are sick of being consumers. And you have a product that can help. Your product will keep them pure. Your product will restore their innocence. Because your product is, in its very essence, the opposite of consumption. Consuming your product is like consuming nothing at all. Keep this in mind always when designing your campaign. Keep in mind how light this product is going to make buyers feel, how free it's going to make them feel—free of people like you."

She takes her seat to laughter and applause. When she sneaks a look over at Chas, he nods approval and gestures with his eyes toward Ed Cabaj, whose face remains slack as he stares, with unconcealed longing, at the picture of the savage girl.

Magic

At night, in bed, Javier's body becomes a lunar landscape of concavities—the hollow of his chest, the widening valley down the middle of his rib cage, the twin gorges beneath his pelvic bones—and she presses up against him, filling the depressions with the length of her own, softer self. If she were very small she would choose the cave of his collarbone to make her home; she'd curl up there against the taut skin of his neck, which has the warm, smooth feel and slightly briny smell of those small flat stones one finds washed up on the beach, baking in the sun. She's developed a theory about his body: On the one hand, all the parts of it he uses to reach out to and apprehend the world—his hands, eyes, nose, ears—are just a little larger and more overdeveloped than average. Even his height seems geared toward this purpose, as though his body were nothing but an ambulatory periscope to bring his head up over the surface of crowds. On the other hand, the rest of it is slimmed down to the barest level of functionality. His torso is just broad enough to contain his organs. His arms and legs are just wide enough around to bundle the muscles and nerves and bones that allow him to dodge and weave on rollerblades through traffic jams and slip through closing subway doors. The logic of his body holds true even for his penis, which is just a little longer than its leanness should allow.

Over the past few weeks this odd little theory of hers has taken root in her mind and grown into an all-embracing explanation of every aspect of Javier's personality and every difference between him and her. If only she had a body like his, she reflects, she just might be able to see life the way he does. She can't escape her body; its presence is too real, too insistent, there's too much of it in too many places, a thousand eyeballs fasten onto every part of it everywhere she goes, mooring it in place, never letting her forget a single inch or gram of it. But Javier's body is so improbable that it's like some trick of the air, a puff of wind in a trenchcoat, a spirit clothed in the merest afterthought of flesh. When they make love, she presses herself hard against him to feel his materiality, to reassure herself that he's actually part of her world. But when they take to the streets together, she finds herself—sometimes exhilaratingly, sometimes even a little terrifyingly—in his world, a mystical wonderland in which people silently passing on the street are anything but silently passing, in which souls are in perpetual communication, whispering to one another in the ubiquitous language of surfaces: a puffy hairdo issuing invitations to contemplate free love and nature worship; a bare waxed scalp humming a counterpoint of quietude, purity, renunciation of excess; a leather coat clamoring for rugged individualism; a transparent handbag retorting with calls for the abolition of private property and a radical rethinking of our attitudes toward death.

This is the world Ursula lives in now, whenever Javier is at her side. Some days they'll sail around on rollerblades; others, they'll proceed on foot, slowly, their faces close to the city's canvas. They may get up well before dawn and claim for themselves an unobtrusive corner in a financial-district diner, or alternatively rise late, pick up sandwiches and iced coffees, and seek out a sunny section of park bench. They'll sit quietly, sketching the way the stockbrokers drape their jackets over their chairs, or the way the high school kids on their lunch hour tie their shirts around their waists. To use the time efficiently they'll multitask, interrupting their sketches to copy down the names of any vacation spots, athletic activities, or concerts the stockbrokers or students discuss. Usually they'll content themselves with silent observation, but if the right kind of person indicates a willingness to talk, they won't fail to make use of the opportunity. Thus in a coffee shop they'll talk to a kid with a one-haired Charlie Brown haircut about the thousand-page tome on yoga he's reading; and on an inner-city basketball court they'll wind up showing some tag-art graffiti figures they've tried doing to a group of kids who will shake their heads pityingly and then bring them up to date on everything from the look of the sneakers to the finer techniques of the drawings themselves.

The airbrushed savage girl has been joined by a whole paradessential clique in Ursula's sketchbook. She's learned how to draw men who look at once edgy and healthy; how to draw utility vehicles both rugged and refined; even how to draw food to make it appear simultaneously filling and light. As she sketches, she often finds herself replaying in her mind her years of struggling to make paintings she hoped would pry open the cracks of the world, expose the contradictions, get at the truth of things, and replaying as well the increasing desolation and powerlessness she felt as time went on. Because people don't want their contradictions exposed, she's decided. They want their contradictions glamorized, valorized, mythologized. Her airbrushed savage girl did precisely those things, and she saw for herself the power it had over its viewers, a kind of primal forcefulness her art paintings never seemed to achieve.

If the painful lesson she learned from Chas was that people want paradessences, the far more palatable lessons she's absorbing from Javier are that she doesn't necessarily have to feel bad about giving people what they want; that contradictions help people cope; that what Chas thinks of as the "broken soul" of a product, if looked at in a more forgiving light, might just as easily be called its magic, its power to suspend antinomies, to let the consumer have it both ways and every way, buying a new pair of sneakers not only to grip the earth but to soar into the air, one foot on the ground and the other transcending on the wings of brand identity, becoming part of that higher mythology of the product, emblazoned in its constellations, bridging with one bold leap of imagination body and spirit, dream and responsibility, phenomena and noumena, life and art. . . .

And perhaps it's this newfound respect for surfaces that keeps Ursula from asking too many questions of Javier or digging too deeply into his problems. She's never once commented on his trembling hands or runny nose. Eskalith, she found out, is a brand name for lithium, used to treat bipolar disorders, but she hasn't asked him about his condition. She never asks about his past, either, anymore. The stories he makes up about his childhood have become a running joke between the two of them. One day he'll tell her his parents were underwater archaeologists and go on to describe how he rode a pair of dolphins across a bay in the Adriatic to school each day. The next he'll say his parents were jewel thieves who trained him at an early age to climb walls using suction cups and to outwit alarm systems. But whatever his childhood was like, she knows now that what directly followed it was far from ideal.

Only minutes ago he told her the story, after she woke him from a bad dream. He has bad dreams often. In the middle of the night comes the sound of his distress, nothing like his waking voice: a soft, high-pitched whine, repeated with each breath, like the whimper of a crying dog, anxious, bereft, and helpless, one of the sadder noises she's ever heard. Waking him from his nightmares has become so habitual for her that she can now do it practically without waking up herself. She shakes him gently, tells him it's OK, then holds him while they both return to their dreams without another word. But tonight when she shook him, his eyes opened and he began to talk. He told her how he ran away from home at sixteen and has been on his own ever since—how he just started walking one day and kept walking all night, crisscrossing streets, avenues, bridges; and how by morning he found a highway that he walked alongside all the next day; and how at dusk a truck stopped to pick him up; and how he slept then and woke up far from home. He told her how he bummed around the country for five years after that, living in squat houses, picking up menial jobs, making a friend or two, then growing disillusioned with the place or the people and picking up and moving on to repeat the process somewhere else.

She was half asleep as he talked, and his words flowed over her, alchemizing instantly into imagery, the way words tend to do in that state, so that by the time he's finished and has gone back to sleep and she is fully awake and begins trying to recall more exactly what he said, she finds that her mind has misplaced his words somewhere and is filled instead with hazy images of dilapidated rooms in busted, postindustrial cities, of bus stations, construction lots, fast-food kitchens, dark basements with folding cots. She concentrates, now, and some of the words come back to her, and she remembers his talking about his strange journey less in terms of physical settings than in terms of the simultaneous progress going on inside him: how the nature of reality was changing before his eyes, the flashes of luminescence, people beginning to glow like stained glass at sunrise, suffused with color and light, meaning and beauty, an ecstatic vision he couldn't understand or control or maintain but that spurred him ever onward from one place to the next.

His quest eventually brought him back to Mid City, where he found a new squat house and moved in with a bunch of street punks much younger than him. He got a library job at the university and began auditing courses, searching for the start of something, some great project to which he might commit his life. And then one day he saw Professor Lacouture walking across the campus and was impressed by the cut of his suit and the confidence of his gait. So he began attending the man's lectures and learned how every surface was a thing of infinite complexity, every surface an aesthetic position, a philosophical argument, a political treatise, and a blueprint for a worthier way of living all at once.

And he went home to his squat and saw his street-punk roommates anew. Their look, he saw, was not just a look: no, it was a vessel, perhaps the only one at their disposal to carry their difference, to keep it alive through the soul-numbing climate of adolescence. And if they could just manage to smuggle it safely through to adulthood, he realized, this difference would develop, flourish, grow into political, cultural, and moral convictions. And the imagination required for these kids to re-create themselves through fashion would heighten their sense of what was possible in adulthood. And the close friendships they learned to make through sharing their fashions would in adulthood give them the skills to forge alliances, movements, communities. And the courage it took for them to bear the scorn of their parents, teachers, and peers would in adulthood serve them as courage to fight for all their visions of what was admirable and beautiful and right.

And this, he told her, was what trendspotting meant to him. Trendspotting meant everything to him. It meant there was so much meaning out there that once he fully knew how to find it he'd never go hungry for it again.

And he sleeps, his jaw loosened, his mouth pulled down once again into that overbitten, sad, and childlike frown. And wide awake now beside him, Ursula watches his face, thinks about his story, and makes out the pattern clearly now. Spirals of depression. Rebounds into mania. Time after time breaking abruptly with his past, abandoning all his old plans, friends, attachments, and beginning all over again down some new path. She wonders how long he's here for this time, how long before she becomes as insubstantial to him as he seems at times to her, how long before they slip through each other's fingers, the haphazard kink of life that brought them together once again smoothing out like none of this ever was.

Plastic

That guy in there," Ivy says, pointing into a room as they walk by. "You see him?"

An Asian teenage boy, lying on his back, staring without emotion at the ceiling.

Ursula nods. She wishes Ivy would keep her voice down.

"He drank a quart of Drāno," she says. "It ate his whole throat away, and most of his stomach, too."

The boy blinks, possibly in annoyance. Ursula takes Ivy's skinny arm and coaxes her out of the doorway.

"He can't eat or drink," Ivy says, fascinated. "He has to get fed through the IV. He can't talk, either." She looks down, watching her slippers slide forward across the floor. The latest cocktail of medications seems to be working, though the side effect of muscular stiffness rather resembles the tendency toward catatonia it helped alleviate. Except for the slippers, she's begun to wear her own clothes again, today a black sundress printed with small white flowers, which Ursula hasn't seen on her since she was fourteen. Apparently she's no longer concerned about being used to advertise for the Bodies or the Antibodies.

"The Drāno hollowed him all out inside," Ivy says. "I know that feeling. To be all hollowed-out inside. Let's ride the elevators."

They pass the front desk. Ivy walks ahead to the lobby and pushes the Up and Down buttons simultaneously. Instantly a car arrives, going up, and Ivy slips in, gesturing for Ursula to follow. A doctor is inside, a slight, serious-looking Indian man, and Ivy presses her hands together and gives him a little Hindu head-bow, then leans her thin, stiffened body back against the stubbled aluminum wall.

"You a plastic surgeon?" she asks the man.

"No," he says. "I'm an internist."

"Our mom's a plastic surgeon," Ivy tells him, "and she had these videotapes she'd make of the procedures to show patients what to expect. Urse and me watched them on the sly. They were gross but kind of funny, too. She drew on the women's boobs with a red Magic Marker. Two circles like eyes around the aureoles."

Ivy traces two little circles on her chest. The doctor, who has already noted her hospital slippers, nods calmly at the information.

"Then she'd cut along the lines," Ivy says, "and she'd vacuum out the fat to make room for the silicone bags. Slurp slurp slurp. Just like that." She snorts. "That was the funniest part, watching her stuff those bags into the women's boobs with her fingers. The bags were so funny, but at the same time it was very serious because our mom was making girls into grown-up women with her Magic Marker and her knife and her little bags of Jell-O."

The doors open. The doctor remains where he is, letting them shut again. Perhaps by now he's figured out who this woman is. Perhaps he's heard the stories.

"'Girls into women,'" he says, playing the psychiatrist. "That's interesting."

"Urse and me used to play plastic surgeon together."

The doctor looks at Ursula, and she looks at the floor and nods, embarrassed. It's all true.

"Urse was always the surgeon because she was the oldest. She gave me nose jobs and tummy tucks and face-lifts and boob jobs. She'd draw lines on me with a red Magic Marker, and then she'd pretend to cut and snip. She'd pinch me to make it seem real. I think sometimes I really thought it *was* real. I think I was a schizo even then. But I'm better now."

"I'm glad to hear that," the doctor says. His voice is soothing. He sounds genuinely glad for her, as though he actually believed her. Ursula wonders about these doctors, wonders about Dr. Shivamurti, who told her this morning that Ivy is almost ready to be released. Ursula isn't so sure. Maybe she's hopelessly cynical, but recently she's gotten the feeling that Ivy is only pretending to be better. This entire conversation taking place on the elevator seems to Ursula to be a case in point, just one more way Ivy has learned to play the game, confessing anything that smacks of childhood trauma to anyone in a white jacket.

"I'm going back to work soon," she boasts.

"That's excellent," the doctor says.

The doors open again. They've reached the top floor.

"Come on, Urse," says Ivy.

She steps out into the lobby and Ursula follows. The doctor remains inside.

"Good luck to you," he says as the doors close in front of him. Ivy leans over and presses the Down button.

"Is that where you got the idea?" Ursula asks.

"What idea?"

Ursula points to one of her scars, the one running along her left arm. Ivy looks at it as though seeing it for the first time. She looks up at her sister, worried.

"Do you think they make me too ugly?"

Ursula knows what she means: too ugly to model, the only thing Ivy cares about these days. All her delusionary talk of trendspotters has been replaced by an ongoing obsessive monologue about being a model again—inarguably a more socially acceptable turn of mind, but almost as troubling to Ursula, because she really doesn't think Ivy stands much of a chance of working as a model now. It's not just the scars on her body; her face, too, is not what it was. If her expression had become merely affectless, it wouldn't be so bad, Ursula thinks—blankness is probably more of an asset than a liability to a model anyway. No, the problem is that her face isn't blank *enough*. Its muscles behave strangely. Her jaw is a little squarer and more pronounced than before. And her mouth turns down at the corners when she isn't smiling. And when she *is* smiling, the muscles around her eyes remain serious, making the smile look oddly haunted. When she smiles like that, Ursula gets the feeling that her sister really does know what it feels like to be all hollowed-out inside. She hopes the end of Ivy's modeling career will mark the beginning of a more fulfilling existence. As Ivy recovers and gets readjusted to the world, Ursula plans to guide her interests in some new direction—something with a future, something down-to-earth that will give her a sense of her real worth.

"You don't look ugly at all," Ursula assures her. "But remember, Ivy, you've got to take this whole going-back-to-work thing slow. You've got to rest, and go to the group sessions, and just let yourself live."

Ivy stares at her, then looks down, her voice low and without inflection when she speaks. "You think I'm gonna be a failure," she says.

"Ivy, no, no, you're gonna do really well. I know you are."

"You'll see," she whispers. "They're gonna help me."

"Who do you mean?" Ursula asks. This is the first time today that Ivy has said something she doesn't understand. "*Who's* going to help you?"

Ivy clasps her hands behind her back and sweeps the floor with an itinerant, slippered foot.

"My loyal fans, of course," she says, looking up with that strange artificial smile.

This is a joke. Ursula laughs, letting herself entertain the far-fetched idea that things may actually turn out all right.

Hitmen

The two of them—James T. Couch and James T. Couch's Irony—adjust their glasses on their nose and peer through the Plexiglas wall at the shadowy forms jerking and bobbing on the cramped, smoky dance floor, James T. Couch looking with interest, James T. Couch's Irony with feigned interest.

"So this savage girl," the two of them say. "What *kind* of fur was it?" James T. Couch sounds like a nervous man trying to sound casual. James T. Couch's Irony sounds like an unconcerned man pretending to be a nervous man trying to sound casual.

And this, she recalls, *was supposed to be the normal one.*

"I don't know, James. Brown fur."

"But it *could* be synthetic, right? I *have* to know that."

Ursula smiles and clenches her teeth. James T. Couch's Irony is every bit as industrious as it's been over the last few days, pressing emphasis onto random words, feigning concern, as though the fur were important to him, as though his reputation were at stake—from which Ursula is invited to gather that the fur is not important to him and that his reputation is by no means at stake, whereas in fact, since the fur flatly contradicts his last report, she knows it's extremely important to him and his reputation is very much at stake.

"It could be synthetic," she mutters. She's due to meet Ivy's friend Sonja Niellsen here; they haven't had a chance to talk since she first got to town. Sonja is Ivy's only friend, so far as Ursula can make out, or at least the only one who visits her—the only nonimaginary one, at any rate. The two of them are planning to get an apartment together after Ivy is discharged, and Ursula wants to make sure Sonja is going to be a good influence. Ivy's going to need all the good influences she can get. In their latest conversation Dr. Shivamurti admitted to Ursula that if her sister's coverage weren't about to run out, they probably would have wanted to keep her in a while longer. She advised her to try to get Ivy into a halfway house, but as it turns out, even the most dubious-looking of these places have yearlong waiting lists. The best that Ursula has managed to find is a couple of day-care centers for the recovering insane, but she's pretty sure the decor of the places alone will be enough to keep her sister from going anywhere near them. So if Ivy is going to have any hope at all of readapting to the world, Sonja is going to have to be helpful, patient, and understanding.

It's a delicate situation, and Ursula was hoping for a bit of privacy in which to sound Sonja out properly, but privacy is something she's had very little of since the day she met James T. Couch, who for some unfathomable reason has latched on to her like a barnacle. The coincidence of his happening to show up here would be downright spooky were it not for the fact that he so clearly belongs in this hellhole of a club. His outfit is even slightly gaudier than usual for the occasion: a pair of tight orange slacks, a pair of Day-Glo high-tops, and yet another of his trademark nonsensical Japanese T-shirts, a garish appliqué of a cartoon car full of cartoon animals, with the accompanying quasi-English slogan *The Driving Life: It's all a fun!* His new glasses are an eyeful as well, shaped like television screens, the black frames wider on the outer sides to accommodate a column of costume knobs and dials.

"You're the *picture* of elegance, as usual," he effuses, as though reading her mind and, ironically, returning the compliment.

"Thanks." It's true enough, though. The Banzer suit has lead to other outfits, purchased with her own money—or her own credit, anyway—from casual to evening wear; tonight it's something in between, a black stretch-silk blouse and a matching skirt. It's been a while since she last wore a skirt. She's also waxed her legs for the first time in years, and they feel pleasantly cool and slippery in the air-conditioning.

"And to think Chas told me you were a slob." He smiles another flash-bulb smile, his thick lenses refracting the reddish light from the hanging Moroccan lanterns and making his eyes look diabolically beady and small.

He leans back against the wall and slides his head around like a charmed snake's to the muted sound of the dance music, a layered agglomeration of record static and tape hiss. The deejay, a girl with short bleached blond hair in a tank top and baggy pants, stationed just beyond the Plexiglas wall, slides her head around in a fashion exactly similar to Couch's. It takes Ursula a moment to realize that this is no accident, for Couch, with derision, or admiration, or both, is mimicking her.

"So what do you *suppose* is keeping Javier?" he says.

"He's coming, too?"

"You don't sound so happy!" he says, surprised and mock-surprised. "Is there trouble in paradise?"

"What's that supposed to mean?"

"Oh, well, you two seem to have gotten to *know* each other pretty well." His miniaturized eyes widen into the most innocent of looks, by which she is supposed to infer that he knows something, whereas he couldn't possibly know anything. Javier wouldn't tell Couch; he doesn't even like Couch. Not that he's ever come out and said it—he never says anything bad about anyone—but she can tell by the way he avoids looking at him or talking to him when they're together in a group. In much the same way, she's come to notice, Javier tends to avoid just about anything that's potentially unsettling or unpleasant. He's never once gone with her to visit Ivy, for instance, insisting he has a phobia when it comes to hospitals. And even talking about Ivy's illness makes him uncomfortable: usually he just nods sympathetically for a while, then takes the first opportunity to change the subject. His emotional evasiveness upsets her sometimes, but at the same time she's learned to appreciate his delicacy, his earnest desire to protect her from anything that might make her feel angry or sad or hopeless, as she's all too prone to do. Whenever her problems start getting to her, he's always at the ready with new counteroffensives of distraction. The latest and most successful of these involves the savage girl. Without the girl's knowledge, the two of them have adopted her. They leave her food—sticks of beef jerky, cans of tuna, Spam, creamed spinach, sliced pineapple—placing them on the pediment of the statue of Guy Banister while she's off foraging. Occasionally they leave her fresh fruit and vegetables from the supermarket down the block, though she's more suspicious of these. They still haven't seen or heard the girl speak, but just the other day, to their immense joy, they witnessed some of the local street punks communicating with her in a crude sign language, bartering food and raw materials for stitched hides and inner-tube slingshots.

Encouraging though this may be for the prospects of a savage trend, things aren't looking all that savage here at the Sarin Spa, as James T. Couch doesn't fail to point out. He makes a taxonomical list of all the nonsavage breeds and species lounging around them on padded couches and little leather-covered ottomans: the ravers, the ragers, the eraserheads; the girls who wear pigtails and over-the-knee stockings; their sworn enemies, the girls who wear ponytails and just-under-the-knee stockings; and finally the inevitable hefty complement of style-challenged flatlanders, looking and feeling like they don't belong, even though they comprise the majority, pay most of the covers, buy most of the drinks. No earth tones here; no sandals, talismans, or bones, it's true. Nothing but bright, unnatural colors, James T. Couchian colors, the kinds of phosphorescent shades found on computer screens. Not that James T. Couch doubts the savage trend, oh no, not for a minute. His tiny eyes widen angelically. Then they narrow devilishly. Then, glancing up over Ursula's head, they bulge.

"Hey," Sonja Niellsen says. She stands with her bare legs pressed together and her arm crooked into a frozen wave. Although her face is recessed in the oversize hood of a black crepe shrug, it's unmistakable nonetheless. She wears that same trademark expression that she and the more famous models she emulates all wear in magazine ads now: half sulky, half afraid, and a little vacant; they call it the kidnapped look. Ursula is surprised to realize that it occurs naturally on her, surprised it isn't something that has to be coaxed out by a team of photographers.

Ursula opens her mouth to speak, but Couch beats her to it.

"James T. Couch," he says, proffering a hand. "I'm a *big* fan of your work." In one motion he hops up and grabs an ottoman out from under a middle-aged couple in tight jeans about to squat down around a neighboring coffee table.

"You know," Couch says to Sonja, sliding the seat snugly up against his own. "I couldn't help *noticing* that choker you're wearing. Where'd you get it?"

The accessory in question sports a constricting-looking phalanx of smoke-colored stones.

"Oh. A friend of mine made it." Absently she pulls down her hood. Her stylist has done her hair in a new way, a short bob that scythes around her cheekbones. Her eyes reflect twinkles of ruddy lantern light but are otherwise dark.

Couch sits down, and Sonja continues to stand there obediently while he questions her about each element of her attire, from her crepe shrug down to her bubble-toe lace-ups and back up to her strapless, knotted sackcloth minidress, the satin-trimmed hem of which he bends to scrutinize at eye level. He adjusts his glasses, nodding at the names of stores and designers tripping off Sonja's lips. To stretch out this sublime moment still further he asks her about her underwear, guessing various brand names. Sonja begins to hesitate, and in his usual emphatic tone, he lets her know he will be using the information for a book he's cowriting, his smile implying that he's joking, whereas of course he's not joking.

"Let me ask you something," Couch says. "How do you feel about fur? Would you ever wear it?"

"Um, real fur, or synthetic?" she asks.

Couch aims a triumphant smile at Ursula. "You see? You see? Am I right or am I right or am I right, come on, hey, am I not right?"

"Do you think you're right?"

Couch smiles, happy to have her play along with his routine. How can she make fun of him when he's already making fun of himself? The man is the Antaeus of Irony. When you try to knock him down, it only makes him stronger. If there's a way to lift him off his surfaces, Ursula has yet to find it.

Javier shows up just in time to place his order with a young cocktail waitress who has appeared out of nowhere to stare at Sonja with awe and resentment. He pulls up a small table, probably mistaking it for a stool, and sits down on it next to Ursula, examining her face.

"How are you?" he asks.

"Fine," she says, startled by his tone of concern.

"Javier," Couch says, "aren't you *surprised* to find Ursula here?"

"Oh. Yeah. That's . . . surprising."

"And I'm sure this *other* beauty needs no introduction."

Javier looks at Sonja without a trace of recognition, and they stare at each other blankly for a moment before he opts to stick out his hand and repeat his own name.

"I'm Sonja," Sonja says. "I know Ivy."

"Oh, oh, sure."

"Javier and James are people I work with," Ursula tells Sonja.

"Trendspotters," Sonja says.

Ursula laughs, confused. "How did you know that?"

"Ivy told me you're working for Chas," she says, her eyes narrowing ever so slightly.

"She . . . ," Ursula begins. "She told you that?"

Sonja nods.

But Ivy can't possibly know that; Ursula has never told her. She feels suddenly out of breath. They all stare at her, unsure what's wrong.

It's just another one of Ivy's paranoid delusions, she tells herself. One that simply happens to be true.

"She . . . she talks about Chas to you?"

Sonja nods.

After the initial shock Ursula decides that maybe this is a good thing. Maybe it's a sign that Ivy really is getting better.

"Speaking of our Grand Inquisitor," Couch announces, "I've just come from a meeting with him. For the last three hours he's been telling me how he wants this presentation thing to go. And I was wondering, has either of you . . . um . . . *seen* this year's trendbook yet?"

"Why?" Ursula asks. "Did it surprise you?"

He looks at each of them, his smile widening tooth by tooth. "That's certainly one way of putting it."

"Javier says he's making a new man out of Chas," Ursula explains.

Couch looks at Javier askance. "*Reeeeealllly.* A new man, you say? How so?"

Javier doesn't reply. Couch seems to be making him even more uncomfortable than usual. Ursula picks up the slack.

"He's making an optimist out of him," she says.

Couch looks genuinely amused, then holds up a finger and takes a sip of his drink so he can spit it out in a simulated paroxysm of hilarity.

"Chas! *An optimist!*" He turns off the uncontrollable laugh, wipes the imaginary sweat from his brow. "Now *that's* funny."

"You've . . . seen the trendbook?" Javier asks, a note of poorly disguised trepidation in his voice.

"Oh, no," Couch replies, lacing his fingers across his chest. "The man trusts no one. I just listened to him talk about it."

"Oh," Javier says, clearly relieved. "Well, you know the way he talks."

The two men stare each other down for a minute, Couch with his phony smile and Javier with forced bravado. Ursula begins feeling uncomfortable and looks off at the dance floor. A new deejay has taken over, a stocky kid with hair in his eyes and a gold tooth who has started fading recent movie tunes into and out of a backdrop of house music. The composition of the dance-floor crowd shifts accordingly, the boys and girls with horn-rimmed glasses and big, clunky shoes departing, the boys and girls with wire-framed glasses and linen jackets tied around their waists arriving. The core constituency of heavyset black men with shaved heads and skinny, androgynous-looking women with close-cropped hair remains constant.

She looks back to find Couch and Javier watching her. She has no idea why. The two of them are beginning to make her paranoid.

"So," she says, trying to grease the social wheels. "What new leads are you guys tracking down tonight?"

"Please," Couch protests, holding up his hands. "I'm just in town to have fun. Streetwork is so outmoded." He leans over and says to Sonja with a vague air of conspiracy, "I work *virtually* nowadays."

Sonja looks at her lemon drop.

"Satellites," Couch says. "I get a thousand channels beamed to my lake house."

Couch has already described his research station to Ursula in painstaking detail: six computers continuously scanning the Web for trendy keywords, a bank of twelve television screens set to switch channels randomly every minute. He watches them all simultaneously, looking for patterns as he rides his Exercycle or his rowing machine or his ski machine.

"I should have you all up to my lake sometime," Couch says. "It's very private. I'm sure you like to get away from your adoring fans now and then, am I right, Sonja? It must get to be a *strain* for you, being adored all the time."

He places a limp hand on her arm and leans close to her as he speaks. Sonja looks at him confused; perhaps she has never until this instant considered the possibility of adoring fans.

It takes Ursula a moment fully to process Couch's invitation.

"*Your* lake?" she exclaims.

"Well, it's a small lake," Couch says, oozing mock modesty. "Not one of the Great ones, you know. But it has its charms. Once Ivy's all better, you *must* bring her along, too. Oh, and speaking of Ivy"—Couch aims his smile first at Javier, who looks ashenly into his drink, and then at Ursula—"allow me to be the first to *congratulate* you on her new job offer."

His face pinkens in the choke hold of his smile.

"Chas finally clinched it for her just this morning," he goes on.

Ursula looks over at Javier anxiously, but he seems suddenly to have become preoccupied with a stain on his sleeve.

"Your *friend* Ed Cabaj is going to use her for the diet-water campaign!"

"What . . . ," she falters, ". . . what do you mean?"

"You really made an *impression* on him at that party, Ursula," Couch continues. "Chas said Ed kept talking about you, saying if only you were a few years younger and so on, or if only Ivy were still . . . you know, compos mentis. And then Chas *socked* him with the big idea: Why not use Ivy anyway? Think of the publicity! I tell you," he says with a laugh, "ever since your sister got put away, I've been worried about our poor old boss. What with his listening to all this Light Age mumbo jumbo of Javier's, I thought our blessed Mother Superior was finally losing it. But he's still the king of all salesmen, we've got to give him that. Do we not just got to give him that?"

She turns to Javier, who sits woodenly, staring at the tabletop.

"Show her the pictures, Javier," Couch urges.

Javier's head snaps up. "No, James, this isn't the time for—"

"Yes, Javier," Ursula says, erecting a smile on her face to match Couch's. "Show me the pictures."

"Chas still has them."

"Oh, stop being so modest," Couch says, innocent and mischievous by turns. "You've still got all the rough sketches. The book's right in your bag. I saw you doodling away in it an hour ago."

Javier turns toward her, prepared to say something, but her smile stops him cold. Silently he reaches into the bag at his feet, brings out his sketchbook, hesitates, then sets it on the table.

The sketchbook resembles all his others, except instead of bearing some abstract, conceptual title like *Elective Affinities*, or *Invented Origins*, or *The New Earnestness*, this one is labeled simply *Ivy*. Ursula opens it. Into the first few pages of the book are pasted a few clippings of Ivy's magazine and catalog ads. The last clipping is from a newspaper, the photograph of her being led by the police out of Banister Park, covered in slashes of blood and paint, wearing nothing but a short, tattered baseball jacket donated by a homeless man. The next dozen or so pages are taken up with rough and mostly incomplete exercises, Javier getting the hang of the physical language of Ivy, the look in her wide eyes, the carriage of her thin shoulders, her body in the midst of various motions and stances, wearing the outfits from the catalogs. Then, suddenly, a change in theme: a series of highly detailed color-pencil drawings of Ivy in savage outfits—hide skirts, one-shouldered tunic shirts, accessories of feathers and shells. The overall style of these pictures is more or less the one that Ursula developed for the presentation; Javier has dressed Ivy up in all the same beguiling contradictions, the voluptuous toughnesses and bold demurenesses and menacing pastels, but he has also gone on to create for her a series of outfits even more daring, revealing, and seductive than any that Ursula imagined for the savage girl. In one drawing she's even topless, and almost bottomless as well, wearing nothing but a loincloth, a bone necklace, and bright-red streaks of paint on her arms, belly, and cheeks. A sheen of sweat glistens on her naked chest. Sparks of reflected fire flash in her brazen stare.

Couch snickers, looking over Ursula's shoulder at the book. "Can't you just see Cabaj's eyes popping out at that one? The old goat."

Sonja stares with her big, dark eyes at Ursula.

"I'll bet your sister's pretty happy—*will be happy*, I mean," Couch goes on, "when she hears the news."

Ursula says nothing.

"Don't you think?" he asks.

She slowly fixes her eyes on Javier, maintaining the smile on her face.

"So . . . how long exactly have you been . . . working . . . on this idea?" she asks him.

"Not . . . I . . . I wanted to surprise you."

"Oh, you sure did that."

She looks through the Plexiglas. The deejay has mixed in a corny tune from a recent fun-loving-hitman movie, and a correspondingly mainstream crowd has poured onto the dance floor in response, happily rolling and snaking their arms.

"Look at that one, with the smirk on his face," Ursula says.

She points out a tall young man with a long blond ponytail. His wide mouth is locked into a wry smile, with a twist at the corner.

"What's he grinning about, anyway?" she asks.

Ursula looks at them, daring them to respond. No one does.

"The music," she says, answering herself. "It's the music. The smile is there to show the rest of them that he's in on the joke."

"'The joke'?" Couch asks.

"The joke," she repeats. "The joke that both the deejay who picked it out and the dancers dancing to it believe themselves to be more sophisticated than the tune. The smirking man smirks in order to show that he's in on the joke, so he can indulge in the fun-loving-hitman fantasy without an overload of embarrassment."

Sonja gazes wonderingly at the dancing man. Couch gazes with amusement at Ursula. Javier stares at the tabletop.

"He's imagining himself to be a fun-loving hitman," Ursula explains, "living in that fun-loving world of fun-loving hitmen and the bodacious babes they meet in the course of their killing various people and the wacky antics that ensue."

Her three listeners venture no comments. Nor do they move.

"Happy homicide," she says. "Harmonious hostility. That's the paradessence of that little smirk, isn't it?"

She directs the question at Javier, who shifts uncomfortably in his seat. Meanwhile Couch looks back and forth between the two of them, a roguish light in his eyes.

"What do you think of him?" Ursula asks Javier.

He clears his throat. "What do you mean?"

"Do you like him?"

"'Like him'? In what way?"

"I hate him," Ursula says, still smiling. "I want to wade through that idiotic mob and scratch that smirk off his face. Isn't that funny?"

No one says anything.

"I sound like my mother," she says lightly. "'Wipe that smirk off your face!'" She passes a hand in front of her face, removing the smile, then staring at them blankly. "She always said that. And you know what? I could never do it. Ivy learned to do it on command, but not me. I could never get rid of that silly, guilty smile. And now Ivy doesn't know how to smile, and I can't stop! Even when I want to be frowning, crying, screaming, even!"

They all jump when she slams her palm on the table. She feels the smile creep back onto her face.

"I smirk and smirk and smirk," she says, "and I feel just as stupid, powerless, and guilty every time."

She stares at the dancing man.

"The whole city's got this fucking smirk."

She passes her hand over her face again, removing the smile.

"Excuse me. I've got to go talk to someone."

She gets up and presses through the lounge crowd toward the door. Before leaving, she stops at the Plexiglas window for one last look at the ponytailed man, who dances with his wry smile in front of a video screen filled with computer-animated naked dancers in gas masks, while all around him people withdraw into their slashing-armed, carved-out spaces, and all around them all, green smoke pours down from golden vents in the ceiling.

Blackout

She finds Chas sitting in his darkened office. A small desk lamp in front of him glows meagerly, leaving a raccoon's mask of shadow around his eyes, while behind him the latticework of city lights spreads out down the slope and blurs into a haze above the flatlands. She knew he'd be here. He's been sleeping here every night since the presentation, finishing that trendbook Javier pertinaciously believes himself to be cowriting. He doesn't seem particularly surprised to see her. He gestures for her to take a seat, and she has just enough presence of mind to remain standing. She hasn't even thought about which allegation to begin with, but already a new one is crowding the others out.

"How'd you know I'd be at the Sarin Spa tonight, anyway?" she shouts. "Are you having me tailed or something? Are you tapping my phone?"

"Christ, Ursula. You sound like your sister."

"Have you been visiting her?"

Chas waves his hand dismissively, leans back in his chair.

"No, not me. I tried once. She went berserk," he says.

"Not you. Who's *Mr. Teeth*, then? Javier?"

"'Mr. Teeth'?"

The answer stabs her like an icicle in the chest. She can barely speak.

"It's James T. Couch," she whispers, and then yells, "It's that . . . *disgusting* Couch! Isn't it?"

Chas squints at the volume, twists a pinkie in his ear. "Couch is good with her," he says. "He's helped her more than you know."

"'Helped her'?"

"That's right. Convinced her to get out of that hospital, out of those sexless clothes, back to work again."

"'Convinced her' how?"

"I don't know. Ask Couch."

Suddenly she remembers what Ivy said when she talked about Mr. Teeth.

"The pictures," she says. "Couch showed her those pictures Javier drew."

"Yeah." Chas nods. "That's probably what sold her in the end. She turns herself on. But who can blame her, right?"

Ursula screams, not with anger but with fright. The room has gone dark.

"What the fuck?" Chas murmurs.

Everything has stopped. The darkness is total. No light. No sound.

"The power," Ursula whispers.

"Wonder if it's the whole damn building," Chas says.

"More," Ursula replies. "Behind you."

She hears him swivel his chair around to face the sector of blackness where the window should be. Meanwhile she says nothing, tries to remain undetectable, the situation sinking in. She's trapped in an empty, darkened office tower with a sadistic madman intent on controlling her sister's life—her own life, too, maybe. What reasons can he possibly have for doing this to them? There are no reasons for this kind of thing. No reasons with madmen. No *reasoning* with madmen. She takes a step back.

"Not again," Chas mutters. "The whole West Slope at least. Suburbs, too. What's it this time? Terrorists or the usual incompetence?"

Ursula says nothing. He's trying to bait her into talking so he can locate her.

"Can't rule out Armageddon," he adds dryly.

Ursula takes another step back.

"Where you going? You feel like walking down a hundred flights?"

"I'm not going anywhere," she insists, sounding like a guilty child.

"Relax. There *is* somewhere we can go."

She hears him get up, feel his way around the desk. She flinches as he finds her wrist and holds it, not tightly. He locates the door for them, then leads her across the reception room, through the front door, and down the hallway. She hears a heavier door open.

"Steps," he warns. "We're going up."

He puts her hand in contact with a handrail, then lets go and starts to climb. He sounds calm, reasonable. She could never get away anyhow. She follows.

"Rare opportunity," Chas says. "They don't like people up there. Suicides. Lawsuits. Etcetera. But the alarm won't sound with no power."

Suicides, she thinks. But he won't kill me, she tells herself. If he did, he wouldn't be able to terrorize me anymore.

"Look," he says. "Enough with the silent treatment. I asked Couch to assess Ivy's stability, that's all. We needed to know if she was together enough to pull this off for us."

"'We,'" she says. "You and Couch and Javier."

"Right."

"How long has Javier known about this plan?"

"'Known about' it?" Chas says. "It was his idea."

"His idea?" she asks, her throat painfully constricting. She knows her voice will sound like a whimper if she opens her mouth again, but she's beyond humiliation. "This whole fucking thing was his idea?"

"Goddamn creative genius, your boyfriend."

She hears him stumble on a step that isn't there. They've reached the landing. He pushes open a metal door. The bottom scrapes against the gravel of the roof. A blast of warmish, bitter-smelling air forces its way down the stairwell. She follows him out.

A flat, black, perfectly circular area about a hundred yards in diameter. They are close to the edge, the lava-rock wall, crenellated like a medieval parapet. Far off at the center of the circular roof stands a penthouse, a miniature black lava-rock castle with exaggerated turrets and narrow Gothic windows.

They walk along the roof's circumference. The rectangular teeth of the wall are taller than she is, but the spaces between are only waist-high. In the blacked-out city far below a few fires set in trash cans now light up small patches of street. Farther down the mountain a block of row houses is on fire. The valleys twenty miles off have regained power and form a gauzy sickle of light around the base of the slope.

As they make their way from the western side to the southern, the Shackley River comes into view, wending its way down through the foothills, its sluggish current of lava illuminating the dilapidated, postindustrial shores in a dim orange glow. On its western face the Black Tower is a hundred stories tall, but the building is set into the mountain so that as one circles around, it shrinks as the urban terrain rushes up to meet it. Looking down from its northeastern quadrant, just before the volcano's peak, the ground is a mere ten stories below.

A few steps farther and the volcano's mouth appears, and the distance plummets again. Chas leans over the wall, gazing down into the blackness, and Ursula, slightly calmer now in the partial light, can't resist the urge to do the same. Half a mile down, through the dark, choking clouds of sulfur and ash, she can make out two small pools of magma, one elongated and snakelike, the other smaller and round, like burning letters in the abyss:

So

In the ruddy illumination the crater wall is visible, smooth and black. At eye level around the rim jut the jagged peaks of buildings, windowless and filmed with soot. Nuzzled between two of these, the asymptotic crest of the Sidney Gottlieb building and the spiraling peak of the Carlucci, stands the statue of God. She's never seen it this way before—from behind, that is, an angle that makes it seem even more twisted and comical, its gaunt, charred back bristling with knobby vertebrae and stooped from the weight of its lopsided, twin-lobed, elephantitic head.

"Man, this stinks," Chas observes.

He's right. The crater fumes are terrible. She knows some poisonous gases occur naturally, but the fact that the volcano doubles as the city dump probably doesn't help matters. Even at this hour of night the conveyor belt at the northern end chugs away, sending a steady stream of trash plummeting silently over the lip and down into the abyss.

My God, she thinks. We're in hell.

She coughs. The stench of the fumes makes her feel faint. She doesn't think she has the strength to move. But when Chas calls out to her, suddenly somewhere else on the roof, she feels her legs moving her toward him.

"Better over here," he shouts. "Some crosswind."

She finds him taking shelter behind a mushroom-shaped aluminum vent, the only one she can see on the rooftop. It's a breezy night, and the ash smell isn't nearly so strong here. She waits for him to speak, to indicate what happens next, but he doesn't say anything, just waits her out, whether patiently or indifferently she can't be sure.

"I don't understand, Chas," she says, striving for calm. "What's in it for you, using Ivy for this campaign? And what's in it for Cabaj? What if she goes crazy again? He knows the story. Why on earth does he want to risk that?"

"What's the risk?" he says, looking off at the whipping ash. "Crazy is good. Crazier the better."

"I don't get it. *Why* is crazy good, Chas?"

Chas shrugs. "Schizos are in."

His squarish profile reveals nothing. She can't make sense of it.

"Schizos are in?" She laughs nervously. "How do you figure that? Name one schizo who's in."

He considers this. "It's more of a hunch kind of thing," he admits.

"'A hunch kind of thing'?"

He turns to face her. "Ivy's the perfect spokesperson for diet water," he says. "That thing she did with the warpaint, Ursula—people still remember that. They'll look at her and they'll think of all the pressures of the world, and how all those pressures can drive even a pretty young girl nuts. But they'll also see that she's happy now. They'll see that all her dreams have come true. That she's got everything she wanted: she's a glamorous model *and* she's a powerful savage. Picture it. There she is, in her little savage dress under all those cameras and lights. Drinking Cabaj's diet water. Queen of the urban jungle. It's the perfect happy ending."

He is almost whispering now, his voice intimate and sly, close enough for her to feel the warmth of his breath on her cheek. He backs away, just a little, to study her face.

"You see it now," he says. "You see the logic of it."

"No," she insists. "You're wrong, Chas. You haven't seen Ivy lately. She can't do it like you think she can. She's different now. She looks different. Her eyes are weird. Her face twitches. Her teeth are yellow from chain-smoking. Her hands are all gnarled up like bird claws. She's schizophrenic, Chas. People will see how General Foods is exploiting her and it'll make their stomachs turn. They'll be disgusted."

Head still tilted back, he dissects her coolly with his gaze. "You'd kinda like that anyway, I'll bet. You'd kinda like them to see how we marketers exploit all manner of human weakness. You'd like to see this whole thing blow up in my face."

She knows exactly what he's doing. He's provoking her, testing her vulnerabilities, feeling around for just the right sales tactic. But he also happens to be right. Maybe she *would* like to see Ivy disgust the world and Chas fall on his face. She says nothing, but he's reading her thoughts.

"Let it happen, then," he says calmly, folding his arms. "We'll see which of us is right."

Let it happen. Now he's laid his cards on the table. That's what this is all about: they want her consent. Maybe they think she could talk Ivy out of it. She could certainly try. And even if she failed, there are undoubtedly other ways she could make it difficult for them. She could go to the press. She could talk to Cabaj's superiors at General Foods, who probably wouldn't want the controversy.

"To think," she says, staring him down, "Javier almost even had me thinking you loved Ivy."

This pricks him. He rubs the back of his neck, his face heating up.

"Look," he says, a low threat of rage edging into his voice. "I'm giving Ivy what she wants. What she needs. What she's demanding in that loony bin day in and day out, in case you stopped listening. Ivy wants to be a model. What else's she gonna do? Go back and live with your nutso mother and watch soap operas all day? Go see a therapist? A *therapist?*" he repeats, the syllables twisting his lips into a sneer. "Is that what you want for her? You want her to hand her power over to some faith-healing quack who's gonna sit there in his big fat chair patting her on the butt and telling her that all she is inside is a hungry, lonely little baby? Strapping her onto his big fat man-tit and telling her to go goo-goo and ga-ga? You think that's what Ivy needs? You think that's what *anyone* needs? To have some therapist turn them into a whiny, wheedling little infant? Your sister can be *self-reliant*, Ursula. Your sister can be powerful in her own right. Your sister can be a fire-eating, ass-kicking *urban savage.* That's what *I* propose to do for her. That's *my* kind of therapy."

His eyes burn. Behind him the rising steam from the crater looks as though it could be coming from his head. She knows what he's doing, knows he's simply justifying his own selfishness, but once again she can't help wondering whether he may not have a point. She can see how role-playing a savage girl *could* be therapeutic for Ivy, how it could help her feel more powerful, more in control of her destiny. And maybe if her modeling career really was to take off she'd have less motivation to live in her delusions.

Chas watches her think it over.

"You see it," he says. "You see I'm right."

"Don't flatter yourself."

"You see what my kind of therapy can do for Ivy," he says. "Now let's talk about what it can do for you."

"Chas, no offense, but you're not really my ideal therapist."

"Why the hell did you come to me for a job, Ursula? You led me to believe you wanted to make a new start, wanted to get somewhere in life. That *is* why you came to me, isn't it? Or was it just to spy on the evil, twisted man who corrupted the fragile mind of your baby sister?"

She backs away, but he closes in on her again as he talks, shoulders squared, as though he were about to take her and break her like a twig over his knee. She steps back again and feels through the fabric of her skirt the cold metal of the vent behind her.

"A little of both, maybe," she says.

He nods. "Thank you for your honesty," he says, his tone calmer. "Now allow me to be equally straight with you. I need Ivy. As far as I'm concerned, she *is* the future, she's everything I'm predicting: tribalism, virtualism, postirony, the whole new era to come. And if I'm right, everybody wins. I win. Ivy wins. And you win, too, Ursula. You win big. The savage look is your baby, and that baby is a prodigy, it's an itty-bitty, speed-reading, concert piano–playing whiz baby. And when that baby grows up and takes over the world, who's gonna be there right beside it? You are, Ursula. You and your sister both, the two of you, rich, powerful, invincible. Think of it. You and Ivy. Queens of the urban jungle."

He's studying every millimeter of her face, alert to the smallest reactions.

"Queens of the *jungle*," he repeats, emphatically. "Killing and eating and playing. Noble and beautiful and strong. No more fear, no more failure, no more rules. Nothing can touch you. It's all yours. No bullshit. That's it. That's the deal. That's the opportunity I've created, for Ivy and for you. And do you know why I've done this for you? Because I respect you."

Despite her fear she laughs, and then immediately regrets it.

"Dammit, shut up!" he bellows. "Listen to me!"

Her heart stops. She doesn't dare breathe. He shakes his head, cools down again, and starts speaking in a level tone:

"I don't compliment people often. I like them to listen to me when I do. So listen. You're a damn quick study, Ursula. And you're an inspired salesman. That stuff you pulled at the presentation was good. You're gonna go far. I guarantee you I will *personally* see to that. I would've brought you in on the high-level planning earlier, except with your sister's being involved I thought it would be better to give you as much time as possible to get to know us and see what we're doing."

"I'm not a quick study. It's taken me two months to figure out I've been used."

"*I'm not a quick study,*" he imitates her voice, an unflattering whine. "*I've been used.*" He lets out a heavy breath through his nose. "Ursula, listen to me." He cups his hands into a megaphone. "THIS IS YOUR THERAPIST TALKING!" he shouts in her face. Then he brings his face within an inch of hers and goes on talking in a rapid whisper. "You're not a baby inside, do you understand me? You're a fucking queen inside. You're regal, powerful, smart, sexy. You've got exactly what it takes to rule this shitheap of a world. I knew that from the day you walked into my office, Ursula. You positively floored me. So much that I didn't believe it. I just thought my feelings for Ivy were clouding my judgment, but seeing you on the job, seeing you day after day in action, proved it. My instincts about you were absolutely right. You've got more style and talent and brains and guts than most of these marketing morons have in their wildest fantasies. You've got it all, Ursula. I know it. I see it. I'm *trained* to see it. Believe me, I've devoted my life to separating out the human garbage from the real potential out there, the potential for *living*, the potential for exercising real power and creativity and *life force*. You have the power to live life to the hilt. And deep down you know you have it, you know it's in you."

He looks at her keenly, taking her shoulders gently in his hands.

"But you're afraid," he continues. "You're afraid to let it out. You're afraid that by showing your power you'll make other people feel inferior. You're afraid they'll resent you. You're afraid of leaving behind the safety of what you know for the uncertainty of all the things you could have. And that's a tragedy, Ursula, an absolute fucking waste of a gorgeous, powerful, brainy colossus of a woman. I want you to discover that power, to own up to it and make it yours. You're not a baby inside. You're a fire-eating, ass-kicking, powerful-as-all-fuck *QUEEN*. You can do it. You can roar like a goddamned lion."

He continues staring at her, his eyes diamond-sharp, his lips pursed with conviction. She knows what he's doing, but it doesn't matter because he's right; whether he actually believes it or not, he's right about her. This person he's describing is who she really is, who she knows she is inside, who she looks for when she looks in the mirror and can sometimes even glimpse for a fleeting moment before the fear and self-hatred chase the vision away.

His eyes lock on something in hers, gauging some minute change in her expression.

"BE THE LION!" he shouts. "Do you hear me? You can *be* the lion! Now tell me. Tell me which you want to be. You want to be the baby or the motherfucking *Lion Queen?*"

His eyes are inflamed, serene, and cool all at once—red, white, and blue in equal proportions. He is offering her power. Whatever else is false, this much is plain to her. All she has to do is take it. All she has to do is make it her own.

"The lion," she says. For what it's worth, this is true. Sure, she'd rather be the lion. Who wouldn't?

"Say it louder," Chas says, standing almost against her so she has to look up to find his eyes. "No one can hear us. There's no one here but you and me."

"Like you have to remind me," she whispers.

"Stop whining!" he says, putting a hand over her mouth, tilting her head back still farther. "Start being the lion! I want you to say it as loud as you feel like saying it. I want you to say it as loud as you can muster. Tell me you want to be the lion!"

He takes his hand off her mouth.

She stands up straighter, getting right up in his face, widening her eyes. "I want. To be. The lion," she replies in a calm, mockingly studious voice.

He turns his head slightly and looks at her from the corners of his narrowed eyes. She laughs at his consternation, feeling a sudden lightness. To her surprise he smiles as well, that sly half smile, his lips parted just enough to reveal the lower parts of his upper teeth on one side of his mouth. That was all it took, she thinks to herself. All I had to do was show him I was unafraid, show him I was his equal, and he relented. She likes this feeling. Likes his smile, the admiration in his eyes. She suddenly realizes she's flirting with him, and he's reciprocating. For a moment she thinks of Javier, but his betrayal smolders in her even more than before. He barely ever even spoke Ivy's name, but her image was running through his mind all that time. She thinks of his fingers, those sensitive, tender fingers, sketching the contours of Ivy's pointy breasts and taut little belly again and again. At least with Chas, she thinks, looking up into his eyes, I have no illusions. At least I know he's a bastard.

"You don't sound like a lion to me," he observes, leaning closer. "You sound like a little pussy."

She laughs at the innuendo as he walks the fingers of his free hand up her leg.

"Nice try," she says, making of her hand a wall to impede the path of his fingers. He's an interesting bastard, she'll give him that.

"Just try it," he coaxes. "What are you afraid of? Say it like you mean it. Say it like you *are* one."

"Sure, Chas, you'd like that. You say 'Jump,' and I say 'How high?,' is that it?"

He walks his fingers up over the wall of her hand and farther up her leg. She makes another wall, a couple inches higher.

"No, that's not it," he says. "This is about you, not me."

"Let's make it about both of us, then," she says. "You go first. Show me how."

He considers, then shrugs. "All right. Like this." He tilts his head up to the sky, takes a breath.

"I AM A LION!"

He shouts it at the top of his voice, so loud she flinches away, but she can't move far because he's simultaneously brought his hand inside her thigh, beneath her skirt, to hold her in place. She laughs and puts her hand on top of his to keep it from moving upward. Or downward.

"Now you say it," he whispers.

"I am a lion!" she shouts.

"No." He sighs, his forefinger edging upward against her thigh. "I was wrong. You're not a lion after all."

"I *am* a lion."

"Are you?"

She takes his hand and puts it inside her panties.

"I just need a little encouragement," she says in his ear.

He smiles. "Try it now."

"I am a Lion!" She laughs.

"Again."

The wind whips up her skirt, and she feels his stiff middle finger finding the wetness.

"I am a LION!" she shouts, a wild tremor in her voice.

"Better," he says. She leans back against the vent as his thick finger begins stroking, pressing, exploring. Life is too absurd for remorse. It's like getting brained by a falling flowerpot, like getting run over by an ice cream truck.

"*I am . . . ,*" he whispers, hovering above her.

"*I am . . . ,*" she whispers, dizzy and cool in the darkness.

Life is too inconstant to be real, a brief glitch in the logic of nonexistence, the moment before the cartoon coyote sees that he's run off the cliff and is hovering in the dubious air.

"*. . . a lion,*" he whispers in her ear, his free hand tracing the curve of her hip.

". . . *a lion,*" she whispers. Life is a contradiction impossibly sustained by belief, belligerence, desire—that three-ring circus of the human will, clowns and lions and trapeze artists all racing and leaping and flying under the big top.

"*I am a lion,*" he whispers, one hand on her ass, the other sliding down the back of her leg, lifting it.

Life is too absurd and inconstant and contradictory to stop her from having it all, having it any way she wants. She can be the lion, can kill and eat and play and be noble and beautiful and strong, with no more fear, no more failure, no more rules.

"*I am a lion,*" she whispers, and licks his ear with the tip of her tongue as he enters her. He grunts and growls as they fuck, a little boastfully, but a little needfully, too, and she likes the sound of it, and she grunts, too, at first half in mockery but soon uncontrollably as their thrusting grows desperate, grunting and growling like lions while all across the city a hundred burglar alarms simultaneously begin their nebulous, tinny clanging.

The power is returning.

Savages

Guru

The Black Tower's conference hall has never been a cheerful place, but for this occasion Chas has taken the gloom to a whole new level, blotting out the already meager daylight with red velvet curtains and banishing the halogen lamps in favor of crudely hewn stone pots from which rise pale, translucent flames, their dim light flickering over the eighty audience members—the corporate executives, marketing directors, account managers, art directors, and copywriters of the various agencies, companies, and departments with subscriptions to Tomorrow's annual Trendpak. This lecture is a new addition to Tomorrow Ltd.'s package of services, and Chas has hyped it extensively through a mouthpiece in the person of James T. Couch, who's been making the office circuit for the last two weeks to drum up an audience. Couch, Ursula knows, performed this duty only reluctantly, harboring, as he does, serious doubts as to the commercial viability of this year's presentation. "I just don't get it!" he moaned, having decided at some point to make a confidante out of her. "Chas is always telling us, Keep it Light! Keep it Light! This is not Light. This is anything *but* Light."

For her own part, Ursula has reserved judgment, but now, watching the clients opening their Trendpaks for the first time, she admits that Couch may have been right. As they peer into those silver-painted, octagonal cardboard boxes, their faces drop like those of children finding their trick-or-treat bags filled with chocolate-covered bugs. Having taken a look at Trendpaks from previous years, Ursula can understand their dismay. Normally this brightly colored box comes packed with quirky, entertaining new products culled from stores around the world—the latest toys, crockery, books, CDs, fabric blends and prints, fun little items they can take home for their spouses and children to play with. But this year most of the items aren't so playful; some of them aren't even readily identifiable; and the tags that come attached to them on gold threads usually only deepen the mystery. There is, for example, a headless, unclothed Barbie doll, her slit-open torso filled with wires, with a tag that says *The Controlling Machine*. The tag attached to a bent butter knife reads *Surgical Instrument of the Tall Grays*. A gob of soft red plastic is tagged *This Is the Color of Electronic Blood. As Any Child Could Tell You*. There is a microcassette recorder with a tag reading *The Voices in Your Head*, which, when played, sporadically whispers put-downs about the listener's appearance, intelligence, and social aptitude in growling male and piercing female voices.

And in the case of the few readily recognizable products, the ubiquitous tags serve only to *de*familiarize. Thus a Burt Bacharach CD is tagged *This Is Not Camp. Irony Is beside the Point*. A key chain of the Pokémon character Pikachu is labeled *I Am Your Aborted Child. I Cry Out for Vengeance. I Order You to Kill! Kill! Kill!* A photo of Jay Leno, autographed to "Frances," is tagged *Frances, You and I Are the Same Person, and We Both Know It, and Any Apparent Difference between Us Is Illusory, a Mere Divergence of Angles. Not Something to Be Proud of, for Either of Us, But There It Is*.

Several explicitly primitivist products have been thrown in for good measure, including a "sacrificial" animatronic Barney doll, rewired to bellow in pain and then speak in tongues; a wooden box containing sealed canisters of "authentic, 100% organic warpaint"; and a book on Santería with a highlighted instructional chapter on the making of charms and spells.

Two of the items come with lengthy explications. The first is a chrome, egg-shaped beeper whose attached scroll reads:

> *This product will alert you when your attention is required in any one of your various virtual lives—when, for example, one of your cities is being besieged by Mongol hordes; or when your manager secures a multialbum*

deal for your rock band; or when your guardian spirit comes under an enemy black-magic assault; or when one of your virtual children is arrested for drug possession; or when you are needed at an urgent meeting of the Council of Jedi Knights.

The other is a set of holographic stills from the TV series *Gilligan's Island,* one of each cast member, oscillating strangely among three stages of a characteristic facial expression, the trees and thatch huts of their jungle island in the background. At the bottom of each picture is printed the name of a deadly sin: the picture of Gilligan is labeled "Sloth"; the Skipper is "Anger"; Ginger is "Lust"; Mary Ann is "Envy"; the Professor is "Pride"; Mr. Howell is "Greed"; Mrs. Howell is "Gluttony." The pictures are about the size of tarot cards; they come in a shallow cardboard box to which is attached an accompanying document:

*A scuffle due to egotism causes your flare to fire into the sea; the search plane passes ineffectually by. Your raft sinks under the weight of your possessions; the cargo freighter disappears over the horizon. If you cup a conch hard against your ear, you may even hear the laughter—mocking, disinterested, divine. As a **citizen** you are trapped in hell, among other citizens whose tragicomic flaws compound your own, ensuring perpetual failure. The only escape from the situation comedy of a dystopian society is into the audience, the position of absolute exteriority. Only insofar as you choose to be purely a **consumer,** limiting your expressions of freedom to acts of consumption, do you remain free.*

At the bottom of the Trendpak box is the trendbook, a manuscript bound by three gold rings. A facsimile of the trendbook's glossy cover is projected on the screen behind the lava-rock podium. The text reads:

THE LITE AGE

*A Trendbook for Survival
in a Bold New Era*

Tomorrow Ltd.

The title arcs in rainbow-striped letters over a computer-generated image of a shimmering silver castle city perched on a sunlit cloud. The subtitle runs beneath the cloud, where the sky is dark and moody. Beneath the subtitle a flat expanse of shadowy, uniform row houses stretches to the horizon. The company name is placed in a darkened space beneath the row houses—at sewer level, Ursula supposes.

I didn't know it would be spelled that way was all Javier said, in a thin voice, when she walked up to him twenty minutes ago. He was sitting at one of the small metal tables in the Black Tower's atrium, where more or less the same people can be seen every afternoon eating their lunches alone. There was no lunch on Javier's table, just the book, and he sat there slumped and expressionless, gazing at the cover. He looked tired—worse than tired. There were deep black crevices under his eyes. His skin was pale, his hair matted and unwashed. She asked him what he thought of the little book he'd cowritten, and the question came out abrupt, sarcastic, and a bit more vindictive-sounding than she'd intended. She was trying to make him feel the full weight of what he'd lost, to make him see how he'd reaped what he'd sown, how his betrayal of her trust had borne karmic fruit in the form of Chas's betrayal of his own. For as it happens, while the trendbook makes extensive use of Javier's ideas, outlining a world to come in which people will be able to use consumerism to create their own ideal "realities," Chas has turned Javier's vision on its head, describing how this relativistic array of lifestyle choices will consist not of realities but of illusions, beneath which a far grimmer, absolute reality will remain. It is to the aim of helping marketers exploit these flexible "realities" in order to thrive in the fixed and far more unforgiving reality that the preponderance of *The Lite Age* is dedicated.

Jaded and invulnerable though Ursula thought she already was by this point, the book has affected her deeply, carrying her beyond even cynicism, into a strange new state of free-floating alienation and detachment that she feels powerless to understand or even question. She's been walking around in this haze for the last few days, and so when she saw Javier and went over to him and asked him what he thought of the book, it was not only because she was seeking revenge but also because she genuinely did want to talk to him about it. Or rather she wanted *him* to talk to *her* about it. She wanted him to invite her to sit down with him so he could refute Chas's argument for her point by point, rubbing the numbness from her mind with the heat of his convictions. But her question came off sounding too spiteful, or maybe it didn't even matter. Javier didn't refute anything. He didn't look at her. He just made that one comment about the spelling and then reverted to silence, his head turned aside as though he'd been struck, his face drained of color, his normally expressive eyes gone dead, looking much as he'd looked the night of the blackout, three months ago, when she'd come home to find him waiting on her stoop, all prepared with a sales pitch of his own for making Ivy their savage girl, and she'd told him not to bother, told him Chas had already convinced her.

"He did?" Javier had said, his face flooding with relief. "Oh. That's good. That's great." He'd let out a laugh and then asked, "How'd he do it?"

"He fucked me on the roof of our office building," she'd replied.

And his lopsided smile had trembled slightly and fallen.

Since then Ursula has been working on her own. Chas has taken up the slack left by Javier in her training, meeting with her a couple of times a week, each time in a different location, each location evoking new little lessons and insights: how aftershaves must burn almost to the extent of hurting to make up for men's shame over using what is essentially a perfume; how 84 percent of receptionists treat people in beige trenchcoats with more deference than they do people in blue trenchcoats; how department stores are designed to feel like cultural institutions, and purchases to feel like diplomas, the culmination of an education in the new good things in life. Their sexual encounter has gone unmentioned and unrepeated; she is still caustic with him, and he is still surly with her; and the only change in their relationship is a newfound complicity between them, based, probably, on the seemingly mutual satisfaction with which they now fall into these comfortable roles.

As for Javier, Ursula now sees him only when their check-ins at the office happen to coincide. They tend to pass each other in silence. In the periphery of her vision she now sees him seated on the opposite side of the conference hall. She makes sure not to look his way. Doubtless he's doing the same.

The room darkens, and the audience falls silent. A moment later the door at the front of the hall swings open, and the man of the hour strides in, broad-shouldered and sharkskinned. She hasn't seen him since the trendbook was couriered to her apartment a week ago. He sequestered himself for the week to prepare for the lecture and also, apparently, to grow a goatee, perhaps the same one he used to wear as an academician. Unlike the hair on his head, the little beard has yet to go gray: it remains fine and reddish brown, as though he'd kept it in a Baggie in the back of his freezer all these years. The goatee doesn't exactly make him look younger—his skin is too creased, his eyes too recessed—but it does throw off death just a little, in a creepy, vampiric kind of way.

He takes his place behind the podium.

"Ladies and gentlemen," he says. "Comrades. I am speaking to you at the dawn of a new age."

He pauses to regard the group, each person in turn.

"A new Dark Age!" he bellows, bringing his palms down hard against the lectern.

No one breathes. The only sound comes from Chas's fingertips, slowly and evenly drumming the lectern. Through slitted eyes he scans the faces in the audience, slowly, one by one, as though mentally picking his listeners up out of their chairs, turning them around, and vigorously kicking them in the ass.

"All right," he says at last, softly. "So what am I talking about?" He nods to himself and leans back from the podium, pulling the audience members forward in response.

"To answer this question I have to back up a bit. To the height of the Preironic Era of consumerism. The late nineteen-fifties. The days of the gray flannel suit, when your typical American ad agency was as bureaucratized as the Department of Defense. The days of the Cold War, which we Americans fought by consuming products, big-ticket items, cars growing longer and heavier and gaudier by the year, tail fins designed to go out of style, engines built to roll over and die when the odometer rolled over a hundred thousand miles. The salad days of consumer-motivation research, when the great theorist Ernest Dichter, in the introduction to his seminal work *The Strategy of Desire*, could pose the question of whether or not it was ethical to wade into the human mind and implant never-before-existent desires for unneeded products—only to respond wholeheartedly in the affirmative by wrapping himself in the flag.

"In the Soviet Union, Dichter argued, advertising was every bit as prevalent as it was in America. The only difference was that the Soviets' advertising campaigns were run by the government and were called propaganda, whereas ours were called marketing and were run by private business. The purpose of propaganda, he went on to say, was to manipulate people into believing that all was as it should be; that the citizens had everything they could want; that they lived in a great country founded upon a great ideal; that their work was important; that their lives were meaningful. In short, propaganda strove to create contentment. The purpose of American-style marketing, in contrast, was precisely the opposite. It existed to create discontent, to ensure that citizens were never happy with their lot, inciting them to crave more money, more property, newer cars, better clothing, better bodies, younger and more beautiful spouses.

Thanks to marketing, American citizens were perpetually unsatisfied, goaded ever onward, ever forward, generating the American advantage, the drive that ensured progress, technological innovation, and a fully stimulated economy."

He pauses for a moment, scanning their eyes. Seated to her left, Ursula recognizes the spiky-haired woman and the grim Asian man with the underbite from the savage-girl presentation. They gaze up at Chas fearfully. He steps out from behind the podium and begins taking measured paces across the stage as he talks.

"In Dichter's own time this theory was not as readily understood as it is today, because on the face of it American-style advertising and Soviet-style propaganda looked and felt about the same: both were utopian endeavors, depicting idealized citizens reaping the benefits of life in their respective societies. Probably even Dichter himself didn't realize how right he was, for no one could have fully anticipated the revolution in marketing-driven dissatisfaction about to sweep the country.

"To appreciate the full impact this revolution had on the popular psyche, you might try a little thought experiment. Try imagining yourself as a factory worker in the Soviet Union in the year nineteen hundred and sixty-one. Imagine yourself standing there on the assembly line, fitting tab A into slot A. And the whistle blows. And you walk into the cafeteria to get your daily ladle of borscht. And you go and sit down in your favorite corner. And your hands are too tired to pick up the spoon just yet, so instead you look out your favorite grime-covered windowpane, and painted on the wall of the local party headquarters across the road there's a new mural of your leader. But something's different about this mural. He's not looking off heroically into the distance like he's supposed to. No, he's looking right *at* you. And his eyes are kind of baggy, kind of like yours when you look in the mirror. And his shoulders are a little slumped. And his gut hangs out over his belt. And below this oddly frank picture is a declaration in block letters that says, 'Attention, Comrades: Vlad Lenin was a craven megalomaniac. Joe Stalin was a tyrannical butcher. Me, on the other hand, I'm just a run-of-the-mill party hack. But hey, at least I'm not ambitious. Yours truly, Nick Khrushchev.'

"You're sitting in that factory, and you see that piece of propaganda, and it's like no piece of propaganda you've ever seen before. In fact, it seems to mock the foundational principles of propaganda itself. It acknowledges that your way of life is far from ideal. It shows a respect for your intelligence that leaves you breathless. Its incisive humor seems to promise a revaluation of all values, to offer the hope of a whole new era of directness, freedom, and authenticity. And there it is, right on the wall, right up there for everyone to see.

"As it turned out, of course, the Soviet worker never saw that mural. Khrushchev didn't put that poster up, and for good reason. Publicly sanctioned ironic doubt would have run counter to the purpose of propaganda, which, remember, is to create contentment.

"But marketing thrives on discontent, which is why in the U-S-of-A, in the year nineteen sixty-one, Americans opened their copies of *Life* magazine to find an advertisement like none they had seen before, an advertisement for that squat little tail-finless car called the Volkswagen. The photographs purposely tried to show the Volkswagen in the harshest possible light. The copy admitted the car was ugly. Follow-up ads not only mocked the Big Three automakers for their showy tail fins and gimmicky gadgets and planned obsolescence, but also directly mocked the deceitfulness of conventional advertising—the impossibly happy nuclear families, the bogus expert testimony, the photographic trickery, the overblown rhetoric of ad copy. By buying a Volkswagen, these ads suggested, you were buying a critique of the entire automotive industry and, moreover, flouting the elaborate marketing system of manufactured desire."

Chas takes his place again behind the podium, presses a button, and the slide of the trendbook cover is replaced by a mathematical-looking formula:

CRITIQUE OF A, B, C = PURCHASE OF D, E, F

"Traditionally, irony has had two major functions in Western thought. The first is what we call ideological critique, the work of analyzing the internal contradictions of ideologies. The second is what we call dialectical reasoning, the work of synthesizing opposites and building new and improved ideologies. But the Volkswagen campaign showed marketers how to short-circuit these traditional world-disclosing and problem-solving functions of irony. It showed them how to co-opt and subvert any ironic critique of consumerism by harnessing it to the support of a chimerical 'alternative consumerism,' as represented by a set of products proclaiming themselves to be free of—even somehow *outside of*—the lies, cynicism, and trickery of commercial culture. Furthermore, by absorbing the critique of the pitch into the pitch itself, they created an environment in which there seemed to *be* no outside to consumerism, no dialectical antithesis, thereby bringing all attempts at dialectical reasoning to a screeching halt. Whatever effects this ongoing shell game of corporate-sponsored irony may have had on *civic* culture—and these are arguable but are generally acknowledged to include increased cynicism, apathy, depression, amorality, and political malleability—its effects on *consumer* culture are very clear. Consumption has skyrocketed. Remember, consumerism thrives on dissatisfaction, and mass, co-opted ironic doubt is dissatisfaction made into a way of life. Which is why it is perhaps not a great exaggeration to say that it was the successful incorporation of irony that won the Cold War."

Chas pauses for a moment. The young Indian executive next to Ursula reels with concentration, one hand clutching the side of his head and the other gripping his mother-of-pearl pen like a set of brass knuckles. She turns around in her seat. The whole audience seems caught between frozen fascination and wide-eyed horror. She locates James T. Couch, lounging in the back row in a neon-blue muscle shirt. He sees her looking at him and smiles and shakes his head, as though to say, *That Chas. . . .*

"So much for the history lesson," Chas says. "Let's move on to the here and now. I'm here today to break the news to you that this forty-year party is *over.*"

He picks up a copy of the trendbook and holds it up as he speaks, his clip now rapid and urgent.

"As you'll see from the charts and sample responses in appendix A and chapter three of this season's trendbook, our research shows that irony isn't working as well on today's younger consumers. In fact, the younger the consumer, the heavier and more virulent the irony has to be to get through at all. More alarming still, in the studies included in appendix B and cited in chapter four you'll find the evidence we've gathered of what we believe to be an entirely new form of consciousness emerging in society at large: a *postironic* consciousness. And in chapter six you'll find our argument that this postironic consciousness is the beginning of nothing less than the next step forward in the evolution of consumer culture." He slams his palm against the unseen button, and a new slide appears:

CRITIQUE OF A, B, C, D, E, F . . . = PURCHASE OF A, B, C, D, E, F . . .

A generalized murmur rises from the audience. The spiky-haired woman turns to the Asian man and whispers a question. The Asian man responds ambiguously, folding his arms and beetling his brows.

"Impossible, you say?" Chas says, stepping out from behind the podium.

"Take a look at our trendbook. Read our case studies. Not only is post-ironic consumerism possible; it's already here. My tireless agent James T. Couch has spent the last six months traveling to the far corners of the World Wide Web, to the outermost edges of the Virtual Imperium, and there has discovered whole new ecosystems of postironic consumers. People who collect Mickey Mouse paraphernalia because they're obsessed with the death count in Disneyland. People who spend all their free time trading and amassing video collections of the moronic TV sitcoms that oppressed them as children. People who forge virtual communities inside Web-based computer games and don't even play the games but just hang out there for six to ten hours a day. These are astonishing developments, developments that are opening up a whole new cosmos of consumption."

Chas begins to pace again. The audience members follow him with their eyes, as if he were a wild animal they dare not let out of sight.

"Make no mistake," he says. "By 'postironic' I don't mean 'earnest.' Innocence lost cannot be reclaimed so simply. This is more than a simple backlash. Our culture has become so saturated with ironic doubt that it's beginning to doubt its own mode of doubting. If everything is false, then by the same token anything can be taken as true, or at least as true enough. Truths are no longer absolute; they're shifting, temporary, whatever serves the purpose of the moment. Postironists create their own sets of service-able realities and live in them independent of any facets of the outside world that they choose to ignore. Ironic advertising is becoming irrelevant because in the new postironic mind-set irony itself is the base condition; it is beside the point. Practitioners of postironic consciousness blur the boundaries between irony and earnestness in ways we traditional ironists can barely understand, creating a state of consciousness wherein criti-cal and uncritical responses are indistinguishable. Postirony seeks not to demystify but to befuddle, not to synthesize opposites but to suspend them, keeping open all possibilities at once. And we marketers, in forging a viable mode of postironic consumerism, must seek to foster in the con-sumer a mystical relationship with consumption. Through consumption consumers will be gods; outside of consumption they will be nothing: a perpetual oscillation between absolute control and absolute vulnerability, between grandeur and persecution."

He walks back to the podium and leans forward, gripping its edges with either hand.

"What is postirony? Postirony is ironic earnestness. Postirony is omnipotent slavery. Postirony is giddy terror. Ladies and gentlemen, postirony, in its purest paradessence—"

He looks at directly at Ursula.

"—is *schizophrenia*."

Perhaps the flaming pots in the sconces are devouring all the oxygen, because the air in the darkened room is suddenly heavy and unfortifying and difficult to breathe, as though she and the rest of these people sealing her in on every side were all neatly seated in the belly of a whale, traveling at some unfathomable, airless, lung-crushing depth. She begins to panic and fights to regain control, telling herself there is no whale, there's plenty of air, she's not underwater but high up in a building. But it doesn't work. It's not good enough. Her heart begins slamming against her chest. She tells herself that it's not just a high building, it's a penthouse at the pinnacle of the silver castle city on the sunlit cloud. It's a sunny day in the Lite Age, and she's at the very top of the cloud castle, and all the bad things are far below. The cement plain beneath them bristles with embedded shards of bone, half-sets of teeth, calcified fetuses, points of hypodermic needles, razor-blade edges, thumbtacks, electromagnetic coils, half-melted pistols with finger bones still coiled around the triggers, but it doesn't matter because from the bay windows of her penthouse at the castle city's pinnacle, all these hard, sharp, or otherwise cruel pieces of debris are visible only as festive, glittering flecks in a gray, frozen sea. Her penthouse is a vast greenhouse, a tropical paradise of tall trees and thick vines and powerful streams of cool, rushing water, misting the air, swirling and eddying and washing everything clean, an endless supply of water, always new and always the same. She doesn't know which is more calming, the ever-newness or the ever-sameness of that water, or whether it is a combination of both of these attributes, but she holds the rushing water in her mind and begins to breathe easier again.

Through the fronds, the hanging vines, and the perfumed air, she watches calmly now as Chas opens his arms in front of him and goes on speaking in a mellower tone.

"Welcome, my friends, to the new age. Study the trendbook. Study chapter six and learn how tribalism and the concept of invented origins will lead us into a period of unprecedented alienation from mass society and a mystified relationship with technology, culminating in the disintegration of civic institutions and all forms of public life. Study chapter seven and learn how virtualism and the concept of elective affinities will lead to radical individualism, or the creation of multiple consumer identities within a single person. Learn how postirony will schizophrenize the cultural unconscious, leading to an explosion in delusion-maintenance industries, throwing imaginative space open to privatization and ushering in the era in which you marketers will come fully into your own, inheriting the mantle of influence from churches and states, becoming the spiritual guides of the masses, caretakers of a new, ahistorical, mystificatory mindset, cultivators of a worldwide amusement park of fantasies and denial. And we here at Tomorrow will be right by your side, always available for private counseling sessions, always at the ready to help you develop strategies for maximizing the potential of this exciting historical moment. We at Tomorrow will show you how the new Dark Age may very well not be all that dark for your business. On the contrary: *this* Dark Age," he says, "just might . . . be *Lite*."

He smiles his harrowing smile. Somewhere a button is pressed, and the heavy velvet curtains move aside, leaving the marketers squinting in the piercing shafts of light. Ursula takes slow, measured breaths, thinking of her streams, her flowers, her majestic, life-giving trees, their millions of leaves sucking in all the toxins and giving back good, clean oxygen to the world.

Famous

The restaurant in the Pangloss Hotel is a five-star affair with five-star prices, but the theme is greasy-spoon-diner all the way. The booths are upholstered with leather dyed the particular reddish hue of vinyl dyed to resemble dyed leather, and the marble tabletops are rimmed with grooved stainless steel, just like the common faux-marble Formica tabletops they strive to imitate. Of course James T. Couch was the one who introduced Ivy to the place, and for the last couple of months it's been her favorite restaurant, the one she insists on coming to time and again. Today, thank God, Couch has other things to do, so Ivy and Ursula are here alone. No sooner is her sister seated across from her in their regular booth than she torches the tip of a cigarette with a new gold lighter, takes a long drag, flips up the hinged lenses of her sunglasses, then turns over her uncannily plastic-looking frosted-crystal water glass and knocks some ash into it, like a cat marking its territory. By now the busboy knows neither to try filling Ivy's ashing glass with water nor to bring her a fresh glass of water, which would inevitably get ashed in as well, and the waitstaff knows not to tell her that smoking isn't permitted. When other patrons complain, the maître d' passes on to them the same sob story James T. Couch passed off on him along with a hundred-dollar bill—that the smoker in the far corner booth happens to be none other than Ivy Van Urden, the renowned schizophrenic fashion model for whom a constant influx of nicotine is that sole and thinnest of threads from which her sanity dangles. For all Ursula knows, it may be true. The medication Ivy takes has been making her increasingly stiff, and the cigarettes, perhaps due partly to the nicotine stimulant and partly to the constant use of limbs, lips, and lungs required to manipulate them, seem to serve her in much the same way a can of oil did the Tin Man, keeping her just limber enough to clank along.

The ceremonial ashing-in-the-cup accomplished, Ivy moves on to her ritual appreciation of the view: the booths are lined with interior windows that look out into the hotel lobby, and for a good five minutes Ivy follows the lobby's various motions as closely as a die-hard football fan watching his home team deploy its offense. She tracks the elevators, rising like air bubbles in glass tubes; scrutinizes the glass-domed fountain, blasting glimmering jets of mercury; then loses herself in the lobby's conveyor-belt product display. Encased in thick, yellowed glass, the conveyor belt rises out of the lobby floor by the far wall, circles around and passes right below their window, then proceeds spiraling along the vast rotunda wall up fifty stories to the glass of the artificial skylights, through which shines the light of three artificial, pastel-colored suns: a red giant, a blue dwarf, and, as the designers chose to call it, a green goblin.

After tracing the path of the conveyor belt as best she can all the way up, Ivy turns her attention to the items themselves, trundling by on the belt just below the window: an endless parade of scarves, hats, blouses, dresses, lingerie, bow ties, wallets, watches, and jewelry, each product riding on its own velvet pillow. She sits very erect, as any good fashion model should, a sign of progress on which the outpatient care staff takes care to compliment her at each bimonthly checkup. Ursula was never even aware that Ivy was taller than her until she became a model, straightening the familial slouch, levitating her head, stretching her neck like a ballerina. She's wearing a low-cut maroon minidress that is really too dressy for daytime but looks good on her nonetheless, nicely contrasting with her skin, which is pale, luminous, and once more devoid of acne, thanks to her renewed regimen of glycolic acid and Retin-A. Today is Ivy's twenty-first birthday, a fact Ursula had forgotten—repressed, possibly—until Ivy mentioned it a moment ago. In a few months Ursula herself will be thirty. The signs of age she sees in the mirror every day are made slightly more galling by the progress of Ivy's body over time, for—though Ursula may only be imagining this—it seems like Ivy just keeps looking younger. The bloating effects of the medication seem thus far to be confined to her face, which in expanding has filled in the worry lines around her eyes and mouth, giving her the soft-focused expression of a much younger girl.

The ads that created her new fame first appeared two months ago, plastered across the sides of Mid City buses. They showed her sprawled out in a tenement entranceway, dressed in a one-shouldered hide minidress, with a back so low and a hemline so high that her bare back touched the moldering door frame and the backs of her bare thighs pressed against the cement stair on which she sat. Her jaggedly chopped hair was pressed down against her temples and forehead by a tight leather band, and her face was made up with slashes of bright-gold warpaint along her cheekbones, mauve eye shadow that gave her eyes a puffy, beaten look, and gold lipstick, sluttishly smudged. The scars on her arms and legs were left visible and unretouched. A wooden spear leaned against the door frame behind her. Beside her dirt-streaked, canted thighs stood the plastic liter bottle, erect and beaded with condensation. The copy bracketed her from above and below:

traveling lite

litewater

From the streets and sidewalks passengers and pedestrians gazed at the savage girl hunched between the wheels and the windows of the bus, her lovely, dirty, naked limbs in a heap, her heart-shaped, gold-painted face tilted to the side: a broken toy. They recognized her—the obscure model who'd gone nuts in that gruesome, titillating, highly entertaining manner a few months back. Those who wouldn't have remembered on their own were helped out by the media which reminded them with a spate of infotainment stories on this daring use of a schizophrenic, the ethical dilemmas it raised, the lingering questions about her present condition. The campaign was a triumph in splitting the difference between irony and earnestness. Some chuckled at the implicit joke—the model who traveled light by jettisoning her mental faculties—while others were simply drawn into the bohemian romance of the image, lulled by the suggestion that the lonely, troubled Ivy Van Urden had at long last found her tribe.

The photo shoot had been a trial. At first it had promised to be a disaster. Ivy had emerged from the trailer confident enough, but then her eyes had locked on Chas, standing off to the side with Cabaj and the other Litewater people. They hadn't seen each other since the day after she was admitted to the hospital, and Chas froze at the sight of her. Odd things began to happen to his face. His normally cool eyes took on a look of fright, and his effort to smile came off as a grimace, a pulsing bulge of tension warping his jawline from one side to the other.

Ursula had been anticipating and even dreading this moment of truth for the previous couple of weeks, so she was now gratified to discover that this demonstration of Chas's love for Ivy caused her nothing more than a slight and relatively toothless bite of jealously. In fact, more than anything, the sight of his reaction soothed her, as she took it as proof of several things at once: he wasn't heartless; she hadn't been completely crazy to team up with him; he really was doing what he thought was best for Ivy; and she herself, in going along with it, was genuinely attempting to help her sister as well.

But as she realized when she finally turned her attention to where everyone else's was, at the moment Ivy didn't look all that helped. At the sight of Chas's face in all its contortions, her posture had degenerated and her features had grown primal, shoulders hunching, head jutting, bottom teeth showing, eyes panicked and wild. The onlookers started to panic as well: they had gotten more of a savage than they had bargained for. The photographer shot a worried look at Camille Stypnick, the Mitchell and Chennault art director, who looked at Ed Cabaj, who in turn tugged nervously at his jowels and looked to Chas for reassurance. Then everyone else began looking to Chas, the orchestrator of the fiasco. Sonja, who now accompanied Ivy almost everywhere, stared at him with a cold, steady enmity. Chas, for his part, continued to watch Ivy.

Ivy began to murmur, a rapid, inhuman monotone, her eyes wide with astonishment, as if she, too, were only a listener:

the the the Bodies, the Bodies, have the girl now the Antibodies they're losing marketshare the Bodies, cannot repeat cannot denominate the girlmarket alert the Monopopolice repeat the system turmoiled the the plot to be foiled the little bitch the little bitch to be loyaled to the equilibriumaintenance

Of course, it had occurred to Ursula that something of this nature might happen, and even that—as Chas had suggested on the rooftop—she might not be unhappy if it did, might not be all that terribly upset to see Chas's scheme blow up in his face and Ivy's career go down in flames in the same fateful moment of truth. But as she watched her sister ramble on, her body frozen in a kind of formalized cringe, her mind once again uncoupled, all Ursula felt was a horrible, bottomless guilt. She had lied to herself about her own motives from the very beginning, she thought. She had come to Mid City not to take care of Ivy but to claim a piece of her, had gotten a job with Chas not to get acquainted with Ivy's life but to ascertain whether a man who found her sister attractive might find her attractive as well.

She wanted to run up and grab Ivy and apologize and plead with her to come back, to give the world another chance, to give *her* another chance. But she no longer trusted herself, suddenly afraid that her own presence could do nothing but harm. Probably all the other onlookers felt the same way; no one dared approach Ivy.

Then Chas turned to James T. Couch.

"Christ. Do something already," he muttered.

Couch smiled. "Not to worry, Boss. I got your back."

Casually, he walked toward Ivy, hands in pockets, whistling some moronic little jingle, drawing out the moment to show them all precisely how dependent on his intervention they were. He stopped directly in front of her, tilted his head a little and studied her bemusedly, then reached out his hand and placed his forefinger over her lips, which soon stopped moving. Smiling placidly, he stroked her hair, then leaned in closer and spoke quietly into her ear. The two of them stood like that for a couple of endless minutes, Couch talking, Ivy frozen in place, still staring at Chas. Couch then turned toward Chas as well.

"Um, Bossman," he said. "Hate to say this, but maybe you'd better, um, *scram?*"

He flashed Chas a toothy smile. Chas glowered back at him and then, infuriated, embarrassed, and possibly heartbroken, turned and stalked off.

Once Chas had left, Couch went back to whispering in Ivy's ear. Gradually, as he talked, her arms and shoulders started relaxing, her posture started straightening. Her eyes closed for a moment and then reopened, still glassy but no longer wild. He placed an arm around her and asked her a question, and she responded docilely with a couple of words Ursula couldn't make out. The two of them began to walk. Cabaj and the makeup artist stepped aside to let them through, and Ivy took her place in the tenement entranceway. Couch motioned for the photographer, and Ivy allowed the man to guide her into position.

The shoot commenced. Ivy's face was as pure and blank as a projection screen. And Ursula knew in that moment that the pictures would be good, and that Chas, despite his present humiliation, would be vindicated, and that Ivy's savage girl would seduce the world. And more than anything else, she felt relief.

The Litewater campaign coincided happily with the introduction of Avon's Tribal Paint makeup, which, according to the trade journals, has been selling out everywhere except the Third World, where it obstinately underperforms. Litewater's own performance began respectably and grows stronger by the day, despite sporadic reports of dehydration and anal leakage. There was a segment the other week on the *Jenny Jones Show* entitled "Hides for Hos," in which prostitutes were given "savage make-overs." The prostitutes entered stage left, one wearing a faux panda-skin top and miniskirt, another a short, low-cut faux lion-skin dress with a lion's tail attached to the back, and a third a sealskin halter top and a walrus-head hat replete with tusks and white marbles with black cartoon-ish *X*s for eyes. They all seemed to take being on TV in stride, strutting in their choreographed paths across the stage with neither hesitation nor enthusiasm.

Cut to the audience members, standing and hooting, standing and jeer-ing, applauding the fact that they're going to be on television applaud-ing.

Cut to the blond, Harvard-educated host, hand over smiling mouth as though someone had made a dirty joke.

And that's the savage trend so far, a small but far-from-insignificant fashion tremor registering a 3.5 on *Trend Journal*'s "Dichter Scale" and, strangely enough, seeming to embrace few to none of the values Ursula originally associated with an interest in primitive peoples—values such as simplicity, autonomy, inner growth, spirituality, self-empowerment, and the idea that in the primitive experience there may be something we have lost, an ability to synthesize materiality and spirituality into a way of life that is dignified, satisfying, and beautiful. Instead, interest has surged in bizarre rituals and acts of bondage and scarification. Theme restaurants with vaguely cannibalistic themes, already popular here in the Mid, have begun opening franchises in other cities across the country. And the "primitive" aspects of savage wear have done nothing to unsnarl the social complexity of dress codes. Hide skirts have appeared in both upscale bou-tiques and ten-dollar-knockoff stores, but it's relatively easy to tell real ani-mal skins and feathers from the synthetic variety, and real ones are of course more expensive, so, paradoxically, the most credible savages are the wealthiest and most refined. To complicate the issue further, there appears to be a burgeoning taste for real skins made to look synthetic, a new, mutant combination of logic and senselessness so virulent as momentarily to have reduced the animal-rights opposition to a twitching, fetal withdrawal.

At first Ursula felt cheated, as though she'd donated a kidney for a sick child and then spotted it a few days later in a pet-supply store being sold as an aquarium ornament. But in the ensuing weeks she's come to be more philosophical about the trend. It's true that as an artist she had a great deal more control over the substance of her creations. But as a marketer she commands a far greater audience. She pictures herself now as a kind of Godzilla in a beret, carving out Rushmores with the point of the Eiffel Tower, chiseling the man from the Moon for an encore. She has the powers of broadcasting, mass production, and corporate capital at her disposal. Already millions of people have taken her creation, Ivy the Savage Girl, into their lives, and surely, she figures, it can't help but mean to them at least a little bit of what she meant it to mean. And even if it really does mean something entirely different to them all, what artist out there, no matter how serious or conscientious or committed, can dictate the personal uses to which his or her work will be put? No, it should be enough for Ursula that the savage girl is an image people value, one for which they have use, whatever that use may be.

The waitress appears. She has long black hair pulled back so tight it might be smoothing out the wrinkles of her forehead. Her white apron and powder-pink work dress are a little too crisply pressed for diner verisimilitude, but she smacks her regulation bubble gum like a pro.

"Bring me one of everything," Ivy says to the waitress, reminding Ursula of the way Javier ordered "everything popular" that one time. But Ivy, in contrast, is not taken seriously.

"One of everything?" the waitress says, folding her arms. "Why not two?"

Ivy covers a grin with her knuckles, clearly tickled by the absurdity of the idea of having two of everything.

"She'll have every scrap of food you've got in the place," Ursula says. "Just cart it all over here."

"Ten of everything!" Ivy shouts. "And a million of nothing."

The waitress puts her hand on her hip. "Do you want the nothing served with the everything, or after?"

"Or nothing first," Ursula says, "then everything?"

"Lunch is nothing," Ivy declares. "Dessert is everything."

A tourist family at the next table laughs, listening in. Others at nearby tables watch as well, their faces lit up with the sense of privilege they feel in being privy to the scene, ready to participate on cue with their own laughter.

The waitress, probably an aspiring model or actress herself, takes out her little white pad. "The usual, then?"

Ivy nods, smiling like a guilty child. All in all, her new degree of fame agrees with her. Whenever people give her star treatment, she shoots Ursula a secret, mischievous, happy look. Finally, the look seems to say, reality is beginning to live up to her grandiose delusions.

"And you, ma'am?"

"The portobello burger deluxe," Ursula says. "And a latte."

The waitress leaves, and Ivy puffs on her cigarette. "*That,*" she proclaims, watching an olive-colored pillbox hat chug by on the conveyor belt. She thinks something about the hat to herself and speaks no more about it. After a moment, her cell phone erupts in an insectile rendition of the soundtrack to *The Good, the Bad, and the Ugly.* She grabs it out of her purse.

"Hello? Sonja Sonja Sonja. Can't talk now, kid. Be home later."

She sticks the phone back in her purse. "She's a good egg," she muses. "I'm teaching her how to be a celebrity." She taps a cylinder of ash contentedly into her glass. As the poster child for the savage look, Ivy herself has attained that odd, intermediate echelon of celebrity in which she has begun to be trailed by the lowest order of would-be paparazzi and called at all hours of the night by tabloid journalists from obscure countries. Her modeling agency, of which Ursula saw no evidence during Ivy's stay in the hospital except for a single get-well card, is now a constant, hovering, mothering, hectoring presence. Her agents have just landed her a contract with Maybelline, which is rushing to come out with a line of warpaint of its own, and they're fielding offers from several clothing retailers. Ivy has formally given Ursula the right of attorney over her career, and the sums of money she can command for these jobs are so staggeringly beyond anything Ursula anticipated that she's finding it difficult to perform her primary, self-appointed duty: to turn down offers and thus keep Ivy's schedule light and her stress level to a bare minimum. This effort is made still harder by James T. Couch, whose own self-appointed duty seems to be to laze around Ivy's loft and feed her ego, which already knows no bounds. She's anything but satisfied with the degree of success she's achieved. Her hunger for one of everything is by no means limited to food. She pillages the world with her wide, alien eyes, scavenging each object—animal, vegetable, and mineral alike—not so much for the thing itself as for the attention it signifies. The ownership of any given thing means that that thing is paying attention to her, just as the service of a person means that that person is paying attention to her. It's not really greed, Ursula has decided. It's of another order. Ivy requires celebrity as others require air; it functions for her as a protective layer, allows her a kind of second childhood, makes strangers indulgent, happy to cater to her whims, and eager to please her. For this reason Ursula has become reconciled to Ivy's notoriety and even grateful for it, and to some degree she's managed to make peace with herself as well, since the evidence would seem to indicate that she really has been helping her sister after all.

Of course, there's ample indication that Ursula has been helping herself, too. The *Trend Journal*'s account of the savage craze went on to credit Ursula personally, dubbing her "the savvy behind the savage girl, her sister, the troubled and beautiful Ivy." It's only a trade journal, but in the small world of marketing it seems to have a great deal of currency. People introduce themselves to her at parties now. New clients ask to meet her. She is the brains behind Ivy's glamour, and as such she seems to have become just a little bit glamorous herself.

Ivy plays with the shiny gold lighter, unleashing frighteningly, ridiculously large torches of blue flame.

"God," Ursula says. "Where'd you get that thing?"

"Chas Chas," she says lackadaisically, perhaps unaware that this is the first time she's mentioned his name in Ursula's presence. Since the night she fooled around with him, Ursula hasn't brought him up, either.

"Chas?" Ursula says, trying to sound calm. "Have you seen him?"

"No. I won't let him see me. He couriered it. He couriers stuff all the time."

"'Stuff'? Stuff like lighters?"

"Sometimes just notes."

Ursula nods, not sure whether to believe this.

Ivy flicks the torch on again and watches it contemplatively.

"I never understood what you two could've possibly had in common anyway," Ursula says.

The flame goes out. Ivy stares at her.

"You're wondering how he could love me," she says.

Ursula opens her mouth, a false denial frozen in her throat.

"Sure," Ivy goes on, "you've always wondered that. To you I'm the dumb blond sister with the cracked head."

"I don't think you're dumb," Ursula insists. "I never thought that. That's Gwennan talking, not me."

"'Gwennan talking,'" Ivy reflects. "'Pull yourself up by your boot-straps!' *That's* Gwennan talking. The bitch. I hear Gwennan talking all the time. Don't talk to me about Gwennan talking."

She picks up her water glass, blows some smoke into it, and turns it upside down, trapping the smoke inside.

"Chas was the same way at first," she adds.

She crushes her gold filter against the tabletop and tosses it into Ursula's glass, where it floats just below the rim.

"He thought I was a box with a big red ribbon," she says. "He thought I was Ivybox. Put things in me and take them out: hair conditioner, hand lotion, cigarettes, bras. Open me up and stuff me with whiskey bottles, toothpaste, TV dinners—that's what *you* think I am," she says, pointing the pack of cigarettes at an imaginary Chas, then turning back to Ursula. "I told him that and his big old jaw dropped open. He admitted it. He said yeah, that was what he was thinking, but not anymore. That was the night we met, at some party. I told him, I know your type, and he said, *I wasn't aware I had a*—and I flipped him off. You pompous ass. Yeah. Like I've got time for you."

Ivy acts out the little scene for Ursula, giving the finger to a nearby sightseeing senior-citizen couple in place of Chas. Ursula leans forward, seeing her sister anew through Chas's eyes: a brazen, whip-smart, beautiful girl, fresh to the city. She has never imagined Ivy could act like that, could be so assertive.

"What happened then?" she asks.

Ivy smiles to herself, arranging her hands on the table. "He showed up the next day, when I was working," she says. "He had a big white box. It had a bright-red ribbon. After the shoot I took it from him and got in a cab and took off. I opened it in the cab. There was nothing in it but a lit-tle note at the bottom. It said, *I'll kill if necessary, to see you again.* With a little smiley face. And a phone number under the smiley face."

Ivy stares off happily into her memories. Ursula waits, so eager to learn more of the secret of Ivy's power over men that she finds herself actually holding her breath.

"We had the future," Ivy says. "That's what we had in common."

"What do you mean?"

Ivy lights another cigarette. "We both knew it. We both knew the future." She crosses her arms over her chest, as though the room had grown suddenly colder. "At first just Chas knew it, and he told me about it. The telling went on and on, day after day, week after week. He told me all about the Dark Age that was coming, and the more he told me, the more I realized I already knew it. It was exactly like the place I'd been seeing in my head for years. And then I realized that the place in my head was a memory, and that I'd been there. I'd been to the future. I didn't remember how or why I'd been there yet, but I knew I'd been there. And then I started telling Chas about the future, and the more I told him, the more I knew I was right."

She catches herself.

"Don't worry." She puts her hand over Ursula's. "I'm not crazy again. I'm *so* beyond that now. I can be crazy or uncrazy. I can sit here and be from the past and the future or be your sister and the bitch Gwennan's daughter, and that's fine, too. It's all the same. Every story is a cover story. That's one thing you learn."

Every once in a while Ivy will say something like this, reminding Ursula that her delusions are not gone but rather just partitioned somehow, kept off to the side. But she's so functional now—more than functional, she's positively thriving—that Ursula has been having a hard time regarding this as a serious health concern. After all, she's begun to think, if Ivy can create a personal mythology for herself that gives her power, why should anyone try to stop her? Shouldn't we all have the right to tell ourselves the story of who we are in our own way?

"So what did you tell Chas about the future?" she asks.

Ivy purses her lips and blows out a long, slow stream of smoke as the waitress sets down their food. "Like, let's see. Like the sloganitions. I told him in the future every word has a sloganition. He loved that so much. He couldn't stop testing me."

"Testing you?"

"Like one morning I woke up and he was lying there looking at me, and he said, '*Awake.*' And I thought about *awake*. I was pretty sure I had computer chips in my head that did the thinking for me. The chip in my right brain thought *awake*, and it thought, Sunshine, breakfast with Daddy at the kitchen table, softball games, picnics, your first kiss, your senior prom—you know, like all the things that are supposed to happen when you're awake? Then the chip in my left brain crunched all the data into the sloganition, and I told him, '*Awake:* Love is calling you.'"

"And his mouth fell open. Then he said, '*Asleep.*' And I closed my eyes, and I thought *Asleep asleep asleep*, go negative, all the crappy things about *awake*—alarm clocks, jackhammers, traffic jams, fat boss yelling at you, bills in the mail, politicians on TV. And I said, 'Experience Freedom. Experience *Asleep.*'

"His mouth fell open even wider. And I thought, Wow, I'm right: I really *do* have computer chips. I really *have* been to the future. I got out of bed, and they kept coming to me. I stood up and I said, '*Standing:* The world at your feet.' I knocked on the wall and I said, '*Walls:* Giving you some space.' I took off my T-shirt and saw him staring at me, and I said, '*Erections:* Feel your power.' And he felt his power. And I felt my power. You get the picture."

She falls silent, shaking her head sadly.

"He told me I was brilliant," she adds softly, biting her lip at the memory. "I said, What if I'm just crazy? But he said no, he said I saw things almost no one else saw. He said I was the most lucid, clearheaded person he'd ever met. His eyes were on fire when he said it. He meant it. No one ever believed that about me before."

She stares down plaintively at the split-open bagel on her plate. The two fat rings stare back up at her like eyes.

She loves him, Ursula suddenly sees, the recollection of her own night with Chas forming a jagged crystal of shame in her chest.

"After that I started to get confused," Ivy says. "I kept seeing weird things and hearing weird voices, so many things and voices I couldn't keep track of them all. Sometimes I saw millions of tiny streets squiggling around like worms, like I was flying above them, and I heard deep voices whispering. Other times I saw millions of tiny trees, swaying like underwater grass, and I heard high voices kind of singing. The deep voices and the high voices were both trying to tell me who I was, but I couldn't make out the words. And then one day I finally figured it all out, and I felt so relieved because it actually made sense then, kind of."

As she talks, she spreads a thin, very even layer of soy cream cheese across a bagel slice, as carefully as a workman plastering a ceiling, trying to get the surface absolutely smooth. Once this is accomplished, she wets the corner of her napkin with her tongue and uses it to wipe away the excess from the perimeter and the hole. She sets down the napkin and examines her work.

"That night I decided to tell Chas," she goes on. "We were in a bar. We were usually in a bar. I said, Chas, I'm not really sure, and I don't think I'm crazy or anything, but I think there's a reasonable chance that I'm a cave-woman who was taken to the future and brainwashed, and that I've been sent back in time to sell things. I think it's possible that people in this time watch me and buy things, and people in the future watch my life here and buy things also.

"He asked me what the hell I was on. I said I didn't know what hell I was on. He asked me where the cavewoman thing came from. And I said, I dream of trees. And he said, Maybe you're a tree, then. And I said, I think I'd rather be a tree. And he said, What would you do if you were a tree? And I said, I'd grow rings. And he said I was outa my tree. He got up to go to the bathroom, and a man came up to me, a skinny man with pock-marked skin in a beautiful gray silk suit. He told me that he'd made a very profitable transaction earlier that day and he was out celebrating, and the thing he wanted most in the world at that moment was to suck my toes, and he'd give me a hundred dollars if I let him. He had a Russian accent. I was pretty sure he was an agent from the resistance and that this was his way of contacting me. I said OK. I reached up under my skirt and took my stockings off. And the man's friends cheered from their table, and he pulled up a chair and looked at me sitting on the barstool and he took my foot and dunked my toes in a rocks glass filled with champagne. It made my toes cold, and then he put them in his warm mouth and I felt his soft tongue going all around them, and my toes felt like pearls the way they feel in an oyster, and I felt his eyes looking up at my pussy as he sucked my toes, one after the other. And then I looked up just as Chas walked into the room and saw me. He looked confused and then angry, and then he walked out of the bar. When the man was done sucking my toes, he stood up and tossed a hundred-dollar bill into my lap and walked back to his table, and he and his friends started talking and laughing again, and I wasn't sure if I'd fulfilled my mission, but then I looked at the hundred-dollar bill and it told me a little story. The story was about a jungle that the Imagineers turned into a park. They took out the trees and put in upside-down trees that grew out of the sky, and the tallest ones brushed the ground. They took out the parrots and put in pigeons. They took out the three-toed sloths and put in squirrels. The sloths kept getting their toes sucked. The sloths were lazy. But their toes sure felt good. The squir-rels weren't lazy. The squirrels climbed to the top even when the trees were upside down. The squirrels fucked as well as sucked."

She stares at Ursula as she speaks, confusion in her eyes and, somewhere beneath that, pain. Ursula reaches across the table and takes her hand, but Ivy doesn't seem to notice. She continues staring at Ursula's face as though it were a movie screen showing her the story as she goes on telling it.

"I walked out of the bar, and Chas was there waiting for me. He brought me to his place, and when we got there he told me I was doing drugs and they were fucking with my head and he was going to keep me locked up in his apartment till I was straight. But I wasn't doing drugs. I begged him to let me go. I told him that the resistance had given me a secret mission, that people needed to see me, that my image was the drain magnet in the glamour continuum, that my image could save the world. And he told me I was crazy in more ways than one, that my image would only make people feel unhappy and lousy about themselves. I didn't know what to do then. I told him maybe I'd cut my face off. I asked him if that would make people happy. And he shrugged. And he said maybe. And I went into the bathroom and I found his straight razor and I came out with it. And I said, I'll cut my face now. And he laughed. Because he didn't believe me. And he was right. I couldn't make myself cut my face. I heard your voice, Ursula, telling me my face was too beautiful to cut. And I couldn't cut it. And he laughed again.

"I went into the bathroom and found a bottle of Mercurochrome, and I used it to mark my thighs, vagina, tummy, arms, breasts, face. I looked at myself in the mirror, and then I took the razor and I sliced along the red lines. I did it quickly, before I could change my mind. I thought about how I could still have plastic surgery and be beautiful again. And then I thought that if I was ugly, I would turn into something new, something dark and slippery like a stealth bomber or a manta ray, and I'd go wherever I wanted and nobody would know, and I'd be happy like I could never be happy before. I went ahead and cut everywhere but my face. I didn't cut that because I didn't want you to be disappointed in me. At first I felt fine. And then I felt the pain and I was scared. It was too much pain, it was like someone was pressing me against a stove burner, it was so much pain I felt my soul fly away from me, back to the long-ago time I came from. I ran after it. I ran through the apartment. Chas was in the bedroom, staring out the window. I ran out the door and down the block and into the park, chasing after my soul."

Ivy's strange stare is too much for Ursula, and she has to look away. Turning toward the window, she finds her sister's image reflected on the pane as well, not just one but two, ghostly and superimposed on the doubled glass. Ursula closes her eyes, and the two Ivys follow her into the darkness, one of them joyful and seductive and strong, the other one sick and helpless and lost. The two visions are so contradictory that she can't begin to reconcile them and is forced instead to let them hang suspended, the two Ivys, side by side in her mind.

"Chas came to see me in the hospital," she says. "He said he'd do anything for me. I knew he'd been surgically implanted with surveillance technology; I could see the time-warp auras buzzing all around him. I screamed until he left. It brought back too much pain to see him. But it was nice that he said he'd do anything for me. I thought about that later, and it made me feel better."

When Ursula works up the courage to look at her again, she finds that Ivy is no longer staring at her. The wide-open look in her eyes is gone, and her attention has returned to the various items on the table. She picks up the bagel but sets it down again in favor of another cigarette, torching the air with the jet of flame, then regarding the lighter with idle curiosity, turning it in her fingers as the smoke leaks from her mouth.

"So what does he say in the notes he sends you?" Ursula asks.

Ivy shrugs, reaches into her rhinestone purse, pulls out a small, square piece of paper, and lays it on the table. The note is laser-printed and centered on the page:

TELL ME WHAT YOU WANT.

NAME IT.

I'LL KILL IF NECESSARY.

"Tell him to make me famous," Ivy says. "That's what I want."

"He did that, Ivy. You're famous."

"No, no. I mean *famous* famous. Famous famous famous. So people have to watch me. You ask me why people have to watch me, and I tell you I don't know. But once they're watching me—I mean really, really watching me—I'll know, Ursula. I'll *know* what it's for. Tell him to make me famous, Ursula."

"Why don't *you* tell him?" Ursula says.

"Why don't *you* tell him?" Ivy replies evenly.

Ursula freezes. If Ivy's implying anything, it's impossible to tell. She picks up Chas's note and folds it lengthwise. She stares at it intently, then carefully tucks in the corners and folds it again and again along a number of invisible axes. She works through the series of folds by rote, the cigarette held between her lips, her mind wandering off into geometry. Ursula has almost forgotten this talent of her sister's. Within a few minutes the object takes shape: a Viking ship, replete with a couple of oars on each side and a dragon-headed prow. Ivy sets the vessel down on the tabletop in front of her and stares at it wonderingly.

"Happy birthday, me," she says.

Invisigoths

The circular stairwell in the statue's copper hull is as hot as a skillet and so tightly coiled that every step requires a pivot. Ursula dislikes the climb, but so do the tourists, which is why the statue of Felix Rodriguez failed as a tourist attraction, which is why the teenagers started to come, which is why Chas, as he told her over the phone, considers it a place worth visiting. She emerges on the observation deck damp with sweat. No Chas, no teenagers, no one at all. She walks to the balustrade and peers down through the bronze licks of thinning, matted hair, tousled to the left by an imagined breeze, while her own hair blows to the right. The jacket of the statue's cheapish-looking bronze suit is blown open by the same false, easterly wind, revealing a bronze shoulder-holstered sidearm the size of a late-seventies Buick.

"I saw a cabbie arranging marigolds in a plastic cup in his drink tray."

The voice belongs to Chas. Suddenly he is right beside her, staring down at the city circuitry stretching down the mountain.

"I saw a shop owner reading a pocket edition of *Purgatorio,*" she replies.

Chas fingers the promontory of his chin. "I saw a woman with her hair in a bun and a Pekinese on a leash stop to sign a 'Legalize Marijuana' petition."

"I saw a woman in a cashmere turtleneck apologize for the sins of humanity to a bank machine."

Chas is impressed. "Not bad. Like a confessional." He nods, clucks his tongue three times. "Pathetic." He turns and looks at her, through her, behind her.

"Invisigoths," he says.

She turns and looks. A group of kids are squatting on their haunches at the other end of the observation deck. She didn't hear them arrive, either, but this isn't surprising because they aren't talking. They sit quietly, looking everywhere but at the view, dressed uniformly in battleship gray—gray trenchcoats, gray boots, gray-dyed hair. One of them, a girl with a pale face and gray lipstick, stares back at them with white, eyeless eyes.

"White contact lenses," he says. "Spooky."

She nods.

"Run three hundred a pair. The dumbasses."

She says nothing. They return their attention to the view, watching silently as a soccer ball soars over the edge of a nearby cliff and plummets down to land on the yellowish grass of Richard W. Held Park, where insectile workers in blue coveralls are cutting down the last of the thin trees.

"Ursula," he says. "I want you and Javier working together again."

"You do."

"Yeah. I do. You're a good influence on him. A stabilizing influence."

"All finished with me, eh?" she says breezily. "Now you're handing me back to Javier."

He regards her with amusement. "'Finished with' you? I haven't even *begun* with you."

"Have you talked to *him* about this?"

"I'm too busy." He rubs the back of his thick neck. "Besides," he mutters, "he's still not talking to me. And now he's stopped coming into the office outright. No reports, no nothing."

She laughs. "My God, Chas, you're supposed to be the boss. If he doesn't talk to you, why don't you just fire him?"

"Javier may be a prima donna, but he's also a goddamn walking zeitgeist barometer. I need him. And he's onto something new. I want you working with him, keeping track of what he sees, what he says."

"What's he onto?" she asks.

"Something about tweens, he said. Something major. Couch bumped into him in an arcade in the South Slope Mall. He said that and wandered off."

"'Tweens'?"

"Preadolescents. Between childhood and teens. Eight-to-twelve-year-olds. Everybody's going apeshit over tweens nowadays. Including the Gap Corporation. They want a fully illustrated report on postirony in tweens for their Old Navy brands. There's a substantial bonus in it for us if we get it to them by the end of the month. So if Javier's really onto something, I'd like to know about it."

"He's not talking to me, either, Chas. And I'm not talking to him. What makes you think I've got a better shot with him than you?"

Chas considers this. "Bigger tits," he hazards.

She aims a look in the direction of the overdeveloped pectorals beneath his shirt. "Not by much."

Chas doesn't deign to reply. Behind him Ursula catches the stares of the invisigoths, all five sets of blanked-out eyes fixed on her. At least she thinks they're fixed on her: it's more of a feeling than a certainty, a quality of attention in their creepily cherubic faces. And maybe she's imagining it, but she senses something accusatory in their stare. They are judging her, she thinks, and judging her guilty, but of what she isn't sure. Are corporate climbers like her deplorable for being cynical or for being naive these days? She wonders which in fact she is, if either, or whether it's possible she's even both. It is possible—more than possible; in fact it's probably the very paradessence of capitalism, now that she thinks of it: *cynical idealism, self-interest for the common good.* And the personal paradoxes don't end there. In the last few weeks she's thought of herself as both a capitalist tool and a saboteur, both a loyal sister and a betrayer, both a glamour monger and a utopian dreamer. She's so many different people she can barely keep track of them all anymore. She wonders whether others feel like this as well. Life is like some frantic bingo game, she thinks, where players try to maximize their odds by tossing down chips on as many sheets as they can before the next number is called.

"So what are you so busy with, anyway?" she asks, moving slightly so Chas's slab of a head blocks the bleached-out eyes from her view. "Is it those Lite Age counseling sessions you've been pushing?"

His jaw tightens; a single vein stands out at the corner of his eye. "They're not biting," he admits.

Ursula is shocked. She didn't think Chas could fail at anything he tried to sell. "They're not?"

"Not yet. Gap thing's all we got right now."

"So the rest of them aren't convinced?"

"Postirony is visionary. It requires big adjustments in thinking, major shifts in strategy. They're all just sitting on their hands, waiting for someone else to make the first move."

"Couch thought the presentation might have been a bit dark," she ventures.

He glares at her. "Of course it was dark! That was the whole goddamned point. Lightness alone won't cut it anymore. In the postironic marketplace darkness will be just as necessary to move products off the shelves."

He shakes his head.

"Our clients will come around. Some of them. The smarter ones." He stares off through the bars. "Maybe."

He makes a fist and socks it into an open hand. "And if they don't, that's fine, too. We've got other business opportunities now."

"We do?"

He smiles faintly.

"You see Ivy today?" he asks.

"I did."

"And?"

"'And' what?"

"She have anything to say?"

"You mean in response to your little notes?"

He turns and stares her down. "Well?"

Ursula sighs, giving in. "She wants you to make her famous. *More* famous."

He nods. "Well, that's the plan. Already in motion."

"'The plan'?"

"We don't need clients, Ursula. We've got the future. We've got Ivy."

Ursula scans his impenetrable face.

"'The future'? Chas? What are you talking about?" she says. "You don't think she's really—"

"I'm talking about *schizos*, Ursula. Ivy's going to be our spokesperson for postirony. I'm cooking up a website deal. One of those things where people can tune in to her whenever they want. All Ivy, all the time. She's gonna live in the spotlight, just like she always wanted."

He thinks for a moment, gives her a quizzical look.

"What are *you* talking about?" he asks.

"For a second there I thought you were crazy like Ivy," she says. "But you're just crazy like Chas."

Chas cocks his head questioningly, and Ursula sees behind him that the invisigoths have vanished. Chas turns and looks as well. He goes on to check in every direction, and then, with a look of mischief in his eyes, he leans over the railing and lets loose a sparkling gob of spit at the crazily canted city below.

Shelter

The front door cracks, and a sliver of Javier appears behind it, bed-headed, unshaven, in a sleeveless undershirt and a pair of rumpled wool slacks. He's come down to answer the buzzer without asking who it was, and when he sees it's her, his face displays a mixture of confusion and embarrassment.

"Expecting someone else?" Ursula asks.

"Just a package," he says. His eyes wander over her outfit before passing through her into some other dimension uncluttered by her presence. Seeing him in such disarray makes her feel self-conscious and a little guilty about her own carefully crafted appearance. She's wearing a new designer skirt suit and has just had her bangs cut jaggedly in a way the stylist told her would look tough and sexy, though she suspects it makes her look merely dour and disoriented. Furthermore, she's had her as-of-late unbitten nails done, her face professionally rejuvenated with the latest muds and scrubs and other assorted snake oils, and she's signed up for, if not actually attended, a power yoga class. She took all these steps yesterday, more or less in preparation for this meeting. She wanted to make sure Javier would see the full extent of her newfound confidence, power, and success and realize that she could be more indifferent to him than he could ever be to her. But what she sees in him instead is something far beyond indifference, something of another order entirely. She never imagined he could look so utterly lifeless.

"Javier," she says. "Can I come up?"

For a moment he doesn't reply. "It's a mess," he finally says.

"I promise not to call the Board of Health."

He doesn't smile at the joke, but nor does he make any protest as she follows him up the stairs. He is barefoot. The soles of his feet are black with dirt. He shuffles into his apartment. She shuts the door behind her and continues following him through the rooms. The place doesn't look messy at all. On the contrary, it looks completely unused. But his study, when he leads her into it, tells a different story. She sees, with a sudden shock followed by a pang of remorse, that the elaborate trend chart that used to cover the walls has been totally undone. The magazine clippings, notes, graphs, sketches, and bits of colored fabric now cover the floor, and the walls themselves have been plucked bare save for bristling pins, staples, pieces of tape, and the ragged corners of paper still clinging to them. The only remaining element of the chart is the words written in gold Magic Marker, still floating high up by the molding:

The Light Age

The long worktable, the room's only piece of furniture, has been turned on its side, and the tabletop now forms the side wall of a kind of tent Javier has made by draping a comforter from the upper edge diagonally down over a twin mattress laid on the floor alongside it. A faint, musical murmur emanates from beneath the blanket, as well as a modulating glow. Outside the tent, strewn among the remnants of the chart, lie several torn-open mail-order envelopes and computer-game boxes; dozens of empty cans that once contained soup, Spaghetti-Os, and franks and beans; and an equal number of plastic bowls and plastic spoons encrusted with the dried residue of his meals, which were cooked, evidently, on the hot plate sitting beside an electrical outlet in the corner by the door. The room is windowless, and the air, while not quite foul, is heady and sickly sweet.

"Maybe I spoke too soon about that Board of Health thing," she says, desperate to keep things light. But Javier remains expressionless. Without looking at her he takes a breath, then slowly gets down on his hands and knees and crawls inside his tent through a flap at the foot of the mattress.

Ursula looks around the room helplessly for a moment.

"Javier," she says, dropping to her knees. "Can I come in?"

He doesn't respond. She pokes her head through the flap and finds him on his back, with his head propped on a couple of pillows and his long, unshaven face angled toward a computer monitor propped on more pillows beside her at his feet. There's just enough space to squeeze inside between the monitor and the tabletop wall. She kicks off her shoes and maneuvers herself in alongside him, moving a joystick out of the way and claiming an unused corner of his pillow for her head. On the screen at the other end the computer plays with itself, running a three-dimensional maze to the tinny sound of an endlessly repeating action-adventure sound track. Every so often an enemy soldier appears, at which point the top of a shotgun barrel rises from the bottom of the screen, a ragged red hole appears in the falling soldier's chest, and the maze-running resumes. Ursula's stockinged feet charge with the static electricity of the screen, and her heart fills with the palpable misery emanating from each of Javier's slightly labored exhalations. She can barely bring herself to speak, but she feels that if she doesn't, the misery will suffocate them both.

"You took down your chart," she says.

Javier attempts a horizontal shrug, bony shoulders bunching.

"Why?" she asks.

He stares at the screen, furrowing his brow. "Tried to . . . just . . . work backward. . . . Figure out where I went wrong."

He speaks with difficulty, as though each word has to be unlocked from its own cabinet. She can feel the warmth of his arm against hers and the low straining of his voice resonating in her spine.

"Did you figure it out?"

He nods faintly. The smell of his sweat is slightly acrid, slightly sweet, and not unpleasant. Being this close to him is an almost unbearable reminder of the physical intimacy they used to have. She resists the urge to press herself against him, to rub the life back into him any way she can.

"So? Where did you go wrong?" she asks.

The screenlight illuminates the cords of his stubbled neck, his Adam's apple climbing into his chin and falling back as he swallows.

"It's a conspiracy," he says.

"*What* is?"

"Postirony," he says.

She waits for him to explain. He doesn't.

"What do you mean?" she asks.

"Against the children."

"Javier, what the hell are you talking about?"

He takes a shallow breath, as though summoning the effort to speak.

"We're eating our young, Ursula," he says at last.

"Javier," she whispers. "You're starting to creep me out a little here."

"We're converting them into revenue streams," he says fixedly. "We're starving them of love so they'll buy more of what we sell them. They think they're buying love, but it *isn't* love. It's . . . it's *this*." He points at the screen. "We're eating our young. And they know it. That's the most terrible thing: they know it."

"Stop it, Javier!"

He closes his eyes.

"You know," she says, "you walk around with this ridiculous rosy picture of life in your head for months, and the next thing I know you're preaching Armageddon. You're so self-indulgent. You fucking fly off to la-la land, and then you wallow in self-pity. Well, it's just not that bad, Javier. It wasn't that good before, and it's not that bad now."

Almost imperceptibly, he shakes his head.

"Listen to me," she says. "I'm finally starting to get my life into some kind of order. I've finally resolved to make a way for myself in the world. Don't try to take that away from me now."

"I'm so sorry I led you astray," he says, his tone determined, his eyes still firmly shut. "But it's not too late for you to go back to painting, Ursula. So what your work wasn't marketable? I'm sure it was beaut—"

"Shut up! I'm sick of this! I can't take any more. *You* go back, Javier. Go back on your lithium. Get yourself on antidepressants. Stop making me feel guilty. Stop manipulating me. It's not going to work."

"Please, just go," he says. "I can't take this . . . torture."

"'Torture'?" she shouts. "The whole time you were sleeping with me, you were fantasizing about my sister—"

He turns to face her, his eyes wounded and shocked. "That's not true!"

"—filling your notebooks with drawings of her in little hide skirts—"

"No . . . that's—"

"—and you lie there accusing *me* of torturing *you?*"

The blanket slips from its mooring at the foot of the bed, collapsing over the screen, which is visible now only as a faint radiance on the horizon where the blanket meets their knees.

He tries to speak, but his voice breaks, forcing him to whisper: "You were my only fantasy."

"Spare me the sales pitch," she says.

If he reached over and touched her now, she might even start to crack, might even start to believe him. But he turns away and hugs himself protectively instead.

"I can't fight this darkness," he whispers.

"All right," she says. "I'm leaving. You got your wish. You can go back to running your little mazes now."

He says nothing, makes no move to stop her, just stares at the fabric in front of his eyes.

Venusians

Ursula wends her way down a steep and curving section of Lansdale Street, staggering a little in the heels that she likes to imagine make her height seem like an exceptional feature rather than merely a peculiar one. Her eyes to the sidewalk, she almost runs into a couple of pay phones, and she considers taking this as a sign—a sign to call Javier and tell him about the kind of day it is. It's the kind of day he would like, there's something whimsical about the sky today—the way the blimps and helicopters and early moon all hang suspended in it like lint caught in a sweater; the way it seems to suck that one slender line of ash from the volcano peak straight up, as though through a straw; the way it's stratified like a candy corn almost, an abstract expressionist triptych of yellow and orange and white.

The last time they walked this beat together, they spotted a line of graffiti, "Just Remember: you live For Ever," scrawled across a paste-up poster ad for a cable-TV movie about astronauts. He stopped to examine it and then remarked how incredible it was that the rocket in the background had not been grafittied into a giant penis squirting jism out the nose cone; no, instead simply the words *SPACE COSMOS ETERNITY* had been penned along its flank like a logo. This was the Light Age, he said, every life a spiritual journey, essential and unique, lone journeys of self-creation that would ultimately bring humanity together out of a common respect for the depth and beauty of the human experience. He said all this quietly, lightly, falling silent with a smile and a little shrug. She asked him if he thought he'd live forever, and he said yes, because it was such a beautiful thing to imagine that it had to be true. He asked her to try to imagine she'd live forever, and she couldn't do it on command, but later, on a crosstown bus, she looked around at the other passengers and saw the slope of a grinning child's nose, and the arroyos of dried skin on an old man's neck, and felt their proximity, their warmth, their inexplicable but undeniable eternality, and she thought to herself something she had never thought before: she thought, *My fellow souls.*

A steady procession of broad-bellied planes vault over the volcano, like ducks circling on a target wheel.

She continues walking, leaving the pay phones behind. Another block and she finds a square with park benches and sits down. Ray E. Carter Square, a triangle actually, as so many squares in Middle City seem to be, this one of cobblestones and bushes landscaped to resemble the surrounding buildings. She crosses her legs and hugs herself in the breeze. Directly in front of her on a cement pediment stands the inevitable bronze statue of a man in a cheap suit. His eyes, set too close together for comfort, stare menacingly at the fenced-in playground opposite the benches, where a little blond boy giggles and flies down the slide to the applause of his young, smiling, blond parents. The second his feet hit the ground the boy runs back around to clamber up the ladder and slide down again, again, again. He laughs joyously every time.

Nearby, a bulky old woman in a babushka and overcoat stands unmoving except for her right arm, which flails out repeatedly from a grocery bag, stocky fingers opening to release showers of gray breadcrumbs into the black, roiling pool of pigeons at her feet. Ursula wonders what a plaza would look like without an old woman flinging breadcrumbs. They must have to fight for their turf. All those lonely old ladies out there, and not enough plazas to go around.

Across the square the blond child tells his parents to watch him go down for the dozenth time. They watch, proud as ever.

A conspiracy against the children.

She keeps hearing him say that. She tries to recall the expression on his face. Was he speaking literally? Has he become truly delusional? She doesn't think so. It sounded more along the lines of a figurative exaggeration, a way of describing the ugliness he now sees everywhere around him.

The blond family strolls off hand in hand in hand. Its place at the slide is taken by a thin woman and her dark-haired son, who climbs the ladder to sit timidly at the apex, clutching the rails. The son and the mother, recent immigrants, perhaps, look at each other with huge, dark eyes. The mother offers a strained smile, and the boy lets go of the rails. He goes down slowly, braking with his clunky black shoes, holding his hands out just over the sides. Halfway down his face lights up with the most heartbreaking, most tremendous smile Ursula has ever seen, as though the child had never before imagined he could ever be worthy of a pleasure so great. Once on the ground, he beams at his mother exuberantly, then takes a last, wistful look up the silver slope, not daring to wear out its patience by using it again.

Ursula walks the remaining blocks to the loft and rings the unmarked bell dangling by its wire from the door frame. A window opens on the second floor, and James T. Couch appears. He turns back toward his listeners inside.

"Just like I said. A Jehovah's Witness," she hears him announce. His face reappears. "Hey, get with it, haven't you heard? The day of Liteness is upon us! The Lord is the corporation, and Lacouture is his prophet! Eternal poverty and Happy Meals to all infidel shmucks! Get lost!"

He grins, teeth and TV lenses gleaming.

"Do you live here now or something?" she shouts up.

"Every great man needs a couple of slavish *disciples*," he replies as the buzzer sounds.

The loft Ivy shares with Sonja is still virtually bare, despite the fact that the girls have been here for almost three months. There are no boxes, no curtains, no foodstuffs in the kitchen cupboards as far as Ursula can see. The only decorations are the magazines strewn around on the floor and the lease agreement sitting on the granite island counter—exactly where it was signed, no doubt. The main area is occupied by a total of two oversized pillows and a giant TV set with an integrated DVD player, which sits like the Tycho monolith in the middle of the floor. There are no other furnishings to get in the way of the streaming skylight and white walls. The place looks disturbingly like a photographer's studio, as though the girls were determined to inhabit the bright, blank world of their photographs. Sonja stands with her back to the wall, dwarfed by the empty space around her, wearing a black T-shirt and a long black skirt. Ivy stands in the kitchen area, gazing into the empty recess of the Sub-Zero refrigerator, a little tuft of hair sprouting like a blond avocado plant from an elastic band at the top of her head. She's wearing a tube halter top, hot pants with a British flag–print crosshairing on her ass, and bunchy white socks. Couch assists with her wardrobe now, whenever she decides to let him. Her feet, however, are still clad in her disposable hospital slippers, a last holdout of unconquered territory. Still bent over, red and blue ass protruding, face hazily backlit by the wisps of cold air and refrigerator light, she looks at Ursula and waves. These days Ivy's every motion seems calculated to appease a hypothetical camera. She smiles or pouts incongruously, holds any potentially striking or seductive stance just a second too long to come off naturally.

"I thought you two were going to go out and get some furniture this week," Ursula says, looking from Ivy to Sonja.

"Taken care of," Couch calls out from his perch on the windowsill. "Picked everything out myself. It'll all be here Monday at four o'clock. Installed by five. Party at six. Orgy at six-fifteen."

"You let James pick out your furniture?" she says to Sonja. "Do you think that was wise?"

Sonja stands straight, legs together, arms at her sides, as though facing a firing squad. "Why?" she asks.

"Look at the way he's dressed."

Couch rises to his feet, mock-indignant, displaying his attire: plaid pants and a Japanese product T-shirt that reads *Black Black Chewing Gum. Excellent. Hi-Technical. Taste.*

"My haberdashery is meticulously calculated," he huffs.

"'Calculated'? It's horrible."

"I'm a contrarian. Plaid is down right now, a once-in-a-lifetime investment opportunity for anyone *man* enough to take the heat."

Sonja stares at Couch's wardrobe, her face suddenly troubled.

"Anyway," Couch says, striding toward the kitchen area, "*someone* had to get the furniture. These girls never leave the house. They're too busy *furnishing* other things. My sexual needs, *par example.*"

"Could you possibly be more repulsive?"

Couch walks up to Ivy, who maintains her pose at the open refrigerator. He studies her ass for a moment, then, with a smarmy smile to Ursula, places one hand on it and the other on her collarbone and straightens her out. Even then, Ivy's eyes stay fixed on the lit shelves until the door swings shut.

"Don't worry, baby," Couch says, slowing down and overarticulating the words to the point of obscenity, "I've got some *hot, hot, spicy* Indonesian food on the way."

"God," Ursula gasps. "Get away from her."

He looks at Ursula innocently, pretending not to comprehend.

"Don't talk to James that way," Ivy says, wide-eyed. "James is our trusted friend." The line seems forced, overdramatic, as though she were reading it from a TelePrompTer mounted on the far wall. Ursula can't shake the feeling that Ivy is only playing a part, approximating emotional reactions appropriate to situations she isn't deeply experiencing.

"See?" Couch says, shaking Ivy by the waist like a rag doll. "I've gained their trust. Pretty soon they'll be walking around naked in front of me. And from there, getting the ménage up and running will be a lead-pipe cinch."

"James is going to make me a star," Ivy says to Ursula, boasting like a child. "I'm going to be a dotcom. I'm going to command serious eyeball hours. Isn't that right, *daah-link?*" She cranes her long neck and bats her eyelashes up at him, replicating his smile tooth for tooth.

"Right you are," he replies in some old Hollywood voice. "Stick with me, kid. We're going straight to the top."

"Like Sonny and Cher," Ivy says.

"Like the Captain and Tennille."

"Like Donny and Marie," she exclaims.

"Like Kermit and Miss Piggy."

"Like the big Schmoo and the little Schmoo!"

"Definitely!"

The unlikely rapport between Couch and Ivy baffled Ursula at first. How could Couch, she wondered, with his lewd smiles and double entendres and the rest of his no less paranoia-inducing behaviors, manage to soothe a paranoiac like Ivy the way he did with such ease at the photo shoot? How did the two of them ever come to bond? As it turns out, they bonded over the same thing most people bond over: pop culture. For them, however, it's far more than just a shared experience: it's a shared expertise, about which they compare notes like specialists talking shop. Their favorite subject is bad TV, past and present. Ursula has listened to entire conversations between them—debates seemingly replete with theses, developments, rebuttals, substantiating evidence, and final judgments—consisting entirely of the names of sitcom characters. They can communicate purely in references, some of them dizzyingly obscure. When Ivy says something too obscure even for Couch, he just smiles brightly, nods, and says "Definitely!" and they go right on talking. He has a way of humoring her that she seems to find reassuring. And for his part, Couch is clearly flattered by the way she sidles up to him, with the half-trusting, half-cunning cuteness of a kitten. Indeed, there seems to be an element of cunning on both sides of this saccharine, cartoonish burlesque of a friendship: they clearly feel they have use for each other. Ivy is cultivating Couch, just as he is her; the other day she all but confessed this to Ursula, whispering, "He's *putty* in my hands."

Her little dramatic scene accomplished, Ivy ambles over and sits down on one of the pillows against the wall. Sonja moves over and slides down the wall to join her on the pillow, and the two of them fix their attention on the TV set. The set's back is to Ursula. She assumed it was off because no sound was coming out.

Or maybe it *is* off.

"Look at those two," Couch says softly. "If you want to know what I think, I think Sonja has a little crush on your sister."

"What on earth gave you the idea I want to know what you think?" Ursula says, orbiting the island counter in a futile search for signs of life. The kitchenware she bought for Ivy and Sonja sits stacked in the cupboards like a museum display. She half believes that this apartment is just part of an elaborate ruse, that every night the two models climb the fire escape to the roof, placidly board their UFO, and speed off to the dark side of Venus, the planet of fashion models, where they serve their triple-breasted, quintuple-buttocked Venusian queen. All things considered, Couch is probably doing them both a service. It's doubtful that either of them ever would have gotten furniture on her own.

"Guess we've got to get cracking on this new tween report," Couch says. "Speaking of which, weren't you supposed to pay Javier a visit this week?"

"I did. Yesterday."

"Well?" he asks.

"Well nothing. He's depressed."

"Who isn't? But did you find out what his big *discovery* was?" His question drips with sarcasm. False sarcasm. He waits breathlessly for the answer.

"He said there's a conspiracy against the children," Ursula replies dismissively. "He says we're starving them of love to make them hungry for products. He says the children know it. It was really creepy."

Couch nods, says nothing.

"He's depressed. He's a total mess. He's been sitting around playing computer games. He just talked nonsense."

Couch scratches his head, indicating contemplation. "'A conspiracy against the children,'" he repeats. "*Hmmn.* The phrase has a certain . . . *ring* to it, a certain *sonority,* don't you think?"

"You're putting me on, right?"

He smiles brightly, as if to say he is, or as if to say he isn't.

The buzzer sounds.

"The geeks!" he shouts, and runs to the intercom.

"The geeks!" Ivy shouts, abandoning Sonja and running up behind Couch.

"Come on up," Couch says to the intercom. He slides open the metal door.

"'The geeks'?" Ursula asks.

"The website guys," Couch says.

Four skinny young men enter the loft, carrying boxes.

"Ivy's room is right over there," Couch says, while Ivy peeks at them over his shoulder. "I'll be right with you."

They trudge across the room and through Ivy's door, and Ivy follows them in. Sonja watches her leave a little dolefully.

"What are they here for?" Ursula asks.

"To set up the computer and all the cameras."

"You mean she's going to do the website from here?"

"Of course. How *else* could people get to watch her take a shower?"

"*What?*"

He covers his smirk with his hand, as though he'd just revealed something he didn't mean to.

"James," she says. "Let me just ask you one thing, OK?"

He shrugs. "OK."

"What do you think of this whole Lite Age idea, anyway?"

Couch smiles. "Well, Ursula, I'm glad you asked, because, you know, I've actually given the matter some thought, and I'd be delighted to share my conclusions with you."

He falls silent, waiting to be prompted.

"Well?" she finally says.

"Conclusion number one. . . ." Couch smiles demurely. "Chas is a loon!" he shouts, waving his fingers in the air. "The sahib has finally lost it. Gone nutso! Deranged! Unhinged! Sans marbles!" He widens his eyes at Ursula.

"That's quite a theory," she mutters.

"Thank you!" He blinds her with a flashbulb smile. "So you like it?"

"I don't know," she says.

Couch grins. "Certain conclusion number two: Our generalissimo may very well be driving our profitable little company into the ground. He's *scaring* our clients, Ursula. As if that demented Trendpak he insisted on weren't bad enough, he had to follow it up with that gloom-and-doom lecture. And the ordeal doesn't even end there for our poor clients. No! Once they finish their community service, it's off to Treblinka! They have to go home and read the trendbook! And they thought the *lecture* was dark. I mean, *come on!* The part about unhealthy citizens' being good for most blue-chip investors? The part about destroying nature to ensure imaginative control of the population? The part about voting based on the number of shares you own in the country?"

"It's pretty over the top, I guess," Ursula says.

"Jesus! I'll say."

"He's got a pretty morbid imagination, I guess," Ursula says.

"Doesn't he? Doesn't he? I tell you, Ursula, our prime minister's got the morbidest mind on earth!"

Ursula laughs, a wave of relief washing over her—and coming from this unexpected quarter, no less. Couch is the only sane one left around here.

"What marketer in his right mind," Couch goes on, "would want to go and say something so nakedly, obscenely, pornographically *true-sounding?*"

"'True-sounding'?"

The wave of hope crashes.

"I mean, what corporate executive is going to want to read 'The Truth'?" he says, forming the derogatory quote marks with his fingers. "Even if he believes it's true deep down, he'll never admit it to himself in a million years. Now, Javier," he continues, waving a finger in the air, "there's a guy who knows how to deal with clients. He can lay it on with a *trowel.*"

"He's not laying anything on," she says quietly. "He believes what he says."

"Well, whatever works. . . . I just wish he were here to go around and smooth things over. And as for the Virtual Ivy thing," he says, "all I can say is, it better work. Our majordomo's prepared to spend a fortune marketing it. More than we've got. He's taking out loans left and right. If Ivy doesn't pick up advertisers fast, we're off to Chapter Eleven land."

Couch pantomimes biting his nails, mocking the whole idea of taking the matter seriously. Having become well versed in Couchese by now, Ursula knows this could very well mean he actually *is* nervous about the possibility of Tomorrow Ltd.'s going bankrupt. If so, she wonders why he cares, owning, as he does, an entire lake and all. She herself feels strangely detached from the situation, experiencing the half-queasy, half-giddy fascination of a little girl who sets a snowball rolling down a mountain and watches it grow into something beyond anything she's anticipated. Maybe she could still stop it somehow, run ahead and throw herself in front of it, but the gathering mass is hypnotic, and for the moment the impending havoc seems every bit as alluring as it does appalling.

For better or worse, this snowball keeps right on rolling.

"Hey, James," she says. "One last thing I've been meaning to ask you."

Couch lowers his head and opens his hands, indicating his willingness to serve.

"What did you think about all that stuff Chas said about irony?"

He sighs. "Oh, I don't know. *Irony* this, *irony* that—I've never understood the first thing about irony."

He looks up at her, eyes wide and innocent. For a moment the performance strikes her dumb.

Scars

I'm *So* SCHIZO!" is the title of a photo essay in the fragrant new issue of *Mademoiselle.* The spastic, jaunty letters of the capitalized word stagger across a two-page spread showing the glamorous, eccentric Ivy Van Urden sprawling against a white padded wall in an eggplant linen straitjacket, her legs bare. Other portraits follow, including a second spread taken in her bedroom, newly redecorated in an appropriately schizophrenic half-past, half-future motif, the left side sporting potted tropical plants, animal-skin rugs, and clay-colored walls hung with reproductions of cave paintings, and the right featuring burnished aluminum walls hung with stills from *War of the Worlds*, *Fahrenheit 451,* and *1984,* intrusive cameras on adjustable metal stalks, a steel-framed single bed as high as an operating table, and a giant monitor displaying Ivy's back as she sits at her computer terminal in a backless stretch camisole.

The accompanying article is grudgingly accommodated in two-inch columns along the margins of the pictures. Ursula has diligently set out to read it, but there's so little friction to the syntax that after a few sentences she can't slow down and ends up skimming. The reporter's "angle" is to take a lighthearted tack in discussing Ivy's delusions. Ursula spots the word *kooky* and stops, dumbfounded, to check her vision. *She knows folks think she's a little bit kooky,* the line goes, *but she's not letting the naysayers get in her way. The savage girl is going high tech, with a new website to get her message out and save the world from the evil Imagineers. For Ivy, being a star is a matter of life and death. "My image is the drain magnet in the glamour continuum! I have to get famous as fast as possible!" she says, checking her reflection in a pocket mirror. "And money. I need money. A lot of money, fast. Take another picture of me," she tells our photographer, Giambattista. She pushes out her hip, tosses her hair. "Like this!"*

Ursula closes the magazine. She can't stand Ivy. Around her on the subway car a few people look her way, perhaps discovering in her a resemblance, albeit haggard and flawed, to the glamorous, eccentric Ivy Van Urden. She adjusts her oversize sunglasses and disappears behind the magazine again. She can't help admiring Ivy, of course, for the same reason she can't stand her. Ivy has become the queen of paradessences, an absolute master at having everything both ways and every way and getting everything she wants. She gets power by being a victim, attention by being elusive, respect by being irresponsible, success by being a basket case.

If there's one thing she's learned from Ivy, it's that contradictions stop only the people who stop and think about them, who stop to question the consistency of their various desires instead of simply forging ahead and fulfilling them all. Indeed, the only real gains Ursula herself has made in the last few years have come over the last few weeks of not stopping to think, of letting go and letting the tide of events carry her mysteriously toward both shores at once: a successful career *and* an admirable mission in life. They may seem to be in opposite directions, but that's just faulty thinking, a symptom of her pedestrian skepticism, puritanical conscience, overweening pride, just an antiquated flat-earth logic that has failed to take into account some additional dimension, some heretofore unapprehended curvature that makes east merely a different degree of west, that makes the apparent contradiction consistent after all.

She has picked a direction and set sail, and the horizon shimmers with possibilities. The savage trend may not have become everything that Ursula wanted, but it has undeniably become something real, and in so doing has given her confidence in her own ability to carry on and maybe even escalate her secret guerrilla campaign against consumerism. The tween report that she and James T. Couch have just completed may turn out to be the perfect way of doing precisely this. Together the two of them have confirmed the existence of a burgeoning substratum of tween paranoia: they've talked to child psychologists about the increasingly violent impulses of the very young; researched the growing popularity of cartoons with complex, convoluted, and dystopian story lines; correlated rising sales figures with advertising that pits individualistic children against robotically antagonistic adults. And based on these findings, she and Couch have created the blueprints for superstition-wear, conspiracy-wear, persecution-wear: miniature trenchcoats with tall collars and protective lining against evil rays, talismanic accessories, arcane labels, badges with meaningless but ominous-looking insignias. They've advised the Old Navy people to be intentionally obscure, to pepper their campaigns with unexplained inconsistencies and seemingly unintentional patterns; to play on their young customers' fears of being watched, scrutinized, laughed at; to play to their solipsism, facilitating fantasies of heretofore unimagined control, of being at the center of all things, all consciousness, all existence.

For the last two weeks they've been consumed by the job. Ursula has spent her days scanning the streets and her nights sketching, making notes, and brainstorming over the phone with Couch, who has continuously surfed the Net on his dedicated line while chatting with her into the early hours. Somehow they managed to meet the deadline, just this morning handing in their report to Chas, who is now editing and synthesizing it into something slick enough to justify the sizable price tag. And what's more, they managed to do it without the help of Javier's manic motivational enthusiasm. In the last three weeks he hasn't checked in once at the office or returned a single one of Couch's or Chas's calls.

Nevertheless, they weren't entirely lacking in Javier's help. In fact, he was the inspiration behind the report's unifying theme, recurring catchphrase, and eye-catching title: "Conspiracy against the Children." At first Ursula thought Couch and Chas were even crazier than Javier for wanting to run with his idea, but after a while she began to see how it really could work. And the more they developed it, the more enamored of the concept she herself became. The conspiracy trend, she realized, could provide children with a means of expressing their mistrust of the adult world, enabling them to carry out a subversion of the brand imaging that surrounds them by wearing meaningless insignias instead of product slogans and corporate logos. Of course, she's not unaware that the kids who'd buy this stuff would be supporting precisely the consumerism they wanted to protest, but at the same time, she can't see how a campaign so transparently cynical could fail to allow at least a fair number of the children to see right through it. For these children it might even become a kind of living proof of what they've long suspected, evidence of the endlessly recursive ways in which their attempts at rebellion are diverted back into the currents of the revenue stream. In this way the conspiracy trend could begin to bring the problem into plain view, sparking a debate or even engendering new forms of resistance to the very consumerism it purports to serve.

As Ursula gets off the subway and finds her way up to the daylight, her hopeful reasoning spins off into daydreaming. She pictures a day when the world has woken up and taken notice of her guerrilla campaign, a day when that campaign has proved so effective that popular attitudes have begun to change. She pictures her commercial artwork being compiled for museum retrospectives, analyzed in academic journals—the Van Urden brand of insurgency marketing, they'll call it, the marketing that helped transform the global marketplace into a kinder, friendlier place. She has gone for it all and gotten it all: the career *and* the mission, the material *and* the spiritual rewards, the power *and* the love. She is sought after by intellectuals and celebrities alike, sought after for romance and artistic collaboration, for interviews and lectures and in-depth discussions about the state of the planet. Of course, in the era she pictures there will still be many battles to be fought, but through her work she will have at least provided the individual workers in the corporate world with a renewed sense of their own power—power to follow in her footsteps, to form resistance cells of their own and carry on the war until it is finally won.

It is raining lightly as she reaches Banister Park. The day has turned cold and gusty as well, and the park is practically empty, but the savage girl is right where Ursula left her, sitting at the base of Banister's statue, with a large black garbage bag propped in a mound beside her. She has been meaning to come and visit her for a long time. She's been wondering if the savage trend has had any effect on the girl, whether it's done her any good—speculating, for instance, that with the recent popularity of her style she may have managed to make some friends. Indeed, Ursula has half expected to find her newly surrounded by a small tribe of urban savages. Either that or that she has moved on to some totally new style, fancying herself some other kind of creature now, a robot girl, a tall gray alien, a Trappist monk, a new source of inspiration for yet another guerrilla campaign.

But she's still on her own, still a savage, and Ursula finds this just as comforting.

"Still just you and me," she whispers to herself.

She picks out a relatively hidden bench, spreads out the *Mademoiselle* on the damp slats, and sits down on it. She takes a pair of binoculars from her purse and brings the girl into focus.

Something is wrong with the image. She adjusts the focus again.

But it isn't the focus, it's the girl.

It seems like some kind of rash or skin disease.

But no.

With a surge of terror Ursula realizes that the markings are deliberate: small, red, sickle-shaped scars, densely packed, all over her face, the sides of her shaven head, the length and circumference of her neck. The welts appear on her bare arms as well. A leather jerkin covers her torso, and fatigues and bands of pelt cover her legs, so Ursula can't know how much more of her body she has mutilated. For all she knows, the scars are everywhere, and the metamorphosis is total: a pretty young woman transformed into an armored reptile of ruddy, uneven scales, nothing recognizable save her eyes, which are still unscarred, untouched, eerily calm.

Ursula lowers the binoculars. The savage girl is remote again, a solitary figure seated next to a lumpish garbage bag billowing in the misty breeze. The girl looks up, and Ursula flinches when her eyes pass over her, but if she even sees her, she doesn't seem to care. She looks back down at her garbage bag, then lifts it by the bottom and dumps out a mass of something on the cobblestones: a heavy, darkish mound. Ursula raises the binoculars. The dark mound is a dead dog with longish, matted gray hair. Its eyes and narrow, oddly delicate snout are open in a crazed sneer. The savage girl kneels beside the corpse and turns it on its back. The legs stick up stiffly at bent angles. She undoes the dog's collar and tosses it aside. The throat gapes with a wide wound. Dried blood surrounds the opening, covering the ridge of the dog's chest like a bib.

Holding the carcass between her knees, the savage girl unwraps a bundle of cloth on the ground, a collection of knives and sharpening stones. Among them are a couple of double-edged razor blades, bent into curving shapes that roughly match the scars on her body. The backs of her hands, Ursula can now see as the girl spreads the knives out on the cloth, are scarred as well.

She picks out a box cutter, grabs the dog's chest with her free hand, and begins to cut down the center, bending down over her work like a jeweler cutting a diamond, eyes inches from the blade. Perhaps she is myopic. Her face, covered with its scrollwork of scars, reddens still further with the effort, as her scarred, red hands rip open the gray, papery skin of the dog's groin, and after that the binoculars are too heavy to keep holding up.

Ursula roots through the purse on her lap. She finds her wallet, pulls out all the bills. Quickly she spreads them in her fingers. Two hundred and change, trembling in her grip.

She gets up and walks toward the savage girl. As she approaches, the girl struggles with one of the dog's stiffened forelegs, trying to peel off the skin but succeeding only in pulling free some tufts of salt-and-pepper hair. She pauses to stare at the mauled leg, blinking occasionally. She isn't so expert at this yet, clearly. Ursula wonders what's going through the girl's mind, wonders if maybe she is at this moment trying to ascertain what's become of her life, if maybe she's observing herself as Ursula is, from the outside, seeing herself with a mixture of bafflement and outrage, seeing herself pretending to be something she isn't, a savage, in hopes of having what she assumes savages have, seeing herself having forsaken everything, even scratched out her face, all in return for nothing but a dead dog that's resisting her with every follicle of its fur.

The savage girl picks up a butcher knife and hacks away at the leg. Ursula stands over her now. She has to know Ursula's there, but she still doesn't look up. Ursula extends her arm, holding out the wad of bills in front of the girl's nose.

Then the savage girl looks up.

Her gaze wanders from the bills up along Ursula's arm, around Ursula's breasts, up to her hair, and then back down again, backtracking along the same route—breasts, arm, bills. Her face is broad, with high cheekbones and a high forehead made much higher by the Mohican. The scars on her face and neck are still scabrous, crusted with blood and grayish pus. Her mouth is set in a line, small, like some atrophied, vestigial organ. Her eyes are almond-shaped and blue, displaying nothing, registering no difference between Ursula's money and Ursula's arm, between Ursula's arm and Ursula, between Ursula and the trees behind her. The possibility that she doesn't even recognize money is more shocking to Ursula than the possibility that she can simply choose not to see a person who's standing right in front of her.

The savage girl goes back to what she was doing, yanking the leg back and forth with one hand and pressing down on the knife with the other. As Ursula watches, she cuts through the tendon and pulls the limb free. Ursula half expects her to fall upon the exposed meat with her teeth, but she simply holds the leg up in front of her face and gazes at it. Ursula gazes at it as well, mesmerized by the brightness of the colors, the redness of the muscle, the slick white nub of bone. . . .

Chat

The revelers at Camille Stypnick's upslope, split-level townhouse have come to celebrate the launch of Betancourt Rum and its concomitant ad campaign, scheduled to hit the phone booths and bus stands next week. Placards bearing the ads dangle just over the partygoers' heads from long threads affixed to the ceiling. The lead image is of Fidel Castro, his perennial fatigues cashed in for a pink Hawaiian shirt and purple Bermuda shorts. He stands on a Florida beach, a makeshift raft pulled up on the sand behind him. A bulky camera hangs from his neck, and a frayed stogie rises like an erection from his teeth. His smile has been morphed unnaturally wide, along with his eyeballs, at the sight of a model in a string bikini stretched out on a blanket before him. The follow-up ads are variations on the theme: Che Guevara as rock star, Huey Newton as pimp, V. I. Lenin as oil tycoon, and Crazy Horse cruising down Route 66 in a '57 Chevy, all of them armed with eerily morphed smiles and cadres of nubile women. The supporting slogan, plastered across the tops and bottoms of the ads, makes Ursula's brain hurt. For the life of her she can't figure out what it means.

IT'S MORE THAN REVOLUTIONARY

IT'S *COUNTER*REVOLUTIONARY!

She considers turning around right here and leaving, going to find some anonymous bar where she can spend the night drinking herself sick and fending off men with supersized lecherous smiles. But then she thinks of the savage girl, her skinny body covered with scabs and pus and scars, and she starts making her way through the crowd. She's been feeling those scars acrawl on her own skin for the last day and a half. Those scars, she has decided, originated in the depths of her own twisted, selfish brain. She turned the girl's self-expression into a commodity, forcing her to differentiate herself even further by doing something no one else would do. Ursula has stopped sleeping, stopped eating, but her weariness makes her anxious rather than drowsy, and the emptiness in her stomach makes her want to retch rather than eat. It's like she's trapped in some nightmare in which she walks up a hundred flights of stairs only to find herself in a dank subbasement farther underground than before: everything she does seems to produce an effect opposite to the one she intended.

Present at the party are several of the nubile models and none of the revolutionaries. Sonja didn't make the cut for the campaign, but she's here nonetheless, commending to the public a short mesh dress of interwoven bird bones and a long pair of legs. Ed Cabaj and his colleague Lucien have her cornered, and next to them stands Chas, aloof and uninterested, in a pair of lightly tinted sunglasses. With a twinge of panic Ursula looks around for Ivy, but she doesn't see her. Deciding she needs a few more minutes to gather her courage, she steers herself toward an arrangement of bottles beckoning from the dining table. She pries through the crowd, fixes herself a triple vodka on ice with a lemon twist, takes a swig, then makes her way around the room the long way, scanning for Ivy some more, then loitering for another couple of minutes on the periphery of a small group of people scrutinizing another of Camille's campaigns, a series of subway ads mounted in curved light boards along the wall, in which severe-looking fashion models pantomime pleasureless sex with one another. It isn't clear what the product is. Clothing, maybe. Or perfume.

The onlookers murmur in vague appreciation and venture no comments. These are my people, Ursula thinks with self-loathing.

But not for much longer.

By the time she reaches her associates, James T. Couch has arrived as well, dressed in an eye-searing, wasp-waisted white suit and T-shirt that reads *GROOVY: An Airily American Restaurant.*

"How do how do," he says, wedging himself between Lucien and Sonja and switching on his thousand-toothed fluorescent grin.

Introductions and greetings ensue, and then Cabaj takes Chas by the arm and makes a joke about how Ivy beat out Sonja for the Litewater campaign and about how jealous Sonja is. Sonja looks at the floor and shakes her head, an unconvincing and altogether unnecessary denial. Chas ignores them all, lost in thought. He's dressed in a new suit, too, of dark wool, with a loose weave and a flowing cut that drapes augustly from his boxer's frame. But his face is wan and creased, and Ursula wonders what state his eyes are in beneath those sunglasses. She's heard through Couch that though a few more clients have signed on for personalized reports next year, most are still uncomfortable with the prospect of presiding over a new Dark Age, and that Chas has been compounding the problem by arguing with them and offending them, effectively driving them away. Perhaps with this in mind, Couch now snickers loudly at Cabaj's joke to make up for Chas's unsociability. Cabaj, meanwhile, squeezes the entire left half of his puffy face into a wink at Ursula.

"I'm sorry your sister isn't here," he burbles, "but you know, seeing you absolutely makes up for it. We've got to get you in an ad sometime. Two beautiful Litewater-drinking sisters. What do you think?"

He crumples his bushy brow and smiles slyly. He's probably been drinking since happy hour. Ursula's own glass is already empty. The sweet heat of the booze smolders in her chest.

"Forget about Litewater, Ed, old boy," she says, slapping him on the back. "I've got a great new product idea for you."

"Is that right?" Cabaj says. Lucien inclines his head with interest.

"It's a simple idea, really," she says. "It's called Shit."

Couch widens his eyes, and Chas turns toward her slowly. Cabaj recovers from a moment of uncertainty.

"Shit, eh?" he says, smiling and undoing the top button of his silk shirt. "Tell me about it."

"I think it has tremendous potential," she goes on. "I mean, hey, think about it. It's easily produced. Pure profit, in fact, minus ads and packaging. Would you like me to describe the campaign?"

"By all means."

She makes a frame in the air with her hands. "Imagine: A row of sexy women in little booths squatting over Baccarat fruit bowls."

Cabaj guffaws. "Perfect. But what's the slogan?"

"'Shit,'" she announces. "'Everybody's doing it.'"

Cabaj and Lucien laugh, and Couch follows suit, glancing nervously from them to her.

Chas folds his arms, straight-faced. "'One hundred percent natural,'" he says with a knowing nod. More laughter.

"'Low in fat,'" Ursula responds.

"'Each bolus individually crafted.'"

"'*Lovingly* crafted.'"

"'One a day for good health.'"

"'Because at General Foods we *do* give a Shit.'"

"'Do the Doo,'" Chas says.

"'Eat Shit,'" she counters.

The group laughs at their routine and then falls silent.

"I like that one," Chas says, thoughtful.

"People would do it just for the irony," Lucien says.

"There's another product for you," Ursula suggests. "Irony. 'Double your consumption potential with Irony. Is that movie you saw last night too dumb and offensive for you? Go see it again with Irony and enjoy yourself. See it again and again. Again for the bad acting. Again for the sociological implications. And if you're tired of being a snob, well, then, try *Postirony* and see how badness isn't really bad, it's just another kind of good. It's *all* good. There's a real art to badness. Buy a cup of Postirony and a bucket of Shit at the concession stand and munch your heart out as the fun-loving hitmen blow people away to the sounds of your favorite retro pop songs.'"

Cabaj looks around, sensing malice.

"Seriously, though," Chas says, "maybe something *could* be done along those lines."

"Seriously, though," Ursula says, "shut the fuck up, Chas."

The laughter becomes a little uncomfortable as she and Chas stare each other down. She's going to get herself fired tonight if she can. And if not, she's going to ruin everyone's evening trying.

"Sure, Chas," James T. Couch says. "*Splendid* idea. Just drive the last nail into our coffin, why don't you?"

"What's this?" Cabaj asks.

"Couch thinks I'm bankrupting the company," Chas explains, still facing Ursula.

Cabaj nods. "Well, are you?"

He shrugs. "Maybe."

The group laughs again.

"Sounds like you guys are having fun."

Camille Stypnick has appeared. She's a large woman of about fifty with a cubic yard of black, frizzy hair flowing out from beneath her cap. She's dressed exactly like Chairman Mao, except for the wide flare of her pant legs, and the plunging neckline of her worker's shirt, and the puffiness of her red-starred hat, and the dye on her entire outfit, which instead of being blue is particolored, covered with reproductions of Warhol's silk-screened Maos.

"Now that's what I call a *party* dress," Cabaj says.

"Ha!" Camille mocks, her laugh overloud and intentionally false.

"Revolutionaries," Lucien says to Chas, his voice as soft as a buttered razor blade. "You trendspotting folks pick up on this one?"

"Bah," Chas grumbles. "Revolutionaries go in and out like clockwork. Dependable as the seasons."

"Well," Lucien says with a sigh, "maybe we can get a little more play out of this savage trend, at least."

"No, it's a flash in the pan if I ever saw one," James T. Couch says. "No offense," he says, turning to Ursula. "Although I *did* see the most eminently shaggable high school vixen the other day at Henry the Eighth. You'll never guess what she was wearing."

"Let me see," Ursula says. "Sweatshop worker–skin pants?"

"No. An accessory."

"A see-through mask?"

"No."

"Paste-on bullet entry wounds?"

"No."

"A colostomy bag?"

Couch sighs melodramatically. "You're not trying, but I'll tell you anyway. A bow."

"How festive. Did you offer to unwrap her, or did her father chase you off?"

"No, no. A bow—you know, the weapon kind. And a quiver of arrows."

Ursula considers this factoid. "How festive," she says.

"And don't forget Sonja here," Lucien says, eyeing her bone-mesh minidress and matching choker. "She's still into the savage look."

"She's into Ivy's castoffs is what she's into," Couch says. "She's into anything that's touched that girl's creamy, delectable flesh. Right, Sonja?"

Sonja looks down at her body. "No," she says.

"Oh, come on, I see the way you look at her. I see the dirty looks you've been giving me lately for taking up so much of her time. But who could blame you? We're all in love with Ivy, right?"

She reddens, smoothing the ragged hem against her thighs. "No."

"Oh, you liar," Couch says, grinning his impossible grin. "Oh, girl love. It gets my blood going. How about I take you little savages down to my altar room and make a virgin sacrifice?"

Cabaj bursts out laughing.

"Well, that explains it," Ursula says. "I always wondered what you were saving your maidenhead for, James. I'm sure the gods will be appeased."

More laughter all around. Camille excuses herself to check on her other guests. Couch eyes Ursula, displaying his teeth.

"Well, we can't *all* be as sexually liberated as some people."

The group falls silent, looking expectantly from Couch to her.

"'As some people'?" she says.

"Yes, you know: some people just are, some people just aren't. Javier, for example—he's just not sexually liberated at all. He's so touchingly traditional. Like a knight of old. Totally smitten with one woman. All he talked about was her, all he did was rave about her, how incredible she was, how smart and caring and beautiful and blah blah blah. We couldn't get him to shut up about this woman. And when it turned out that he was just a stepping stone—you know, that this woman was just sleeping her way to the top—"

"Excuse me," she says, looking at Chas, his eyes evasive behind the tinted lenses, and then back at Couch. "'Sleeping her way to the top,' you say?"

"Exactly," Couch says. "See, she wasn't only sexually liberated, this woman; she had a keen business sense as well."

"Sounds like a ballbuster, all right," Cabaj opines.

Couch grins. "She sure was. Broke Javier's big, sappy old heart right in two. And now he's gone, and there's nothing anyone can do to help him."

"What do you mean 'gone'?" she asks in a low voice.

"'Gone' meaning 'gone,'" Couch says with a shrug. "Vanished. Condo's empty. Up for sale. Not a scrap in it. I just stopped by today and found out. They told me he moved out a week ago. No forwarding address."

His little eyes watch her, serenely afloat in their fishtank lenses. She looks at Chas. Chas nods. Then shakes his head.

"Where the fuck is my drink?" he mutters. "Anyone want anything? Sonja?"

"Lemon drop, without the alcohol," Sonja says.

Chas considers the request, shakes his head again, and walks off.

Cabaj and Lucien begin chatting Sonja up again, and Couch leans over and whispers in Ursula's ear:

"Good thing your kind of sex isn't Chas's bag. Otherwise you might have even broken *his* big old iceberg of a heart, too."

Ursula grips his arm tightly and pushes him a couple of steps away from the group.

"What do you mean, *my* kind of sex?" she demands.

He gives her an innocent look. "You mean you didn't know?"

She backs him against a wall.

"Well . . . ," Couch says. "I probably shouldn't be spreading gossip anyway."

She digs her fingernails into his arm.

"Ouch!" he yelps. "That hurts! OK, if you insist."

She lets go. He inspects the synthetic material of his sleeve, rubbing it smooth with his palm as he talks.

"Ivy told me she and Chas never did it," he whispers. "She said Chas thought she was too beautiful to touch." He smiles, shakes his head. "Apparently Ivy agreed with him. So they'd do it without touching. She'd get herself off in a mirror, and he'd get off looking at her, like a picture in a girlie magazine! That's the only way they ever did it! Funny, eh?"

Ursula nods. Couch returns the nod, staring at her coolly and matching his rate of nodding evenly to hers.

"Well," he says, "I guess that goes to show there *is* such a thing as being too beautiful, eh? Good thing most of us don't have *that* problem!"

"Good thing," she repeats, refusing to look away, refusing to show anything. She channels it all into her fists, into her legs. Her toes curl until they cramp in her high heels, and her face, just maybe, shows nothing.

Couch is lying, she thinks. But then she remembers part of the story Ivy told her about her and Chas, something about her feeling her power and him feeling his power.

Couch isn't lying.

"And speaking of Ivy," he announces in a louder voice, "what say we pay her a little visit tonight?"

"Ivy?" Cabaj erupts, turning from his huddle with Lucien. "We can go see her?"

Couch lets his gaze linger on Ursula for another moment before turning to Cabaj.

"Well, virtually," he concedes.

"Ah. Virtually," Lucien muses.

"We'll have to find Camille and get her permission."

"I know where to find her," Lucien says. He turns and floats off through the crowd.

"Interesting guy, that Lucien," Couch says to Cabaj. "Although maybe a little, I don't know, effeminate?"

Cabaj doesn't seem to know how to answer this. Chas returns with a couple of drinks, and the group goes on talking. Meanwhile, Ursula breathes in. She breathes out. She breathes in again. The gist of the conversation permeates her skin. Ivy's website is about to go on-line. The only thing this means to her at the moment is that she can't slip away, that she's trapped here with Couch and the rest of them, because she has to act normal, and being normal means wanting to look at more pictures of her "kooky" sister.

Lucien returns with Camille, who leads them, her anklets clinking, up the spiral staircase to her study. A bulky computer occupies the middle of a long glass table. The monitor plays a silent screen saver showing Middle City being slowly devoured by giant cockroaches. Camille sits down at the terminal and opens the browser, and Couch leans over her and types the address, then proceeds to navigate them through the various entertainments of the site: a short biography of Ivy written by "fashion expert James T. Couch," replete with childhood pictures; a section on her mental breakdown, containing a couple of newspaper articles and the famous accompanying photograph; and the transcript of a brief interview, conducted, of course, by "fashion expert James T. Couch." It flashes by too quickly for Ursula to discern anything other than that the questions are on the whole longer than the answers.

He then takes them to an on-line chat with Ivy, already in progress. The left half of the screen displays Ivy's ovoid face, garishly made up with red and black warpaint and slightly elongated by some imperfection in the feed software, which also makes the video jerk along at about a frame every three seconds. Ivy scans the questions at her own terminal and types responses into her keyboard, and the chunks of resulting text stagger up the right side of the screen:

Ilse:	What kind of fondation do you use.
barb:	So are you still kinda crazy? (smiling!)
tom:	hey stand back a little let's see what ya got on
ivy:	**no foundation.**
H#(F77:	what were you thinking when you cut youresefl up ivy
purv:	have youever done it witha transvestite?
ivy:	**had to appease the Antibodies.**
tom:	what clubs you hang out at
H#(F77:	who are the Antibodies?

Mr.Beeg:	who you callin ainnobody bich
barb:	Why isn't anyone screening out these JERKS?
ivy:	**antibodies fight the Bodies for marketshare.**
tom:	why dont you take off your cloths we cant see anyway
Mr.Beeg:	hey you like to 8>>>> (o) ?
Ilse:	how did you become a modl.
ivy:	**sometimes i'm too body. sometimes i'm too antibody.**
BODIES:	We the BODIES order you to shut up and take off your Top NOW.
Ilse:	I mean model
H#(F77:	Sounds like you've got a tough job.
((((@))):	ivy we got a party going on kick*ss DJ & lots of dr*gs. wanna cum?
ivy:	**my sister helps me. she is a trendspotter. she protects me from the Imagineers.**

The others in the room turn to watch Ursula's reaction. She feels her face flush. She fights the urge to cry.

barb:	what is your favrite pic of u?
iggi:	dont take these jokers serius :)
tom:	hey @ wherez da par-tay @
momo:	So who are the Trendspotters? Are they Bds or Antibds?
Bqul:	Your sister a hottie too?
12345:	Man, it's not just hype. She really is a loon.
viv:	EARTH TO IVY COME IN IVY
tom:	your sis nuts 2?
ivy:	**she is both Hottie and Antihottie. they will kill her if i make a wrong move.**
Nasir:	fascinating captain
Sheila:	hey ivy can you turn the cam and show us what your wearing?
tom:	Antihottie???????
ANTIBOD:	WE THE ANTIBODIES ORDER YOU TO TAKE YOUR PANTS OFF.
Ynot:	Dude, u r fuct.
H#(F77:	What if Ivy's not crazy? What if she knows the Truth?
MaryD:	it's an act. She's putting all of you on.
AgentK:	I believe her

ivy: i am fuct. but so are u. if u don't watch me you will all
        die. send me yr money. i will save u but I need yr $. i'll
        keep it right here in my room, rt here w me.
tom: hey where u goin

Ivy stands, walks to the back of the room, turns away from the camera,
yanks off her T-shirt, and takes down her cargo pants. She steps out of
them, turns around, and faces the camera again. She is wearing plain
white panties and no bra. She stands rigidly, as though she were being
x-rayed. Frame after frame of her appears, in all of which she remains
wide-eyed and rigid. Text continues to scroll up the left side of the screen.

Camille, James T. Couch, Chas, and Sonja all keep watching, while
Ursula quietly backs away.

"This girl's a gold mine," Camille whispers.

Couch nods.

Sonja looks down at her high-heeled moccasins.

Chas stares as though hypnotized.

Mornings

The shades are drawn, and the computer screen bathes Chas's bleary eyes and papery skin in its pallid light. His head rests heavily in the seat of his hand, which is propped in turn by his elbow on the broad arm of his leather chair. He hasn't looked up from the screen since Ursula came in and sat down, nor has he said a word, and after another minute she gives in and repositions her chair to face the screen, the staggered feed of Ivy, putting on a show for her worldwide audience of ironists and perverts. Ivy paces back and forth in her underwear, singing some tune in her whispery little voice. Occasionally she jumps, or pirouettes, or windmills her arms—the little rituals that help transform her delusions, one by one, into reality. She really is under constant surveillance now. Her every move really is scrutinized by unseen masses. And when she talks to the cameras about her invented origins in the magical past and the mercenary future, people respond in kind, via e-mail and chat lines, asking her to elaborate, pretending to be good witches or nefarious Imagineers or trickster trendspotters. In that little room, reality for Ivy has become something entirely malleable under the force of her will. All she has to do is imagine something, and people around the world will strive—whether out of sympathy, or for the sake of amusement, or for the sheer drama of the thing—to make it so. In her debut performance she requested money, and now, three days later, she has money: half a million in small bills, scattered on the bed and all over the floor. This money came from Chas, who apparently got a fraction of it from his personal accounts and the rest from James T. Couch, in the form of a business loan. The gambit seems to be paying off: Ivy's viewership has already gone up a hundredfold. At any given moment a little box at the top of the screen counts the audience: 140,209 people watching her kick up clouds of tens and twenties as she skips around her room; 140,214 people examining the delicate tracework of pink scars on her thighs, forearms, and belly; 140,200 people unable to touch her—she's untouchable, too beautiful to touch, all pixels and light—140,211 people touching themselves instead, and discovering that they actually prefer it this way.

Ursula watches Chas watch Ivy, feeling her own eminently touchable, demonstrably unbeautiful flesh hanging from her like a weighted net, while the heaviest weight of all, the one in her chest, becomes more and more unbearable.

"I assume you've come to hand in your resignation?" Chas says.

"That's right. I'm quitting," she says.

"Whatever. You guys time it or something?"

"What do you mean?"

Chas reaches into his top drawer and pulls out a piece of stationery covered, she sees, with Javier's unmistakably ornate, almost calligraphic handwriting. He leans back in his chair and begins to read it aloud.

"'Dr. Lacouture: In light of the recent yak yak yak, I feel I must protest the yak yakity yak and the future of etcetera in particular the yakity yakity the children of the world yak yak I am personally ashamed to have yakitied sincerely, Javier Delreal.'"

Listlessly, he crumples it into a ball and tosses it in a lazy arc across the room, then goes back to watching the screen.

"You got that today?" Ursula asks.

He nods.

"Was there a return address? Was there a postmark?"

"Mid City. He's still here somewhere."

He's still here, she thinks with relief. It's not too late. She can still find him.

Chas leans in closer to the screen.

"There. Watch," he says.

To the right of the window containing Ivy's image, between flashing banner ads for a porno site and an on-line brokerage above and below, a message begins to scroll and repeat:

Ivy needs more money
to complete her mission.
Become one of Ivy's Friends
with a donation of any size.
Donate with your credit card
on our secure server.
Or send a check
or a money order.
Ivy will thank each donor
with a personalized blessing.

"That's it," Chas says quietly. "The perfect demonstration of post-irony."

"You actually think people will send money?" Ursula asks.

He nods wearily, massaging his temples. "That's my professional opinion."

"Why? You've filled her room with money. Why would people send her more?"

"Well, you've just asked two questions, the first being why *I think* they will, and the second being why on earth they *would*." He leans back in his chair again, stroking his goatee. "The answer to the first question is that it's a well-documented phenomenon. Which is why at Caesars Palace in Vegas they roll the house's winnings across the floor in a giant glass tank on wheels. They do this every night at midnight, when most of the people there have been gaming and losing for hours. It's counterintuitive. You'd think they wouldn't want to rub the losers' noses in it. But when those gamblers see this huge tank full of the profit they've helped create, you know what they do? They reach into their buckets and grab handfuls of quarters. They reach into their wallets and take out their dollar bills and crumple them into little balls. And they toss those handfuls of quarters and balled-up dollar bills into the money tank as it rolls by."

"They do?"

"Yes, Ursula, they do. But to get to your second question, we aren't sure *why* they do. Behavioral psychologists are of two minds on the issue. One view is that it's a form of ritualized submission, like beta monkeys' bending over to take it in the ass from the alphas. The other view compares it to

Stockholm Syndrome, the phenomenon of hostages' identifying with their captors."

"Which one do you believe?"

He scowls at her.

"Neither, of course," he replies. "What kind of academic would I be without a theory of my own?"

"Which is?"

"It's rendering unto Caesar, so to speak. It's kicking the moneylenders out of the temple. It's a rebellion against the power those little bills have over our fate. Purely symbolic, of course. Fleeting. Ineffectual. Utterly moronic any way you slice it. But nevertheless. That's the essence of it. It's a rebellion against Mammon." He looks up at the ceiling, shaking his head. "Who would've thought I could ever be part of such a thing? It's humbling, really."

He goes back to watching the screen, eyes misted with wonder.

"Chas," she says. "Let me ask you something. Do you care about Ivy at all?"

He says nothing, but she sees him stiffen.

"How can you do this to her?" She's promised herself she'd keep her cool, but her voice now starts to tremble. "You see how crazy she is. She needs help."

"Don't patronize her, Ursula," he says evenly, turning to face her. "You see all that money? That's help. That's more help than most little schnooks out there'll ever get."

"How long do you think she can keep this up?"

"However long she feels like it. And when she feels like doing something else, I'll help her do something else. Whatever she wants. She can do whatever she wants, Ursula. How many people on this shitball of a planet can say that?"

"And what if she feels like destroying herself?"

Chas studies her for a moment, then props his forearms on the desk and leans closer.

"What if?" he says softly. "You think that's what I want? You know how I spend my mornings nowadays? Dreaming away about those other mornings I had before, the ones where I could lie there in bed watching Ivy put herself together piece by piece—towels, toothpaste, hairpins, stockings. It took her forever. I didn't give a fuck."

He shakes his head, staring at Ursula, his eyes bright and wondering.

"I realized that was all I ever wanted," he goes on. "Just to watch that weird girl put herself together, with the sun shining on her wet, showered body and the scent of her all around me in the sheets and the radio blabbering on about traffic delays and temperatures at the airport, just like it does for every other pie-eyed, addle-brained couple in America. And then we'd eat breakfast, and that would take forever, too—coffee, toast, even some eggs, because she liked big breakfasts, and so did I then, because real food didn't make me nauseated the way it does now; it actually tasted pretty good. But Ivy wasn't meant for mornings like that. People destroy themselves, Ursula. All the time. Sometimes that's what it takes to keep themselves entertained. If Ivy wants to destroy herself, that's her call. She knows what she needs to do. And if she doesn't, I'm gonna be right here, waiting for her, with a pile of money so fucking high we can disappear into it and never be seen again."

He rests his head in his hand again.

"You're using her, Chas," she says. "You're driving her like a mule. She can't take this kind of pressure."

"Don't get in our way, Ursula."

"Consider me in your way."

"Yeah, whatever. Consider your resignation accepted. Go find Javier and help him save the motherfucking children. Start an orphanage. Raise us up a whole slew of discriminating consumers. Make us proud."

He swivels around, showing her the back of his chair.

Conspiracy

The tips of Ursula's fingers and toes charge with static electricity as she walks through the Plexiglas-lined cavern entrance to the South Slope Mall, the way a cockroach might feel crawling through the innards of a television set. Five levels of dimly glowing stores line the lava-rock corridors, snugly crowded beside and atop one another like skulls in a catacomb, receding toward an intersection a quarter of a mile off.

Stereorama, Le Clique Chic, Jujuland, Rocket Sport, Bestsellers, Veronique's Boudoir, The Sole Man.

Everywhere shadowy forms mill about, hauling gargantuan bags along the serpentine corridors, wandering into and out of doorways, pausing to lean over the balustrades, gazing down at the shoppers below. Still others slouch on benches and over eatery tables, seemingly having given up all hope of ever finding their way back to the city above. The Underworld theme is spoiled, perhaps, only by these shoppers themselves, who are on average fleshier and more rotund than would seem permissible for undead shades. And yet the necessity of lugging around all that extra weight could be seen as a kind of infernal torture in itself, as if for every fraction of eternity longer they spent here, an imp would scuttle up and stuff another pound of fat into their voluminous shuffling buttocks and sagging abdomens.

Tenderbird, Juanita's Golden Taco, Mermaid's, Long Yum Lick, Sofruti Treats.

The names of the stores grow more senseless the deeper into the mall she gets, gradually losing any definite connection with the merchandise, as though they had been spontaneously and randomly generated by some long-obsolete, overtaxed computer spinning its tape reels and spitting out slotted cards in a room the location of which no one even remembers.

Boogalooga, Nice n' Stuff, Qwertyuiop, Take Me Here!, Biggy Barn, Gotta-lotta, La Bonne Storé.

If her will to survive were stronger, she would turn and run to the near-est exit, wherever that is—these places are designed to disorient, and the exits are kept well hidden. Probably she would end up taking the wrong staircase anyhow, and ending up in one of the subbasements where men-tally handicapped workers are paid two dollars an hour to toss all the separated items from the public relations–contrived recycle bins into a heterogeneous pile for shipment in unmarked trucks to the volcano's mouth.

Haha Lala, Pretty Neeto, Bungalo Hut, Sneejak's, Whatsamattayou, Quickel-nickel, Fimsolec, Ocneskow.

The endless corridors remind her of the mausoleum where her grand-mother's ashes are stored, a place at once unmanageably vast and meticulously organized, with all the ashes distributed according to religious affiliation: Catholic halls lined with suffering Christs, Protestant halls adorned with simple crosses, Hindu halls bristling with Siva arms, atheist halls deco-rated with abstract paintings and potted plants. It's in one of these last, godless hallways that Gwennan put her own mother, and there that she fully expects her daughters to put *her* when the time comes, and there that she fondly hopes they, too, will join her one day. She has reserved spaces for them all. This plan for their eternal storage was the issue of utmost importance in Gwennan's mind last night when Ursula called her to talk about Ivy. Ursula's idea was that if the two of them confronted Ivy together, they just might be able to cajole or if necessary even bully her into committing herself. But as it turned out, Gwennan not only already knew about Ivy's website, but was an avid fan.

"Commit her?" she exclaimed in a way that made Ursula feel like a criminal. "She's an *artist*, Ursula. She's a performance artist, and she's *good*. I knew she wasn't going to be in that hospital for long. I always thought she had this in her. You should be out there supporting your sister, not try-ing to put her in a nuthouse."

Gwennan could have left it there, but then she wouldn't be Gwennan. "Sounds to me like you're just jealous as usual," she added.

The idea that Ivy was doing performance art had not, until that moment, occurred to Ursula, but she immediately understood why Gwennan would see it this way. It fitted Gwennan's definition of art—something done to repudiate the world in a public way—to perfection. And where the Boopleganger had failed to carry out this essential mission, Gwennan must now, in some chilly corner of her mind, be thinking that her own daughter Ivy would at long last succeed. Taken alone, this discovery would have been bad enough, but in fact it led her to an even darker hypothesis—namely, that in a sense Ivy was Ursula's very own Boopleganger, that what Gwennan had done with that deranged patient of hers, Ursula had done with her own sister, helping to turn a beautiful girl inside out in order to make a point about the ugliness she herself saw everywhere. The seeming unbreakability of this chain of logic threw her off balance, and all her ideas about how to get Ivy hospitalized again fell apart. Unable to speak, she was forced to listen to Gwennan rant about her new hobby: day trading Internet stocks. She was making serious money, she said. The trick was not to get stressed out about it, and in this, she contended, her training as a Buddhist helped her immeasurably.

Ursula nodded to herself.

"I'm going to hang up now," she said.

"Fine," Gwennan replied. "Oh, listen, if they go public with Ivy's website, let me know. I want to get in on the ground floor."

And now, lost in the endlessly branching and recessing corridors of the South Slope Mall, Ursula pictures her mother perched at her computer in the study of her suburban house, snatching up and unloading shares of her younger daughter. What a logical next step this would be, people across the globe investing in an image of a crazy girl lighting her cigarettes with their money, her riding on them and them riding on her and everyone together riding the bull market in delusion, a pyramid scheme they all know for exactly what it is but half cynically, half mystically hope to beat, hope to get in early on and get out of before the insanity ends, so they can wind up just a little bit closer to the top than to the bottom.

Ursula timidly requests her limbs to continue moving forward, but they are completely enervated. She collapses onto a nearby bench and watches the shoppers trundle by in either direction. Next to her, on a lighted display, an ad for Calvin Klein shows a very skinny black woman lighting a crack pipe against a white background. Across the concourse, behind the plate glass of the Postmodern Torse of Schwarzenegger Gymnasium, row upon row of mallgoers struggle on silver Nautilus machines to work off their excess weight. Outside the gym looms a limbless and headless bronze sculpture of the movie icon, twelve feet high and almost as broad at the shoulders, muscles squeezed between other muscles and stacked one atop the other without apparent order, like a mammoth accretion of candle drippings. A long bronze plaque curves around the sculpture's base, bearing the words

YOU MUST CHANGE YOUR IMAGE

A teenage boy jostles her knees and mumbles an apology as he is pulled along by his girlfriend. He is busy looking at a light-board ad of a woman in a Naugahyde bikini. He glances at her breasts, then away, then at her legs, then away, then lips, away, hair, away, then breasts again, oscillating compulsively. Ursula wonders if the parts will ever form a whole in his mind, or whether that will even matter to him so long as he can just succeed in retaining for later use the specific breasts the specific lips hair breasts legs breasts. Still stranded by her despair, Ursula trails the kids with her eyes until they vanish into a storefront.

ARCADIA

She was beginning to doubt she'd ever find it. It's a smallish-looking place, situated in a cul de sac where a nameless corridor ends in an unimproved cavern wall. She gets up from the bench and follows the kids inside.

The noise is overwhelming. Beeping, blasting, buzzing, screeching. As if the noise of the machines weren't enough, or perhaps to counter it and carve out a space for their individual identities, many of the kids wear headphones, not up against their ears but around their necks, the miniature speakers leaking vaporous rhythms into the air directly in front of them. She knows she'll continue hearing the noise for hours after she leaves, that it will go away only to come creeping back in the silence of night as she lies in bed, alone, waiting for sleep. She knows that it will combine with that other mechanical noise she's been hearing, the tinny tune of the maze game running in Javier's makeshift tent in his destroyed study. And she knows that in her dreams she will continue wandering through mazes within mazes in search of him.

She walks past a firing range of pistol games: a couple of black boys do battle with the Vietcong, next to an Asian boy fighting Arab terrorists. Farther down the aisle a stocky boy with olive-colored skin and a polyester shirt, possibly an Arab, fights his way through an army of pale zombies in a haunted compound. The zombies grimace and shriek as the gunshots appear in their bodies. They collapse, unwholesome piles of bluish flesh, dead for a second time. The boy grimaces as well, teeth gritted, face stretched in some places and creased in others. A green, bent-kneed troll drops from the top of the screen, teeth bared and claws extended. The boy jumps back. The screen turns red and freezes, and a countdown begins. Without hesitation he reinserts his game card to preserve his life and resume the battle.

The arcade is much larger than it looked from the outside. She turns and walks down an aisle of racing games—steering wheels and gas pedals, twisting roads and straightaways unfurling from vanishing points on candy-colored horizons. A pack of white teenage boys crouch forward on wheel-less motorcycles, tilting left and right and left again to the sounds of gunning engines as the screens light up their greasy, bug-eyed faces. She turns again and makes her way through yet another aisle, past hand-to-hand combat games on one side and a couple of full-environment machines on the other, roped-off compartments that buck and twist on hydraulic jacks. The largest crowds cluster around these, waiting in lines and watching the ongoing penetration of planetary defense systems on the outside monitors.

She looks for Javier, but all she sees is children, awkward, isolate, their bodies crammed to bursting with caffeine and sugar and pop music and cologne and perfume and hair gel and pimple cream and growth hormone–treated hamburger meat and premature sex drives and costly, fleeting, violent sublimations. It's all part of the conspiracy, she sees—all of it trying to convince them that they're here to be trained for lives of adventure and glamour and heroism, when in fact they're here only to be trained for more of the same, for lives of plunking in the quarters, paying a premium for the never-ending series of shabby fantasies to come, the whole lifelong laser light show of glamorous degradation and habitual novelty and fun-loving murder and global isolation.

Cadres in training for the Lite Age.

She turns around in search of a way out. There are no exit signs. The crowds press against her. A gauntlet of screens in every direction.

Order

The savage girl always used to be doing things, making things, but now she's doing less and less. For the last few days her only activity has been chopping the wooden slats off a park bench and then chopping them into campfire-size pieces. Every day Ursula could look forward to another length of bench disappearing, leaving another bare metal ring, shortening the total length of the joined benches and bringing the savage girl, who migrated along with the supply of firewood, a few feet closer to her. In not so many more days—nine, to be exact—they'd have been sitting side by side, and the savage girl would have been forced to acknowledge Ursula's existence. If she'd continued to resist, Ursula could have tempted her with a basket full of savory savage food—fried tarantulas, maybe, or boiled pterodactyl eggs, a roasted bison haunch. . . . But today she hasn't chopped, hasn't moved all day, and now the sun is going down, and the bench remains nine days long.

A woman walks into the park through the West Gate: strawberry-blond hair, a blueberry parka, and pressed blue jeans. Her legs are elongated to spindliness by the sun's glare on the snow. She walks toward the savage girl, glancing nervously to either side. Other than the occasional car sliding down Shields Street, there's no one else around. Ursula looks down to where the savage girl sits cross-legged on the bench, chin resting on fingers clasped over the top of her hatchet, eyes staring straight ahead, as unseeing, probably, as the rotting sockets of the gray-furred dog's head she now wears as a hat. For a moment the savage girl turns and looks in the direction of the approaching woman, but then straightaway she returns to looking at nothing, which presumably she finds more interesting. The woman passes by Ursula, exchanging a cautious, almost pleading glance with her as she continues on, walking slower now, approaching the savage girl, her impeccably shagged hair brushing the back of her coat as she cocks her head this way and that. A few feet away from the savage girl she stops and makes a short sound: *Ahp.* The sound is short because she chokes off the end of the syllable. Simultaneously her arm rises and her trembling, knitted-gloved finger points at the savage girl, who again looks up at her and again loses interest and looks away.

Ah—ohhhhhhhhhh.

It's a kind of whimper coming from the strawberry-blond woman now. She backs off a few steps, almost trips, then turns and runs back the way she came. The savage girl displays no reaction.

Is she *that* grotesque? Maybe Ursula has simply gotten used to that red, scar-encrusted lizard face of hers. Or maybe there's something new in that face that Ursula hasn't gotten close enough recently to see: a maggot eating a hole through a cheek, perhaps, or a gangrenous nose beginning to detach itself from the skull.

Maybe the girl is sick. Maybe that's why she hasn't been doing much lately.

Or maybe not; maybe she's just the industrious ant all prepared for winter, all her provisions carefully stowed away, nothing to do now but wait until spring so she can start preparing for *next* winter. Maybe today was too warm for her to think about firewood. It *has* been unnaturally warm, the sun shining even as a new coat of snow wafted down earlier in the day. Ursula is even sweating a little in her regulation Arctic exploration coat. Olive drab. Not her color. Not particularly well camouflaged, either, but she's long since given up hiding. There's nowhere to hide, anyway. Ursula has begun to entertain her own little paranoid ideas, begun to conceive of the universe as a bounded panoptical dystopia at the center of which sits a cosmic, multidimensional version of Chas Lacouture, watching the human race with a zillion callous eyes, his bloodless superstring lips twisted into a Möbius sneer of eternal contempt as he presses the buttons of a zillion obscuranting Javiers to make them go around and rave about how the world is a relativist utopia of ever-malleable, ever-proliferating realities, a vast playpen with no other purpose than to nurture the divine spark of creativity within each of us and grow the human imagination into godhood. It's kind of a dark little life, she's found, being a paranoiac, but it's also not without its comforts—at least this way she's never alone, never insignificant, everlastingly secure in the knowledge there's someone out there who cares enough about her to give her life some consistency, to arrange it into a definite order, a coherent, comprehensible hell.

The other consolation, of course, is that there's no need for her to try to do anything in particular with her life, since it's all been foreordained to fail anyhow. In a world designed to thwart you, doing nothing isn't a matter of sloth, it's a matter of pride, the only possible expression of personal dignity. She could take up Buddhism, or bridge, or day trading, she supposes. There are all kinds of ways of doing nothing. But this one, for the time being, seems as good as any.

She doesn't really see much else she can do anyway. Without the help of their mother's authoritarian presence, she doesn't have a chance of talking Ivy back into the hospital. She can't even talk to Ivy on the phone without their conversation's being webcast far and wide and itself becoming part of the public drama. Ivy never leaves the apartment and very seldom even leaves the field of vision of the cameras in her bedroom and bathroom. Armed guards stand just outside the front door, and food and other supplies, including money—especially money, more and more of it—are delivered. As far as Ivy's concerned, her bedroom is the center of the universe. And even if Ursula were to resolve to give up on her sister once and for all, to let Chas have his way with her, to let her have her way with herself, where could she go and not have Ivy right there with her, ranting on the nearest computer screen, reminding her of the monstrosity she helped to create?

And then there's Javier. Her only real chance of seeing him again lies in her staying in Mid City, in case he's still here or, if not, in case he decides to return. But she's just about given up hope of either of these possibilities. He sold his apartment. He sent in his resignation. And now he's gone. Once again he has left his life behind, everyone he's known and everything he's built. But this time he's older, and he's left more behind than ever before, and she just doesn't see his finding the strength to start a whole new life all over again.

Somewhere a car alarm begins its unvarying cycle.

The tremulous wave.

The glottal stutter.

The dancing octaves.

The hopeful risers.

She wonders how many people throughout the world at this moment are hearing these same sound patterns, and how much more frustration, anxiety, and wistfulness are born with each new peal. She imagines Javier hearing a car alarm in whatever anonymous hotel room he's come to occupy. She imagines him sitting on the bed of his hotel room as the inescapable sounds of the car alarm wend through the window and wrap him ever more tightly in their silken shroud. He is paralyzed but still conscious. He will never move again. He knows this and waits to be devoured. All activity is restricted to his sad, panicked eyes and the deepening crease in his brow.

So Javier sits, somewhere. So Ursula sits. So the savage girl sits.

The sun spreads across the jagged rooftops. A bloody, runny egg.

A police car climbs the curb at the West Gate and creeps toward them along the cobbled path. As it nears, Ursula discerns two policemen in the front seat and someone in the back: the strawberry blonde, her face bright as a strawberry now as well, crying. She wipes the tears and snot from her face with a tissue as the car drifts past Ursula and stops just short of the savage girl's position on the park bench. The two cops get out, hands on their guns. The savage girl stares straight ahead, as though determined to will them out of existence. One of the cops is a woman, short and heavy-set, with dark hair protruding from the back and sides of her hat. The male cop says something to the savage girl, who doesn't respond. But when he takes another step toward her, in one sudden motion she jumps up to a standing position on the bench and brings the hatchet above her head, where she holds it ready. Simultaneously, both cops draw their guns, and from inside the car comes the stifled scream of the strawberry blonde.

Ursula is up and running toward them, not knowing what she'll do. The male cop looks in her direction, his gun still pointed at the savage girl. His head jerks back and forth between them. He takes a couple of quick steps away from the girl and turns, pointing his gun at Ursula. He is shouting commands at her. His voice is so tight and frayed she thinks his vocal cords might snap.

Ursula stops, raises her hands. Beyond the barrel of the pistol, the cop's eyes are round and his face is square, his bottom lip pulled tight to reveal his yellowing lower teeth, strangely small for such a large, fleshy head. The cop's teeth make her more sad than scared. If she moves, she will be shot, but she knows the situation is really not that much different from many others that people find themselves in every day: if you jump into the tracks, you die; if you turn the steering wheel toward oncoming traffic, you die. She probably won't move her hands and he probably won't shoot. The four of them stand still for a moment—Ursula and the savage girl with their arms raised above their heads, the two cops with their arms extended in front of them, the symmetry of it all rather sculptural—and then the woman cop begins yelling.

"Drop your weapon NOW let go of that ax you want to get shot?"

The savage girl doesn't drop the hatchet. She crouches a little, maybe preparing to pounce.

"Don't shoot her," Ursula says. "She doesn't know . . ."

"'Doesn't know' *what?*" the small-toothed cop shouts at her.

Ursula pauses. *Doesn't know language? Doesn't know what a gun is?* Can a person will herself into forgetting these things? Ursula doesn't know what the savage girl does or doesn't know.

"Is she crazy?" the cop says. "Do you know this woman? Is she nuts?"

She thinks she will say no but the word that comes out is *yes.* Her heart squirms behind the bars of her chest. She looks up at the savage girl, wishing she could apologize. The savage girl stares at the cop pointing the gun at her, who now backs off slowly. Her ravaged face has become strangely expressive. Her lips are bunched into a small, tight ring. Her eyebrows are lowered. Her eyes burn. The expression is rage.

"What about you?" the male cop says. "Are you nuts, too?"

"No, Officer."

"What are you doing running at me like that? You wanna die or something?"

"I'm sorry," Ursula says.

"If I stop pointing my gun at you are you gonna pull any battle-axes out of that big coat of yours?"

"No, Officer."

The gun comes down, but it stays in his hand as he backs up to the squad car and reaches in for the radio. Ursula slowly lowers her hands as he requests assistance.

"What has she done, Officer?" Ursula says.

"Isn't waving an ax at a police officer enough for you?"

"Yes, but—"

"How about killing this lady's dog and wearing it around like a bonnet?"

"Aha."

"Yeah. *Aha.*"

The former dog owner looks at her through the back window of the squad car. She has stopped crying, but her face is still puffy and red. Ursula looks back over at the savage girl. The dog's head is perched on top of her head at a jaunty angle now, wrinkled black nose and hollowed-out snout upturned, gray neck and back fur covering the back of the savage girl's own neck like a foreign-legion cap. Looking carefully, Ursula can make out patches of the gray fur elsewhere as well—around the girl's forearms and sewn together with different-colored hides into the tight-fitting coat she's made. The fur leggings and boots seem free of gray fur; they're mostly brown and black.

Now that the woman cop has backed off and lowered her gun slightly, the scarred material of the savage girl's face has begun to recongeal into an expression of calm, her eyes unfocusing slightly, as though the particularities of the cop were so offensive that the general outline were all she could bear. As the sirens in the distance grow louder, the male cop settles back against the squad car, watching the savage girl with raised eyebrows and scratching the back of his neck with his free hand. He does not immediately respond when the strawberry blonde gets out of the back of the squad car holding a nightstick by the wrong end. He does not yet move, but his face begins to register confusion as the woman screams and charges at the savage girl, a strawberry-blueberry blur, the leather thong of the raised, upside-down nightstick flying behind like a banner.

The savage girl turns to face her opponent, the ragged dog's head turning with her. She leaps from the bench, already swinging the hatchet as she lands. But the berry woman comes up fast inside the hatchet's arc, and the blade overreaches her goose down–padded shoulder as her nightstick connects with the savage girl's side. They grab each other's weapon arms. The savage girl drops her hatchet and grabs the berry woman's hair, and the berry woman kicks the savage girl's shin, and both of them scream even louder as they fall to the snow. As they roll, a tuft of strawberry hair flies free, and the dog's head is left behind in the snow as well, a deflated mass of sockets, nostrils, and fur.

The cops don't move, perhaps waiting for the two more police cars that are now making their way down the park paths. For a moment the sirens drown out the screams of the combatants, and then the cars stop and the sirens stop and two more cops emerge from each car, and the six of them move in together. For a moment Ursula can see the two women being dragged apart, and then they disappear again underneath the blue pants and black leather jackets. The women have stopped screaming, and now it's the cops' turn to scream, shouting instructions and threats, and then, all at once, the cops stand up, leaving the savage girl and the berry woman lying prone with their hands and ankles cuffed. The savage girl wriggles around, testing the strength of her restraints. Her cheeks and neck are streaked with bleeding fingernail welts. Ursula can't make out the berry woman's face, but her hair is a tangled, snowy mess, and her body convulses quietly with sobs.

"What happens to her now?" Ursula asks the original male cop, whose small teeth are again visible in the middle of his red, panting face.

He looks down at the savage girl, considering. "If she's on drugs, they'll get her off. If she's not on drugs, they'll put her on," he says.

Another cop within earshot smiles at the joke. Ursula pictures the savage girl in a dull green gown, queuing in a dull green corridor for her daily paper cup of brightly hued pills. Before long the right combination of pills will be found, enabling her to dress herself, albeit in mismatched clothing, and wander the streets aimlessly for three hours every afternoon. Eventually perhaps an even better combination of pills will be found, one that will push just the right buttons: a neon-blue pill to activate in her a desire to window-shop on Haro Avenue, a fluorescent-yellow pill to trigger the urge to work out at Bally's health club, a nuclear-orange pill to spark an interest in surfing the Internet, a kelly-green pill to make her want to drive a forest-green Saab convertible. And all she'll be lacking at that point is the one pill that would really finish the job of making her like everyone else: the pill to make her love a dog, to love a dog more than she could ever love a human being, to love a dog so much that she'll never *need* to love a human being, so much that she'll risk her life for it, or even just for the idea of it, just for the pure, shining, untarnished principle of the dog she loves.

Jellybeans

The theme is apocalypse fashion today on the *Ricki Lake Show*, and the prostitutes saunter onto the set in catsuits accessorized with thigh-high thermal stealth boots and matching over-the-elbow gloves. These draw excited applause from the studio audience. And when plush gray-white winter camouflage–patterned capes with especially tall collars are added to the ensemble, there are even gasps. But when one statuesque black woman appears on the stage in a galvanized-rubber cloak with a velour-lined burlap hood, and throws the cloak open to reveal a silver, form-fitting, décolleté radiation suit, people begin to rise from their seats to get a better look, starting a chain reaction that turns into a standing ovation. Heedless of the adulation, the tall prostitute calmly goes on showing off the accessories: an elegant pair of wraparound infrared goggles, the lenses no bigger than her eyes; a low-slung side holster, accentuating her hips, from which she draws a chrome-plated .38 special; and finally a hard-plastic bubble helmet that gleams iridescently in the spotlights as she puts it on. It gives her dark-eyed, angular face the look of a rare delicacy under glass. The winter-fashion purveyors have all adopted apocalyptic themes; whether it will be a nuclear winter or merely an ice age is uncertain, but the consensus is that the apocalypse will in any case be cold and, of course, very, very glamorous.

The studio audience applauds, gazing at the prostitute with rapture and even, in a few cases, tears.

Fade to a Lexus commercial animated in the style of van Gogh. The car races through a forest of wildly flaying green trees and giant blue dahlias, under a yellow, pinwheeling sun. The colors clash, but the brushwork is right, and for a moment Ursula remembers that feeling she had as a kid when she looked at the painter's sunflowers, and looked, and looked, staring them down, determined to be affected by a work of art, and for the first time in her life she *was* affected, and it wasn't what she'd anticipated at all. It was so much stranger. It made her feel small and vulnerable and humble. It told her that human life was something incidental in a universe made for far greater things than us, a universe staggeringly wilder, more alien, more terrible and beautiful than we could ever understand.

In the commercial a sexy career woman in a lapis lazuli dress suit drives the car, finding private gratification in the gentle curvature of the road and the controlled power of the engine, while the car's various technologies protect her from the roiling chaos outside. Technical animation, also in the style of van Gogh, demonstrates how the computer-assisted suspension cushions her from the precipitous hills, and how the shaded sunroof and the climate-control system shield her from the unrelenting divine sunlight, and how the custom-designed Bose stereo system insulates her from the insanity of that limitless silence. The sexy career woman drives off into the whirling, radiating sunset. It's a happy ending, a warm, safe feeling: a beautiful woman in a beautiful car in a beautiful landscape in an ugly television set in an ugly living room in an ugly world with so little beauty to go around that it seems downright soul-killing not to take what the commercial has to offer, not to snatch up whatever beauty there is, wherever one can get it.

She gets up off her legless couch, waits for the dizziness to subside. She didn't sleep more than an hour or two last night. After the police took the savage girl away yesterday afternoon, Ursula lingered in the park, playing with the equipment she'd left behind. There was a wineskin made from inner-tube rubber; a blowgun made from the pole of a floor lamp; darts made of pins, erasers, and feathers; and a collection of knives, pliers, needles, and thread. Ursula drank from the wineskin, blew darts at a nearby tree, whittled sticks. When midnight came and the police closed the park for the night, she carried the girl's belongings outside the gate and bedded down in her patchwork bedroll. It was warm enough, but it stank of sweat and decay and sported a squarish patch of wiry gray fur at the bottom that was all too recognizable. When dawn came, she slung the belongings over her back and walked home and turned on the television, which she's been watching ever since.

She heads into the kitchen and opens the door to the pantry, a room she uses not to store food or cooking supplies, of which she has virtually none, but rather to house the remnants of her former life: her art supplies, books, and slides. She reaches into a box of old sketchbooks and picks one out at random, an artifact of her high school years. She switches on the overhead light and begins turning the pages. It's been a long time since she looked at anything she did before the onset of her triptych phase, those obsessively repeated utopias and dystopias and purgatorial middle kingdoms, and she's surprised by how colorful and intricate these earlier pieces are. She didn't remember them that way. She can scarcely believe there was a time—really not that long ago—when she was capable of thinking and feeling in so many hues and in so much detail. She goes through the work again more slowly, recalling the sensibility she was trying to express, a sense of the dynamic life of all things, of consciousness on scales civilized society had never thought of: the consciousness of subatomic particles, the consciousness of bodily organs, of beehives, of cities, forests, oceans, galaxies. She imagined she was making art not for the present but for the future, for a society in the future that would understand these things, people who would understand that they were not unique and not independent and would not be bothered by these facts, because they would know, as a central tenet of their existence, that they were not alone.

Funny, she thinks, how all that exuberant mysticism of Javier's was once a part of her, too—a part she's since abandoned and forgotten.

She finds what she's looking for: an X-acto blade. She walks back to the living room, stopping at the secondhand bookshelf she bought shortly after moving in, still mostly devoid of books but brimming over instead with a miniature colony of action figures, stuffed animals, bird-call clocks, gyroscope paperweights, and checkout-counter horoscope booklets. Javier would pick up these impulse items and novelties for her wherever he went. She misses getting these little gifts. She misses his broken, vulnerable smile, and the way he held her hand tightly when he talked, and the way his eyes teared up like a child's at the first sign of trouble—a contagious condition, she's discovered, as her own now invariably do the same. They're doing it now, as she turns her and Javier's breakup over in her mind. She wonders how much her own personal neurosis had to do with her anger at him for drawing those pictures. It's possible he wasn't infatuated with Ivy.

It's possible he appreciated her beauty, her youth—possible that he found her attractive, even—without being infatuated with her. Men are always making this distinction. Maybe they honestly believe in it. And in a way those drawings were just making explicit the link Ursula had intuitively made from the start between Ivy and the savage girl. In a way Javier was simply being helpful, completing Ursula's own thought.

She pictures herself going off in search of him. Pictures herself finding him and committing herself to the project of his rejuvenation. He'll become the person he used to be, and they'll go on with their relationship as before. Eventually she'll marry him, join with him in a perpetual, mystical union, sacrificing a part of her own identity to take on a part of his, becoming henceforth no longer Ursula per se but half of the combination of the two of them, sharing everything, climbing so deeply into each other's lives that they'll never again be alone, they'll grow old together, wandering the streets, witnessing the continually unfolding beauty of the world, perfecting their love for humanity, for each other, for themselves.

She lets the reel unspool itself in the darkened theater of her mind until a car alarm goes off in the distance and she remembers the blade in her hand. Her plan is to cut her left underarm. The place she's aching to make the cut is the pit of her chest because that's where all the pain is. As recently as three days ago the pain in her chest was not something she would have called pain as such, not physical pain, but by the day before yesterday the two kinds of pain were becoming difficult to distinguish, and since yesterday she's been unable to tell the difference anymore. It is pain, it is here, and it is unbearable. Sometimes it feels like a tumor that needs to be carved from the cavity of her solar plexus. Other times it feels like a fluid buildup that a simple puncture would allow to ooze out of its own accord. But she's too afraid actually to put the knife in her chest. She's new at this and doesn't want to injure herself too badly. She's decided that if she makes a cut somewhere else and it hurts a great deal, if the pain is very sharp and lasts a while, then the pain in her chest, thus starved of her attention, might atrophy and go into remission. She isn't sure why, but it feels like it will happen this way. It's worth a try, anyway. She's decided on her underarm because it's a place where a scar won't mar her too noticeably but where she suspects a cut will hurt a great deal nonetheless.

The car alarm issues two subdued chirps and stops. She sits down on her couch and takes off the sweatshirt she's been wearing for the last few days. She's already shaved her underarms to make sure she'll be able to see what she's doing. The bottle of rubbing alcohol sits ready on the coffee table. She opens the bottle and pours some alcohol out over the blade, letting it spill onto the table. It's good to have a plan finally. After she does this, she thinks, maybe she'll have the strength and presence of mind to get her life in order, to get her place cleaned up, to wash and dress herself, to get a new job, a nicer apartment, new furniture, a nice, normal friend or two.

Almost immediately the car alarm takes up its familiar tune again. She sings along with it this time.

The tremulous wave.

The glottal stutter.

The dancing octaves.

The hopeful risers.

She picks up the blade, still singing. But then stops, wondering what the scar will look like. Still holding the blade, she gets up and walks around her desk into her little home-office space. On the monitor is a screen saver of Middle City being decimated by a steady bombardment of meteors. She presses the space bar, and the screen becomes a window into her sister's bedroom. Ivy sits on the floor on a pile of money, wearing a short silk camisole. Her hair is festooned with dollar bills, ruffled and knotted like little bows. To the right of the picture window a long list of names scrolls upward, taxonomized into their various levels of sponsorship by a series of headers:

> *Ivy's Fellow Shamans ($5,000 and up)*
> *Ivy's Soul Warriors ($2,500–$4,999)*
> *Ivy's Time Scouts ($1,000–$2,499)*
> *Ivy's Glamour Shock Troops ($500–$999)*
> *Ivy's Past-Life Lovers ($100–$499)*
> *Ivy's Spirit Familiars ($50–$99)*
> *Ivy's Tribespeople ($5–$49)*

For the most part the sponsors are individuals, though a few Internet start-ups have contributed as well, probably as a form of advertising. Beneath the scrolling list a message runs horizontally across a ticker:

> *Join the Fight. . . . Help Ivy Help You. . . . Join the Fight. . . .*

Meanwhile, above the list, the counter flickers: 446,737 people watching Ivy hold a flaming twenty-dollar-bill up to her face and light her cigarette with it; 446,802 people watching her toss the burning bill into a big metal salad bowl filled with ashes and butts; 447,010 people watching her light up another bill and walk toward the camera, her bare midriff filling the screen, watching her pass the flaming bill in a ritualistic circle around the long scar below her belly button. The scar is thin and pink. It is vulgar and delicate. Indelible and ethereal. Ugly and beautiful.

Ivy turns around, takes one step away from the camera, and pulls down her underwear, doubling over at the waist.

She pulls the panties back up, straightens out, walks away.

447,181 people watching.

Ursula grips the handle of the blade. A fiery metal ingot throbs in her chest. She will carve it out and feel light and cool again. She will become a brand-new person, a better person, transcendent, mystical, spiritual, shorn of cynicism, the person she always wanted to be. Like the savage girl, like Ivy, she will achieve a spontaneous, unreflective existence within her fantasies, living as simply and perfectly in her lies as a goldfish in its goldfishiness, a pebble in its pebblitude, a rhododendron in its rhododendrocity.

She raises the blade, but at that very moment Ivy turns and stares at her, looking suddenly so tired and old, like a tired-out old elephant locked in a lifelong cage. Her sister keeps staring into the camera, frame after frame of vacant eyes, darkly ringed, and with a chill Ursula begins to wonder if she's been totally wrong about Ivy all this time, wrong about her and about the savage girl, too. What if they don't live simply or perfectly in their delusions? What if neither of them, in fact, really believes her delusions at all? What if detachment, and not immersion, is the actual engine of delusion? What if they both observe their lives with even more detachment than Ursula does her own; what if they believe not in too many things but rather in too few, believing in nothing at all, living in a state of absolute disbelief, disbelieving the ground beneath their feet, the air they breathe, their breath itself, the existence of other people, the existence of themselves, the provenance of their very own thoughts, living in permanent exile from every aspect of their own lives, seeing the entirety of existence as nothing but lies, lies within lies on top of lies surrounding lies, no truth anywhere to be found . . . ? *Is this what Chas means by postirony?*

Ursula looks at the little blade in her hand, an animal fright welling up in her. She looks around at this apartment she no longer recognizes. She begins to pace. Her reflection in the bathroom mirror stops her cold. Half naked. Hair matted in some places, frizzed out in others. Eyes wide, face sallow, nose crinkling in disgust at the smell of herself, a sour stink of sweat. She doesn't believe what she sees. She doesn't believe it's her. What if she herself is going crazy? What if it's too late to stop it? What if she's *already* crazy?

She takes a trembling breath, then another.

The car alarm starts up again. She didn't register its stopping.

The tremulous wave.

The glottal stutter.

The dancing octaves.

The hopeful risers.

She raises her left arm and presses the X-acto blade hard into her skin and draws it along. Two inches. Pulls the blade quickly away.

Nothing happens for a second. Long enough for her to laugh.

Well, you've joined the trend, she thinks. Fashion's little slave.

The blood beads. Trickles. A rising throb of current.

This is what they wanted? This is what Ivy and the savage girl wanted?

The pain surges, and then she understands: the real pain, the real existence of her body, grotesquely needful, bleeding, in an ugly room. The rush is reality itself.

She grits her teeth. Why do all the women she knows hate themselves so much?

She moans in agony, a moan rising almost to a scream, and then she begins to cry, pressing her balled-up sweatshirt against the cut.

A loud thumping startles her. The door. She freezes, holding her breath.

"Ursula! Are you all right?"

Javier.

She looks around the debris of her living room.

Javier.

"Ursula!"

"Fine. I'm fine!"

The blood bleeds through the fabric of the shirt.

She wonders if she cut too deep, hit an artery or something. She's so stupid. She should have researched this more carefully.

"You don't sound fine, Ursula."

"I'm busy now," she says, her voice trembling. "Come back later, OK?"

"Ursula, I'm not going away unless you open this door and tell me you're OK face to face."

"Javier, just go—" She rises unsteadily to her feet, tripping and upending the coffee table.

"Ursula?"

"I'm OK," she calls out. "Just tripped, I'm fine."

"Open the door, Ursula." His voice is calm, certain. He's not going away.

"Give me a minute," she shouts.

She runs to the desk and gets a roll of masking tape from the drawer. Then she runs to the bathroom and crumples up a big wad of toilet paper. She has let the sweatshirt drop to the floor, and the blood now dribbles down her arm and her side. She presses the wad against her underarm and wraps the tape tightly around and around. She stuffs a towel in the sink, turns the water on, lets it soak, and then uses it to sponge herself off. There's blood on the waistband of her carpenter pants.

"Ursula?"

"Just a sec."

She runs to the bedroom, grabs a button-down shirt out of the hamper, and squirms into it as she heads to the door. Just as she's about to open it she spots the bloody X-acto blade on the coffee table, where she dropped it to pick up the sweatshirt. She runs back and grabs it, looks around, runs to the desk and shuts it in the drawer, runs back to the door and opens it.

Javier, in a forest-green wool overcoat, a cloud-white tie, a sky-blue shirt. All neatly pressed. Hair actually brushed, pulled back into a short ponytail. Face serene, eyes sympathetic, concerned.

"Um, this is Eeven," he says.

"Sorry? What?"

He motions downward with his eyes. Standing in front of him, not much taller than his waist, is a small black boy, eyes now downcast with embarrassment.

Javier repeats the boy's name and spells it for her. The boy is slight, with narrow shoulders, but his head is comparatively huge, a strange, hovering planetoid, mostly Afro, containing at its center a tiny face like a doll's, with a negligible bump of a nose and a mouth no larger than a quarter.

"He's ten years old," Javier adds.

Slowly the child looks up. His eyes are strikingly like Ivy's, not the same color but just as wide-set, so much so that when they blink in sync, it comes as a mild surprise: she was almost expecting them to operate independently of each other.

She clasps her shirt closed and clamps her arm against her side. Javier crouches down behind the child. "I told you she was beautiful," he whispers in his ear.

She hugs herself, fighting back tears as the absurd pain throbs in her armpit.

"I'm his big brother," Javier says. "It's this inner-city program. I applied months ago. It was pretty grueling—orientations, background checks, interviews. They even visited my place. Lucky I still had a place at the time. Anyway, it finally came through. So you're a big sister now, kind of."

From waist level the two of them look up at her, Javier admiring and Eeven fearful, making her doubly conscious of her appearance. She brushes the hair from her eyes, tries to will her face into some shape that won't necessarily give a child nightmares.

"Ursula," Javier observes, "you cut yourself."

Panicked, she looks down and checks her shirt. She doesn't see any blood.

"Let me see that," he says, standing up and taking her right hand. Her thumb, she sees, is bleeding. She must have picked up the X-acto blade the wrong way just now as she went to hide it. He licks his thumb and uses it to brush away the blood on hers, then inspects the cut, cradling her hand in both of his. The boy watches, their hands inches from his eyes.

"Just a little nick," Javier says. "Nothing to worry about. I'll get you a Band-Aid. You got some in the bathroom?"

She nods, hypnotized by the comfort emanating from his hands. She wishes she could curl up in those hands and sleep for a year. But when he lets go and begins to make his way past her, she remembers the bloody towel.

"No! I'll get it!" she says.

She retreats to the bathroom, reeling with fear and joy, her every sense overcharged, confused. She doesn't quite trust what's happening, doesn't quite trust her own mind. Her mind made her cut herself with an X-acto blade and then made Javier appear in her doorway like some kind of saintly apparition. But no, her mind had nothing to do with it. He's returned. He's really out there. And he really does look fine—better than fine: he looks like nothing bad has ever happened in human history.

She inspects her makeshift bandage. So far it seems all right. She allows herself to look in the mirror one more time and be frightened by what she sees there one more time. Keeping her left arm clamped at her side as much as possible, she washes her face, buttons her shirt, runs a brush through her hair, hides the towel in the cabinet beneath the sink, and finally, almost as an afterthought, sticks a Band-Aid on her thumb. She does all this as quickly as she can, half afraid he won't be there when she comes out.

But he is, and so is the strange child, the two of them now seated side by side on her couch. Javier has produced a bag of jellybeans and something

else, a red fruit of some kind, about the size of an orange, and is now placing the two foods on the coffee table in front of them. Ursula pauses in the
bathroom doorway, watching as Javier prompts the child with a question,
listens attentively to the answer, and responds. He emanates strength, stability, and calm. His face is kindly, his voice soothing, his entire attention
focused on the child. Then he looks up, and his eyes brighten at the sight
of her. Having just seen herself in the mirror, she can't for the life of her
understand why. She wonders if he's back to the way he used to be, back to
seeing the best in everyone, back to seeing the world on the brink of some
marvelous transformation. For his sake, she hopes so.

Javier opens the bag of jellybeans, offers Eeven some, and tosses a few
into his own mouth. He holds the bag out to Ursula, and to her surprise
she discovers herself to be deeply hungry. She sits down next to him and
takes a handful, and for a minute the three of them sit there chewing.

"Sorry the place is such a mess," she says to the child.

"'s OK," he whispers around the gob of jellybeans in his mouth.

"Sorry it's such a dump, too," she elaborates.

"This is nothing," Javier reassures her. "This apartment. This city. Just a
stopover. We're on our way out of here."

"We are?" she asks. God, she hopes so.

"You'll see."

"I will?"

He nods, popping a few more jellybeans into his mouth and putting his
arm around her.

"I smell bad," she warns him.

He draws her closer, and she leans into him, her head resting just inside
his shoulder. Eeven seems calmer now, seems perfectly content to be sitting there chewing the jellybeans with them, doesn't seem to care about
the messiness of her apartment or of her person; and this, combined with
the food settling in her stomach, helps make Ursula feel calmer as well.

The three of them swallow in unison, and then Javier picks up the red
fruit and rips it open, a pomegranate, and they all gaze at the clusters of
glistening red seeds. He picks out a seed, puts it in his mouth, moves his
jaw around for a while, then takes it out of his mouth and shows Eeven
how he's scraped off the pulpy red coating with his teeth. He gives half
the fruit to Eeven and holds the other half between Ursula and himself. She reaches for a few seeds, and he does, too, and their fingers brush
each other's inside the fruit. She puts the seeds in her mouth and sucks on
their sweetish, watery pulp. Eeven watches them, then follows suit, albeit

warily, and the three of them sit there moving their jaws around exaggerat-edly.

"Which do you think tastes better?" Javier asks Eeven after a moment. "Pomegranates or jellybeans?"

Without the slightest hesitation Eeven points to the bag of jellybeans.

Javier turns to Ursula. "What about you?"

"No contest," she says, reaching into the bag.

He nods. "I've always harbored a tremendous respect for the jellybean," he says, holding one up before their eyes. "It's a truly magical thing, the jellybean. You know what that word means, Eeven? *Magical?*"

Eeven nods.

"Tell me."

"When lightning come outa they eyes and you go *hwaaaah* try to karate chop but they fly up in the air," Eeven replies. Despite the drama of his imagery, the words themselves emerge curiously uninflected, compressed in a kind of rapid, breathless monotone.

Javier scratches his head and looks to Ursula for guidance. She offers none. But then he nods, a light going on in his eyes, and he turns back to the child.

"Yes," he says. "Yes, that's right. It's an unnatural power. Jellybeans have an unnatural power. They're supersweet and all different colors and flavors and so much easier to eat than pomegranates. Pomegranates aren't even half as sweet, and they're a real pain to eat, and they come only in one color and flavor. And you know, I've only eaten one other pomegranate in my life. And I've eaten many, *many* bags of jellybeans in my life."

She senses that he's talking partly to entertain the child but also partly to soothe her, and it's working. His voice, the warmth of his body, the child contentedly eating beside them—all these things she finds immea-surably calming. She chews a few more pomegranate seeds, spits them into her hand, and puts them on the table.

"But you know, the thing I realized," he says, "is that I like pomegran-ates better anyway. Jellybeans may be magical. But pomegranates are sub-lime. You know what that word means? *Sublime?*"

Eeven nods.

"You do? Tell me."

"When they eyeballs go *pshwshwshwhsh* and you cut off they hand but they hand go *vwoop* round your neck and you cut off they head but they head go *gneow* and bite your nose," he says matter-of-factly.

Javier ponders the response. Ursula laughs.

"Well, all right," he says. "Point taken. I guess there really isn't much difference. But there is one difference, I think. One big difference that makes all the difference. You don't just consume a pomegranate, you know? You enter into a compact with it. You scatter its seed. You make its life a part of you, and it makes your life a part of it."

As Eeven watches, Javier carefully picks the seeds off the table and puts them in his pocket. He looks at Ursula, offering her his old, crooked-toothed smile, his eyes cloudless, bright. He seems totally at peace. It strikes her that she's never seen him like this, neither manic nor depressed but somehow perfectly balanced. He sees it all, she thinks; he sees all the sadness of the world, but he can take it, he can contain it, and realizing this, she feels the weight in her chest lift with buoyant, giddy, almost irrepressible hope.

"I wonder what they'll be like, the next generation," he says to Ursula. "The ones who'll have no sublimity at all, only magic. What do you think they'll be like?"

She thinks about this. "A lot like us, probably."

"Like us," he agrees. "Only more so."

The three of them sit there side by side on the couch, saying nothing, staring at the opened, brightly jeweled fruit in Javier's hand.

Fishy

James T. Couch leans back in his chair, his pale, naked arms folded over the white towel tied snugly around his rib cage. The two eyes tattooed on his nipples stare wide and crazed at Ursula, while his real eyes, from behind his thick lenses, regard her with a wide and crazed imitation of the tattoo. His festively toothy smile, equally wide and crazed, gives him the overall demeanor of a paper dragon in a Chinese circus.

"Your finest Chianti," he announces to the crew-cut waiter. "And I think I feel fishy today. Bring me a fish. I don't care what kind. You choose. And bring my lovely friend a great big, thick steak of some kind. She looks like she hasn't had a decent meal in a while."

The waiter nods his beefy head and spins away.

"So, Ursula," Couch says. "Ursula, Ursula, Ursula." He scratches his bare chest with his insectile fingers. "I'm so glad you agreed to come meet me. We've got some *awfully* serious business to discuss. You've seen the latest development on the webcast, I assume."

Two salads float down to the tabletop. Couch is already chewing. Ursula can't think on what until she sees for the first time the basket of bread. The world has become crisper and jumpier, moments falling through the cracks here and there in that way they always do when she hasn't slept. Since Javier showed up yesterday she's been too excited to sleep, too impatient, she feels like she's been sleeping for years and now finally she has woken, and she doesn't want to waste another moment. The minute he left to take Eeven home, she took a shower, redid her bandage, put on some clean clothes, and went shopping for furniture. She bought a new couch and a big pillowy chair, a couple of throw rugs, a new coffee table, a new kitchen table, a bed and a mattress and a box spring and new linen and many other things, little kitchen and bathroom items she'd been meaning to get forever, been putting off getting, dreading all the time it would take, but she actually got it all done in a matter of hours, and for a little extra money the store delivered everything that very night. She split the purchase between two credit cards and paid the delivery men an extra hundred to take her old furniture down to the curb, and once all the new items were in place she began cleaning up her apartment like she'd never cleaned it before, scrubbing the tops of cabinets and behind the toilet and all those other out-of-sight places she'd previously chosen to ignore. She cleaned one-handed, no less, keeping her left arm pressed close against her side to help the healing along. She worked all night long, kept company by a portable radio she brought along from room to room. She hadn't enjoyed pop music in so long that she was surprised to find she still could. The tunes were ineffable and sweet like cotton candy, and she glutted herself on their sugar-spun yearning, singing along as she worked.

She didn't finish cleaning until after sunrise, but still she felt incredible. Her apartment, like the day, was clean and new. It still needed some stuff—nicer window curtains, a paint job—but she knew she could knock these things out in short order, and for now it would certainly serve. This place was only a stopover, as Javier had said, but it didn't have to be an unpleasant one. She could barely wait for him to see it. Maybe when he did, she thought, he'd feel so at home he'd want to move in, at least until they got new jobs and could afford something better. She wished he could see it right now. She was tempted to go across town to the Pangloss, where it turned out he'd been staying all this time, and drag him back over here to take a look. But he'd told her he had some things to take care of—it was time for him to prepare himself for the future, he said—and they'd made plans for lunch at the hotel in two days. The prospect of the wait disappointed her a little but also made her feel glad, glad to know that he, too, was taking care of things, putting things in order. And soon they could face the world together, look for work together, take Eeven to the zoo and baseball games together, help each other rebuild their lives. She didn't even care whether they'd be lovers. They could be friends. That would be fine, too. He was a good friend. He hadn't abandoned her. Just like he'd promised he wouldn't the morning after they first made love.

She was trying to decide upon the most productive way of spending her day when Couch called and implored her to drop everything and come have lunch with him. He said it was urgent, critical, an absolute emergency. His tone of voice was playfully mock-nervous, purposely undermining the words, as though deriding the very notion that a hardened sophisticate like himself could get worked up about his job. In the end she opted to trust the words rather than the tone and agreed to meet him.

"Earth to Ursula," Couch says now, passing a hand back and forth in front of her. "Do I assume wrong? I think I do. You haven't been watching, have you? Ivy's destroying the money. *Destroying* it."

He forks the dark, oily leaves into his mouth, smiling as he chews.

"Sure," she says. "She lights her cigarettes with twenty-dollar bills."

"Oh, no no no," he says with a little laugh. "You haven't been paying attention lately. That's just her warm-up routine, now. For her main act she's making little campfires out of twenty-dollar bills and setting them ablaze with her big gold lighter. She's making little stacks of twenty-dollar bills to try and see how many she can tear in half at once. And if you tune in at just the right time, you can see her wipe her little behind with twenty-dollar bills and flush them down the toilet!"

"That must be quite entertaining," Ursula says.

"'Entertaining,' that it is. It is that," Couch agrees, dredging a piece of bread through an olive-oil slick on his plate. A woman with jet-black hair wearing a long, blood-red smock takes a seat beside him on a small folding stool and begins rubbing an alcohol pad on his left bicep as he eats. Her nose is rhinoplasted, long but scooped the way only short noses are naturally.

"But it gets better," he goes on, his mouth full of food. "The other day a couple of FBI agents came by the office. They're mad as hell!"

Ursula looks up. "FBI agents?"

"They're threatening to lock Chas up!"

Couch beams at her with delight, and she feels herself returning the smile, a sudden, dizzying lightness taking hold of her.

"They are?" she asks.

He nods.

She can't believe it. Someone is finally coming to help.

"So they really think what he's doing to Ivy is illegal?" she asks.

Couch guffaws. "Oh, now, that's *good* you think that. That's so *very* good of you. But to answer your question, *hell no,* you silly goose. Not what he's doing to Ivy—what Ivy's doing to the money! She's destroying currency. Which, aside from being rude, is unpatriotic, highly illegal, and, the way the Feds see it, an act of economic terrorism! And they're holding Chas accountable. They think he's a Communist! They want to fry him like the Rosenbergs!"

"A Communist," Ursula repeats, getting her mind around the concept.

Couch chuckles. "Chas! A Communist! Rich, ain't it?"

She shakes her head and laughs. In spite of her disillusionment, she can't help seeing the humor in this.

The woman fans Couch's arm with a sheet of card stock to dry the alcohol, then takes a tube of K-Y Jelly from a silver cart parked beside her, squeezes out a dollop onto a ruby-nailed finger, and rubs it over the same area. Couch glances down at his arm, then down the front of the woman's smock.

"So can't he just apologize and shut the stupid thing down?" Ursula asks.

"Well, he could, but then he wouldn't be Chas. He's dragging his feet, talking to lawyers. Every extra day he keeps the thing going, viewership goes up and money pours in. He's proving his theory. That's all he cares about. He doesn't care that it can't last. He doesn't care that the sponsors are bugging out and the last of our regular clients are running like hell. The Gap just dropped us like a hot potato, even after telling us they're going to follow us word for word on the 'Conspiracy against the Children' report. We're getting badmouthed on radio call-in shows, on talk shows— *Jesus,* even the E! network thinks we're creepy. Which is all fine and synergistic as far as ratings go, but when the moral-outrage industry is done having us for lunch, it'll hand us over to the camera-mugging, I-can-fight-communism-as-good-as-the-next-guy career politicians, and those people will have us for dinner. This couldn't be happening at a worse time, Ursula. Chas really broke the piggy bank promoting this website. He's put the company in debt, and not just to me personally but to several far less forgiving creditors. At the moment there's enough money in that room to pay off enough of our debt to make it manageable and keep us afloat. But between Ivy's flushing it down the toilet and Chas's courting a costly and protracted legal defense, you, me, and Ivy aren't going to have a pot to piss in by the time this blows over."

With a histrionic flourish he wipes his high, flushed forehead with a table napkin, distancing himself, through parody, from what Ursula perceives to be a clearly heartfelt anxiety. The red-smocked woman presses a sheet of tissue paper to Couch's bicep, smoothing it on with her fingers. When she pulls it off, the design sticks to his arm: a woman in short shorts, long legs, spiked heels, no shirt, with breasts shaped and dotted like a pair of dice, and a barbed tail snaking out of her behind.

"Well," Ursula says. "Ivy listens to you, for some reason. Can't you convince her to go and do something a little less disruptive? Can't you convince her she can save the world through macramé or basket weaving or something?"

"She doesn't trust me anymore," Couch says sighing.

"Why not?"

"She says I'm in *cahoosion* with the Imagineers. I don't have to tell you how much it hurt me to hear her say that."

"Well, what do you want *me* to do? You think she'll listen to me?"

Couch holds up his hands. "Let's just assume," he begins slowly, "just for the sake of argument, mind you, that I had a surefire little idea, an idea about a little speech you could make to Chas. And let's just assume that this surefire little speech *could not fail* to convince our dear old boss that it'd be in his own best interest to step down—you know, sign over the company, for a nominal buyout fee, of course; I mean, we're not *monsters* or anything—but anyway, to pass the baton, so to speak, to make way for some new leadership in the outfit."

In front of Ursula steam begins to rise from a steak au poivre that has just appeared. A thin blond waitress in a white shirt and apron manipulates a knife and fork over Couch's plate, cutting his fillet into bite-sized pieces while he eyes Ursula through the steam. He has a plan, she thinks. From the sound of it, an underhanded one. And he needs her help to carry it off.

"'New leadership,'" she says. "Meaning you?"

Couch performs a little pantomime of modesty, looking down at his plate and blinking. "Well . . . I'm really honored you'd think of me in this connection, Ursula. And what's more, by the way, I must compliment you on your sound business acumen."

"Sure," she says, playing it cool. "That would be pretty nice for you, wouldn't it, James? You'd not only get to run the company, you'd get back all the money you loaned him—and it was a great deal of money, wasn't it? Close to half a million dollars, if I remember correctly. But I guess that's just a drop in the bucket to a rich man like you, owning a whole lake and all that. I guess you'd probably just forgive the loan outright and use the money to repay Ivy for her services?"

"I . . . er . . . well, actually, Ursula, I'm not quite so rich as all that. Or nearly so liquid." He tugs at an imaginary collar, loosens an imaginary tie, while at his side the red-smocked woman continues to fan-dry the design on his arm. "I made that loan out of desperation. I had to take out a second mortgage on my lake, in fact, just to make it. Chas promised me quadruple my money back in a year. You see, that lake, well—oh, well, you don't want to hear about my little financial problems."

"Oh, no, James, please, unburden yourself. I'm here for you."

He treats her to one of his relatively anxious, lower-teeth-only smiles. "Well, that lake—you see, when my grandfather was getting on in years, getting more than a little senile, clearly, he turned into one of those kooky nature nuts all of a sudden and put in one of those horrendous conservation-easement clauses on the lake property, stipulating that it could never be subdivided. Of course, I've got a team of lawyers working to overturn the thing. I'm pretty sure they can do it, but it could take another couple of years. Anyway, to make a long story short, I'm at the end of my credit, and if I don't get that loan back and then some, I'll have to sell off the property before the clause is stricken, which means I'll end up getting not even a twentieth of its real value. You see what a . . . what a *shame* that would be, right? Of course, I'll make sure Ivy gets properly reimbursed for her work, in due course. You have my word of honor on that. But in the meantime the important thing to keep in mind is that the website will get shut down, and you'll get your sister back."

Couch presents her with an earnest, puppy-dog face as the waitress in the white apron ties a starched white bib around his neck.

Ursula shrugs, hiding her excitement at the prospect. "If the FBI's getting involved," she says, "I'll get Ivy back anyway, won't I?"

"That could take months, Ursula. Who knows what kind of things she'd be believing by then?"

This may be true, but she takes care not to look impressed by the argument. Couch continues to look at her as the red-smocked woman tilts his seat back into a semireclining position. Meanwhile, the blond waitress skewers a piece of fish with a fork and, holding a spoon underneath to catch any juices, carries it to Couch's mouth. He chews quickly and swallows.

"And also, of course," he says, "you'd have your job back."

"Working for you? No thanks. No, I think I'm better off just washing my hands of all of you."

Couch coughs. The waitress wipes his mouth. "I see," he mutters.

The woman in the red smock raises the left armrest into position and guides his arm into place. She then opens a lacquered wooden box on the silver tray and using a pair of long silver tongs extracts a writhing leech. She sets the leech against Couch's shoulder, just above the design. It quickly affixes itself to his flesh while he regards the process, his face undisguisedly troubled now. He remains silent for a moment and then, rallying his impossible grin, turns back to face her.

"You know, Ursula, one thing that's been bugging me about this little idea of mine is that I really don't know if I'm enough of a . . . well . . . a *people person*," he says, smiling broadly, "to be out front running the company on my own. Really, I'm too terribly shy. I'm much better as a behind-the-scenes kind of guy. Now, you, on the other hand, you've got the kind of panache it takes to be a good front man for an outfit like this. So how about it? How about seeing yourself as president and co-owner of Tomorrow Limited?"

Ursula stares at him wide-eyed, her effort to appear nonchalant forgotten.

"You're kidding" is all she can manage to say.

The red-smocked woman places a second leech below the design on Couch's arm.

"As you see," Couch replies with a little laugh, "you're in an excellent bargaining position. I can't pull this off without you, and I don't know what more I can offer. The company isn't worth terribly much in its present condition, of course. We'd be starting out with some debt, and it might be an uphill battle at first to regain our client base. But with a little of the old elbow grease there's no reason we couldn't be in the black again in a couple of years' time."

He looks at her searchingly. She lets him wait, picking up her knife and fork and cutting into her steak. For the first time in days, years, maybe for the first time ever, Ursula feels totally in control of her life. She knows she'll help him carry out his plan, whatever it is, if there's any chance at all it'll get that website shut down and Ivy safely back in her care. She knows, furthermore, that she's in a position to make Couch pay for her services. But she also knows she has no interest in running a trend-spotting agency, not with James T. Couch or anyone else. She's through with marketing. This much she's sure of, even if she hasn't the faintest idea what she wants to do instead.

She looks around the room, stalling for time. At a nearby table a middle-aged woman with blond ringletted hair lies prone on a padded, inclined bench. Her earth-tone cashmere sweater is pulled up, revealing the small of her back; a white towel like the one Couch wears is draped over the back of her legs, leaving one buttock bared. As a waiter feeds the ringletted woman spoonfuls of soup, a burly man in a red smock extracts a metal rod from an open cart full of hot coals. At the end of the rod is a brand glowing bright orange, too bright for Ursula to make out the design or even discern whether it is image or text. Holding the rod firmly in both hands, the red-smocked man presses the brand into the woman's buttock. The woman lets out a shriek, not quite loud or long enough to cover the sound of sizzling flesh, and the sight reminds Ursula of her own recent scarification, so vividly that her underarm throbs with pain. The man removes the brand and then, before Ursula can make out the pattern of the red welt, slathers the woman's wound over with white ointment. It looks so cooling, so soothing, the man's fingers caressing the salve into her skin, that Ursula's own sympathetic pain instantly subsides.

Then she smiles, the answer having come to her.

"Javier," she says. "I want Javier to be the president."

Couch barks out a laugh that stops abruptly when she doesn't join in and he sees she's not kidding.

"Javier? Ursula, look, Javier's a good field agent, but, well, you know, a president has to inspire confidence, make strategic-type decisions, you know, that sort of thing."

"You haven't seen him lately," she replies calmly, cutting herself another hunk of steak. "He's transformed himself, James. It's incredible. You'd barely recognize him. He's stable, he's responsible, he's all into preparing himself for the future—he's even doing some inner-city program, taking care of a kid. I mean it, James. Javier would be perfect. And you said yourself the clients like him."

Couch thinks about this. "Well, that's true. He's certainly personable enough. And I could still take care of all the tricky wheeling and dealing stuff, I suppose." He grins. "Sure. President Javier. That works for me, Ursula. I'm a reasonable man."

"And we have to talk about my fee for services rendered—"

His grin melts into a theatrical pout.

"—which I'll be requiring forthwith."

The woman in the red smock turns on the tattoo gun and presses its rapid-fire needle into Couch's arm.

"Um," he says, "*how* forthwith?"

There is no blood, just ink and then clear fluid weltering from the punctures in the skin. No blood. The man doesn't bleed.

"Get out your checkbook," she says.

Business

Chas stands facing her in a white bathrobe, his neck and face red, heavy bags under his eyes, his wet gray hair combed back.

"We need to talk," Ursula announces. Her heart is pounding. Unless she's bleeding again, the bandage in her armpit is already sopping with sweat. He hesitates. Clearly, he doesn't want to talk to her. But he leaves the door open, turning and walking back toward the kitchen.

She follows him in. His apartment is undecorated, modernistic and swank, with few interior walls and an almost paralyzing overabundance of open space. A wall-to-wall window looks out across the volcano crater at the crest of the Black Tower, which at the moment nudges the underside of a lone cloud like a gun muzzle to the chin of heaven. The stainless steel dining table is piled high with take-out containers. A set of free weights takes up a choice area by the window, gleaming in the sunlight. In the far corner a very large computer monitor sits on another stainless steel worktable; on the screen a cartoon Middle City is being slowly eaten away by acid rain.

She takes a seat at the kitchen counter. He keeps his back to her as he fiddles with the coffee maker. His big stone block of a head juts forward as though it might slide from his massive, hunched shoulders. He looks worn out, even more so than when she saw him in his office. She wonders if he's been sleeping as little as she has lately, wonders whether it's the company's recent troubles or Ivy's round-the-clock performances that have been keeping him up. His haggard and persecuted appearance makes her feel momentarily ashamed of what she's about to do.

"Go ahead," he mutters. "Talk."

"I've come to make you an offer, Chas," she says. "It's not a bad one, under the circumstances. And I think by the time we're done talking you'll see you're in no position to refuse."

Chas doesn't look up from the percolating coffee, but he stops moving.

"'An offer,'" he says. "What kind of offer?"

"An offer to buy your company."

He turns to face her, and she looks quickly down into her new briefcase, purchased specially for the occasion, trying to draw from it the confidence she desperately hoped it might give her. She takes out a stack of papers and a cashier's check and lays them side by side on the counter. She readies a steely stare and looks up. But his stare is steelier than anything she can muster. Like a crowbar prying open her brainpan. Her eyes snap back down to the papers.

"I have here a check for a hundred thousand dollars," she goes on, her nervous energy tripping the rehearsed words into motion. "From what I understand, you put fifty thousand dollars of your own money into Ivy's bedroom. So what you see here is a check for twice that amount."

In the periphery of her vision she sees him approach. He stands opposite her and sets his palms down on the counter.

"Yes," he says evenly. "That's twice what I put in the room. And a small fraction of what the company is worth."

"Be that as it may," she says, "that's the highest your prospective buyer is prepared to go. It's going to take a lot of work to free the company from all the debt and bad publicity you've saddled it with. Tomorrow may not be profitable again for some time."

She feels him looming over her.

"My prospective buyer," he says quietly. "Who would that be?"

"That would be James T. Couch," she says. "As you can see from the check."

In the ensuing silence the back of her neck charges with static electricity, the same feeling that she once got driving through what would momentarily become a lightning field.

"And why," Chas says, "did James T. Couch send you, of all people, to waste my time with this ridiculous offer?"

Because the smarmy bastard was scared shitless, she thinks, but says instead, "Because I'm the only one who can properly underscore the dire consequences of your failing to accept."

He leans down, bringing his head within inches of hers. His narrowed eyes bore into her.

"These 'dire consequences,'" he says slowly. "Please explain, Ursula."

"You're aware, I take it, that the FBI is building a case against you for willful destruction of currency."

"Frankly, I wish they *would* prosecute me," he says. "But they never will. They know if they do they'll just be giving us free publicity. The money'll come rolling in by the truckload."

Ursula takes a breath.

"Which is probably why they're getting ready to bust you on kidnapping charges instead."

Chas cocks his head, startled. "Kidnapping?"

"They think Ivy's the next Patty Hearst," she says. "And they think you're the Commie scumbag who's brainwashed her into committing acts of economic terrorism."

He stares at her, his eyes wide and incredulous. She holds her breath, not daring to move lest some random bit of body language betray her.

He shakes his head. He's not buying it.

"That's positively asinine," he says.

She flinches but holds his stare.

"What a bunch of baboon butts," he goes on. "To think our tax dollars support those shitheels."

He's buying it, she realizes. The story fits snugly into his overall conception of human intelligence.

"It doesn't sound all that asinine to me," she says, her nervousness putting a sharp edge in her voice. "In fact, to me it sounds pretty damn close to the truth. And with my help they say they won't have any trouble making the charges stick. They're pressuring me to testify against you, Chas. And you know, I'm really having a hard time figuring out why I shouldn't."

Chas leans forward, flustered. The accusation seems to hurt him more than she anticipated. "Ursula, listen to me. Whatever else you end up believing about me, you've got to understand, except for getting Couch to convince her to model again, I never put any ideas into your sister's head. If anything, *she* put ideas into *mine*."

"Well, you know, Chas, I've been working pretty closely with you and Ivy both, and I'm beginning to remember the course of events very differently from you!"

Her tone has become increasingly shrill with agitation and she's ended up yelling in his face, her shame and fear turning to rage.

"You're blackmailing me," he says, astonished.

"I want my sister back!" she shouts, a feverish tremor in the words. She's half crazy with adrenaline. A part of her even hopes he'll spring on her, just so the tension in her can find some release. She'll put up a good fight. She'll scar him for life before she goes down.

But he doesn't spring on her. To her utter bewilderment his thin lips curl into a half smile, and his eyes sparkle as he lets out a voiceless laugh, a slight rush of air. Then he turns, walks back to the coffee maker, and pours out two cups.

"Cream and sugar?" he asks.

She's too startled to reply at first. He turns and looks at her questioningly.

She swallows, feeling for her voice. "Yes. Please," she says.

He opens the refrigerator, takes out a carton of half and half, and pours some into both cups. He seems more than anything else relieved to have found out she doesn't actually believe he brainwashed her, relieved to know he's dealing with blackmail, pure and simple.

"I started taking cream a while ago," he informs her. "Helps a little. Think I'm getting an ulcer. Been working too hard, I guess. Taking it all much too seriously."

He brings her cup over along with a sugar bowl and spoon, sets them gently in front of her, then gets his own cup, carries it around the counter, and sits down in the stool next to her.

"Nice briefcase," he remarks, caressing it lightly with his fingertips. "Very businesslike. Lambskin?"

She nods, feeling herself blush.

"Appropriate," he muses. "Ursula Van Urden. Wolf in sheep's clothing."

He brings the cup to his lips. "I probably need a little vacation anyway," he says, taking a sip. "Damn. That first cup of coffee. Really clears your head."

She says nothing. His sudden solicitude is more terrifying than his previous anger. It's a trap of some kind, a trap she can't see but knows is there, a pair of steel jaws already underfoot, all set to snap her in half. A frantic electricity sears her nerves, and there's no release for it now. She feels Chas's warm bulk pressing against her side as the two of them shift and settle into the same pose, forearms resting on the countertop, shoulders hunched, staring at the range top.

"OK," he says, his tone measured, reasonable. "I can see you've got me in a bind. I can see you're gonna go through with this fiasco to the bitter end if you have to. So what do we do now?"

She stiffens, feels her muscles getting sore. The trap is there, all set and waiting; it has to be. But what can she do? She reaches for the coffee but sees that her hand is trembling and quickly pulls it back. There's no choice now. She has to go forward.

"All you have to do is sign these papers, and then you're done," she says.

He nods, angling his whole upper body toward her to make a study of her face.

"And what if I say I need some time to think it over?"

She faces him squarely. "There's no time left, Chas. If you don't sign these papers now, I'll walk right out your door and right over to my appointment at the Phillips Federal Building."

"I see," he says, his eyes completely placid. "And what makes you so sure you'd make it as far as my door?"

He says this so softly—almost seductively, with that little pursed smile on his lips—that it takes her a moment to process the threat. Then her heart jumps, slams against the wall of her chest. And in the midst of her utter terror, she can't help smiling, that scared, guilty smile of hers that surfaces at the most inopportune moments.

"Come on, Professor," she says, going with the smile, struggling to keep her voice even. "Cut the tough-guy routine."

They stare at each other, smiling. After a minute Ursula begins to admit to herself that his smile seems genuine. The discovery makes her more confused than she's ever felt, but also a little less afraid, and she begins to breathe again.

Chas nods, as though acknowledging some change in her expression, and then laughs. He picks up the papers and begins to sign after the *X*s without reading so much as a word.

"The point is, Ursula," he says as he signs, "you don't know *what* I'm capable of."

The words are as matter-of-fact as they are nebulous. But he's signing.

"Well," she ventures, "you didn't know what I was capable of, either."

"No," he says, a hint of ruefulness in his smile. "I knew. You're a lion, kiddo. I told you. I knew it all along."

He signs the last paper with a flourish.

"No hard feelings, Ursula," he says, and to her astonishment she sees sincerity in his eyes. "And tell my worthy adversary James T. Couch I wish him the best of luck with his new company."

He picks up the check, looks at it with amusement, folds it neatly in half, and drops it into the pocket of his robe.

Ice

In the cab Ursula and James T. Couch sit very still, staring straight ahead. Slowly Couch turns his head to face her. She glances over and finds his face plasmatic with teeth.

"Hey, Ursula."

"What?"

"You look pretty good in that suit. That's the one Javier got you, right?"

She nods.

"It really says *I mean business.* Very sexy, too."

She has nothing to say to this. Her thoughts are humming along fine without him. She still can't quite believe she stood up to Chas like that. She repeats the events of the last half hour in her mind again and again and has just as much trouble believing it each time. She keeps looking for the trap, wondering why it never sprang. He tried to scare her; was that the trap? She honestly can't think of anything else he could have done under the circumstances, but still she doesn't quite believe it. But that must have been the trap. And she avoided it. She called him Professor. That was good. She showed him she wasn't afraid. Which of course she was. She was terrified. He must have seen that. But all the same, she stood up to him. She made herself immovable. And he saw she couldn't be scared off. And he accepted his defeat with grace. And he actually congratulated her. He really did seem proud of her. She still can't quite believe the rest of it, but she has to admit he really was proud of her; she saw it in his face. So that was what happened. Or was it? It was. It had to be. The signed papers are right here, safe in her briefcase. And here she is as well, safe in the back of a cab on her way to the Pangloss, safe in a daze with her newfound sense of power, her sister soon to be freed, money in the bank, a company for Javier to run. It's really happening.

"Hey, Ursula, can I ask you something?"

"What?"

"Have you ever *done it* in a taxi?" His eyebrows inchworm over his glasses. His high-wattage smile heats up his cheeks.

"Not that I can remember."

"Oh, ho! So I've got to get you drunk, is that it?"

The eyes of the cabdriver swivel toward her in the rearview.

"You'd have to get me a lot more than drunk, James."

"OK. What else? You name it!"

"Get me a lobotomy—that might help your chances."

"*Touché!*" He shakes his head, still smiling. "Oh, I'm sorry. Intrigue just gets my blood flowing."

The cab turns onto Conein Avenue, and Ursula tries rolling her head around, but it's too painful; her shoulders are as taut as steel cables. Excitement wells up in her as she thinks about seeing Javier. *President Javier.* She wonders how he'll take the news. He won't believe it at first. She'll have to convince him it's true. He'll look from her to Couch, and gradually he'll start to believe, and he'll start smiling that heartbreaking smile of his, and his eyes will tear up, as hers are doing now just picturing the scene.

The car slows, pulls to the curb outside the Pangloss. It seems darker than when they got in the cab a few minutes ago. James takes a twenty-dollar bill from his wallet and slips it into the cabby's outstretched hand. The fare is $19.65. "Keep the change, my friend, you deserve it," he says, patting the man's shoulder steak of a shoulder. He pushes Ursula out onto the sidewalk, hops out behind her, and shuts the door just in time to muffle the cabbie's curses.

"You're a real smooth operator, James."

"You're too kind," he replies, sliding his arm under hers as they traverse the hotel's gargantuan atrium. A glass-walled elevator arrives; they board, and immediately the lobby floor sinks away, a living mandala of shopping, dining, loitering. They look up and watch the rotunda ceiling approach, the red, green, and blue suns blazing merrily away in the artificial sky like the lights of some cosmic projection TV set.

They disembark on the fortieth floor and make their way along the curved terrace walkway, the conveyor-belt product display keeping time with them just below the balcony rail, a bulky platinum watch and then a silver-lined fog-free shaving mirror happily riding along on dark velvet pillows. Far below, on the atrium's floor, the burnished steel of the Pangloss Restaurant gleams in the indoor lighting, each of its four sides resembling a giant silver trailer home seen lengthwise. When they get to Javier's door, Couch sidles up beside Ursula and sneaks his hand up to the small of her back. She reaches behind her, removes the hand, and knocks.

No answer. She knocks again.

"Javier?"

They wait a moment longer, then Couch tries the knob. "It's open," he whispers. He gives it a push and lets it swing inward.

"Javier?" she calls out.

They step in. A suite, with white carpeting, white furniture, pearl-white walls. The view from the floor-to-ceiling windows takes advantage of the hotel's odd position at the foot of Conein Avenue, looking straight up the canyon of office buildings to the volcano's peak. Stark against the sky at the very top of the avenue, the statue of God stoops rheumatically atop the volcano's rim. The soot has recently been cleaned from his face, making his features—the bulging eyes, the broom-bristle eyebrows, the two oversize front teeth—discernible for the first time in years. His translucent, twin-lobed head pulses its usual dull red light, barely visible in the bright-gray daylight.

Couch lets out a little whistle, looking around.

"Dude. Killer digs," he says, taking off his fitted leather overcoat and tossing it on the couch. His unflattering purple muscle T-shirt reads, simply and inexplicably, *SHOOBY-DOOBY.*

"How *does* the man afford it?" he exclaims. "That's what I want to know. This place must run him four hundred a day at least."

Ursula has wondered about this herself. He's probably living off the proceeds from the sale of his condo. But he must be going through the money pretty fast. She walks into the bedroom, calling out his name.

The bed is made, the room empty.

"Ja-vi-er," she hears Couch calling, knocking on a door. *"You in there?"*

A large cardboard box sits on the white dresser, its top open. She walks over and looks inside, finding a number of items: A laptop computer. A few boxes of educational software and computer games. A floppy-eared silver robot dog. A pair of silvery, high-tech-looking, child-sized sneakers. A bag of jellybeans. An envelope, addressed to her.

"Ursula," Couch calls out. "Um, I . . . I found him."

Something odd about his voice. The way he paused.

A cold sickle of fear cuts through her.

"James?" she calls out, moving toward the sound of his voice.

"In here."

The bathroom door is open, and Couch stands just inside, looking down and to the left.

She edges in, then starts to scream but abruptly stops, unable fully to process what she's seeing. The sight is too strange. Javier is lying in the Jacuzzi, immersed in ice cubes. The only parts of him not entirely submerged are his bent knees and his dead, gray-white face. Empty plastic bags that once contained the ice litter the tile floor around the tub.

"What the *hell*," Couch murmurs.

Javier's eyes flutter open, then close, and Ursula shrieks.

"Jesus," Couch says. "He's still alive."

"*Get him out of there!*" she screams.

Couch shakes his head, still blinking with disbelief, then bends down and begins digging through the ice. He pulls Javier's arms up to the surface, first one, then the other, then grabs hold of them and starts to tug his body out, struggling mightily against the weight of the ice. Ursula moves in to help, digging away at the cubes, and Couch finally hauls his torso clear. Javier is dressed in a black suit, a white shirt, a scarlet silk tie, all soaked through from the melting ice. His head, neatly combed and slicked, lolls to one side.

"Javier! Javier!" she shouts.

Couch slaps his bloodless face repeatedly as Ursula shouts.

His eyes flutter open again. His bluish lips move.

"What's he saying?" Couch says.

Ursula bends down to hear but can't make anything out.

"Help me get him out of the tub," she pleads.

Together they heave and drag his limp body all the way out, his heels falling first against the tiles as they lay him down on the bathroom floor. Couch's foot knocks an empty pill bottle, which skitters under the sink. He reaches over and retrieves it.

"Sleeping pills," Couch says, an odd, troubled grin on his face. "I guess . . . I guess I'll call an ambulance."

She kneels beside Javier and rubs his face, trying to warm it. She loosens his tie, rips his shirt open, presses her hands against his clammy chest. His body is cold, limp. She clambers on top of him, pressing her entire trembling length against him. She puts her ear to his chest, her hands to his neck. She can't tell if there's a pulse. She begins to shake uncontrollably.

"Ursula," he whispers.

She looks up at his face, not knowing if he really spoke. She presses her ear to his chilly lips and feels them moving.

"I can't hear you," she sobs.

This time she hears.

"Freeze me," he whispers.

Praying

Javier sleeps surrounded by machines, ventilating his lungs, drip-feeding his veins, stimulating his brain stem with gentle sound waves, committing each heartbeat to memory on some deep electromagnetic abacus. For millennia, Ursula thinks, our wayward, lonely race has been dreaming of an entity that would cherish our existence enough to number our heartbeats, and here it is, of sorts. Perhaps the day is not far off when we'll have machines capable of counting our good deeds; capable of sensing when we're in a down sort of mood and stepping in to show us, with full-color flow charts, precisely how special we are; capable of loving each of us more perfectly than we've ever succeeded in loving one another, or ourselves.

He is brain-dead, the doctors say. Ursula knows it isn't true, though. His poor, foolish brain is just overtaxed; he's resting it.

The amount of frostbite, they say, was minimal. He may lose a few toes, nothing more.

It always happens on the upswing, they say. Not during the depression but after, when the energy is there to make the plan and carry it out.

His letter to her was not a suicide note, or so he insisted in the letter itself. It was a set of instructions for his body to be cryonically preserved.

He had made all the arrangements, and all she had to do was call the enclosed phone number, and the cryonics people would rush to the scene, pack him in dry ice, and whisk him off to their facility, where, after carefully removing his fluids and filling him with antifreeze, they would store him in a tank of liquid nitrogen. He explained to her in the note that the process was very scientific, that he was not crazy, and that he had requested to be revived in five hundred years, by which point he was certain the Lite Age would be ancient history and his own more hopeful predictions for humanity would have been realized. He had not been wrong, he assured her, just a little premature, a little ahead of his time.

The other contents of the box were for Eeven, he wrote—just some little things he'd picked up with his last unmaxed credit card.

Last, he wanted her to know that he hadn't abandoned her, that he'd purchased a cryonics plan for her as well. He wanted her to live out a long and happy life in this time and then to die of old age and have herself frozen. Her tank would go right next to his, and when the day came they would be revived together, and the future technicians would reverse her aging, and the two of them would emerge from the facility together, hand in hand, into a whole new lifetime of brightness and joy. He was praying she would follow these instructions, he said, because that way it would be only an instant before he'd see her again.

The first time she read the letter was in the ambulance, and she couldn't even think about it. The second time she was sitting here alone with him, and she cried for hours. Not only because she saw how much he loved her—though this alone would have been enough—but also because the thought of going through the pain of living a whole other life not only didn't appeal to her but actually horrified her. Even in his attempt to kill himself Javier had displayed more love for life than she herself had ever felt. She had pretty much always equated living with suffering, and now for the first time she fully felt how wrong this was, and how sad. Given a dozen lives, a hundred, a thousand, she'd probably never appreciate a single one. She'd probably drive poor Javier to misery and self-destruction every time around.

There are no windows in the intensive care unit, but Ursula can tell from the increased bustling of the ward that it's probably late morning. The light from the hall casts shadows on the curtain pulled across Javier's little space, and Ursula watches them pass: the briskly moving shapes of nurses, the lazy, fluid shapes of orderlies pushing carts, the sagging, shuffling shapes of visiting family members. She wishes he would wake up.

She's pretty sure she's ready to start loving life now. Once he wakes up—any minute now, she's sure—she thinks it won't be so very hard any longer. In the half darkness she keeps thinking she sees his eyes flutter, his mouth move. She leans over and puts her ear to his lips, listening to the sound of his breath, waiting for him to speak.

A short, squarish silhouette looms larger on the curtain. A hand appears and pulls a bit of it aside, revealing the florid face of a nurse Ursula recognizes from yesterday.

"Ms. Van Urden," she says. "I was wondering if you are related to Ivy Van Urden?"

It would be simplest to lie, but the nurse's tone suggests something more than mere curiosity.

"She's my sister," she says, straightening out.

"I thought so, maybe. You look so much alike. The reason I asked is she's on the morning news. She's got a bomb. It's on TV in the waiting room."

Remembering

Policemen move the outer barricade, and the squad car taking Ursula to the scene inches through but doesn't make it much farther. They've cordoned off the block to car traffic, but the pedestrians continue to stream in unabated, mingling with the firemen and paramedics and news crews, some of them leaning on parked cars, others huddling for warmth around doorways and laundry steam vents, all of them looking up at Ivy's window and waiting for something to happen. The amount of activity on the street overwhelms Ursula's drowsy senses. She can barely make her eyes focus on anything. The atmosphere, she thinks, seems festive. She can't help thinking the police have accidentally brought her to a block party.

Ivy's threat to blow herself up along with close to two million dollars began last night, apparently, but didn't generate any widespread attention until eight-thirty this morning, when she stepped through the computer screen and into the real world by tossing a small homemade bomb and a couple of hundred twenty-dollar bills out the window. The only casualty from the explosion was an unoccupied, illegally parked Jaguar. The largest beneficiaries of the rain of money were a group of teenage squatter punks who had been camping out on the street, perhaps with the idea something like this might happen sooner or later. The punks, solemnly brandishing handfuls of the half-burned bills, were being interviewed on TV when Ursula hurried into the waiting room. She recognized them from Banister Park; they were the ones who'd bartered with the savage girl, trading food and raw materials for her handcrafted garments and armaments, which they now wore beneath their long military overcoats. One boy had on an amulet made out of beer-bottle glass, and strips of pelt tied around the shins of his camouflage pants; another wore a black baseball cap to which had been sewn a squirrel's pelt, its sneering face and little clawed feet splayed forward atop the visor; and a girl, her face streaked with bright-violet warpaint, leaned on a gnarled wooden staff with a spiked metal head. Then the report cut back to the live Internet feed: Ivy staring the camera down, a single, huge, green, slightly blurred eye filling the screen.

Walking through the crowd now, a policeman to either side, Ursula reaches the inner barricade. Beyond it, in the space between a haphazardly parked sedan and a bomb-squad van, stands James T. Couch, comparing trenchcoats with a man next to him. Looking up, Couch spots her and points her out, and the other man motions to the cops at the barricade to let her through.

"How's, um . . . Javier?" Couch asks, stepping up to her with his nervous, bottom-feeding smile.

"He's fine," she explains. "He's just sleeping. He's so tired."

Couch nods uncertainly, his lower teeth pressing deeper into his upper lip. The other man approaches behind him. He has an effete, catlike face and a long, flat nose. His trenchcoat, she notices, sports an eye-catchingly tall collar, turned up around his cheeks like a vampire's cowl.

"Follow me, please," he says, his voice liquid and nonchalant, then turns and leads them toward a building across the street from Ivy's loft.

"What's happening?" she asks.

The catlike man opens the door and begins leading them up a flight of stairs. "We've got your sister's accomplice up here," he says. "And more information about the bombs."

"I'm going to kill him," she mutters to Couch. "That *bastard*."

"Who?" he asks.

She doesn't bother to reply. They follow the man into the front apartment, a domestic loft filled with a couple dozen men, some in police uniforms, some in sweatshirts and sneakers. A couch, a piano, and a couple of broad-leafed potted plants have been hastily pushed to the walls to give clear access to the windows, which overlook the street and the windows of

Ivy's loft directly opposite. Stationed at the window is an unmanned long-lensed camera on a tripod.

"Sister's here," the trenchcoated man announces, and a ravenously thin man with sallow skin and salt-and-pepper pompadour steps up and puts out his hand.

"Miss Van Urden, I'm Agent Dellaqua. I'm coordinating the situation here."

The man has a tense way of speaking and dark circles under his watery blue eyes, one of which is slightly lazy and floats off somewhere to the left of her. He starts walking her and Couch toward a long mahogany dining table covered with radio equipment, clipboards, Styrofoam coffee cups, and two notebook computers with Ivy on their screens, talking directly into the webcam. Sitting at the computers are two men in dark blue jackets, the arms of which bear the yellow block letters FBI, and below those, the smaller letters VTU, printed in shimmering bondi blue.

"Your sister has four homemade bombs," Dellaqua goes on. "They're small and crude, but more than enough for her to blow herself up."

Ursula looks around the loft, a knot of helplessness rising in her throat. She remembers his sinuous smile, the seduction in his voice: *The point is, you don't know what I'm capable of.*

"Four?" she asks, her voice breaking. "Chas put *four* bombs in my sister's room?"

Dellaqua blinks, looking from her to Couch and back.

"Not Chas," Couch tells her. "Sonja."

Couch motions with his head toward the kitchen area, where still more men lean against counters and appliances, looking grimly down at Sonja Niellsen, who sits in a wooden chair with her hands cuffed behind her. She wears an army jacket with three black and white feathers pinned to each shoulder, a long black dress, and combat boots. Her head is angled downward, her face obscured by a curtain of straight black hair.

"James," she whispers, "how can they think Sonja did this? It was obviously Chas. Look at the poor girl. They've got her handcuffed."

"Any information you have on Chas Lacouture's involvement in all of this will be appreciated," Dellaqua says. "But we're certain Miss Niellsen was the one who bought the materials and assembled the bombs. We've got eyewitnesses, receipts, and her own confession."

"That's crazy. How could Sonja make explosives?"

Dellaqua bridles at the word "crazy," retracting his chin into his neck and staring at Ursula coldly. "Those bombs have two ingredients. One is sugar, and the other is something you can pick up at Home Depot. The recipe is available on several thousand websites."

"But why?" Ursula says. "Why would she do it?" She peers into the kitchen area, trying to get a glimpse of Sonja's face.

"Because Ivy asked her to," Dellaqua snaps. "And because she wanted their names to be linked for all time. That's what Miss Niellsen says anyway. It was a suicide pact. She was planning to be there when Ivy set them off, but we picked her up when she left the building to buy breakfast."

Couch sighs. "I told you Sonja was ga-ga for Ivy." He chuckles nervously.

"It's possible Ivy brainwashed her," Dellaqua goes on. "She shows some of the classic symptoms, but our experts need some time with her to be sure."

"You think Ivy *brainwashed* her?" Ursula erupts.

Sonja looks up and sees Ursula, causing the other heads in the kitchen to turn toward her as well. Her little mouth is set in a firm line. Her eyes are steady and clear and unyielding. She actually looks less brainwashed to Ursula than she ever has before. The "kidnapped" look is entirely gone; and in its place Ursula finds what can be described only as the look of a full-fledged savage girl.

Sonja looks back down at the floor. Agent Dellaqua starts talking again, scratching his head and looking around anxiously.

"Ivy's objectives, on the other hand, aren't so innocent. Definitely political."

Ursula stares at Dellaqua, her focus oscillating between the serene laziness of his right eye and the utter turmoil of the rest of his face.

"How do you mean, political?"

"Destruction of currency is a serious crime. Your sister is attempting to undermine the economy."

"Oh, come on."

Dellaqua fixes his good eye on her. "Money is the lifeblood of our society," he says. "Even purely symbolic attacks on it can lead to copycat crimes, crises of confidence, chain reactions we can't even begin to anticipate. Is Ivy involved with any groups or organizations, to your knowledge?"

"You mean like, is she a Communist?"

"Who are these people called the Trendspotters, anyway?

"*We* are," she shouts. "Me, James, Chas. We're not political. We're businesspeople. Agent Dellaqua, please, she's just a schizophrenic. She's not a terrorist."

"I'm not denying your sister's mental condition. But you have to realize that these days terrorism is everywhere. It's in the air. People can be terrorists without even knowing it."

"Can you please get her out of there and talk politics later?"

"I'm trying," he says, his face pained and exasperated. "I spent the whole morning on the phone with her. She says she's going to blow herself up at noon, which gives us an hour and a half. She's been insisting on seeing you, in person. I told her I'd let her talk to you on the phone—which is what I brought you here for—but she said we were trying to trick her and it wouldn't really be you. Then she pulled the phone cord out of the wall. Until she calms down a little all we can do is watch her on the computer screen, like everyone else."

"You have to let me go in there and talk to her," Ursula says. "I can stop all this."

Dellaqua shakes his head. "Right now the only threat your sister poses is to herself. I'm inclined to keep it that way."

She fights the urge to throttle the man. "Sir, please," she says instead. "She'll listen to me. I know how to talk to her."

Dellaqua studies her face. "Your friend here, Mr. Couch, has been telling me the same thing for the last hour or so. He says she trusts you. You protect her from . . . who is it?

"The Imagineers," Couch says.

Her plaintive look seems to soften him. He thinks for a beat. "Is that true?"

For a moment she wonders which he means—true about Ivy trusting her or true about Ursula protecting her from the Imagineers. She decides for the present purpose it doesn't matter.

"It's true," she says.

Dellaqua looks away, pawing his jaw. He turns to a man sitting at the far end of the table. "Wire her up," he says. "She's going in."

A young agent with patchy, hipster sideburns and sweat stains on the underarms of his shirt comes over and asks her to pull the bottom of her blouse out of her pants. Wearing a wire seems like a dumb idea to her—after all, the agents can simply listen in on the webcast like they're already doing; and if Ivy happens to discover the wire on her, who knows what delusions it will reinforce?—but she decides not to waste time arguing. As the sideburned agent tapes the transmitter to her back, she looks again at the iridescent blue letters on the jacket of the men watching the computers.

"What's that stand for, anyway, 'VTU?'" she asks no one in particular.

"Virtual Terrorism Unit," Couch whispers in her ear. "Sexy, eh? This ain't your dad's FBI, that's for sure. Pretty soon they'll be funding themselves through merchandising alone." He rocks back on his heels, looking around the loft with approval.

Dellaqua comes back over and begins coaching her on the kinds of things she should say and not say, equivocating on every point, telling her to be firm but polite, respectful but not indulgent, rational but not provocative, and on and on. Each new vacillating, contradictory instruction adds to her anxiety, so that by the time the wire has been tested and Dellaqua is done talking she's sweating and can feel blood drumming in her ears. He then walks over to one of the computer screens. Ivy is silent now, writing frantic messages in the air with her cigarette. Most of the former garish Flintstones and Brave New World furnishings are gone, and except for the computer and mounted cameras and money everywhere, her room is arranged eerily like the one she had as a child, with a single bed, a little writing desk, and a wooden dresser with large round knobs, all in the same positions. Dellaqua toggles to an overhead view of the room, taking advantage of a recent innovation of the website, and points out to Ursula the four pint-sized thermos bottles packed with explosive powder, fuses stuck through holes drilled into their caps. The thermoses lie on their sides on serving plates covered with more of the grayish powder, like entrées in their sauce. Next to each of the plates burns a lit candle in a silver holder. One bomb is positioned near the bedroom door, another is by the window, the third is in the bathroom, the fourth is on the floor beside the bed.

"Listen," Dellaqua says. "If you get the opportunity—" He stops, looks her up and down critically, his eyes lingering on her breasts for a moment, then goes on: "Remember, you're um . . . a *bigger* girl than she is. If you can grab her real tight and hold her by that far wall over there between the bed and the dresser, our men will have the door down and the fires snuffed and you girls safely out of there in ten seconds. Can you do that?"

She nods, and Dellaqua spends a minute locating his suit jacket, a double-breasted number, surprisingly crisp, which he buttons in a mirror by the door, squaring his shoulders and running a practiced hand over his pompadour.

"Let's go," he says.

Couch gives her the thumbs-up, and Dellaqua walks her down the stairs and across the street. To either side of the barricades camera bulbs flash and people shout things to her, but she can't pick the words out of the overall noise. And even the noise she hears only distantly, as though through a thick sheet of glass. She is exhausted, in shock, barely even conscious, in that state just before sleep when dreamthought begins taking hold. She can barely feel her legs; rather, it seems to her as though she were being slowly trundled along past the eyes of consumers on some giant conveyor-belt product display. She floats past the group of street punks, who watch her with silent expectation. She watches them back, and with a surge of drowsy pleasure and pride, she decides she likes their look: it's striking, challenging, and in its crude, savage way, even beautiful. From behind the safety of her sunglasses she goes on to examine the rest of the crowd, and she's amazed to see how colorful they are, all of them, so harmonious and yet so variegated—all in winter coats, but each coat unique in hue and cut and fabric; all wearing bright, curious hopeful expressions, but displaying such a kaleidoscopic variety of hopefulness: hope of getting a final glimpse of the glamorous Ivy Van Urden in her window, hope that Ursula will talk her to safety, hope that they themselves may be called to acts of heroism, hope for a big, bright explosion, hope of scavenging money from the wreckage. Witnessing this dizzyingly, almost gruesomely gorgeous collage of hopefulness, Ursula for a moment can't help admiring her little sister for putting this whole spectacle together, and moreover can't entirely bring herself to hate Chas for it, either—Chas, who, even if he wasn't directly involved, must have at least known about the bombs, must have known when he signed those papers that soon there would be no room full of money, no company for her and Couch to cheat him out of, no Ivy to watch putting herself together on calm, sunny mornings. She remembers what he said that day in his office about letting people destroy themselves if they want to. It's a terrible notion, perverted by an individualism gone disastrously awry. But it's not devoid of love. A wayward, twisted kind of love. For a wayward, twisted kind of world.

Dellaqua escorts her past the police guard at the entrance to Ivy's building, then leads her up the stairs. Just outside the open front door stand four men in freshly pressed black fatigues, helmets, and tactical vests, resting a matching black iron battering ram on end in their midst. Three firemen stand behind them, with extinguishers ready at their sides and a fire hose snaking out through the stairwell window.

She and Dellaqua step through the open door into the front room of the loft. The furniture Couch picked out for the place almost makes her laugh: a sofa upholstered in bright-blue fur; bulbous silver floor lamps on long, bending stalks; a round dining table topped with a mesmerizing black and white spiral. The granite counter actually shows signs of use—on it are a large porcelain mortar and pestle, a mixing bowl, and a couple of empty sugar bags. For a moment she savors the marvelous image of the two girls placidly baking something, but then she spots the electric drill and the duct tape and remembers the bombs. Next to the drill stands a small cardboard box, opened at the top, on which is printed a scene of cartoon weeds fleeing a plot of neatly furrowed soil in bug-eyed, mouth-agape panic. Beneath the surface of the soil, the product's brand name, KaOX, sends off shimmering tendrils of radiance in all directions. More empty boxes and sugar bags litter the floor around the counter.

"Don't forget," Dellaqua whispers. "Take any opportunity. Get her against the far wall and hold her. We'll radio the men and they'll be in there in no time."

"I hear you out there!" Ivy screams from behind her bedroom door.

"Your big sister's here," Dellaqua calls out. "She wants to come in and talk to you."

"Ursula? You out there?"

She takes a breath.

"I'm here, Ivy," she says. "Will you let me in?"

She and Dellaqua stand unmoving, waiting for her response.

"Hey, dickface!" Ivy shouts. *"I'm unlocking the door for my sister. Don't try any funny business! I'll blow this place sky-high!"*

Funny business, sky-high, Ursula thinks, wondering exactly which of a thousand interchangeable TV dramas Ivy thinks she's in. Doubtless, she'd be pretty disillusioned if she could she Dellaqua or his strangely alienated and maladjusted crew face-to-face. They fit Ursula's idea of substitute high school teachers more than of law-enforcement agents.

She hears the sound of locks' being undone.

"OK, Ursula, come in slowly. Slowly!"

Ursula walks across the room and opens the door. Inside, Ivy squats over one of the plaid thermos bottles, holding her lit cigarette above it. The light from the window above her is blotted out by a thick blanket hung from the curtain rod. The piles of money eddy slightly in the draft from the open door.

"Lock it behind you," she says.

Ursula turns. Across the main room Dellaqua stands with his arms folded. None of the other men is visible. She closes the door and locks it.

"OK," Ursula says, turning back around. "We're safe now. You can get away from that."

Ivy leans her head back against the windowsill and takes a drag on her cigarette, the bomb centered on its plate between her bare, skinny ankles. She's in her usual webcast attire: white cotton panties, a V-necked undershirt, and no bra, her nipples clearly outlined above her folded arms. Her bangs hang raggedly over her eyes, and the rest of her hair has grown out enough to be gathered in back with an elastic band. She uses the gathered hair as a kind of bandoleer for her pastel-colored cigarettes, several of which are lodged loosely above either ear.

"Ivy," Ursula says, stepping gingerly over the mounds of bills and sitting down on the edge of the bed, "that thing could go off by accident with you so close to it. Come and sit on the bed with me."

Ivy doesn't move, "You look nice, Urse," she says.

At once Ursula remembers the cameras. She looks around and locates them, six in all—one in each corner, a small one on top of the computer monitor, and one bracketed to the ceiling and angled down at the bed. Almost against her will her posture straightens, and she feels her face muscles go rigid; millions of people, she thinks, are evaluating her skin, lips, breasts, hips. Ivy, in contrast, scratches her underarm unself-consciously. A couple weeks' worth of hair is visible on her legs, and the acne has returned to her face: two pimples stand out prominently on her chin.

"Can I get you a cup of tea?" Ivy asks.

Ursula looks around. "You have a hot plate in here? That might be dangerous."

Ivy gets up, steps over the bomb, and walks toward Ursula, her hands in front of her as though she were carrying a tray. "Here you go."

"Oh. OK, Ivy." Ursula pretends to pick up a cup from the imaginary tray. "Thanks."

"Milk?" Ivy says, smiling brightly and motioning with her head at the space between her hands.

"No thanks," she replies, returning the smile.

"Sugar?"

"No, plain is fine."

"Lemon?"

Settling into the routine, Ursula reaches into the space Ivy indicates with her eyes and pantomimes picking a lemon wedge out of a bowl, then squeezing it into her tea. She strives for verisimilitude. It's almost even fun. It reminds her of the games they played as kids.

"How is it?" Ivy asks.

Ursula brings her hand to her mouth, tips it, swallows, licks her lips. "Good," she says. "Hits the spot."

Ivy nods.

"You going to have some?"

"No," she says. "I'm not going to have some. Because there isn't any!" She throws up her hands. "You're so full of shit, Ursula. Look at you!"

Ursula looks at her hands, still daintily poised in front of her, holding the imaginary teacup.

"Why are you so full of shit?" Ivy shouts. "When did you turn into such a phony? Look at you, sitting there all prim and proper in your blue suit. All made up for the cameras! Your big day as a star!" She lets out a long, cackling laugh, then screams, "You look like a fool!"

Ursula drops her hands, her eyes filling with tears. She suddenly realizes that this is exactly how the whole world must be seeing her now—as the less successful, aging, camera-hungry sister who took the time to dress up like a Barbie doll while her younger sister was threatening suicide. How can she explain she's been wearing this fancy suit since yesterday? She could never explain. It would sound like an excuse. And to top it all off, she's starting to cry.

"Ursie!" Ivy says, in a wholly different tone. "Hey, don't cry. Don't be sad. Please." Ivy plops down on the bed and puts her skinny arms around her. "Hey, I didn't know it was you. I thought they'd gotten to you. I thought you were one of them. I thought they put a chip in your head. But it's you! I'm so happy it's you!"

Ivy hugs her tightly, and Ursula knows that this is the moment, that all she has to do is grab Ivy and push her to the wall, and the door will come crashing down and this farce will be over, and she'll be the hero after all. But even as the hero, she'll still be the fool, she'll never shake the humiliation. She lets her arms hang uselessly, lets herself become an even bigger fool, sees in her mind Agent Dellaqua cursing her, sees the experts explaining her failure in tedious detail on the nightly news. She doesn't care. She doesn't want to go back out there, now or ever.

"I'm so happy you're here," Ivy whispers. "You can help me now."

Ursula wipes the snot from her nose with the sleeve of her twenty-five-hundred-dollar suit. "Help you how?" she mumbles.

"Help me deliver my message. Will you do that, Ursula? Will you help me? We can do it together!"

Ursula looks up. Ivy's smile is so hopeful that she can't help returning it with a miserable smile of her own. She wipes her eyes. "What do you want me to do?"

"Here," Ivy says happily. "Lie down next to me on the bed."

Ivy lies down on her back. "Hey, dickface!" she shouts at the ceiling.

"No funny business! I got a big-ass fucking lighter and a lit candle and a bomb right here next to the bed!" She turns to Ursula again, pats the space next to her. "Right here," she says softly, "on your back, like me."

Totally docile, Ursula lies down on her back. The ceiling, she notices, is covered with little glow-in-the-dark stickers of stars, moons, and shooting stars.

"OK," Ivy says. "Now look into that camera right there." She points out the ceiling camera. Ursula stares at its luminous, recessing, glassy eye.

"They're all watching us now," Ivy whispers.

"I know, Ivy."

"They're seeing us all over the world."

"I know."

"You look really pretty, too," she says.

Ursula's heart sinks and rises in her chest. "Thanks, Ivy."

"We're going to deliver the message now, OK?"

"OK."

"You looking into the camera?"

"Yes."

"So am I. OK. . . ."

Ivy takes a breath, and begins to talk to the camera, her voice clear and calm.

"I suppose you're wondering why my sister Urse and I gathered you all here today," she says. "We did it because we have something really, really important to say to you."

She plucks a fresh cigarette from her hair, the old one still burning between her fingers, and lights it with the massive jet of flame from the gold lighter Chas gave her. Without getting up, she reaches over and stubs out the old cigarette in an ashtray on the nightstand. She takes a quick puff and goes on.

"We're here to tell you we know about you. We know how you look at your life sometimes and feel funny. Like it's not your life at all. Like it's someone else's life. No matter what you do, you feel like you weren't meant to be here at all, like you were meant to be somewhere else but you don't know where, and you don't know who you were meant to be or what you were meant to be doing. All you know is that everything just feels all wrong. And it makes you sad. We're sorry you're so sad. But you'll be less sad when you know the reason you feel like you do. And that's why we brought you here: to tell you the reason."

Ivy sucks her cigarette, brings her knees up, and hugs them to her chest.

"The reason is, you *don't* belong here. None of us do. We're all from somewhere else, somewhere very different."

Ivy pauses. Ursula turns her head and looks at her sister's profile. Her expression is relaxed and serene, all the unnatural strains and stresses gone.

"We come from another time," Ivy says, "long ago in the past. We were a great tribe, a powerful tribe. We hunted and gathered. We prayed to the spirits. We lived in harmony with the land. If you think hard enough, you can remember. Do you remember? *I* remember. I remember it all. I can tell you all about it, and then you'll remember, too. We rode around on woolly mammoths, and we flew over canyons with hang gliders we made from the skins of giant manta rays. Some of us lived in houses that we built way up high in redwood trees, and some of us lived all together in giant tepees the size of a whole town, and some of us lived in warm, roomy homes we burrowed into the sides of hills. And when we were happy we danced, and when we were sad we rolled around on the ground, and that was all we needed to be happy again. And then we danced again."

She thinks for a moment, puffing her cigarette, and goes on.

"We had big musical instruments. Do you remember the big musical instruments we had? We had horns the size of school buses, and we had harps made from dinosaur skeletons, and we had drums the size of ponds. And we danced on the pond drums and swang from the dinosaur harps, and a hundred of us blew into the school-bus horns, and that was how we made our music. Are you starting to remember now? Doesn't that just feel right to you? Doesn't that just feel so much righter than what you have now? Just keep thinking about it. The more you think about it, the more you'll remember. I promise."

She lets her legs back down and reaches a hand up to Ursula's head.

"You've got such nice hair," she says.

"Thanks," Ursula says, lulled by the gentle twining and untwining of her sister's fingers in her hair. It reminds her of the way Javier caressed her in bed, running his long fingers through her hair and down the side of her cheek, whispering in her ear words every bit as hopeful as the ones Ivy is saying now. For the first time she admits to herself that Javier is gone. He's really gone. A couple of tears make paths down her temples as Ivy goes on with her speech.

"It's hard to remember because the people from the future don't want us to remember," she explains. "They took us out of the past and put us here in this time and gave us new memories. They needed people in this time so they'd have people to sell things to, because all the real people from this time committed suicide way back in nineteen-eighty, because life sucked so much back then. So the people from the future went and got us from the past and put us here in the present to watch commercials and buy things and keep the future in business. Are you remembering now, Ursula?"

Ivy turns to face her, eyes shining with anticipation.

"Not yet," Ursula admits. "I'd like to, though. It seems like a nice thing to remember."

Ivy nods understandingly, then turns back to the camera.

"This is very important," she says. "Look deep into your souls and try to remember the old ways. We were a great tribe, living in harmony with the land. Try to remember. You've been hypnotized, but try to remember, and try to bring back the old ways. They'll try to stop you. They'll give you money and they'll take away the money. They'll give you fame and they'll take away the fame. They'll keep doing it over and over. They'll keep you spinning and make you dizzy. But we were a great tribe. We need to forget about all this and go back, go back home where we belong. If we all get together and decide to go back, there's nothing they can do to stop us. There won't be anything they can do then."

Ivy falls silent for a minute.

"OK," she says in Ursula's ear. "I'm done."

Ursula takes a breath. "OK, Ivy. What now?"

Ivy scratches her head. "I dunno. How about some Kentucky Fried Chicken? There's one just around the corner. You wanna?"

"OK."

Ivy gets up. "I should put on some pants, I guess." She reaches under the bed, grabs a pair of jeans, and shuffles herself into them, pulling them up and rolling them down at the waist. She steps into a pair of sneakers and bends over again to squeeze her heels in.

"We're gonna need money," Ivy says. "You got any?"

Ursula laughs, wiping her eyes with her sleeve. "You're standing ankle-deep in twenty-dollar bills."

"Oh, this stuff? This isn't real."

Ivy sounds just assured enough for Ursula to doubt herself and take a second look. The bills are entirely regular, as impossible to impersonate as lifelong acquaintances. Their smell is unmistakable, overwhelming, and now that she's focused on it, even sickening.

"Don't worry, Ivy," she replies. "I've got enough."

The two of them walk to the door hand in hand, and Ivy undoes the

locks. Just beside the spot where Ursula stands, a candle burns on a tall silver holder next to a thermos bottle lying in its plate of powder. Ivy opens
the door, and without looking down, Ursula swings out her step a little
wide and knocks over the candle. She hears the satisfying whoosh of flame
behind her as she follows Ivy out.

Gift

I saw a woman flirting with a bearded academic on the subway," Chas says, his voice made even drier and more acerbic through the phone connection. "Told him she had a thing for *cunning linguists*." He gives her a deadpan look, his eyes rimmed with redness behind the thick, smudged pane of glass.

"I saw a woman wearing baby socks as earmuffs," Ursula replies.

Chas considers this for a moment, tossing the phone receiver from hand to hand.

"I saw a bum try to lick a frozen candy apple he found in the snow," he says, running a thumb and forefinger over the stubble to either side of his goatee. "His tongue got stuck to it."

Ursula toys with the cord of her phone. "I saw a bald bodybuilder look suspiciously from side to side before displaying his vintage Pez dispenser to a friend," she says.

Chas laughs to himself, an almost silent rasp.

"Which dispenser?" he asks.

"Goofy. Why?"

He shrugs. "No reason, no reason. Just curious."

The little booths stretch across the room. To either side of her women sit talking over the phones to their husbands, brothers, fathers, sons.

"They're letting you out, Chas," she says. "There's nothing they can do. No one's testifying."

Chas seems unimpressed by the news. "Figured as much."

"They're not bringing charges against Ivy, either," Ursula says.

"Or you?"

She shrugs. "They reviewed the footage and decided it was an accident."

"'Accident,'" he repeats, weighing the word. "Too bad for Couch about that accident. All that money of his."

"Yeah, too bad," she agrees. "I guess there's a lake out there somewhere that won't ever get subdivided."

Chas gazes at her admiringly, his sinuous smile appearing.

"I'm not too worried about James, though," she goes on. "He's already going around chatting up the clients, restarting the business from scratch."

He nods. "Sounds like Couch."

They sit in silence for a minute.

"Me and Ivy are taking a trip," she says. "Getting out of town for a while."

Perhaps he knows she wouldn't tell him, or perhaps he himself thinks it's better for him not to know. Either way, he doesn't ask where.

"She'll like that," he says.

"What about you, Chas? What are your plans now?"

He steeples his fingers, regarding with distaste the dirt beneath his manicured nails. "I'm thinking Japan," he says. "That's where the action is. They're gearing up to dominate pop culture the same way they did with electronics a generation ago. They're rewriting the English language as we speak."

He reaches behind his back and pulls from the waistband of his orange prison pants a thin stack of white paper, folded neatly down the middle into a little booklet. He holds it carefully by the edges, perhaps to keep it clean.

"I want you to give this to Kyle Dice at Nestlé."

He holds the papers up to the glass. They are filled with precise, minute handwriting, penciled in evenly spaced lines, adhering neatly to the same invisible margins on every page.

"I'd appreciate it if you could type it out first," he adds. "But the main thing is to get it to him ASAP."

Ursula shakes her head wonderingly. Chas still has an angle, even now.

"So you've gone right on doing business from prison," she says. "Just like a drug lord."

"No, not business. I expect no payment. It's a gift."

"'A gift'?"

He nods, flipping through the pages and regarding them with something akin to tenderness. "Seeing this product hit the shelves will be all the payment I need. Actually," he says, looking up, "it was really your idea, Ursula. I just ran with it."

"My idea?" she asks. "I don't remember having any idea."

"Shit," he says matter-of-factly.

She waits for him to say more. He doesn't.

"'Shit,'" she repeats.

"Yes. But not just Shit. *Nestlé* Shit. The perfect kid food. It can work, I'm sure of it." His crystal eyes sparkle through the glass. "I want people to eat shit . . . ," he says contemplatively, nodding to himself as though he has just articulated the most rationalistic and soothing of utopian visions. ". . . Then my work here will be done."

Cyborgs

Interface

Ursula closes the station door behind her and crosses the small clearing, settling her pack on her shoulder. The rain forest greets her with its thick, sweet aroma of orchid and plum. Breathing is more like drinking here, and walking is more like swimming, especially just after dawn, as the cool fog heats and gently spirals up through the subcanopy branches and the dark spaghetti of vines to the luminous green of the canopy ten stories above, where the leaves interlock in jagged, crystalline patterns veined by the brightness of the sky and the blooms of even higher trees, sparkles of yellow, magenta, violet, winking through the green like daytime stars. Looking up induces the same feelings in her that it has every day for the last ten months, a mixture of dizziness, humility, sadness, and hope—sadness because of course it is disappearing, and for all the reality it represents the teeming life around her might as well be a painted backdrop; but hope simply because a place like this is actually possible.

She picks her way between the trees along a paca trail, feeling as tiny as a termite in a patch of tall reeds. She is not even exactly at ground level but rather at root level—the giant trees stand on their roots here as if on tiptoe. The hum of insects is constant, louder than rush-hour traffic, punctuated by the squawks of parrots, the howls of howler monkeys, and the twittering of small birds passing under the canopy. The noise was one of those things she hadn't expected, but now she can't imagine living in a silent room, without the noise of life communicating with life, noise not only of sound but of sight and smell as well, creatures calling out for friends and mates with the bright jewels of their coloration, the enticing perfume of their secretions. Fashion is everywhere, programmed into every living thing, down to the smallest of insects. Even creatures without brains at all have a fashion sense, a better one really than the rest of us. Nothing is more fashionable than a flower; it is the perfect advertisement, the perfect transmitter of desire. No wonder the women of the Yanomama tribe wear flowers in their ears.

An enormous particolored moth flutters past. If she'd brought her net with her she would have snagged it just in case, but being netless she is content to watch it wend around a few slender trunks and then loft upward to disappear in a fan of palm leaves.

She stops at the base of a giant fig tree that is being slowly imprisoned by the roots of a strangler elm. The struggle has probably been going on for a hundred years already, and in the normal course of events it would go on for another hundred before the fig tree perished. But in this case both the attacker and the defender will be destroyed in the same quarter of an hour.

She may as well begin here today. She kneels down between the splayed, lichen-covered roots and examines the forest floor. A scatter of leaves as big as welcome mats lie in a sheen of rainwater. She takes the edge of one between her fingers and holds it up to the diffuse canopy light, which shines through the missing sections—the feeding patterns of skeletomizer insects—as it would through the missing panes of a stained-glass window. Putting the leaf aside, she studies the thin layer of ochrous soil under a fine tangle of roots and white fungal threads. A Hercules beetle is struggling to move a fig ten times its size. She removes another leaf, and a frog, black with fluorescent-yellow racing stripes, sits there for a moment before hopping away, not too concerned. Just like back home, the fluorescent colors advertise caution: predators know that these frogs are fatally poisonous if eaten. The Yanomama cook and dry their skin and stick it to the tips of the darts they blow through hollowed-out stilt-palm roots. They say a single dart can paralyze a paca in minutes.

She tears off a chunk of moss from the grappling roots and finds what she's looking for: at least a dozen different creatures are crawling around in the underside of the moss. She sets it down gently and digs the collection kit out of her pack. With a pair of elongated cup-ended tweezers she begins with the largest species, some kind of bright-red plant bug. She collects three of them for the sake of genetic diversity and seals them in a plastic compartment.

Next she tries for a spade-shaped cockroach. These are fast, just like their urban siblings, and for a moment she considers leaving it out of her collection. Perhaps all the other gatherers will omit the cockroaches, too, out of simple prejudice, thus clearing the way for a future cockroach-free jungle. Maybe while they're at it they could leave out the mosquitoes and the ticks as well. Back at the station they all joke about this, but they know that for every species lost, a dozen others that feed on it will be likewise doomed.

She works her way down to the smaller bugs, which are far more numerous. Even after all these months she still hasn't learned enough about entomology to know whether some of these smaller ones are just baby versions of the larger ones she's already gotten. For that matter, she doesn't know for sure that every creature she will manage to collect today hasn't already been gathered a half dozen times by other gatherers. It's unlikely, though, since at any given time a single tree can house ten thousand different species of insects. If she'd wanted to she could have spent her whole time here on this tree alone, working her way up from the roots all the way to the canopy branches, where the spider monkeys, hanging by their tails, would watch her hanging from her cords and pulleys, netting wasps and butterflies.

Working at the canopy level is tricky and requires a lot of practice. Almost all of the collectors get up there from time to time, but some of them have come to specialize in the task, working up in the high branches every day. Ivy is one of these specialists. Over the last ten months she's built up great networks of bright-yellow nylon cords running up and down sets of trunks at various elevations and spanning from one tree to the next. In the mornings she floats upward, hoisted by a gas-powered motor to her perch, and then spends the rest of the day checking her snares, edging out on slender branches to pluck eggs from their nests with her mouth, sliding down along cords strung between the trees like some cross between Tarzan and James Bond, collecting birds and butterflies and iridescent mosses and plants whose roots never touch the ground. Ivy is good at her job, is generally acknowledged to be the best there is, and she takes tremendous pride in it. Her mind remains something of a weather system, but the latest medication, combined with the respect and support of her coworkers, seems to buffer her from the worst of the winds and storms.

Ursula prefers variety, and like most of the other collectors she chooses not to specialize but rather just to do whatever's needed. Occasionally one of her supervisors tells her to try to find more grubs, or worms, or katydids. Sometimes she's instructed to walk in a straight line and collect everything in her path. Other times she's given self-dispensing canisters of KaOX Mist to send up through the breezeless air in order to drop a column of insects onto her collection mat. At the end of each day the supervisors make a cursory examination, jot down a few notes on their clipboards, and pack the samples into watertight crates to be shipped downriver and stored in giant freezers at the Ark, Inc. headquarters. The idea is to save as many species as possible. It doesn't matter so much if in the process they collect a thousand of the same kind of insect, or so the thinking goes. In the future there will be plenty of time to sort them all out. Or even better, there will be a robot programmed to perform the task at an amazing speed, an enormous robot with built-in cyclotrons, microscopes, cameras, computer-imaging equipment, a built-in library containing every known gene, a built-in nanogarage full of nanoforklifts, nanocranes, nanobulldozers, nano–arc welders, a well-stocked supply of the building blocks of life, a built-in primordial pool, petri dish, fish tank, birdcage, terrarium, greenhouse, and a couple of built-in plasma bulbs, buzzing with purple and blue rays, just for show. And when the time is right the mayor of the world will cut a ribbon and a crowd will cheer and a multicultural team of technicians will flick the On switch and the robot will go to work, re-creating the Amazon rain forest and shipping it piecemeal to a freshly cleared two-million-square-mile swath of Brazil, or if the bidding is higher elsewhere, to a climate-controlled Canada, or a climate-controlled China, or a climate-controlled North Pole. In the end there will be no shortage of Amazon rain forests—there will be plenty of them to go around.

Spotting some movement, Ursula looks past the tree trunk and sees a Yanomama man making his way toward her, carrying a bow in one hand and a red, blue, and yellow macaw in the other. He holds the dead bird out for balance as he steps over a fallen tree. He is naked, his genitals darker than the surrounding skin. His face and body are painted with the serpentine patterns of the Patahamateri tribe. As he gets closer, she recognizes him.

"Hi, Walter," she says.

Walter waves. "Yo, Ursula, how's the bug business?" He squats down next to her. From up close she sees that his long, pale body is covered with more red bites and scratches than usual.

"The bug biz is booming," she says. "Thanks to you—looks like you're feeding half the bugs in this jungle."

Walter laughs and nods, scratching a bite on his chest and smearing the seed-paste pattern in the process.

"I hear you'll be leaving us soon," he says.

"Tomorrow."

"Going back to the big-city life, eh?" His voice carries a note of derision.

Ursula nods, preparing to explain, but Walter doesn't ask.

"Why don't you come and say good-bye to the tribe? Dan's doing a new ceremony today. It might be cool."

"Dan? I thought Günter was your shaman."

"His malaria got bad a couple weeks ago. Had to go downriver." Walter slaps the back of his skinny neck, looks at his hand.

"What's the ceremony?" Ursula asks.

"We're honoring the spirits of dead tribesmen."

"Why? Has anyone in your tribe died?"

"Well . . . ," Walter says, shifting uncomfortably on his haunches, "not *recently*. We're contacting *past* members. *You* know. . . ."

"Oh, you're honoring the *real* Patahamateri," Ursula says. She knows this is a bit cruel, but she can't help it.

Walter pokes around the ground leaves with the end of his bow. "We prefer not to think of ourselves as *unreal*, actually."

"Oh, sure. I'm sorry."

"Well, I'd better be on my way." He stands, his penis at her eye level. Walter is pretty well endowed. No doubt the ego boost his nakedness provides him with compensates somewhat for all the scratches and bug bites. "You coming?" he asks, as an afterthought.

"Sure."

Walter turns around, displaying his fuzzy, clenched buttocks, and starts walking. Ursula repacks her kit and follows. His blond hair is bowl-cut in the Yanomama style, the base of his skull and the back of his neck bright pink from shaving. His hair's golden hue attracts bees by the dozens, forcing him to shoo them continually with his free hand.

"Is this going to be an actual Yanomama ritual?" Ursula asks.

"Well, they didn't use to have much in the way of religious ceremonies," Walter says. "We kind of felt that it would be a good addition. But there will be plenty of authentic aspects—chants and dances and stuff. We're pretty sure they're authentic, anyway. We damn well paid enough for them."

That the real Yanomama are at least making a bit of money off this whole charade is the one indisputably good thing about it. The shanty-town villages of the settlement program are atrocious: the former tribes-people have no work and nothing to do. The men and boys take turns hunting for free pornography on the village WebTV, while the women and girls hang out by the logging road all day, begging for money and prostituting themselves to the loggers. Ironically enough, the dark Avon eye shadow, blush, and lipstick the women now pay so dearly for looks far more savage on their round, childlike faces than the vivid seed paste and flowers they used to wear. The only remaining bright spot in their lives is when one of the neo-Yanomama like Walter emerges from the jungle seek-ing authentic folklore, herbal remedies, food sources, and, especially, ritual ceremonies. The villagers, dressed in T-shirts and poorly made cutoff jeans and skirts, gather round the naked, painted American or European, and when they've finished laughing their heads off, the naked white man tells them he wants to buy a ritual, and the oldest among them nods sagely, negotiates a price, and then explains the appropriate chants and move-ments. Whether he is giving him actual ceremonies or just making them up off the top of his head is anybody's guess. The neo-Yanomama long ago gave up trying to get the real Yanomama to abandon their shacks and join them in the jungle. The real Yanomama, particularly the young ones, now regard nakedness, communal living, and Indianness in general as embar-rassing and even shameful.

Walter and Ursula enter the neo-Patahamateri village, a large clearing surrounded by a *shapono*, a single ring of thatched roofing jutting from the ground, propped up by palm slats. In the circular, wedge-shaped space beneath the roof, eighty or so neo-Patahamateri live communally, without a single wall to divide them. They lounge in hammocks, the flaccid white flesh of their bottoms pressing through the netting like threaded balls of cheese. Although the sight of them fills her with the usual mixture of pity and frustration, she's glad she has come, if only so she can see for one last time the thatched structure itself. Like the rain forest surrounding it, the *shapono* will have ceased to exist within a couple of years. But Ursula will at least be able to carry the memory of it back to the city with her. And liv-ing in whatever anonymous apartment she finds for herself—surrounded by walls thick enough to isolate her from but not quite thick enough to block out the presence of neighbors she'll never even know—she'll remember the *shapono* and remember that once there were people who were never alone, who spent their entire lives in the company of their tribe, and that this gave them strength, and a deep understanding of their interdependence, and yes, sometimes even happiness. And she knows that when she tells people about this they'll roll their eyes and say it sounds like hell and that they'd never want to live with *their* families. But hell is not necessarily other people, no, not necessarily; hell is being surrounded by people who share no solidarity, it's like dying of thirst on the bank of a contaminated river. Hell is the Middle City metropolitan area and ten thousand other metropolitan areas just like it, ground zeros of densely packed buildings, each surrounded by a hundred-square-mile radius of flat suburban sprawl, as though our race had been so filled with the fear of a nuclear apocalypse that, like a return of the repressed, we'd ended up acting out the devastation of it by other means, making of our lives a living monument to death.

And tomorrow she's going back.

In the middle of the *shapono* clearing a large campfire blazes, an absurd waste in the heat of the daytime. Near the fire a dozen tribespeople prepare for the ceremony, adorning one another's hair with white down. Walter and Ursula walk toward the group.

"It seems weird to do this kind of ceremony in the daylight," she says. "Is this when they told you to do it?"

"They didn't really say. But at night we can sleep. In the day we've got to fill the time somehow."

"Don't you people have to hunt? Or do you just order out for Chinese?"

"Nowadays, with all the logging, the animals practically leap into the pot."

Ursula points to the campfire. "And I suppose you're not too concerned about the waste of wood," she says.

"With half the forest burning up north? What difference could *this* possibly make?"

He's right, of course, but still, the carnivalesque atmosphere here in the village makes Ursula uncomfortable. Probably half of these neotribespeople are serious, at least according to their own skewed reasoning, about preserving a culture and a way of life; the other half are just the latest brand of ecotourists. The whole forest, or what remains of it, is steadily filling with thrill-seekers of all kinds, from weekend campers to apocalyptic cultists. Ursula can't blame any of them, really. She can't even bring herself to hate the people who come here to hunt the remaining leopards, or the speculators who bottle rain-forest air and laminate leaves in plastic. She can't blame people for wanting to experience this place in whatever limited way they can. After all, consumption is a kind of love, she thinks, the only kind most of us happen to be any good at.

"Yo, Walt." The shaman takes a couple of steps toward them. His balding head is blanketed with white down, and his face is painted brown, with an orange stripe running down the center. He is short and thickly built, and his large, hairy belly is peppered with short, impressionistic paintstrokes. His penis is thicker than it is long, as though it had gained muscle mass from the daily exercise of resisting the crushing weight of his belly.

"Yo, Dan. You ever meet Ursula?"

"Yo, Ursula," he says, holding up a meaty hand. Coincidentally, *Yo* is an actual Yanomama word, used in greeting. Not surprisingly, it's one of the few Yanomama words that have caught on here.

Dan turns back to Walter. "See you got a bird."

"Threw itself on my arrow."

The shaman nods somberly, then leads them back to the rest of the group, who are now sitting cross-legged in a circle. All of them are already painted and topped with down. The women's bottom lips are pierced in the traditional three places, and the holes have small sticks stuck through them; the large holes in their earlobes are filled with red and yellow flowers. Their breasts have already begun to make peace with gravity, aureoles turning toward the ground. The owner of the breasts she's staring at waves, and Ursula looks up, embarrassed. The woman's name is Giselle; they've talked before. Giselle makes room for her and Walter in the circle.

Walter begins to pluck the bird, doling out feathers that the tribespeople proceed to dip in paste and affix to their shoulders in fanlike patterns. Dan walks into the middle of the circle, carrying a long stilt-palm root and a wooden bowl full of powder. He sits down and snorts some powder from his pinched fingers, then packs the end of the tube with the stuff and holds it out to a tribesman, who guides it to his mouth. Dan blows on the other end while the tribesman inhales. He then repacks the tube and holds it out to Giselle.

"What kind of drug is this?" Ursula asks.

"Ground-up *epene* seed," Walter says. "A hallucinogen."

"Very trippy," Giselle croaks, massaging her throat.

The tube comes Ursula's way, and she declines. It moves on to Walter.

"So are you looking forward to going back?" Giselle says.

Ursula looks at Giselle's prismatically decorated face. "I know I'm going to miss this place," she says.

"Why don't you stay, then, join the tribe?"

Ursula follows the smoke rising from the fire. The sky is beginning to cloud over, soaking up the forest moisture for the afternoon rain.

"Giselle," she says, "where will you go when the forest is gone?"

"What are they going to do, run their bulldozers right over us?" After she speaks her eyes betray a glimmer of uncertainty, as though her question had been posed in earnest. But then she smiles, gathering in the mounting euphoria of the *epene* seed. "Let 'em try," she decides. "We'll give 'em a faceful of darts."

For all these people's apparent flakiness, Ursula knows this isn't an idle threat. They *will* defend this place however they can. They'll make of their bodies links in the human chain and fight for every last tree. And at night they'll sleep soundly, secure in that rarest of modern-day certainties, the conviction that their lives, if not necessarily helping the world, at least aren't making it any worse. For these reasons Ursula finds the invitation to stay with them more than a little tempting, but she knows this isn't her tribe. Her tribe, she's pretty sure, is back in Middle City, and in other cities and suburbs and towns—a tribe of scattered, isolated individuals, a tribe that doesn't yet know it is a tribe. With any luck, though, she'll find at least a few of its members. And in the meantime, she has her plans. Back at the station she has a small box containing a few sample materials she's culled from the forest over the last few months—cloudy cocoons, diaphanous webs, blood-red root systems, pale fungal threads—and even more important, she has her sketchbooks, filled with studies for the new work she's planning, not a painting this time but an installation. The webs, she imagines, will ensnare. The cocoons will pacify. The roots and threads will connect the webs to the cocoons. It will be a system by turns breathtaking and baleful, but not, in the end, incomprehensible, not inescapable. From an outside vantage point—a platform, she imagines, at the far end of the room—the work will be wholly graspable in a single insight, a single moment of recognition. In this way she believes, it will be empowering. In this way, it will give people the courage to go on trying to understand and master all those other forces acting on them that at first seem too pervasive and too insidious ever to take on.

Squatting on his haunches, the shaman begins to chant in a basso voice she wouldn't have thought him capable of:

"Aaaah krashiii, aaaah krashiii, aaaah krashiii. . . ."

Without warning the tribespeople around her shriek with delight, then jump up and start running around the *shapono*'s central plaza, red feathers bristling on their shoulders, down flying from their heads. Some of them flap their arms and make shrill noises. Others sway their arms above them as though swinging through vines. One man crawls on the ground in painstaking slow motion, turning his head very slowly and smiling exactly the way sloths do. Most of their animal imitations are eerily accurate. She can even recognize Giselle's imitation of a plant-cutter ant.

Then one after another they flail about and fall to the ground as though struck by lightning. From the family areas of the *shapono* other tribespeople come out and carry the limp bodies back to the shaman, who continues to chant as he walks around the fire, lighting a stick wrapped in some kind of leaf. The stick doesn't catch fire exactly but just glows at the tip and smolders like incense. He walks over to the recumbent tribesmen and chants over each of them in turn, waving the smoking stick. One by one they reanimate, sit up slowly, and stare searchingly into the fire, imbuing it, she assumes, with whatever personal meaning they choose. Until recently Ursula didn't think people could assemble their own religions and go on to invest in them even the slightest amount of actual belief. But observational evidence, it seems, is proving her wrong. Perhaps what she's been witnessing is the birth not only of a new religion but of a new *kind* of religion, an ironic religion—one that never claims to be absolutely true but only professes to be relatively beautiful, and never promises salvation but only proposes it as a salubrious idea. A century ago there were people who thought art was the thing that could fuse the terms of this seemingly insuperable oxymoron, and no doubt art is part of the formula. But maybe consumerism also has something to teach us about forging an ironic religion—a lesson about learning to choose, about learning the power and the consequences, for good or ill, of our ever-expanding palette of choices. Perhaps, she thinks, the day will come when the true ironic religion is found, the day when humanity is filled with enough love and imagination and responsibility to become its own god and make a paradise of its world, a paradise of all the right choices. It will be in such a world, she likes to think, that Javier will awaken. She knows, for his sake, that she'll do her part to help that future along.

It was with a little ad hoc, new-time religion of their own that she, Chas, and James T. Couch said good-bye to him. They went to the cryonic facility not knowing exactly what to expect. What they found was oddly unspectacular but at least clean and well maintained, an industrial basement housing a hundred or so stainless steel cylindrical tanks standing on end. A manager led them to the one in which he assured them Javier was now being maintained at a constant temperature of minus 196 degrees Celsius, the temperature of liquid nitrogen. He pointed out the LED temperature gauge and described the thoughtful combination of computer monitoring systems and live inspections, as well as the failsafe wiring in back connecting the tank to an on-site backup power generator. The manager was a technician, of course, and not a priest, so when he'd finished describing the operations of the facility, he judged his duties fulfilled, wished them well, and left them alone with Javier's tank.

For a while no one said anything.

The surface of the tank was featureless and smooth.

The closest thing to an interface with Javier was the temperature gauge, and it was to this that their eyes gravitated, the number -196, lingering for a few seconds at a time before disappearing and immediately reappearing. For a long time to come, maybe centuries, this would be all anyone would know, or need to know, about the man inside.

It was Chas who broke the silence.

"I saw a kid with a tire-tread haircut," he said, bringing his piercing eyes to bear on the tank. "He had on a black T-shirt that said, 'I Won't Go Down in History, But I'll Go Down On You.'"

He folded his arms, and waited.

-196... the gauge flashed. -196... -196. ...

Couch spoke next.

"I saw a highly delectable cyborg girl in the park the other day, in a minidisk-sequined cloak and a fiber-optic drape choker."

He shared a moment of all-embracing mockery with the tank, his eyebrow creeping over the frame of his TV glasses.

-196... -196... -196...

"I saw a poodle with dreadlocks," Ursula gushed, breaking into a smile at the memory. "I looked it up later on a dog-fancier website. It's an actual breed of dog. Not a poodle at all. It's called a puli."

She fell silent, blushing with exhilaration. She was pretty sure that this little piece of information would be too much for Javier to resist, that even now his eyes must be popping open, that at any moment the top of the tank would begin to unscrew, and out he'd come, raving about all the supercool things they had in store.

Acknowledgments

Among his many sources, the author wishes to acknowledge Lynda Edward's vivid article "I Have Seen the Future and It Is Puce with Aquamarine Accents" (*Spy* magazine, March 1991); Thomas Frank's thought-provoking book *The Conquest of Cool* (University of Chicago Press, 1997); and David Langendoen and Spencer Grey for the harrowing concept of trans-temporal marketing; and to thank Dr. Susan Stabinsky for helping him gain access to the lives of victims of schizophrenia. The epigraph on page vii is from *Paris Spleen,* by Charles Baudelaire, translated by Louise Varèse (New Directions, 1970).

The author also acknowledges the support of the Michener Center for Writers; the Wurlitzer Foundation for the Arts; and the University of Illinois at Chicago; and extends his profound gratitude to the many people who helped make this book what it is, especially Joseph Skibell; Cris Mazza; Gina Frangello; Martin, Diane, Greg, and Mary Shakar; Olivia Block; Bill Clegg; and Robert Jones.